KAY HOOPER
IRIS JOHANSEN
FAYRENE PRESTON

The Delaney

Christmas Carol

BANTAM BOOKS

AUTHORS' NOTE

It's difficult to remember just when it all began. The first set of our Delaney stories, our Shamrock Trinity, was published in 1986, but the idea for what we then assumed would be a simple trilogy of books had come to us some considerable time earlier.

And it *was* a simple idea originally. We were all three going to attend an upcoming writers' conference in Arizona. We thought it would be fun if all three of us could "get a book out of it."

But we were all authors for Bantam's Loveswept line of contemporary romances, and we agreed that for three authors to turn in three books at roughly the same time with a virtually identical setting would probably not be a good idea.

Unless . . . we found a way to turn that negative into a positive.

Many phone calls ensued in those days before e-mail. Living in three different states, we discovered the wonders of the conference call. Our phone bills began to assume the proportions of the national debt. Suggestions and ideas were tossed back and forth. Titles, characters, an innovative way of connecting three separate stories.

And out of those early discussions the seeds of a dynasty were planted.

Our publisher, at first somewhat disconcerted and rather worried (collaboration between disparate authors being a somewhat tricky beast), got behind the project with enthusiasm once our determination became obvious. And we settled down to write our stories.

Collaboration was new to all of us, so we had to learn how to work together. To say we enjoyed the process would be an understatement, but what we enjoyed most of all was the opportunity to create a truly unique family.

We gave our Delaneys a rich and colorful history, with a detailed family tree stretching back to 1828. We gave them triumphs and tragedies as well as epic love stories. We sent them to war, tested their strength and will, sent them to the heights of human achievement, and broke their hearts. They became as real to us as our own families.

Our "simple" project grew, and we created an Australian branch of the family for our Delaneys of Killaroo. Then we went back into our family's vivid, colorful history for two sets of our Delaney Historicals as well as Iris's *This Fierce Splendor*.

But there were still more stories to tell, more incredible Delaneys we wanted to write about. And finally, perhaps lastly, we teamed up to produce the three novels you're holding in your hands, our *Delaney Christmas Carol*, first published in 1992.

Three friends began, all those years ago, with a very simple idea. Roughly seven years later we had created sixteen complete novels about one truly amazing family.

We hope you enjoy our Delaneys and their *Christmas Carol*. They're some of our favorite people.

Kay Hooper
Iris Johansen
Fayrene Preston

FOREWORD

Like many stories surrounding the Delaney family, the truth of the mirror was somewhat clouded by conflicting tales. That wasn't unusual, particularly given Shamus Delaney's habit of freely embellishing his family's history, but it did sometimes cause problems for succeeding generations.

Even the most likely explanation as to how the Delaney family came to have the mirror was vague, yet colorful. Stripped of all but the barest bones of the story, however, it seems that in his youth in Ireland, Shamus performed some service—about which he was uncharacteristically silent, even in his private journal—for a mysterious tribe of Gypsies. In return, a Gypsy artisan carved a lovely and elaborate frame from bogwood for an oval mirror of exceptional clarity.

Was the frame so special, or the mirror itself? In all the years afterward, no one was prepared to guess. Nor would any Delaney have dared to separate the dark bogwood from the brilliant perfection of the mirror in order to know for sure. For most, that question hardly mattered, because the undeniable fact was that the mirror was far more than glass and wood.

It was a window that offered brief glimpses into the past, present, and future of the Delaney family. But it was a capricious thing. The mirror revealed tragedy as often as triumph and refused to be mastered even by the willful Delaneys. Only some Delaneys saw anything other than their own reflections, and few indeed saw what they wanted to see even when the mirror opened its window into time.

Many of his descendants were divided on whether Shamus knew the true nature of the Gypsies' gift. Some said that he accepted the mirror and stumbled on the truth later, while others were certain that the Gypsies themselves had explained in language fanciful enough to satisfy even the most romantic the true nature of their gift when it was given.

Whatever actually happened during that presentation, time revealed the truth of the mirror. And no doubt there were many Delaneys in the years that followed who believed it was a window best left shuttered, because it wasn't wise for mortal eyes to gaze into the future.

Still, not even the Delaneys who might have wanted to dared to destroy the mirror. They might well put it away, but it became as much a part of Delaney heritage as the bogwood clock. However, as things put out of sight sometimes fade out of mind, the mirror was either deliberately or accidentally forgotten by the family at various times through the years. Tucked away in an attic or shoved back into a dark corner, it waited patiently to be discovered or rediscovered.

Bits of its history were lost, for a time or forever. Whole generations of the family lived without knowing anything at all about the mirror. But then a curious explorer would find it again and become intrigued. It would be dusted off and polished and brought forth to be exclaimed over.

It possessed its own sense of timing. It always seemed to reappear in the family at critical moments. And, oddly, it favored holidays, particularly Christmas—perhaps because of the holly carved so intricately into its frame, or perhaps simply because Christmas was innately a magical time. In any case, the holiday seemed a perfect time to hang so lovely a thing in a room or hallway of Killara.

And who could resist a glance into a mirror of such exceptional clarity? Few. Most saw only their own reflection, but some saw more. . . .

IRIS JOHANSEN

*Christmas
Past*

PROLOGUE

December 24, 1883

HE WAS COMING!

Zara was elated, but anxious. The young priest was moving slowly up the aisle toward the pew in which she huddled. She suddenly went rigid with panic. The scent of incense and wax that had seemed so pleasant was overpowering now, and she could scarcely catch her breath. She watched wide-eyed as he stopped at each tall wrought-iron candlestick, its flame briefly illuminating his smooth, beardless cheeks, carrot-colored hair, and broad, freckled hands as he reached up to extinguish the candle.

In another moment he would see her. There was nothing to fear, she told herself desperately. She had sensed only kindness, compassion, and . . . discouragement in him during the Mass.

Still, she *was* afraid. The compassion he felt for his flock might not include her. Why should he be different from the others? He would probably mock her and send her back to her people. It was not too late to escape being hurt, and it was not too late to run away.

She would *not* run away. She must not lose her courage after all these hours of waiting. He could not hurt her any more than the others, and perhaps he would be kind. After all, it was the season of goodwill, which was the reason she had chosen to approach him on Christmas Eve. Her gaze went to the splendid ivory and mahogany crucifix on the wall above the altar.

He had not been afraid.

Her panic began to ease as she waited for Father Timothy to reach her pew.

Two more candles to extinguish and then he could go to his bed, Father Timothy thought wearily. Had he reached any of those poor souls tonight? He had wanted to comfort and cheer his people in this year of famine and want, to give them something to hold on to in these lean months. But, he feared, he had failed them. Their faces revealed no inspiration, only reserve and doubt. And who could blame them? He could not offer them a lifetime of experience and dedication to God as their former priest had been able to do. They thought he was too young to understand their—

"Father!"

He froze, his gaze flying to the far corner of the last pew beside which he had stopped. A child, a girl of perhaps seven or eight was staring at him, her blue eyes wide with fear. It appeared his bed was not to be as near as he had hoped, he realized with resignation. "What are you doing here, child? The Mass was over hours ago. Did you fall asleep?"

"No, I have waited to see you." Her voice was tremulous. "I need to ask something of you."

Children were always full of questions about the Nativity at this time of year. "It's almost midnight and your parents will be worried about you. Come back tomorrow."

"My parents are dead. No one cares where I am." She moistened her lips. "And we won't be here tomorrow. Our caravan leaves at dawn and we won't be back until spring."

"Caravan?" Gypsies traveled in caravans and the Branlara tribe had come to take Communion tonight. The presence of the wild Gypsy folk with their bold, bright clothing, shining boots, and arrogant airs had made his parishioners bristle with resentment and his own task of putting his people at ease with him even more difficult. His gaze traveled over the child's ragged brown skirt and bony shoulders. A huge black shawl covered those shoulders and her head with only a fringe of red hair protruding from it. Her attire was not so different from the other poor folk of the parish, and she appeared more fearful than bold. He asked doubtfully, "You're one of the Gypsy children?"

She stiffened warily. "Yes."

It seemed the Branlara were more careless with their children's well-being than he had supposed. "Well, you're still too young to be out on the streets at this time of night."

"I'm nearly nine." She motioned impatiently with her hand. "And this is the only time I could see you alone. I've been waiting for hours."

Perhaps she was bolder than he had thought. "Then it must be very important to you. What is your name, child?"

"Zara."

"I'm Father Timothy Reardon."

"I know." She nervously clutched her shawl more closely about her. "Old Father Benedict died two months ago and you were sent here to take over for him. You've never had a parish before."

"You know a great deal." He smiled ruefully. "Have even the Gypsies been gossiping about me?"

"No." She drew a deep breath and went on in a rush. "I need your help. I cannot read. And I want—no! I *must* learn how."

"Cannot your own people teach you? I've heard the elders of the Branlara are not without learning and give regular lessons to their children."

"Not me." She looked away from him, her knuckles turning white as she grasped her shawl even tighter. "They will not teach me."

"Why not?"

"Because I'm not . . . I'm different."

"Different?"

"What does it matter? They will not do it." She went on hur-riedly, desperately. "I learn very fast and I wouldn't trouble you for long. We come to Dublin twice a year. If you teach me, I will come here and work to pay you for the lessons. I can scrub floors and run errands and—"

"Wait." He held up his hand to stop the frantic flow. "Just tell me why it's so important to you."

She didn't speak for a moment. "Magic," she whispered.

"Magic?"

"Around campfires some storytellers give us tales from the books of the elders. Wondrous tales." Her eyes were shining, her thin face suddenly alight with eagerness. "When I listen, it's as if I go away to another land."

Pity surged through him as he looked at her. His every instinct told him this child had need of such escape. "And you wish to read these books yourself?"

"They would not permit it. They would punish me if they even knew I left the wagon to listen to the storytellers. It's forbidden for me."

"Forbidden?"

She ignored the question and went on eagerly. "But if I could read, I'd find a way to get books of my own and then I wouldn't need to break the *Malan*."

"And this magic is the only reason you wish to learn?"

"Yes. Why else should I—" She stopped, her eyes widening in sudden fear. "No. But I can't tell you the other reason."

"Why not?"

She didn't answer for a moment, and when she did, it was barely audible, a breath of sound. "Because then you'll be like all the oth-ers and won't want to be around me anymore."

A world of desolation was in that simple answer, Father Timo-thy thought, and felt a sudden tightness in his throat.

"Please. Believe me," she whispered. "No matter what anyone tells you, I'm not bad. I'm *not*."

"I know you're not bad," he said gently. "Perhaps whoever said that to you meant only that you're sometimes naughty, as all children are."

"No, that's not what they meant." Her scrawny hand reached out to clutch his arm. "Then, if you don't think I'm bad, will you teach me? I'll work so hard for you."

That was all he needed, this Gypsy waif wandering about the parish and further alienating his flock. Not to mention the difficulties he might encounter with the Branlara for interfering with a member of the tribe, even such a neglected one as Zara appeared to be. Yet the child touched his heart. She was so lonely, her wistfulness so poignant. He sighed heavily. "Why did you have to choose me?"

Her stare shifted to the crucifix and then to the statue of the Madonna and Child to one side of the altar. "Because you believe in magic too."

His gaze followed hers and suddenly his weariness and discouragement lightened. "We call them miracles," he said softly.

"But you believe?"

"Yes, I do believe."

"Then you'll help me?"

She was holding her breath, her face pinched, her expression heartbreakingly anxious in the candlelight.

Suffer all the little children to come unto me.

Was he to flaunt Christ's example and send her away just to make his own path easier? "I suppose I must," he said gently.

Joy illuminated her face. "Thank you, Father, you won't be sorry. I'll come back in the spring and work so hard. I'll even learn to read your scriptures." Her brow furrowed. "Though I've heard they're very boring."

He repressed a smile. "You most certainly will read them and they're not at all boring." He stood up. "Now, wait here and I'll get my coat and take you back to your people. It's very late and the streets aren't safe this time of night."

"No!" She jumped to her feet. "You don't need to go with me. I can run fast. I'll be fine. Better than fine!" She darted up the aisle toward the vestibule, then whirled at the door, to say, "And they don't think you're too young."

"What?"

"The people of the parish are glad you're here. Father Benedict was too crotchety and stern, and most of them like the idea of breaking you in to suit themselves. You have nothing to worry about."

His eyes widened. "How did you know I was—"

"Magic." She smiled with delight. "Miracles! I'll see you in the spring. . . ."

1

Killara, Arizona

December 15, 1893

"Blast it," Zara muttered. Her foot was bleeding again!

Holding on to the corral post for balance, she scowled at the lacerated flesh on the bottom of her left foot. The rags she had tied around her shoe hadn't protected her wound, and the rocks on the trail coming down from the foothills had done their worst. Even though it was bleeding again, she couldn't be bothered with it now. She was too close to reaching her goal. She quickly shifted the rags to cover the cut, then paused a moment to catch her breath and look at the large adobe ranch house a hundred feet away. It rose out of drifts of snow and only glimpses of its red-tiled roof could be seen through the heavy white mantle atop it.

Killara. The house was more imposing and intimidating than she had imagined. For a moment she felt thrill of fear at what she was about to do. These wild inhabitants of Arizona had no more liking for housebreakers than the people in her native Ireland and were reputed to be much more violent in dispatching them.

Nonsense, there was no reason to fear. From a high lookout she had watched people depart and was sure the house was deserted now. It was well after midnight; the servants and ranch hands slept in the village over the hill and would not venture out on so frigid a night. She had ascertained before she left Hell's Bluff that afternoon that the savage was planning on indulging his lustful appetites at Garnet's bordello and would pose no threat. She had all night in which to search for and find the treasure—and get away with it, of course.

The icy wind quickened, chilling her to the bone yet bringing with it the faint musical jingle of wind chimes from the front porch. Comfort flowed through her as she realized they reminded her of the chimes during the Mass at Father Timothy's cathedral. Surely this was a sign that what she was doing was not unforgivable and all would be well.

She darted toward the front door, her heart pounding, her breath visible in the clear cold air.

Green eyes glared malevolently at her in the darkness!

She stopped short in shock and then drew a relieved breath.

It was only a huge black cat curled up on the doorstep.

"Have you no sense?" she whispered. "You're no guard dog. You'll freeze out here. Go to the stable, where it's warm."

She stepped forward and the doorknob turned easily under her hand. She had learned the doors of Killara were always left unlocked. Who would dare to steal from the all-powerful Delaneys?

The cat leapt to its feet, arched, and hissed at her.

"Go away. That man is not coming back tonight, and he does not deserve your loyalty if he left you out here in the weather to fend for yourself."

The cat's paw darted out and raked her ankle.

She bit her lip to keep back the cry of pain. The animal's claws were exceptionally sharp.

The cat hissed again, its eyes glittering in the moonlight.

"You're cursed with a foul disposition and a foolish nature."

She was the one who was being foolish, she realized, talking to the dratted animal to avoid taking this final step. She must not waver at this crucial moment. She could feel exhaustion seeping into her muscles, the throbbing in her foot increasing with every step. The deed must be done quickly or not at all. What did she care if the stupid feline froze to death? He was clearly as much a tomcat as his master and every bit as wild. She opened the door, hesitated, and then motioned impatiently. "I suppose you might as well go in."

The cat immediately abandoned the attack and ran ahead of her into the hallway. She slipped silently into the house and closed the door. Not softness but good sense had inspired her to let the cat in, she assured herself. Now the animal would not be outside howling. How that dreadful noise would wear on her already frayed nerves!

She identified the scent of lemon wax, pine, and oak in the darkness. She pulled a candle and matches from the deep pocket of her skirt and knelt; the light from the candle seemed bright in the large foyer. A massive copper chandelier hung above her and fine pictures filled the wall space. She had taken pains to learn everything she could about the interior of the ranch, but hearing was not seeing. It was truly a grand and wondrous place. She felt another jolt of fear. The fineness of her surroundings compared to her own ragged attire and dirty face made her all the more aware she did not belong there. What if someone—

She *did* belong there. At this moment and for this purpose she did belong at Killara. She straightened her shoulders and marched toward the beautifully wrought oak staircase.

At the head of the staircase she paused uncertainly, peering down a long hallway. She knew most of those doors led to bedrooms, but there should be a small door in the alcove to the left....

There it was!

Stale, damp air assaulted her nostrils when she opened the door to the attic.

Darkness. Cobwebs. Dust.

She drew a deep breath and braced herself, suddenly feeling very much alone as she started up the long flight of stairs. This attic held more than the treasure; it held memories and perhaps even ghosts of those who had gone before.

She crossed herself and muttered an incantation at the thought. What if the vengeful spirit of Malvina Delaney waited for her at the top of those steps? Who knew what caused a spirit to linger. The old woman had died over six years before but she had possessed a strong soul and would have been fiercely opposed to what Zara was about to do.

She paused on the fifth step as she heard a hiss from behind her. She looked back to see the cat crouched at the bottom of the stairs, glowering at her.

"Well, aren't you coming?" She tried to keep her voice from trembling. "Not that I care, you understand, but there are probably some fat mice for the taking up here."

The cat didn't move.

"You might even get a chance to claw me again."

The cat glared at her in the darkness.

"Suit yourself." She started up the stairs again. "I have no use for your company anyway, you stupid animal."

Soft fur brushed her ankles as the cat darted past her up the steps.

Relief and hope surged through her. If there had been ghosts in the attic, surely the cat would have known. Everyone knew cats were canny creatures blessed with knowledge of ghosts and the little people that common folk did not possess.

There were neither ghosts nor demons guarding the attic, and she had nothing to worry about but finding the treasure and getting away from Killara before the servants came back from their village at dawn.

Hell's Bluff, Arizona

"You must stop this foolishness and go home, Kevin." Silver Savron jerked her head at the pretty, fair-haired strumpet in the bed beside her cousin. "Leave us."

Kevin Delaney sighed in resignation as he lifted his tousled dark head from the pillow. His indomitable relative stood in the doorway. "Hello, Silver."

"Who are you to bust in here?" The strumpet glared at her indignantly. "Get out!"

"Hush." Silver closed the door. "This doesn't concern you. Run along. He has no further need of you."

"That's hardly a decision for you to make, Silver." Kevin raised himself on one elbow. "Did it ever occur to you that you might have interrupted a very delicate moment?"

"Did I?" Silver's glance raked his face. "Nonsense, you've obviously had enough of her for the moment. She looks content. You're not content but the edge is off." She plopped down on the chair by the door. "I must talk to you."

"At a whorehouse in the middle of the night?"

"Where else could I see you? The first thing I heard when I got to town was that you've not left this place for the last week."

"Who is this shrew?" the harlot demanded.

"Easy." Kevin's soft drawl suddenly held a biting edge. "I can see how her intrusion may have annoyed you, but I can't allow you to abuse her." He smiled at Silver. "I reserve that privilege for myself."

"Who is she?"

"My esteemed cousin, the Princess Silver Savron." Kevin waved his hand at the naked woman. "Miss Hester Jenkins."

Hester Jenkins's eyes widened. "A real princess?"

"Oh, very real. Sometimes she makes other realities pale in comparison."

"I've never noticed you paling," Silver said dryly.

The strumpet studied her before nestling closer to Kevin.

"Princess or not, she's too old for you. Send her away and I'll show you a way to—"

"Old?" Silver shot the woman an outraged glance. "Get her out of here before I scalp her."

"Out." Kevin patted the woman on her round behind. "She means it. She may be a Russian princess by marriage, but she's also half Apache. I'll call you after my dear cousin has the courtesy to depart."

"Don't count on him," Silver said as the woman reluctantly scooted out of bed and wrapped a shawl around her naked body. "You'd do better to find another client to fill your coffers tonight."

Hester Jenkins ignored her and smiled at Kevin. "Don't be long. I'll wait for you."

Silver should have expected that reaction. Whether they were soiled doves or respectable ladies of the town, they all chose to wait for Kevin. "Women spoil you. I'm sure it's not good for your character," she commented as the door closed behind Hester.

"I'm a rich man and pay well for my pleasure." Kevin smiled crookedly as he sat up in bed and leaned back against the headboard. "Hester's a very greedy lady and knows she won't lose by waiting."

It was the first time since she had entered the room that she had seen that jaded cynicism he showed the rest of the world. It was a natural armor for the heir apparent to a vast fortune, but she still felt a pang of regret. She could have told him it wasn't the money that drew women to him, not even the classic perfection of his face or the whipcord strength of his body. It was the reckless intensity, the flashes of wicked humor . . . and the hunger. The hunger had always been there since he was a small child. He had always had a tremendous appetite for learning, for affection, for living. Now that he was a man, his hunger included a voracious appetite for the carnal pleasures.

He was wild, hard, and sometimes bitter, and yet Silver's husband, Nicholas, said he saw many of her own qualities in Kevin and perhaps that was why there existed this special bond between them. Why else was she there when she should have been home with her own children waiting for Nicholas?

"Does Nicholas know you're here?" Kevin asked as he tossed aside the sheet and got up. He crossed to the table opposite the bed and poured himself a whiskey. He still had an Indian's lack of shame in his nudity, she noticed with approval, and his dissipation had not as yet had any effect on his physique. His body was as tight and muscular as when she had last seen it two years ago on the day they had bathed in a stream at the tribal encampment.

"Nicholas is in San Francisco." She added quickly, "Not that it would make a difference. He never interferes with what I want to do."

He lifted the glass to his lips and drank deeply. "Not in any obvious manner. However, I can't imagine him letting you come here alone."

"Nicholas knows I can take care of myself." She shrugged. "But I admit I was glad he was out of the picture. Nicholas believes you should be allowed to sow your wild oats."

"And you do not?"

"You've sowed enough wild oats in the past three years to cover half of Arizona with fields. You drink too much. You've had four gunfights in the last year, and you spend more time in this whorehouse than you do on Killara."

Kevin took another drink and then made a face. "Well, I won't be drinking much more of this whiskey. Lord, it tastes foul."

"How can you tell? It must all taste the same when you drink as much as you do. It's time you tempered that Delaney wildness with good Apache discipline."

He chuckled. "Only you would claim it was my white, not my red blood, that's troublesome."

"I am a half-breed too. I know the conflict you face." She met his gaze. "And I know what Malvina and Joshua tried to do to you. But you did not let them succeed. You are not a false-faced white.

You are yourself, Kevin Delaney, and there will always be people who hate you for your Indian blood. It does not mean you have to shoot all of them."

"I don't shoot all of them. Just a selected few." He lifted a brow. "Is that what this is all about? Plainfield deserved to be shot."

"So I understand. I hear Jud Plainfield is a terribly unpleasant man." She frowned. "But you handled it very poorly. If a man deserves shooting, he deserves killing. You only wounded him, and as soon as he heals he will come after you again."

He threw back his head and laughed. "Lord, there's no one like you, Silver. It's not every lady who would chide me for *not* killing a man. I assure you, it was purely a miscalculation. I was drunk at the time."

"I told you that you drink too much."

"Perhaps." He smiled mockingly. "Or maybe it's my Indian blood. You know we heathens can't handle our fire water. I did pretty well considering my condition. Plainfield has been laid up for over a month."

"But any day now he will be well enough to come after you."

He smiled coldly. "Good, I hate to leave loose ends dangling."

"I thought that was why you were still here. I want you to leave for Killara tonight."

"And I will do what I choose. I'm no longer a child you can order about, dear coz."

No, there was nothing childlike in the fierce man who was glaring at her now. He was totally adult, totally male, and frustratingly stubborn. "I never ordered you about and I never treated you as a child."

His ferocity vanished. "No, you never did. You shouted at me, you showed me, but you let me choose." He set his glass on the table and fell to his knees in front of her chair. "Which brings up the question of why you're not letting me choose now. Are you, by any chance, worried about me, Silver?"

She scowled at him. "Why should I be worried about a libertine who cannot even properly finish off a man?"

"I'll try to do better next time." He lifted her hand and laid it on his cheek. The hardness was completely gone from his face and his expression was as full of mischief and affection as it had been when he was young. "Forgive me?" he coaxed.

Silver felt a melting deep within her as she looked at him. At that moment she could see the remnants of the boy he had been in the man he had become. He was as beautiful and loving as his mother, Rising Star, and exerted the same Irish charm with which his father, Joshua, had lured her kinswoman to her destruction. But she must not soften toward him if she was to get what she wanted. She jerked her hand away. "I will forgive you for not killing Plainfield if you tell me why you goaded him into a fight."

His expression instantly became shuttered. "I told you, I was drunk."

She shook her head. "You may embrace trouble when it comes to you, but you do not seek it out."

"How do you know? Maybe I've changed."

"Why?" she persisted.

"Silver, I don't see why I—" He stopped. "You're not going to give up, are you?"

"No."

He shrugged. "Dominic."

"What?"

"He was boasting that he wanted to bag the famous Dominic Delaney."

"That's ridiculous. Dominic hasn't been a gunfighter for over twenty years."

"His reputation is very much alive, and there are quite a few young guns willing to face him down to gain a reputation of their own."

"He's not even in the state."

"He'll be here at Christmas. Everyone knows Dominic and Elspeth always come home for Christmas."

"So you decided to be noble and take this gunman down and save your poor uncle Dominic."

"Noble?" He said the word as if it left a bad taste in his mouth.

"Is *stupid* a better word? It's all the same. You think because Dominic is not in his first youth he can't guard himself?"

"I didn't say that."

"But in your arrogance you thought it."

"Stop spitting at me," he said roughly. "It was no trouble, so I diverted his attention."

"With a bullet. Dominic would not thank you for it."

"Dominic won't know." He paused. "If you don't tell him."

She had no intention of telling Dominic. Sweet Mary, she should have guessed what Kevin was up to. Beneath a cynical exterior he was passionately protective of the people he cared about, and he had always loved Dominic. Well, she *would* be foolish to give up the weapon Kevin just had handed her. "There is a possibility I could be persuaded not to tell him that you consider him too ancient to defend himself."

Kevin gave a low whistle. "You little devil."

"Don't be disrespectful to your elders." Silver grinned at him. "Go home tonight before this Plainfield recovers his strength and decides to come after you, and I will remain silent."

"It will do no good. He'll only follow me to Killara."

"But you'll be on your own ground."

Kevin muttered a curse beneath his breath. "I'm not going to be railroaded by you, Silver."

"Yes, you will." She stood up. "You were very unwise to tell me this. You should have known I'd use it against you." A sudden thought occurred to her. "Or perhaps that was why you told me."

He frowned. "Why should I do that?"

"Men often have to give themselves reasons for doing what they want to do."

"That sounds very obscure. You're telling me I want to go home to dear Killara and leave all these splendid pleasures of the flesh?"

"How do I know? You tell me."

His lips tightened. "I care nothing for Killara. I could walk away from it and never look back."

"You say that because your grandmother Malvina and Joshua drummed it into you that you must love it. It was perfectly natural for you to go in the other direction to spite them. I would do the same."

"Yes, you would." He lifted her hand to his smiling lips. "We're very much alike, Silver."

"Except I have more sense." She paused. "But I regret we let them hurt you."

His expression became impassive. "They didn't hurt me. You and Patrick fought well for me."

"Not well enough. We did our best, but we are not saints and our own lives got in the way." She touched his cheek with her forefinger. "And you are no Don Quixote. Leave the windmills alone. Go home to Killara."

"Home?" He shook his head. "Killara is damn boring."

"Because you don't let yourself become involved in the running of it."

"I have a foreman who does the job very well."

"It's not the same."

"Drop it, Silver."

"When you go to Killara."

"And be bored to perdition? I'd rather you tell Dominic and have him curse me for it."

"Then do it for another reason."

"What reason?"

"Do it because I've never asked a favor of you before," she said softly.

He was silent a moment. "Damn you, Silver."

"You will leave tonight?"

"Tomorrow. It's freezing out and I'm a little too drunk to ride. I'll wait until—"

"You weren't too drunk to fornicate," Silver interrupted. "And the principle is basically the same. As for the cold, it will do you good while keeping you out of that *young* harlot's nest. I wish to know you've gone before I leave Hell's Bluff."

"Then stay in town until morning. You shouldn't be riding without an escort anyway. I'll take you to Tucson before I go back to Killara."

She shook her head. "I wish to be back home before dawn. I'm not expecting Nicholas before tomorrow evening, but sometimes he arrives early and I wouldn't want to be away when he returns."

"Impatient?" Kevin teased.

"He's been gone two weeks and you are not the only Delaney with a healthy appetite for bed sport." She added tartly as she moved toward the door, "In spite of my advanced age."

"I believe I'd better warn Hester to avoid you in the future. She seems to have wounded you."

"She did not wound me. I just do not like her. You would do well to find someone else to bed. She is not only greedy, she is stupid."

"I agree her judgment is at fault." He bowed and somehow managed to make the gesture look graceful in spite of his nakedness. "You'll never grow old, Silver."

"It is my firm intention not to do so. You will give me your promise to leave at once?"

He hesitated and then shrugged. "If it will put your mind at ease."

"It will." She started to open the door and then turned to face him. "Christmas."

"What?"

"You have not kept Christmas at Killara since Malvina died. You must do it this year."

"No," he said flatly.

"The old traditions are not bad because Malvina and Joshua insisted on keeping them. You quite enjoyed them as a boy."

"No, Silver," he repeated.

She hesitated and then decided to yield the point as she saw the hardness return to his face. Kevin could be pushed only so far, and she had already gained more than she had hoped. "Oh, very well. Then I suppose we'll just have to go to Patrick and Etaine at Shamrock. But next year . . ."

* * *

A smile tugged at Kevin's lips as he slowly started to dress. It was no wonder Nicholas had given up his country to be with Silver. She was bold and honest with a mind sharp as a hatchet and a will strong as weathered rawhide.

Too strong. Why the devil had he allowed her to wring that promise from him? He was always restless and bored when he was at Killara, and going there would only delay the inevitable confrontation with Plainfield. Silver's notion that he *wanted* a reason to go back to the ranch was pure nonsense. Malvina had seen to it that Killara would never feel like home to him.

"She's gone." Hester came back into the room and closed the door. "And good riddance to her. You should see the look she gave me when I passed her on the stairs. Cold as frost it was—what are you doing?"

"Getting dressed."

"Why?"

"Because I'm leaving." He peeled four bills off his roll, tossed them on the table, and replaced his money clip. "I'll see you in a week or two. I'm going back to Killara."

"Now?" She moved close to him. "Not now. I haven't had enough and neither have you."

For a moment he was tempted.

"Don't pay any mind to what that bitch said," Hester whispered. "I'll make you feel so good that— What's the matter?"

Kevin had stepped back and away from her. "The matter is that you've made a mistake."

"What mistake?"

"Never again refer to my cousin in that fashion. In fact, never speak of her at all." He put on his shirt. "I thought you were only greedy, but I believe she may be right about you. You lack a certain basic intelligence." He sat down on the bed and pulled on his boots. "Go away, Hester."

She scowled. "So much for that damn potion."

"What?"

To cover her slip-of-tongue she hastily said, "You don't mean that. You *need* me."

"Another mistake. I don't need anyone." He stood up and pulled on his leather coat. "And I've taken a sudden dislike to that viper's tongue of yours."

"I didn't mean it," she said quickly. "Stay and I'll..." She ran to stand before the door, deliberately letting the shawl fall away from her naked breasts. "Don't go."

His hands closed on her shoulders and he shifted her to one side. "Good-bye, Hester."

She finally realized he meant it, and her anger flared. "Then go, you dirty half-breed. Do you think I care? You think I like being touched by a damned Indian?"

There it was, out in the open, cutting. It always came out sooner or later, he thought wearily. "Oh, you liked it." He opened the door. "You may not have wanted to like it, but I've become very skilled at reading the truth from the lies over the years. This 'damned Indian' gave you one hell of a good time, my dear."

He closed the door behind him, shutting away her curses as he shut away the pleasure she had given him. Both were behind him now and both were empty of meaning.

He was very good at shutting emotion away, a skill he'd developed over the years. Silver thought him wild and uncontrolled, but the life he had lived had taught him discipline. Now he would set about concentrating on closing out the cold, his need for a woman, his anger, and everything but the long ride back to Killara.

The door leading to the attic stood open.

Kevin tensed, his gaze flying to the darkness beyond the open door. It could be nothing. Consuelo could have left the door open before she left for the village at sundown.

But why would she have been in the attic? She never went up there.

And there was a smudge of blood on the floor just inside the threshold.

Blood.

Plainfield was wounded. Ambush?

Kevin blew out the candle, set the holder on the floor, drew his gun, and stepped silently into the darkness.

But he could see a faint haze of light, like that thrown by a candle, in the attic above him.

Two steps.

No sound from the attic.

Another step.

A rustle of cloth touching cloth.

He pressed against the wall and took another step and then another.

He could still see a halo of light. Plainfield must not know he was in the—

The light disappeared!

He crouched low and bolted up the rest of the stairs. At a dead run, he threw himself to the side to avoid a hail of bullets as he reached the top.

Pain!

His gun flew out of his hand.

But it wasn't bullets that had struck his arm, he realized as a heavy metal object clattered to the wooden floor.

A shadow rushed at him!

He launched himself to tackle Plainfield. He knocked him to the floor, mounted, and reached for his throat. His hands tightened savagely, cutting off the man's breath. "Plainfield, you bastard, I'll—"

Plainfield was muttering a curse. No, it was an incantation or a prayer.

And it wasn't Plainfield's voice, it was a woman's.

His hands froze on her throat.

"Don't toy with me," the woman gasped. "If you're going to kill me, do it and get it over with."

"Who are you?"

The woman was silent.

"Dammit, why were you lying in wait for me?"

He heard a snort in the darkness. "Don't be foolish. If I were lying in wait for you, it wouldn't be in an attic. What are the chances you'd come bounding up here?"

Something about the tartness of her tone reminded him of Silver, and his grip on her throat loosened. "Are you alone?"

"Yes, and if you're not going to throttle me, get off my stomach. I cannot get my breath."

"In a minute. I'm not taking any chances." He jerked his muffler from around his neck. "You damn near broke my arm. What the hell did you throw at me?"

"A frying pan."

He grabbed her wrists, quickly knotted the muffler around them, and then swung off her. "You had a candle. Where is it?"

"On the floor by the big chest against the wall."

"Stay there." He moved toward the chest.

"Who are you?" she asked.

"You don't know?"

"I cannot *see* you."

He found the candle on the floor and reached into the pocket of his jeans for his matches. "You will in a minute."

"That's not what I mean." The woman's voice was impatient and held the hint of a brogue. "The light will help only a little. You're dark to me."

He lit the candle and turned to look at her.

"Good God." A cloud of auburn curls framed a thin, pointed, dust-streaked face. Small, delicate, sitting huddled on the floor enveloped in a stained and ragged plaid shawl, she looked very young, twelve or thirteen years old. "You're only a child!"

"Nonsense, I've reached my nineteenth year." She scrambled to her feet, her enormous blue eyes searching his features. "I know you. You're the savage."

He felt a flare of anger. "How pleasant to be so readily identified. I do have a name."

She nodded. "Kevin. But Malvina always called you the savage."

"Not only to others. You knew my gentle-natured grandmother?"

"Only through her letters." She gazed accusingly at him. "You're not supposed to be here."

"You're not the first to state those sentiments," Kevin said. "And I tend to agree, but I believe I have a greater right than you. Who are you?"

She didn't reply.

He took a step closer and stared down at her. "I'd advise you to answer me," he said softly. "My shoulder hurts damnably, I'm cold through and through, and I'm still a little drunk, all of which contributes to making me extremely bad tempered."

"I was responsible only for your shoulder. You can't blame me for the rest."

"I can blame you for breaking into my house, presumably with the aim of robbing me. Do you know what we do with thieves here on Killara?"

"Something unpleasant."

"Extremely unpleasant. We take them out and hang them."

"I came only to take what is mine," she said fiercely. "You have no use for it. Why shouldn't I have it?"

"I have no idea what you're—" He clenched his teeth and then asked again, "Your name?"

She didn't answer for a moment, and then said reluctantly, "Zara."

He waited.

"Zara St. Cloud."

"You're a foreigner?"

"Why do you say that?"

"You have the same slight accent my grandmother had. Irish?"

"I just speak properly. It's you Americans who speak queerly. So flat and odd. I am Gypsy."

"Why are you here?"

She glanced away from him. "I belong here. I'm a Delaney."

He shook his head. "You can't get out of this by claiming kinship or friendship with my grandmother. There are no St. Cloud Delaneys and definitely no Gypsy Delaneys. Now, why did—for God's sake, why are you trembling? I'm not going to hang you." He added grimly, "At the moment."

"I'm not trembling." Her teeth sank into her lower lip. "I'm shaking. There's a difference." She rushed on. "But it's not because I'm afraid of you. I'm not afraid of anything. I'm just a little cold."

He touched her cheek. Underneath all that dirt it was silkier than Hester's, he thought absently, smooth and chilled as marble. "More than a little. You feel like an icicle." He was abruptly aware that it was as cold in the attic as it was outside. "How long have you been up here?"

"I don't know. Hours..." She backed away from him. "I couldn't find it. She told me she...hid it...but I couldn't—"

"She?"

"Malvina."

He stiffened. "Another lie? My grandmother's been dead for six years."

"I know she's dead." Her words were slurred. "And her spirit isn't here. I was afraid.... But the cat would have known...."

"Cat?"

"Cats always know." She looked dazedly around her. "I don't see him. He was here just a minute ago. Do you suppose..." Her knees buckled and she started to fall.

He muttered a curse beneath his breath as he caught her before she hit the floor.

2

────────────

SHE WAS BEING CARRIED DOWN THE STAIRS, ZARA REALIZED DIMLY. Strong arms holding her, the smell of soap and leather, the feel of a steady heartbeat beneath her ear. Safe. Everything was all right now. No need to fight anymore. He would take care of her. He had been angry, but he wasn't now, and everything was as it should be. Kevin would— Dear Lord in Heaven above, what was wrong with her? He was probably going to take her out and hang her! Her eyes flew open and she started to struggle.

"Be still," he said curtly. "It's hard enough getting down these stairs with no light without you causing problems."

"Then let me down."

"And have you faint again?"

"I didn't faint. I would never do such a thing."

"You fainted," he said flatly.

"Perhaps I was a bit dizzy, but I'm over it now." She added quickly, "But I wasn't afraid. It wasn't because I was afraid of you."

"You said that before."

"It's true," she whispered. "I'm not afraid of anything."

"Not even Malvina's ghost?"

"It's a stupid person who is not wary of spirits."

He set her down as he reached the hall and closed the attic door. "Can you stand for a minute while I light this candle?"

"Certainly." She leaned back against the wall, watching him bend to light the candle in the candelabrum. She would not fall. She mustn't show him how weak she was at this moment. "I told you I was fine."

"Why should I believe that any more than the other lies you've been telling me? Hold on to this." He thrust the candelabrum into her hand and picked her up again.

He was carrying her down the hall instead of down the stairs. Perhaps he wasn't going to hang her after all, she thought with relief. "Where are we going?"

"To my bedchamber."

Her heart leapt. "You're going to *ravish* me before you hang me?"

"Lord no, why should I want to ravish a little girl who's thin as a rail and badly in need of a bath? You smell to high heaven."

"That means nothing when a man wishes to rut with a woman."

He glanced down at her face. "That's been your experience?"

"Yes. If you don't wish to ravish me, why are you taking me to your bedchamber?"

"You ask a lot of questions."

"It's perfectly natural to be curious in these circumstances. Why?"

He scowled. "Because I remembered that blasted blood on the steps. It was your blood, right?"

"Blood?" She tried to think through the haze of weariness surrounding her. "Oh, yes, my foot... What has that to do with anything?"

"I can't bandage the damn wound without water, can I?"

"It doesn't seem reasonable to bandage my wound if you're going to hang me."

"Savages are seldom reasonable. Ask anyone." He opened a

door on his left, strode into the room, and deposited her in an over-stuffed chair. He untied her wrists and tossed the scarf on the floor. "Anyone at all. Damn, this room's as cold as the attic." He crossed the room to kneel before the logs laid in readiness in the fireplace. "What happened to your foot?"

"I cut it a little." She moistened her lips. "I don't think you're really going to hang me."

His lean face was suddenly illuminated as the kindling caught and she inhaled sharply. She had seen him in town at a distance and this was the first time she had seen him up close. By all the saints, he was as beautiful as Lucifer.

He said, "Give me a reason why I shouldn't hang you."

"It wouldn't be proper to hang your own kin."

He cast a reckless smile over his shoulder. "I've never been known to do the proper thing."

"I heard that in town."

"And what else did you hear?"

"That you do little but whore and drink and shoot people."

"You have an acid tongue. I'd curb it if I were you. Which foot is—"

"The cat!"

"What?"

"You left the cat in the attic. He'll freeze up there."

He frowned. "I saw no sign of him. He probably ran down when you were trying to break my arm with that skillet."

"But what if he didn't? You shut the door and he can't get down. Go let him out."

"You expect me to leave you here without a guard to go chasing after a cat?"

His tone was dangerously annoyed and she knew she shouldn't pursue it. She should save her strength for her own battles. Yet she had taken comfort from the blasted cat and it wasn't fair to leave him in the freezing attic. "I don't expect any kindness from a man who would leave his animal out in this weather, but even you must have some mercy."

"I did *not* leave him out and he's not my cat. Beelzebub belongs to my housekeeper, Consuelo."

"You're still responsible for him. Are you not master of the house?"

"Consuelo can get him in the morning. I have no intention of going back up there and—" He broke off as he met her reproachful stare. "Oh, dammit to hell!" He rose and walked quickly to the door, slammed it behind him, and an instant later she heard the key turn in the lock.

She leaned back in the chair and closed her eyes. Dear God, she was frightened, but she must not let him see it. It was never wise to let the enemy see weakness. One must always keep a bold front and not show the hurt. She supposed she should be trying to think of some plan to escape, but she was too weary. She could use this time only to regain her strength.

She guessed that ten minutes or more had gone by before she heard the key turn in the lock, and she hurriedly sat upright in the chair.

He did not look any better tempered than when he had left as he went over to the washstand.

"Did you find him?"

"Yes." He held up his right hand, which was scored with four bloody scratches. "Satisfied? He was curled up warm and tight as could be in that big chest and didn't appreciate being moved."

"I'm sorry," she said haltingly. "Thank you for getting him out."

He glanced at her. "Thanks?"

"You think because I'm Gypsy I do not have manners? I know you didn't have to do it."

He knelt in front of her and set a basin and towels on the floor beside him. "I didn't do it for you. Consuelo would have scalped me if anything had happened to that cat. Which foot?"

"Left. You're afraid of your housekeeper?"

"She's full-blooded Apache, not just a half-breed like me." He smiled sardonically. "One has to be wary of savages, you know."

She realized she had hurt him, and for some reason that knowledge disturbed her. "I didn't mean...it just came out. Whenever Malvina wrote she always referred to you as—"

"That ignorant savage," he finished.

"Not ignorant. She told me you went to a fine school in the East but it didn't help to—" Malvina's words had been brutal, and she decided not to repeat them.

"You needn't spare my feelings. She never believed any education could tame the barbarian in me." He shrugged. "And I always gave her exactly what she expected."

For an instant the darkness surrounding him shifted and Zara thought she sensed a terrible loneliness beneath the bitterness. She suddenly wanted to show him he wasn't alone, to share something, anything, with him. She said impulsively, "The cat scratched me too."

"Indeed? Then I wouldn't have thought you'd be so eager to rescue him."

"He can't help his nature." His long hair, tied back in a queue, was black and shiny as the cat's fur as he bent over her foot, and she had to suppress a desire to reach out and stroke it. What a stupid impulse. Kevin Delaney was much wilder than the cat that had already wounded her. "This isn't necessary. My foot is quite—"

"Lord Almighty!" He had untied the rags around her shoe and was gazing at the bloody flesh revealed by the gaping hole in the sole. "I'm surprised you could walk on this at all. How did you hurt it?"

"The rocks on the trail from Hell's Bluff. I had a hole in my shoe when I started and the leather ripped."

"You *walked* from Hell's Bluff?"

"A farmer gave me a ride in his wagon for part of the way."

"And I suppose you walked across the ocean from Ireland as well?"

"I would have walked it if I could." She made a face. "It took me four years of working as a kitchen maid to save enough money to travel steerage on that ship, and by the time I reached New York I had enough money left for a railway ticket only as far as New Orleans. It took me another three months to get the fare to Hell's Bluff. I arrived there four days ago."

"How did you get the money? You don't appear too adept at thievery."

"I don't steal." She met his skeptical gaze and repeated hotly, "I *don't* steal. Tonight was different."

"I agree it wasn't commonplace. Why did you stay in Hell's Bluff for three days instead of coming directly here?" He unbuttoned her shoes and took them off.

"I had to ask questions. I had to make sure you weren't planning on coming back here."

"And who did you ask?"

"Those women in Garnet's house. It seemed the most reasonable course. Everyone says you spend most of your time there." She smothered a gasp when he began to wash the torn flesh. His gaze flew to her face. "It didn't hurt," she said quickly. "You only surprised me."

"It doesn't hurt and you're not afraid," he said caustically. "What a brave lass you're being. It must be the Delaney blood you brag about."

"You don't believe me."

"We've already established that. However, there are probably a few grains of truth among the lies, if I can sift them out. I do believe you were in Hell's Bluff asking questions, but I doubt if they were answered. Though I'm not held in any great love by the ladies of that establishment, they do respect my money and it's not their custom to open up to strangers."

"They talked to me." She amended, "Well, not truly to me. I just placed myself in a position where I could hear them talk among themselves."

"And how did you do that?"

"I sold them love potions and told their fortunes."

"What?"

"You heard me."

"I find it difficult to believe the ladies of the brothel wanted your love potions. Love has very little to do with their profession."

She shivered. How peculiar was his touch. His hands cupping her foot were hard, callused, and yet generating an odd tingling warmth that was spreading up her ankle. Perhaps he was gifted with the mysterious healing power she had heard tales about from the elders of the tribe.

"Well?" he asked. "Do you deny it?"

What had he said? She jerked her mind away from the disturbing nature of the feel of his hands and tried to recall. "They weren't exactly love potions. I told them they were potions to make men unable to resist them and they sold very well. Every single one of them bought a vial."

His head suddenly lifted. "All? Hester?"

"I don't remember any of their names."

He swore beneath his breath. "That damn foul-tasting whiskey."

"She used it on you?" She smothered a smile. He clearly would not appreciate her laughing at him, and it was not a moment to make him any more angry than he already was. "She should have put it in something else. It never works well in spirits."

"I noticed that."

She quickly changed the subject. "But they were really more interested in the fortune readings. Everyone always wants to know what the future holds."

"And you told them?"

"No, I cannot see the future. I told them only what they wanted to hear."

"Riches, a fine marriage, long life?"

She shook her head. "Not all people want the same things. I looked deep into their souls, plucked out their deepest desire, and told them they could have it." She added quickly, "I know it seems cruel when I do not know it will come to pass, but it does no harm to make them happy."

He finished tying a strip of linen around her foot, sat back on his heels, and looked at her. "You're saying you can tell what people are thinking?"

"Most people. I have to try hard to actually read their thoughts, so I rarely do it. Emotions are easier. They just spill over and can be scooped up and sifted. You're dark to me, but that doesn't happen often. I am Gypsy and have the power, you see."

"The power?"

"Magic."

"Magic," he repeated. "You're a sorceress, I suppose."

She ignored his mockery and shook her head. "A sorceress uses her magic, I do not."

"Not even to tell fortunes?"

"That was different. I had to know whether you were going to be here tonight."

"You could have looked into your crystal ball."

"I told you, I can't see the future. I had to rely on what people told me." She pressed back against the chair; it was getting harder to sit upright. "Most unreliable. They said you would be staying at that bordello until the man you shot recovered, and yet you're here."

"My plans changed." He paused. "Fortunately. Otherwise I would never have apprehended such a heinous felon. What were you looking for in the attic?"

"Something that belongs to me."

"What?"

"The mirror."

"What mirror?"

"Malvina's mirror." She threw up her hands. "You see, you don't even know about it. It means nothing to you and it's doing no one any good there. I came all the way from Ireland to get it. It should belong to me."

"Malvina's mirror?" he repeated.

"Well, it's not really Malvina's. It belongs to the family. But your grandfather Shamus gave it to Malvina and she was the one who put it in the attic. She had no right to—"

"I don't know what the hell you're talking about," he said impatiently. "You're telling me you came all this way to try to steal a mirror that Malvina regarded so lightly she stored it in the attic?"

"She thought a great deal of the mirror, too much. That's why she put it in the attic." She swayed in the chair. "But she was wrong, she should have sent it to me. I *begged* her to send it to me."

He frowned. "You're turning pale as a sheet. Are you going to faint again?"

"Of course not, I told you I never faint. I'm just growing... sleepy... the fire..."

"And walking from Hell's Bluff with no shoes to speak of and breaking into my home. You've had quite a day." He hesitated a moment and then muttered a curse. The next moment he stood up, gathered her in his arms, and was striding toward the bed.

"What are you doing?"

He tossed her on the bed and threw an afghan over her. "Go to sleep."

"Here?"

"Do you think I'm going to let you out of my sight? Not likely. A woman who is determined enough to travel halfway around the world to steal a damn mirror wouldn't cavil at making another try. I'm too tired to go chasing after you tonight." He crossed to the door, locked it, and came back to her. "I'll get to the bottom of this idiocy in the morning."

"You're going to sleep with me?"

"You bet I am." He lay down on the bed beside her. "And I sleep light. Try to leave, and I'll tie you to the bedpost."

Minutes passed as she lay rigid, acutely aware of him beside her.

"Stop lying there like a poker," he snapped. "I'm not going to touch you. I must have more finicky tastes than your other paramours. Even if I could overlook your smell, unwilling women have no appeal for me."

"I see." She turned on her side and closed her eyes. She would pretend to sleep until she was sure it was safe to creep out of the chamber. It would not be possible to go back to the attic this night to look for the mirror, but she could hide somewhere on the property until she could manage to come back. "It's the talisman."

"What?"

"The smell." She yawned. "I don't usually smell so foul, but I made a talisman to bring me good fortune on my journey and hung it about my neck in a bag made of sheep's bladder."

"Sheep's bladder," he repeated distastefully.

"It protects the spell from drifting away."

"And does the same for the odor."

"You don't believe at all in magic?"

"I don't believe in anything I can't see or touch. I'm surprised you do. Your magic evidently isn't very strong if your luck in this enterprise is anything to go by."

"You can't say that for sure," she protested. "Perhaps if I hadn't had the talisman, you'd have shot me instead of just knocking the breath out of me." She yawned again. "And you haven't hung me yet."

"That's true. Hanging can be a strenuous occupation, and I'm not up to it in my present condition. I'll consider it tomorrow."

But she would be gone tomorrow, she thought drowsily. He would soon drift off to sleep and she would be able to sneak out of bed and . . .

She was asleep.

He could see the rhythmic rise and fall of her slight breasts beneath the afghan, the shadowy sweep of dark lashes on her thin cheeks. She was slumbering as deeply as an exhausted child. He felt an inexplicable flicker of tenderness followed immediately by frustration and impatience. This Zara wasn't a child but a woman, and he would not be softened by the fact that she appeared to be a youngster. Gypsies were notorious thieves, and she had come to steal from him, had plotted and planned with cold determination to—

No, not cold. There was nothing cold about Zara St. Cloud. She was maddening, frustrating, an explosive mixture of earthy bluntness and wide-eyed superstition, but there had been no doubt of the passion in her voice as she had spoken of the mirror. What mirror could be so valuable that it would bring a woman across an ocean and a continent to find it?

Passion. His lips tightened grimly as he shifted on the bed. He wished he hadn't thought of that particular word. It brought to mind his own present physical frustration. Blast Silver. If she had not decided to take a hand in his affairs, he would be enjoying Hester's lush favors instead of lying here next to this aromatic woman-child and contemplating the coming week of boredom while he waited for Plainfield to make his appearance.

Yet he hadn't been bored tonight, he suddenly realized. Since he had gone up those attic stairs, he had been angry, intrigued, frustrated, even amused, but not bored. If Zara St. Cloud could accomplish this particular magic, perhaps he should make use of her.

Physically?

Maybe. He needed a woman frequently, and all cats were gray in the dark. As far as he could tell, the woman wasn't actually ugly under that coating of dust, and her skin had felt quite pleasant to the touch. It should not be too difficult to strike a bargain that would include her easing him of his lust. He was not unskilled, and she was obviously used to the men of her tribe who were less than gentle in their rutting.

She murmured beneath her breath, turned, and suddenly rolled sidewise to rest against him.

Mother of God, the *stink!*

He firmly pushed her to the far side of the bed.

The sheep's bladder would definitely have to go.

"You get up now."

Startled, Zara opened her eyes. A woman was staring down at her, her sparkling black eyes almost lost in the creases surrounding them.

"Who are you?"

"Consuelo." The woman's voice was as without expression as her face. "You get up now and come with me. I have a bath ready in the kitchen."

Zara shook her head to rid it of sleep. Consuelo, the housekeeper who owned the cat, she remembered. The woman before her was enormously plump but gave no impression of softness. She appeared to be as implacable and dangerous as the other inhabitants she had encountered in this house. Zara's gaze searched the room. It was flooded with sunshine, but there was no sign of Kevin Delaney. "Where is—"

"Kevin is having breakfast. He said he will talk to you again when I have rid you of your stench." She sniffed experimentally. "He is too particular. It is not so bad. No worse than a cow that lays dead on the range for a week." She jerked the afghan off Zara. "But we will rid you of it all the same."

Zara sat up, swinging her feet to the floor. "Where are my shoes?"

"You will not need them. The señor said I should find you others." The housekeeper's left hand suddenly emerged with a butcher knife. "Lean your head back, I need to see your throat."

Zara stiffened, her eyes on the gleaming blade.

"You're afraid I'm going to slit your gullet? Why would I do that, when I just told you I must give you a bath? You think I like to bathe corpses?" Consuelo bent closer and with one stroke severed the leather cord holding Zara's lucky charm.

"No!" Zara's hand flew upward even as Consuelo grabbed the charm and threw it on the floor on top of the pile containing her shoes and shawl.

"Give it back!"

Consuelo shook her head. "Kevin said it must be thrown away."

Zara glared at her. "I want it."

Consuelo took a step back, but her expression did not change. "You are younger than me, but I weigh as much as a young pony. You would not like to feel my knee on your chest." She turned and moved toward the door. "You will not touch it again."

Zara stared mutinously at the woman's back. She felt naked and defenseless without the charm. Perhaps Kevin was right and the magic was not as strong as it should have been, but it was all she had.

"Come," Consuelo said as she opened the door.

Zara cast a longing look at the sheep's bladder pouch and reluctantly got to her feet. Even if she no longer had the talisman on which to rely, she had keen wits and determination. That might be enough.

A fleeting memory of Kevin Delaney's fierce, mocking face suddenly came back to her.

Still, a little magic never hurt. She would make another talisman at the earliest opportunity.

"She is clean." Consuelo threw open the door to Kevin's study and pushed Zara ahead of her into the room. "And fed. She ate her eggs like a starving coyote. Did they not feed her at that place?"

"What place?" Kevin's tone was absent, his gaze on Zara.

"Garnet's. Isn't that where you found her?"

"No, I found her in the attic." She didn't look like the same defiant waif of last night. Zara St. Cloud's auburn hair blazed in the early morning sunlight and her skin glowed with a silken sheen. Consuelo had dressed her in a simple blue skirt and white blouse belonging to her daughter, Isabel. Isabel was considerably more robust, but the garments almost fit. Almost. His gaze lingered on the delicate shoulders, the well-formed arms, the slender neck bared by the loose cotton blouse.

Consuelo frowned. "The attic?"

He tore his gaze away from Zara. "Thanks, Consuelo. You've done a good job."

Consuelo shrugged. "It was no trouble. She did not fight me. I think she is not stupid."

"Of course I'm not stupid." Zara stepped forward. "Do you think I don't like clean clothes and ridding myself of those fleas?"

"Fleas?" Kevin hadn't thought of that possibility. "Consuelo, perhaps it would be a good idea for you to go to my room and launder ..."

"It's already done." Consuelo turned and lumbered toward the door. "I thought you'd brought her from Garnet's and I don't trust those Chinese who take care of her house."

"They're as clean as you are."

"Maybe." She turned to look curiously at Zara. "The attic?" When Kevin did not answer, she again shrugged, then left the study.

Kevin's stare shifted back to Zara. "Come here and let me look at you."

"You're already looking. You can see me well enough from there." She sat down in the chair by the door. "Consuelo said you would talk to me when I was clean. I'm clean. Talk."

"Is that an order?" he asked silkily. "May I remind you that you're the one at a disadvantage here? I believe it's my place to ask the questions."

Her grasp tightened on the arms of the chair, but she said defiantly, "You will not harm me. If you'd intended to hang me, you wouldn't have had Consuelo go to all this bother."

"A bath and a meal are no bother. Neither is hanging a thief."

"I didn't steal. Well, perhaps I intended to steal, but I didn't get the chance so I'm really not a thief." She lifted her chin. "And the mirror should have been returned to me anyway."

"Why?"

"My people, the Branlara, made it for the Delaneys to use, not to be stuck in an attic." She leaned forward and tapped her breast with her hand, her voice vibrating with intensity. "*This* Delaney would use it as it was intended to be used."

Her motion had caused the blouse to slip farther off her shoulders, revealing the upper slopes of her breasts. Kevin forced himself to look back up into her face. "Just how close are our family ties?"

The question took her aback and she tilted her head to look at him in bewilderment. "We were talking about the mirror."

Lord, she had a wonderful neck. "And now we're talking about your claim to be a Delaney."

"You said you didn't believe me."

"I'm not sure I do, but there could be a certain awkwardness if it were true."

"If you hung me?"

He ignored the question. "How close is the connection?"

"Your grandfather, Shamus, had a cousin, Donal. Donal was my grandfather." She rushed on. "He denied it, but my grandmother swore it was true. I know I have Delaney blood."

"Shamus's cousin . . . that means, even if it's true, it makes you only a very distant cousin."

"You don't wish to claim kinship with a Gypsy?"

"That has nothing to do with it." He smiled bitterly. "Most people around here would claim your pedigree far superior to mine."

"Then, why do—"

"The mirror. Tell me why you want the mirror so desperately?"

Her gaze slid away from him. "Because it's magic."

She wasn't telling him the truth. He probed, "Like your talisman?"

"Don't laugh at me. It's magic, I tell you."

His smile still lingered. "What kind of magic?"

"It tells the future."

"Then, I can see why you'd want it. Such a tool would make your fortune-telling a much more profitable endeavor."

"I told you to stop laughing. The mirror would do no good to me in that way. The mirror tells only Delaney fortunes. And only a Delaney can see the visions."

"What a temperamental object."

"It's true," she whispered. "I tell you, it's true."

She believed it, he realized. She was not telling the entire truth about her reason for wanting the mirror, but she did believe it was magic. Why was he surprised? Gypsies were traditionally superstitious, as she had already demonstrated with her charms and belief in spirits. "And you think if you look into that mirror you can see your future?"

"Why not? I'm a Delaney. Malvina saw her future in it."

"What?"

"She saw her two sons being killed in an Indian raid. At first she didn't believe it, but it came true."

"So she hid the mirror in the attic."

"She wrote me that only hurt comes from seeing the future and that no one must ever look into the mirror again."

"Then perhaps she destroyed it."

Zara's eyes widened in shock. "Not even Malvina would do such a thing. You don't destroy magic. It might rebound and bring down a curse on you."

"You couldn't find it in the attic."

"It has to be there," she said stubbornly. "If you hadn't disturbed me, I would have found it."

He bowed. "My profound apologies. I should have let you rummage through my home in peace."

"I suppose I cannot blame you," she said grudgingly. "I would probably have done the same if it were my home." She added matter-of-factly, "Though I can't be sure. I've never had a home."

He firmly suppressed a pang of pity. He would *not* feel sorry for this urchin. He would think only about how his body had readied the moment she walked into the study. He still felt heavy and aching. She had caused him nothing but turmoil since the moment he had met her and would not hesitate to do so again to get her hands on that damn mirror.

Which made his next words as much a surprise to him as to her. "If I let you go, will you promise me you'll go away and forget about the damn mirror?"

Her eyes widened. "You'd let me go?"

"Answer me. Will you forget about the mirror?"

She opened her lips and then closed them again. "I cannot," she whispered.

A surge of relief flooded him. "Then I'd be a fool to let you go, wouldn't I? I guess we'll have to strike a bargain."

"I don't know what you mean," she said warily.

"You want to search for the mirror. I might be persuaded to let you do so."

"Why would you?"

"I don't believe in talismans or mystical mirrors. What would I care if you found it?"

Hope lit her face. "You would truly let me—" She stopped and then asked cautiously, "Bargain?"

"I'm forced to stay here for the next week or so, and I'm not looking forward to it."

"Why not?" she asked, startled.

"I have no liking for Killara."

"Then you're a fool," she said bluntly. "I've never seen such a fine, grand place. What else could you want?"

"A lack of boredom." He smiled crookedly. "And I've decided you might provide it. Stay with me for the next week and furnish me with diversion and I'll let you look for your mirror. No, I'll even help you look for it."

"And if I find it, it's mine?"

He shook his head. "You may look into the mirror, but it will remain mine."

"You said you didn't care anything about it," she protested.

"But I'm as possessive as all the other Delaneys. *If* you find it and *if* you decide you want it, then there's a possibility we may strike another bargain. We shall see."

She frowned. "It doesn't sound a very good bargain to me."

"It's the best you'll get."

Her teeth nibbled at her lower lip. "What do you expect from me?"

"Anything I want." He smiled. "Everything I want."

A flush touched her cheeks. "Fornication?"

"A blunt term."

"That's what all men want from women. You'd be disappointed. I'm not pretty and I don't know any of those tricks the women at Garnet's know."

"But I'm not at Garnet's and I'm willing to tolerate a lack of skill . . . if you display appropriate enthusiasm."

"You'll be disappointed there too. To me it's always seemed . . . awkward."

"Indeed? Then our time together may be more interesting than I thought."

She frowned in puzzlement. "Why do you— You won't change your mind?"

"Oh, no, the situation is becoming more intriguing all the time. Will it help you make up your mind if I assure you I'll wait until it no longer seems 'awkward' to you?"

A relieved smile immediately came to her face. "Oh, then there's nothing for me to worry about."

"No?"

She got to her feet. "Men are always boasting what great bulls they are, and it all comes to naught. Most of the time women only pretend to like it. Can we go look for the mirror now?"

He felt a flicker of outrage mixed with amusement. "I take it you're agreeing to the terms?"

"To the bargain? Of course. Why not? I have nothing to lose." Her bearing was charged with bravado as she swaggered toward the door. "I'll have a warm house and food in my belly and opportunity to look for the mirror. And when the time comes, I'll have no trouble making another deal for the mirror. You're clearly not a good trader. Carlo would have no trouble selling you Gento."

"Carlo?"

"My stepbrother. He did the horse trading for our tribe. Carlo is very clever."

"And Gento?"

"An old plug of a horse. Even Carlo's not been able to sell him to anyone."

He was no longer amused. "But you think me gullible enough to purchase this nag?"

She caught a hint of his displeasure and didn't answer him directly. "Let's go look for the mirror."

"In a moment." He moved leisurely across the study. "First I must prove to you that I'm not such a fool as you think me. I don't think it would bode well for our bargain for you to lack respect." He stopped before her and said musingly, "Now, what signs would a canny horse trader look for? Turn around."

"Why?"

"I have to see how you move, don't I?"

"This is foolishness."

"Turn around." His voice was still soft, but a steely note edged his tone.

She shrugged and turned in a circle. "Satisfied?"

"No." He knelt and lifted her skirt. He heard her sudden intake of breath and felt the muscle bunch beneath his palm as his hand slowly, sensually, caressed her calf. "Your legs seem sound, but that torn foot would indicate a lack of care given by your previous owner." Rubbing, exploring, his hand moved to her upper thigh. She uttered a sound low in her throat and made a motion to step back. "No," he said warningly. "Don't move. You agreed, remember?" His thumb and forefinger gently pinched the flesh. "Velvet-soft, but you're too thin. I'll probably have to put good money into feeding you if you're to be of any worth to me. I doubt if you would stand the pace I'd set...at first." He stood up and his hands framed her face. "Open your mouth."

She kept it closed, glaring at him.

He pressed his thumb to her lower lip. "Open. I have to see your teeth, don't I? That's a very important part of any transaction of this sort."

"I'm not a mare."

"You're the one who compared our arrangement to a horse trade. I'm actually being much kinder to you. As I remember, you termed me a bull, and surely a mare is more intelligent than a bull." His thumb pressed harder. "Open."

Her lips parted.

"Good strong, white teeth." His hand moved down to stroke her neck and then to cup her breast. He could feel her heart pounding wildly beneath his palm and suddenly his irritation and outrage were gone. Soft . . . warm and so alive. He had never seen a woman more vibrantly alive. Only the thin cotton on her blouse separated his hand from her flesh, and he felt her nipple harden. Even the frail barrier of the fabric was too much. He wanted to slip the neckline down and look at her, lower his head and— Lord, in another minute he'd be pulling her down to the floor and mounting her like the mare he'd been mockingly treating her as. His hand dropped away and he stepped back. "Maybe I've not made such a bad bargain after all."

Her cheeks were flaming and she was looking at him as if she were a startled child. She didn't speak for a moment. "Have you—" She paused to steady her voice. "Have you finished with me?"

"No, we've barely started. But it's enough for now." God should strike him dead for that lie. He'd not had anywhere near enough of her. He opened the door and bowed. "The attic?"

"What?" She squared her shoulders and whirled on her heel in a flurry of blue skirt. "Oh, yes, certainly, the attic."

3

THE ATTIC OCCUPIED THE ENTIRE TOP OF THE HOMESTEAD AND WAS crammed with a forbidding variety of furniture, trunks, and boxes.

"Lord, what a mess. No wonder you didn't find the mirror. What does it look like?" Kevin asked.

"It's oval with a carved bogwood frame, about three feet tall and two and a half feet wide." She was already burrowing in the huge trunk she'd had to abandon searching when she had heard him on the stairs the previous night.

"No mystical carvings or incantations?"

He was laughing at her again. "It's decorated with holly carvings." The mirror wasn't in the chest. "There's nothing here."

"On the contrary." He was kneeling beside her, his hands rapidly rummaging through the piles of clothes in the trunk. He pulled out a voluminous moss-green velvet garment and draped it around her. "All treasures aren't necessarily bound to the mirror. Warmth can be very precious when it's as cold as it is up here."

It was a splendid velvet cloak, trimmed in ermine. She looked down at it. "I can't wear this."

"You took Isabel's clothes from Consuelo."

She reached up tentatively and gently stroked the softness of the velvet. "That was different. Isabel's clothes are . . . She's like me. This is . . . wonderful."

"My cousin, Brianne, evidently didn't agree with you, or she wouldn't have left that cloak up here."

"You know who this belonged to?"

"I assume it was Brianne's. She has red hair too." He touched a springy auburn curl falling over her temple. "And she wears green a lot."

"I can't wear it." She started to shrug off the cape. "It's too grand for me and would only get dirty."

He stopped her. "No, keep it on. I like you in it." He pulled the hood over her hair. The gesture was oddly possessive, and she was suddenly afflicted with the same breathlessness she'd experienced in the study. "You look splendid in velvet." He fastened the button at her neck as he added musingly, "I wonder how you would look on it."

"What?"

"Never mind." He stood up and turned away. "Let's find that blasted mirror and get out of here."

"Wait." She tore through the trunk until she found a man's yellow rain slicker and handed it to him. "Here. It may take longer than you think."

He took the slicker and smiled curiously. "I thank you."

"Don't just stand there. Put it on."

He slipped it over his head. His dark hair and tanned skin gleamed in vibrant contrast to the yellow of the slicker. He looked lean, tough, and yet as beautiful as one of the statues in the cathedral in Dublin.

"Does that please you?" he asked, intrigued by the expression on her face.

"Yes." It pleased her too much. She wanted to keep on staring at him, but she had no time for such indulgence. She tore her gaze away. "I'll take the south side of the attic. You take the north."

"It's time to stop. We've been searching all day," Kevin said. "It may not even be here."

"It *is* here." Zara pushed aside a brass-bound trunk to get to an armoire in the corner. "It's got to be here. She wouldn't have thrown it away. It would be—"

"Bad luck," Kevin finished.

"Yes." She tried in vain to open the door of the armoire. "It's locked. Do you have the key?"

"No, stand aside and I'll break the lock."

"And ruin a fine piece of furniture?" She shook her head. "Someone has to have a key to it."

"It might be with the household keys. Consuelo keeps the rings on a hook in the kitchen."

"Then let's go get it."

"Tomorrow." He held up his hand as she started to protest. "It's getting dark, we haven't eaten since breakfast, and you're so cold you're turning blue. We'll start again early tomorrow morning."

"I'm not cold." She tossed the cloak away from her shoulders to show him and suppressed a shiver as the chill penetrated her thin cotton garments. "We're so close. I want to—"

"You don't know if we're close or not. There could be nothing in that armoire but old clothes."

"Then why lock it?"

"True." He frowned thoughtfully. "Perhaps there's a skeleton in it."

Her eyes widened. "What?"

"It would be one way of disposing of a body. My grandfather and grandmother weren't the tamest people in the world."

"Why would they want to kill—"

"Perhaps they found someone rummaging in their attic." His lips quirked.

"Oh, you're joking." She turned back to the armoire. "But it's certainly big enough for a body."

He took her hand and pulled her toward the stairs. "Tomorrow."

His touch was generating that same sense of disturbing warmth as before. "Let me go." She disengaged her hand. "If we keep looking, we might find it now."

"And if we don't, we'll find it tomorrow or the next day." He met her gaze. "I don't intend to spend all night searching for your magical mirror. I have other activities in mind."

She felt the breath leave her body. His tone was deeply sensual, and she was catapulted back to that moment in the study when he had knelt at her feet and his hands had . . .

"Don't look at me like that," he said roughly.

"I don't know what you mean."

"I'm not going to jump on you. I told you I'd wait, but how the hell am I supposed to wait if you—"

"What do you want of me?"

"Conversation. A companion at the supper table. Is that too much to ask?"

"No, I suppose not." She started down the steps and looked back at him over her shoulder. "But we'll have little to talk about. We have nothing in common. I don't come from a grand home, nor do I have a fine education. I've always lived in a wagon traveling from place to place with our caravan. A priest, Father Timothy, taught me to read and write but little else. I love books, but I've not been able to lay my hands on as many as I'd like."

"Then you may be interested in seeing the study. I'll take you there after supper." Kevin followed her down the stairs. "My mother was a great reader. My cousin, Silver, said it was her salvation."

"Why?"

"She was Indian, and it was not easy living as an outcast."

"She had you, didn't she?"

"She died when I was born. You might say I killed her." His lips twisted. "In my grandmother's eyes it was the only worthwhile thing I ever accomplished."

Zara felt a deep sense of shock. "She actually said that?"

"No, but she made her feelings very clear." Kevin closed the attic door and indicated a door on the left down the hall. "You might as well use Brianne's room while you're here. After you wash the dust off, join me in the dining room."

"A room of my own? I thought . . ."

"That you'd be occupying my bed? Not yet."

She stared after him as he went into his chamber and closed the door. She should have been thinking about the mirror but found herself wondering about the women who had lived in this house. Brianne, Silver, and Rising Star . . .

A portrait of an Indian woman hung over the mantel in the library. The painting dominated the room and was the first thing Zara saw when she entered it after supper that evening.

"Rising Star?"

Kevin nodded. "My mother. Brianne painted it from memory after her death and gave it to me for my eighth birthday. Malvina smiled politely, and when Brianne left she put it in the attic out of sight."

Another wound. "Then how did it get down here?"

"When I was twelve I brought it down and hung it there."

"And she let you?"

"No, she tanned my hide and took it down." He went to the fireplace and stoked the fire to life. "And I promptly put it back. She took it down again. The fifth time I hung it there, she left it."

"Why did she hate her so?"

He shrugged. "Indians had killed her two sons. She was Indian."

"It wasn't your mother's fault."

"People don't always think with their heads."

Zara was well aware of that fact. She had encountered prejudice all her life because she was Gypsy, but it somehow hurt her to realize how Kevin and his mother had suffered. How terrible to live as a captive in a house where you were hated. At least she had been surrounded by other outcasts, free to travel from place to place.

"Did you hate Malvina too?"

"No, in many ways I admired her. She and Shamus came to a hard land and tamed it. She was no monster. She loved and protected her own children as much as she disliked and rejected me."

She was surprised he could be so fair in a situation that must have been terribly painful for him. It was not the first time he had surprised her that evening. During dinner he had been almost silent but had ignored her uneasiness with the gleaming cutlery and had been as polite as if she were a fine lady. He had been . . . kind.

"When did your grandfather Shamus die?"

"When I was five." He crossed to the leather chair before the hearth and sat down. "And no, I didn't hate him either. Sorry to disappoint you."

"Why should I be disappointed?"

"A savage should always display the appropriate ferocity, shouldn't he?"

"I said I meant nothing by it." She lifted her chin. "And I refuse to apologize again because you're ashamed of what you are."

Anger flickered in his expression. "I'm not ashamed. I'm more proud of my Apache blood than my white."

"Then why do you keep harping on it?"

"I don't harp—" He stopped, surprised. "Perhaps I do. Silver said as much."

She nodded. "I was the same before I realized it didn't matter what anyone thought. I know what I am."

"And you think I don't?"

He was watching her with narrowed eyes, and she decided it would be best to change the subject. "Who is Silver?"

"My cousin, a half-breed like me. A very unusual woman."

"Did Malvina—"

"I believe we've talked enough about me. Come here and sit down."

She moved forward to stand in front of him. "I'm tired. I believe I'll go to bed."

"Not yet. It's my turn to ask questions."

"What questions?" she asked warily. "I've told you why I'm here. Why should you need to know anything else?"

"Curiosity. Sit down."

She plopped down on the floor at his feet.

"We do have chairs."

"This will do." She turned around to face the fire and crossed her legs tailor-fashion. "I won't be here long. You cannot be very interested in me."

"Why not? Aren't you my cousin?"

She darted him a surprised glance over her shoulder. "You believe we're kin?"

"I haven't noticed you being less than truthful so far. On the contrary, you appear to be honest to the point of pain. *My* pain."

"I do tell the truth. I am a Delaney. I swear I am."

"Such passion." His hands were suddenly on her nape. She stiffened and he said impatiently, "Relax. I'm only rubbing your neck. The texture of your skin is exquisite." He began to massage with his thumbs. "I'm surprised Malvina didn't give you the mirror. She thought the Delaneys were next only to Gabriel in the heavenly firmament and obviously approved of you if she returned your letters."

"She cared nothing for me. The only reason she answered my letters was that I gave her news of her people in Ireland. I wish you would not do that. It feels ... strange."

"Am I hurting you?"

"No." And yet that was not the exact truth. Though he was only gently stroking her neck, his touch was sending currents of heat through her shoulders and breasts that caused an aching sensation. How odd, she thought.

"Then I see no reason why I should stop. You knew Malvina's people?"

She shook her head. "When I was eleven I wrote Malvina for the first time. When she didn't answer the next time our tribe was in Dublin, I went to her old home and asked questions until I found them. Malvina had a younger sister and a nephew when she left Ireland. Her sister died fifteen years ago, but her children and grandchildren are still alive and were spread throughout every county in Ireland. I wrote Malvina and told her if she would write to me, I'd visit her kin whenever our caravan passed by and send her word. I received a letter three months later. Every time she wrote me I sent her little bits of information about the doings of her sister's family. Not too much. Just enough to make it worth her while to keep answering me."

"Very clever. Family was everything to Malvina."

"It was the only thing I could think to do. Most of the time her letters just rambled on about Killara, but every now and then she would mention the mirror."

He brushed her hair to one side and his index finger began to trace patterns on her sensitive flesh. "Why is the mirror so important to you?"

A hot shiver went through her and she had to take a deep breath before she could speak. "I've already told you."

"Not everything."

She didn't answer.

"Then tell me about your own people. Your parents must be singularly lacking in judgment to let you run around the world with no protection."

"My parents are dead."

"Do you have brothers and sisters?"

"No, there's only Carlo, my stepbrother."

"Ah, the canny horsetrader. How could I forget about Carlo?"

She felt the heat fly to her cheeks as she remembered what had transpired after she had told him about Carlo.

"Are you fond of each other?"

"Yes."

His hands on her neck tautened for an instant. "How fond?"

She swallowed. "Fond enough."

"Enough for what?" His voice turned silky as his hands slid down over her shoulders to rest on the upper slopes of her breasts. "Is he as skilled with women as he is with horses?"

"Better than most." She was scarcely aware of what she was saying. "May I go to bed now?"

"No," he said a little too loudly. "You're not holding to the agreement. I'm not amused."

So he was displeased, was he? Well, she couldn't worry about it—not when she was in such turmoil herself. She slid out from under his hands and jumped to her feet. "I told you that you'd not find me what you wanted." She turned to face him. "You'd do best to—" She broke off and inhaled sharply at what she saw in his face.

"You were saying?"

"Nothing." She whirled and fled toward the door. "I'll see you in the morning."

"I didn't say you could go."

Anger flared. "Then throw me out of your house, take me out and hang me. I don't care. I'm weary and you're most unsettling. I'll take no more."

"You've not taken anything yet." His tone was deeply sensual. "But you will, Zara." Then, as he studied her, his expression changed. "You *are* tired. Get out of here and get some sleep. I'll comfort myself with a bottle of whiskey tonight."

She looked at him, wondering why she couldn't leave him. She wanted to go. He had filled her with fear and disquiet, and she wanted none of it. Yet something twisted painfully inside her as she saw him sitting there beneath the portrait of Rising Star. Mother and son both had the same air of strength . . . and loneliness. "You should go to bed too. Carlo says liquor addles the brain and makes a man as stupid as an inbred horse."

"I'm not interested in the opinions of your Carlo," he bit out. "Though I fully intend soon to be able to match him in experience with you. I'd advise you to leave me now if you don't wish that experience to occur immediately."

Relief poured through her. The loneliness and vulnerability in him had vanished, and now she could see only the reckless, sensual man. Both aspects of Kevin held a threat, but this one did not hurt her heart. Hurt her? She dismissed the thought impatiently. He could not hurt her. She would find the mirror tomorrow and soon would be gone from his life. "I really do not care if you drink yourself silly. Good night." She suddenly turned back to him. "Did you find the key to the armoire?"

"Yes, Consuelo had it."

"Then we can go up to the attic tonight and see if—"

"No, we cannot," he said with precision. "I'm well aware of where your interest lies, but it can wait until morning."

"But I wish—"

"Tomorrow."

She was tempted to argue with him, but there was so much leashed ferocity in that one word, she decided it would be best to let him have his way. "Oh, very well."

Kevin reached for the bottle of whiskey on the table beside him and poured a stiff drink the moment the door closed behind Zara. He needed it. He drained the glass in two swallows and filled it again. He wanted to follow Zara up those stairs and into her bed. Her body had responded to his touch with an alacrity that had fed his own lust to fever pitch. Why wait? She might not be ready yet, but he could make her ready. Evidently her dear, clever bastard of a stepbrother had been able to perform the feat with no trouble. Why shouldn't he be able to do the same?

He drained the second whiskey even quicker than the first.

Jealousy. He had never known jealousy before, but now it was tearing him apart. He kept seeing her lying naked, her red hair spread on a pillow, a man over her, moving. . . .

He wouldn't think about it, dammit. He would finish the blasted bottle and then go up to her and—

Liquor addles a man's brain.

And Plainfield was out there somewhere just waiting for him to make a mistake.

He could risk a mistake. He had managed to put down Plainfield before with no trouble and he'd had more than one bottle under his belt. If Plainfield appeared, he could do it again.

But Zara was in the house and Plainfield would be a threat to her also. Kevin was risking her safety as well as his own.

She was nothing to him though, a Gypsy who had appeared in the night and touched him and tormented him. She must take her own chances. He would *not* be responsible for her.

But how would he feel if Plainfield hurt her?

The thought inspired such rage and terror that he was stunned.

His glass crashed down on the table and he jumped to his feet. He should send her away. Somehow she was gaining too much of a hold over him and so quickly it was making his head swim. Ridiculous. He could satisfy his lust with any woman.

But he didn't want any woman. He wanted Zara St. Cloud—and he would have her. Then he would send her away and this fascination she had for him would fade.

But he couldn't risk Plainfield hurting her, dammit. He cast one frustrated glance at the bottle of whiskey on the table before he strode out of the library and up the stairs to bed.

4

THE ARMOIRE DOOR SWUNG OPEN.

"There's nothing here," Zara said, disappointed.

"That's not quite true." Kevin wrinkled his nose at the musty smell assaulting them. "It's packed to its top with old clothes." He pushed aside several hangers. "Evidently Malvina never threw anything away."

"Naturally. She was thrifty. She grew up in a poor family and was a housemaid in Dublin." Zara's tone was abstracted as she caught a glimpse of something cream-colored that looked soft. "What's this?" She pulled out a beaded leather garment from a pile on the bottom of the armoire. "It's beautiful beading. Who did—" She stopped as she saw his expression. "Your mother?"

"Possibly. Or it could have belonged to Silver." He shrugged. "I'm surprised Malvina didn't burn those things instead of just shutting them up here and hoping they'd rot. At least it explains why the armoire was locked. Forbidden fruit." His expression suddenly changed from bitterness to recklessness as he began to pull out other leather clothing. "But this particular forbidden fruit has proven tougher than she thought. It's about time it saw the light of day again."

"What are you doing?"

He pushed the pile of garments toward her. "Do you want them? Take them." His eyes glittered a mocking challenge. "Or perhaps you wouldn't want to be seen in them . . . you might be mistaken for a savage."

Perhaps he wasn't as dark to her as she had thought, for she sensed his hurt again as if it were her own. She felt compelled to ease it. She said quickly, "Don't be foolish. Why shouldn't I want these lovely things? They're as fine as this velvet cloak you let me wear, and I like them better."

"You have unusual taste. Doeskin over velvet?"

"Velvet is for fine ladies. I'll be much happier with this." He was looking at her with an expression that made her uneasy, and she hastily lowered her glance to the beaded tunic. "If you truly wish me to have them."

"Oh, yes, I truly wish you to have them." He smiled curiously. "I find I derive an inordinate amount of pleasure from giving you things." He pulled out a pair of doeskin knee boots and tossed them on the pile. "But I believe we'll have to find you someplace appropriate to wear them. We can't have—what's this?"

The removal of the boots had revealed something dark and gleaming beneath the stack of clothing on the bottom of the chest.

Zara's heart gave a leap, and she frantically began pushing garments aside. A faint silvery glimmer . . . Could it be? "It's the mirror!"

"So it is. How appropriate. The forbidden with the forbidden," Kevin murmured. "I'll get it." He nudged her away, pushed garments to the side, and managed to pull the mirror out of the armoire. "Where shall I put it?"

"Against the wall, by the window." She scurried at his heels as he carried the piece across the attic. "Be careful. Don't drop it."

"I'm not going to drop it. It's not that heavy." He set the mirror down on the floor and leaned it against the wall. He dropped to his knees, took his handkerchief from the pocket of his jeans, and started wiping the dust off the surface. "You wouldn't think it could get so dirty locked in—"

"Let me." She snatched the cloth from his hands, knelt beside him, and carefully began rubbing the smudged surface. Her hand was trembling so badly she could hardly hold the cloth. After all these years of waiting it was here before her. In a moment she would see, she would know....

The mirror free of dust, she sat back on her heels and closed her eyes.

"You're not going to see anything with your eyes shut," Kevin said dryly.

"I'm afraid to look. What if..."

"What if?" he prompted.

"Nothing." She could not avoid the test forever. She opened her eyes.

She saw only her own reflection cloaked in green velvet, her eyes big with apprehension, and Kevin beside her gazing at her with a quizzical expression. Disappointment overwhelmed her. "No!"

"What's wrong?"

"There's nothing there." Her nails dug into the velvet of the cloak. "But there has to be. It *has* to happen."

"No magic?"

She suddenly turned on him and said fiercely, "Stop staring at me and look at the mirror. What do you see?"

"You, me, the attic."

Relief poured through her. "Then it's all right. If you can't see it either, then it's not me. It's not because I'm—" She stopped. "It's just not ready to show me anything yet. I was told it wouldn't always tell the future; sometimes it will tell the past and sometimes only reflect the present like an ordinary mirror."

"Have you ever considered the possibility that it *is* an ordinary mirror?"

"No, and I shall not. It has to be magic." She jumped to her feet and went back to the armoire. "You take the mirror and I'll carry those clothes you gave me."

"I'm surprised you even remembered the clothes. Isn't the mirror the only thing that's important to you?"

She was surprised herself but had acted instinctively to avoid wounding him. What idiocy, when he was more enemy than friend. Still, she gathered up the leather garments. "Magic is important, but so are warm clothes and a full belly. You were kind to give these to me and I would be ungrateful not to appreciate them."

"Kind? I don't recall being overly kind to you."

"Well, you've not been unkind. Stop arguing with me and take the mirror."

He picked it up. "And where am I taking it?"

"To the chamber you gave me. It would be stupid to stay up here in the cold now that I've found it. I'll hang it on the wall."

"And I suppose you intend to sit before it until something miraculous happens?"

"Certainly."

"No." He strode down the steps. "An hour a day. No more. The rest of your time belongs to me."

"An hour? That's not enough." She followed him down the steps. "The bargain was—"

"As you haven't complied with any part of the bargain, I wouldn't bring up terms." He shot her a glance. "One hour."

She scowled mutinously. "That's not fair." She followed him down the hall. "You said I could look at it."

"And so you will." He opened the door of her room. "Where do you want it?"

She pointed to a landscape painting hanging on the wall beside the door. "Take down that picture and put it there. But I still—"

"You said you believed the mirror was magic."

"I do. It is. What does that have to do with anything?

"Then don't you think if the mirror wanted to show you something, it would do so? How could one nonbeliever like me keep it from happening? However, if the mirror isn't ready to reveal these great and wondrous secrets, I doubt if staring at it the entire day will force them into the open." He replaced the picture with the mirror and set the picture on the floor. "Do you ride?"

"What?" She tore her gaze from the mirror. "Horses? Of course I do. Carlo taught me."

Even through her absorption she was aware of his sudden tension. "And I wonder what else he taught you," he muttered as he turned away. "Never mind. I believe it best not to discuss your Carlo at present. I'll meet you downstairs in twenty minutes." He nodded at the doeskin garments in her arms. "Change into those. Be sure to wear the cloak. It's cold as bejesus."

"Where are we going?"

"Out."

"That's no answer. Where—"

"Away from attics and magic mirrors and this damn house." The door slammed behind him.

He was angry again, and she had an idea it had little to do with Killara and much to do with her. She was tempted not to obey him. She didn't want to go with him and face his mockery and anger or the wild mixture of disturbing feelings she always experienced when she was with him and, blast it, she didn't wish to leave now that she had found the mirror. She took a step closer and eagerly gazed into the gleaming surface.

Nothing. Just her own disappointed face and the velvet-draped canopied bed and gauzy white curtains behind her.

Perhaps Kevin was right and the mirror's magic could not be forced. Maybe when she least expected it the reflection would change, shift, tell her what she wanted to know.

In the meantime she had made a bargain, and bargains must be kept. Kevin had kept to his word about helping her find the mirror and, if he demanded her presence, she must accede. He would probably grow bored with her company soon anyway, and then she would be free to come back and try again.

She cast one final wistful glance at the mirror before turning away and pulling the cotton blouse over her head.

"Very nice." Kevin's gaze ran over her, from the doeskin-beaded boots peeping from beneath the hem of the velvet cloak to the hood sheltering her head from the bitter wind. "I half expected you to come down wrapped in a bedspread just to spite me."

"That wouldn't have been sensible." She nodded with approval at the two horses he was leading toward her. "Fine animals."

"Your Carlo would approve?" He heaved her up on the back of the mare. "I'm honored."

"He would approve, but I think we'll not talk about Carlo. For some reason it puts you in a bad temper." She watched in admiration as he mounted the stallion with economical grace. "You did that very well. Perhaps you can do something beside whore, drink, and shoot people."

"Perhaps." He turned the horse and kicked him into a gallop, flying down the north road.

He rode as if pursued by a demon, and she had all she could do for the next thirty minutes to keep him in view. They streaked past a frozen lake and over stark terrain bordered by tall evergreens heavily laden with snow. It wasn't until they were in the foothills that she finally pulled even with him. "You're clearly not riding for pleasure. Are you going to tell me where we're going?"

"Not far." Kevin didn't look at her as he spurred ahead again. "Just over the next hill. Don't worry, I'm not taking you out to lose you."

"I didn't think you were. I've got the mirror, but you've received nothing in return yet. It's not human nature to give and not want to wrest something for oneself."

"How wise of you to realize that."

"It seems a long way to go for a ride. I don't see why you can't—" She stopped as they crested the hill. In the valley below them was spread a small village, a jumble of tepees and a corral in which horses jostled one another to reach bins of corn. Men, women, and children were dressed in garments like the one she wore. "Indians?"

"Apaches." He reined in and gazed down at the village. "My mother's tribe."

"On Delaney land?"

"I brought them here three years ago. It's better than the reservation the government gave them. There was no game and the land was barely able to grow cactus, much less crops. Whites stole their birthright and gave them—" He stopped and shrugged. "I couldn't stand it, so I gave them this valley."

"Are we going down?"

"No, I just wanted to make sure they were still here and all right. It's been a hard winter. I ordered wagons of food and grain to be brought to them a month ago, but . . ." He sat there looking down at the village. "The tribe used to be located south of the Dragoon Mountains. Silver used to take me there every summer and we'd spend a month with them. Malvina would spit and hiss but Silver never cared."

"And you liked it there?"

He nodded. "We stayed with Consuelo and her family. I was more at home there than I ever was at Killara."

The wistfulness in his expression touched her. "Then let's go down." She impulsively kicked her horse and started down the trail toward the village at a gallop.

"No! Wait, it's not—"

"Come on. It's foolish to come all this way and then go back without seeing—" She stopped, weaving in the saddle, feeling as if she had been clubbed. "No!"

"What's wrong?" Kevin pulled up beside her, grasping her arm and steadying her. "Are you sick? You look like you're about to fall off the damn horse."

The waves of emotion assaulted her, tore at her. "Sad," she whispered. "So much sadness." Her eyes stung with unshed tears. "Hurts."

"What are you talking about?"

"Them." She nodded at the village. "Don't you feel it? So sad..." She tore away from him, and the next minute she was urging the mare up the hill, away from the village, away from that overpowering agony of melancholy.

Kevin muttered a curse and rode after her.

She reined in at the crest of the hill, her breath coming in gasps. "Better now. Out of range."

"Out of range from what?" Kevin frowned. "What the devil is wrong with you?"

"They're sad.... They mourn." She motioned helplessly. "Their thoughts..."

"You claim you're reading their thoughts?"

She shook her head. "Too far away. I'm only...waves of feeling." She swallowed. "Too strong." She gazed up at him and said defensively, "It's true. I do have the power. You can believe it or not, as you like. Most gadjos don't."

He was silent a moment, gazing at her. "I believe you."

"You do?" she whispered.

"I'd be a fool not to realize you felt something. You're white as a sheet and you're still shaking." He looked down at the village. "And sometimes I think I can feel the same sadness. It doesn't take anyone with 'the power' to sense what they're feeling, experiencing." He turned his horse. "Let's go."

"No." She drew a deep breath. "You care about them. You must want to visit with them. I'll stay up here and wait."

He ignored her and headed back the way they had come.

"Didn't you hear me?" she said as she caught up with him. "I want you to go on down. It's not as—"

"I said I wouldn't visit the village."

"But why not? I told you that—"

"You say a great deal but you don't listen. I'm not going."

"You're not being reasonable. Why don't you—"

"Lord, you're persistent," he said, exasperated. He didn't speak for a moment and then burst out, "I'm not welcome there, dammit."

"Of course you are. They must be very grateful to you for taking care of them."

"Charity?" His lips twisted with bitterness. "They don't want charity. They want their chance to live with freedom and dignity as they once did. They treat me with courtesy, but when they look at me they see just another white man."

"But you said you once felt at home with them."

"Everything changes. It was a different time." She could sense his pain as poignantly as she had the villagers'. "I didn't share their defeat and humiliation, so how could I be one with them? I don't share in the white man's desire for conquest, so how can I be one with *them?* I don't belong to either people."

"I don't understand."

"My mother once told my cousin Patrick about an Indian proverb that says no one must run headlong toward the sun lest the demons steal his shadow. She said because she had married a white man and tried to be like his people she cast no shadow at all, neither Indian nor white. She asked him not to let anyone steal my shadow."

"I don't think you would allow anyone to take anything from you," she said quietly. "So he must have succeeded."

"Did he?" He suddenly smiled recklessly. "You're right, of course. No one steals anything from me these days. I do what I like and I'm not chained either to that Indian village or to Killara. I cast my own shadow and I take what I want."

She felt a mixture of relief and apprehension as she realized his sadness was gone, replaced by the wild hard man she had first glimpsed in the attic. "That's good," she said cautiously.

"It may not be what my mother meant, but it's how I learned to survive." He leaned forward, his hand encircling her throat and his voice velvet soft and infinitely sensual. "There are many interesting ways of casting a shadow, Zara. I think it's time I showed you a few of them."

She couldn't look away from him and felt her heart throbbing wildly beneath his touch. "A shadow is . . . I don't know what you mean."

"Yes, you do." His hand fell away and he turned his horse. "And if you don't, you will soon."

Kevin lifted Zara off the mare and threw the reins of the horses over the hitching rail in front of the homestead.

"Come on." His hand gripped her wrist and he urged her up the steps, then into the foyer. "Hurry."

"Where—" Zara broke off before she finished the question. There was no need to ask. She knew where they were going and what they were going to do. She had sensed the recklessness and the need in him every minute of the ride back from the village. It was going to happen. "You said you wouldn't—"

"Until it didn't seem awkward to you." He was pulling her up the stairs. "It's not going to be awkward, dammit. If it is, feel free to stop me."

That was easy to say, but his hand on her wrist was an unbreakable manacle and she felt as if she were being swept away by a storm wind.

"You will not want lunch, I suppose?" Consuelo stood in the hallway calmly looking up at them.

"No." Kevin paused on the steps to frown down at her. "And stay out of this, Consuelo."

"I have no intention of interfering. I was just asking." She shrugged and plodded down the hall toward the kitchen. "It is what I expected. . . ."

His hand tightened even more possessively around Zara's wrist as he hurried up the steps and into her room.

He slammed the door, his hands immediately going to the button of the cloak.

"No!" She backed away from him. "Don't do that."

He went still. "You're breaking your word?"

"Don't be ridiculous. I keep my promises." She felt the heat in her cheeks. "It's just . . . not here. I don't want to do it here."

"Why the hell not?"

She nodded at the mirror a few feet away. "What if it remembers everything it sees?"

"Oh, for God's sake!" He grabbed her wrist, and once more they were striding down the hall. In a moment they were in his chamber, the door locked.

"No mirrors," Kevin muttered as he unbuttoned her cloak. "Does that make you happy?"

She was too frightened and unsure to know what she was feeling. The green velvet cloak was now a bright pool on the carpet, and he was lifting her, carrying her toward the bed. "Shouldn't you draw the drapes?"

"Why? There are no mirrors to see you. There's only me." He smiled mockingly. "And how can I cast a shadow without light?" He set her down on the bed. "Besides, I want to see every inch of you."

"With daylight streaming in, you'll certainly do that. I would think—"

"Did your Carlo prefer darkness?"

"Carlo? What does he have to do with this?"

"Not a damn thing." He slithered the soft doeskin tunic over her head. "So shut up about him."

She thought about pointing out that he was not being fair. After all, she had not been the one to bring up Carlo. Then she forgot about fairness as his hand cupped her breast. Amazingly, she felt the nipple swell, harden beneath his touch. "How odd."

"How lovely," he corrected her hoarsely, his head bending slowly toward her. "Small and perfect." His tongue touched her nipple.

Heat jolted through her, and she felt the muscles of her stomach clench. She cried out, her back arching as sensation after sensation tore through her.

He was making low sounds of need and pleasure deep in his throat that were as erotic as the touch of his mouth on her breast.

"You like this?" He lifted his head and smiled with primitive satisfaction as he saw her dazed expression. "Not awkward?"

She didn't trust her voice so she simply shook her head.

He took a step back and stripped off his shirt. "Hurry. Get undressed," he muttered. "I can't wait any longer."

She tried to obey him, but her hands were trembling so badly, he was completely unclothed while she was still struggling with the doeskin boots. Her eyes widened as she stopped to look at him. It was not the first time she had seen a nude male. Living in a caravan made modesty impossible, and Carlo was proud of his body. Carlo was a handsome man, but he did not possess Kevin's lean, golden symmetry of form. Her gaze went over strong thighs and tight buttocks, the triangle of dark hair on his chest, the taut abdomen.

"What are you waiting for? For Lord's sake, let me do it." A slide of straight dark hair fell over his forehead as he bent forward to help her with the boots. He pulled the boots off and tossed them aside. He was breathing hard, his chest rising and falling with every breath as he looked at her. "Now stand up."

"What?"

"I want to *feel* you." He slid her off the bed to her feet. His hands clasped her waist, pulled her into the hollow of his hips, and slowly rubbed her against his body.

She bit her lower lip to keep from crying out.

His grasp on her waist tightened and he squeezed gently.

His breath flooded out shakily. "Do you know how this excites me?"

She couldn't speak. She could barely breathe. Her knees gave way and she had to grab him to remain upright.

"Do you?" he persisted hoarsely.

He was clearly going to insist on an answer, she realized with exasperation. "Of course I do," she said tartly. "What a foolish question. It could not be more obvious."

He began to chuckle. "Granted. I'll try to be less foolish in the future." He pushed her gently down on the bed, parted her thighs, and moved between them. His lips tightened. "I hope to hell you're ready. I can't wait any longer."

It was starting. Her palms nervously clenched on the sheet. She hadn't thought she would be this frightened. She must not let him see it.

He suddenly plunged forward, filling her completely.

Her cry was more in surprise than pain. She had expected discomfort, but not this fullness, this sense of total joining.

But the satiation was gone almost immediately. She needed more.

She was vaguely aware of his sudden stillness. "What's wrong?" she murmured.

"Plenty." He drew a shuddering breath.

The motion sent a tingle of need through her. She reached out blindly, her hands grasping his hips. "Do . . . something."

"You want it?" He stared down at her, his cheeks hollow, his eyes glazed, wild. "You want me? I warn you, I can't be gentle."

"I don't care," she whispered. "I don't think I can either. I feel most . . . strange."

"You feel most . . . wonderful." He closed his eyes and began a slow, deep rhythm that caused her nails to dig into his hips.

Wave after wave of pleasure thundered through her as he moved her, shifted her. He was murmuring words but she couldn't distinguish their meaning. Her heart was beating so hard, the drumming seemed to fill the room.

She felt as hot and disoriented as she had once when she had contracted a fever. Her head thrashed back and forth on the pillow, and she heard her own voice gasping, begging, but she didn't know for what she pleaded. The sense of union was so strong now that she felt as if they were one body and the tension and fever were mounting until she couldn't bear it. "Kevin . . ."

He moved faster, harder, deeper.

The fever broke and she half lifted off the bed with a low cry.

He collapsed on top of her, his entire body shaking. She dimly felt the impulse to hold and comfort him, but she was too dazed to move. A moment later she felt him move off her.

He lay there breathing hard, staring straight ahead. When he could speak he raised himself on one elbow to look down at her. "Why?"

"I had to have the mirror," she said simply.

"Enough to give up your virginity for it?"

"My people do not consider a woman ruined because she gives herself to a man. Only gadjos are that unfair to women. Besides, there was a possibility it wouldn't happen."

"You're wrong. From almost the first moment that possibility did not exist." He sat up and pulled the cover over her. "And what about Carlo?"

"What about him? Oh, you thought..." She shook her head. "Carlo would never look at me. He likes big, robust women. He says small women are like ponies, fit only for young boys."

"I'm beginning to think that Carlo isn't as canny as you make him out to be." He went over to the fireplace and stoked the logs. "I'm no boy and I found you very...fit."

A surge of pleasure went through her. "I thought you found me pleasing."

"Oh, yes." His voice was thick. "You might say that."

"I guess that's good. It's always nice to be considered..." She frowned. "Or perhaps it's not. You might want to do it again, and I don't think...it was a most unsettling experience."

"In what way?"

"I felt...bound to you. I'm sure we'd both feel much more at ease if we don't—"

"I disagree." He turned to look at her.

Breathlessness. Tingling. Heat.

"I won't be at ease until I'm in you again." He moved toward her across the room. "As you can see."

She saw bold arousal, glittering eyes, cheeks hollowed as if from a terrible hunger. The air in the room seemed to crackle like that in a forest after a lightning storm, and she could feel the same weakness she had experienced before drawing her toward him into the storm. She moistened her lips. "I suppose once more would do no harm if you truly require it."

"Yes, Zara." He moved over her and slid smoothly into her depths. "I truly do require it."

"It's very interesting, isn't it?" She could barely speak, her breath was coming in little gasps. "It felt like—" She paused. "It's difficult to put into words. Is it always like this?"

"If it were, I wouldn't waste my time doing anything else."

"According to what I heard from the women at Garnet's, you do expend a great deal of time and energy on it." She wished she hadn't thought of Garnet's; it brought an odd, fierce hurt. "I think you lie when you say this is different."

"I don't lie." He leaned down and lazily licked her nipple before moving off her. "I wish to hell I did."

"Why?"

She raised herself on one elbow to look down at him and suddenly understood. "Oh, you feel it too."

His expression became wary. "Feel what?"

"Bound. It isn't a pleasant feeling, is it? It makes the heart beat fast and this funny, queasy flutter in the belly. Don't worry, I'm sure it will go away once we're no longer together. It's just part of the spell."

His brows rose. "You're saying you cast a spell over me?"

"Good heavens, why would I wish to do that? No, it's only . . . I believe sometimes these spells fall naturally on people. It's not really magic. I remember once Kasan, a friend of Carlo's, went crazy over a woman from another tribe and threatened to kill her husband and take her for himself."

"And did he do it?"

"No, our caravan moved on and the madness faded. I'm certain it will be the same with us."

"How comforting."

"And besides, Kasan thought he loved the woman. We feel only passion, and that should make the spell weaker."

"It doesn't feel weak." He took her hand and placed it on himself. "Does it?"

"No." He wanted her again and, dear heaven, she wanted him. "But I'm sure that's only part of the spell. It's more powerful in the beginning, and then lessens."

"Then perhaps we'd better take advantage of it now." He pulled down the coverlet and moved over her. "Be sure to tell me if you see any signs of weakening."

There was no weakening, she realized in despair as the rhythm started. The spell was growing stronger, the bonds tighter with every time together.

Then she could no longer think at all.

"Let me in." A loud knocking at the door. "You must eat now."

Zara was barely aware of Kevin's muttered curse as she fought her way through heavy veils of sleep. Consuelo. It was Consuelo's voice, she realized dimly, Consuelo banging on the door.

"Go away," Kevin shouted.

"Pepe is bringing up the tub for the woman, and I have the water poured in a tub for you in the kitchen. You must rouse yourself now. I will have supper ready in forty minutes."

"I don't want—"

"Perhaps you do not, but the woman is as skinny as a starving heifer and should eat. Forty minutes."

They heard her heavy footfall in the hall and then her yelling on the stairs. "Why are you resting on the landing, Pepe? Have you no strength? Bring up that tub."

"Blast her." Kevin sat up in bed. "One of these days I'm going to send her back to her people. If I don't massacre her first."

"We don't have to do as she says. I'm not hungry." She could not imagine ever being hungry again. She was filled with an unbelievable languor and satiation.

"No?" He turned to look at her with narrowed eyes and suddenly she was no longer satiated. She could feel her breasts swell as if at his command and the heat start once more. "Lord, what's wrong with me?" he murmured. "I can't get enough. It's as if I've never touched you." He reached out and stroked his index finger along the line of her cheekbone. "So delicate. There's nothing to you. When I hold you I feel as if I could break you, and yet when I'm inside you there's such strength."

She could sense the now-familiar tension and expected him to come back to her, wanted him to come back to her. She shivered in anticipation, waiting.

He frowned. "What's wrong? Are you cold?"

She had never been less cold. "No, I just—"

"Dammit, you wouldn't tell me if you were." His hand dropped away from her cheek. "Oh, no, you're not afraid and you don't feel hunger or cold. You accept everything I do to you for the sake of that damn mirror." He got out of bed and stalked naked toward the door. "You need to eat. She's right . . . damn her soul."

The door slammed behind him.

She had only time to sit up on the bed and drape the sheet around her before Consuelo stalked into the room, closely followed by her black cat, Beelzebub, and a short, muscular man carrying a porcelain tub.

"By the fire, Pepe." Consuelo motioned to the hearth, and while Pepe was depositing the tub she strode over to the bed. "You look as drained as a plucked chicken. Why did you not tell him you were hungry?"

"I wish you would not compare me to animals. I'm not a starved heifer nor am I a plucked chicken. And why should I have told him I'm hungry when I'm not at—" But she *was* hungry, she realized incredulously. A vast emptiness was yawning in her stomach. "I didn't know I was."

"Then you'd better learn your requirements quickly. You can't expect a man to pay attention to any need but his own when the heat is on him." Consuelo moved over to the bureau to fetch a brush. "Your hair is tangled. We'll have to wash that too. Be quick with that water," she said over her shoulder to Pepe. "And see that Kevin has all he needs downstairs while you're about it."

Pepe grumbled something and left the chamber.

"Now, let's get to it." Consuelo began running the brush through Zara's curls with more speed than gentleness. "You look like you've ridden through a tornado." She grinned. "Or maybe ridden a tornado. Kevin can be as rough and lusty as a bull when he's rutting, but his women never seem to mind."

Bull? It seemed even Kevin wasn't exempt from her comparisons. "He wasn't rough with me."

"No? I'm surprised. He had the wildness in him when I saw him drag you upstairs."

Kevin had been wild, but after that first time there had been no roughness. At times he'd been too deliberate for her, teasing her until she thought she would go mad. "I don't want to talk about it."

Consuelo shrugged. "It's nothing to me." She glanced over her shoulder at Pepe, who was now back and pouring a pail of water into the tub. "Kevin does well?"

The man nodded sourly. "Well enough to curse me and tell me to get out and leave him alone." He poured the other bucket of water into the tub. "He said to tell you to hurry and get her downstairs."

"Impatient," Consuelo murmured. "It will take as long as it takes, but maybe we will indulge him by being quick this time." She threw the brush on the bed. "Get out, Pepe."

Pepe gave her another scowl and left the chamber.

"Come along." Consuelo jerked the sheet from around Zara. "Into the tub. We'd better get you finished before he comes after you, or we might not get you fed after all."

"I can bathe myself." The water was hot and blissfully soothing. She leaned back and closed her eyes. "I don't need your help."

"Be quiet." Consuelo knelt in back of her and took up the sponge. "Kevin has you so limp you may go to sleep before I get you out of here." She lifted Zara's hair and briskly scrubbed her neck and casually commented, "You have bruises."

"No, I don't." She opened her eyes and saw to her amazement the faint blue smudges on her breasts and hips. "He didn't mean to—"

"I know," Consuelo interrupted. "He's not a harsh man, but he feels more strongly than most. It was good you were here to take the wildness from him. Most of the time when he comes back from the village he drinks a bottle of whiskey and then goes back to Hell's Bluff." She dipped the sponge and scrubbed Zara's face and back. "This time maybe he'll be content to stay until it passes, if you give him what he needs. Dip your head."

Zara obediently dipped her head in the water. "I don't know what he needs."

"To forget for a while, to laugh, to lust."

"How did you know we had come from the village?"

Consuelo brusquely lathered soap into Zara's hair. "He's always like that when he returns. I can see it in him."

"What do you see?"

"The hurt, the bad feeling. I tell him to stay away, but he cannot. He is very foolish. He feels he must protect them even if they reject him. Kevin will never ignore a responsibility even if it brings him pain." Consuelo pushed her head into the water to rinse it.

"Are you trying to drown me?" Zara sputtered when she was allowed to lift her head.

"No, that would be stupid, when I have use for you."

"What use?" Consuelo did not answer, and after a moment Zara said, "Kevin told me you belong to that tribe."

"Yes, he brought me here the year before he moved the tribe to the valley. I changed my name to one whites can pronounce and have never returned to my village."

"Why not?"

"All of us must make choices. My husband was killed when he chose to follow Geronimo, but I have a child and I wish her to live a good life. She cannot if she clings to defeat and the old ways. The first year I spent here was hard. I had to learn many new things." She made a face. "Some of them I thought very stupid, but I learned them anyway. It was worth it. Here at Killara Isabel will have a chance. Kevin is very good to her and next year will send her to school in the East." She got to her feet and reached for a towel. "Stand up."

Zara stood up and was immediately wrapped in the huge towel. "You don't need to dry me as if I were a child."

"You're right. I have no more time for this. I must go tend to my stew. Hurry and dress." Consuelo turned at the door to look soberly at her. "He is a man worth saving. You must keep him here."

"What?"

"Silver sent me a message before he returned to Hell's Bluff. It is dangerous for him to return to town. There is a man who wishes to kill him."

Her heart gave a jerk. "Plainfield."

Consuelo nodded. "Yes, that is the name. Silver says this man has no honor. Kevin must stay among his own people, where at least the fight will be fair. Keep him here."

"I cannot keep him anywhere against his will. He's the one who holds the power."

"He is a man. He clearly finds you pleasing in bed, where a woman always holds power. Keep him occupied there and all will be well."

Zara did not move for a moment after the door closed behind Consuelo, her mind a jumble of confusion and fear. She had heard in town of the gunfight that had wounded Plainfield, but events had moved so swiftly since she had arrived at Killara she had almost forgotten it. Yet now she remembered Kevin's murmured words in the attic. Dear heaven, he had expected her to be his enemy laying in wait for him. He had expected Plainfield to follow him to Killara and try to kill him.

The knowledge brought panic that in turn ignited frustration and anger. She did not want to feel this fear for any man. She had come to Killara only to find the mirror and what it held for her, and it was not her responsibility if the stupid man got himself killed. The bond between them was only of the flesh, and she would not have it mean more to her than it did to him. She was accustomed to armoring herself against loneliness and rejection, but this was different, baffling, more frightening.

The bond was becoming too strong.

5

"IT'S ABOUT TIME." KEVIN FROWNED AS ZARA CAME INTO THE DINing room. "Consuelo not only had time to give you a bath but perform purification rites." His gaze traveled over her. "Blast it, your hair is still wet. Does Consuelo want you to catch pneumonia?"

"It's only a little damp." She stared back at Kevin. The black shirt, trousers, and boots he wore lent him an air of tough, sinister elegance. She had a sudden memory of another Kevin, naked, barbaric, both captor and captive as he moved between her thighs. She came forward, feeling awkward and a little shy. "And your hair is wet too."

"That's different." He picked up a chair and moved it from the table to the hearth across the room. "Sit down, I'll bring your food to you."

"This is foolish," she protested. "This is a fine, tight house. There are no drafts here." Yet she still felt a warm glow at the caretaking gesture. "I've bathed in a spring in the dead of winter and come to no harm."

"Be quiet and eat." He thrust a bowl of stew and a spoon at her, then took his own bowl and sat cross-legged on the hearth a few feet from her. "I'm not doing it for your sake. I don't want Consuelo yelling at me for misusing you."

"She wouldn't do that. She cares nothing for me."

"No?"

"Not that it matters," she added hurriedly.

"No, of course not. Why should it matter that you're alone and defenseless in a strange country?"

"I'm not defenseless."

"That's right, I forgot. You could always cast a spell or put a hex on her."

"I wouldn't do that. Loyalty is a fine quality. I like Consuelo."

"Then I'm sure the hex would go on me." His lips tightened. "You can't say you like me when I've taken your virginity and your body as if you were one of Garnet's women."

Like? She did not know how she felt about Kevin Delaney, but *like* was entirely too tame a word for the emotions he inspired in her. "No, I don't think I do like you."

Some indefinable emotion flickered in his expression before he smiled crookedly. "But you liked what I did to you in that bed upstairs, didn't you?"

She could feel the heat in her cheeks as she lowered her eyes to her bowl. "You do ask stupid questions. You know you gave me great pleasure. I told you, it was almost like magic."

"I'm weary of this talk of magic. There's no magic in the world but what we make for ourselves."

"You're blind. It's all around us. You just have to let yourself see it."

He shook his head.

"Truly," she insisted. "You said you believed I felt the sadness in the village. What is that but magic?"

He shrugged. "I'm not sure. A talent, perhaps. Mozart composed a symphony when he was only five. He didn't call it magic."

"I've never heard of this Mozart."

"No? There's a book about him somewhere in the study. I'll try to find it for you."

"Never mind. It wouldn't prove anything. We would still disagree." She took another bite of the stew. "Have you never believed in magic?"

"Oh, yes," he said self-mockingly. "When I was a boy there was a shaman in the tribe who I believed could do anything. He would make great medicine that would save the Apache and their lands from destruction, he could stop the killing of buffalo, he could make me accepted by white and Indian alike. But it didn't happen, did it? It took a long time but I finally realized when we look at magic we see only what we wish to see."

"You're wrong."

He shook his head. "I'm right, but we won't argue about it. At least we both agree on one kind of sorcery. Will you find it too onerous to know I fully intend to take you back upstairs and spend the night performing the same magic?"

She didn't look up as she took another bite. "Another foolish question. I made a bargain and I must keep it. After all, you helped me find the mirror."

"Oh, yes, the mirror. How could I forget the all-important mirror?"

A bitter rawness lay beneath his mockery but she would not let it touch her. "It is important. It's the mirror that brought me here. It's the only reason I stay."

"How kind of you to remind me. Look at me."

"I'm too busy. Can't you see I'm eating?"

"Look at me, Zara."

"You told me to eat and yet you—" She glanced up at him and lost track of what she was saying. His hair shimmered raven black in the firelight, as dark as his eyes, as dark as the spell he wove so deftly around her. He exuded sensuality, beauty, and a power that made her feel as weak as she had in his arms.

He said softly, "It hurts my pride that you consider my prowess in bed so insignificant in the scheme of things. I believe I'll have to exert myself to change your mind."

Her hand was trembling as she put her spoon in the bowl. "Now?"

"Why not?" He started to rise to his feet and then stopped. "No, finish your stew."

"I've had enough."

He scowled. "I said finish it. I can wait."

But she could see he did not want to wait any more than she did. What a strange man he was. Ruthless and hard one moment and the next displaying a consideration and disciplined control that surprised her.

His smile instantly cloaked that moment of softness. "The food will give you strength and you'll need it."

She couldn't get her breath as wave after wave of pleasure cascaded over her.

"Unimportant?" Kevin murmured as he swung off her and settled on the bed beside her. "Now, tell me how unimportant it is."

Dear heaven, the bond between them was strengthening. When he had been inside her this time it felt as if they were one, as if their two souls had flowed together.

"Tell me," Kevin repeated.

"So you can preen like a peacock?" She turned away from him so he couldn't see how shaken she was. "I shall not flatter your vanity by—"

His hand cupped her breast, bringing instant response. A shudder went through her.

"Tell me," he said softly.

"It was extremely . . . interesting. Does that content you?"

"No." He nibbled at her earlobe. "Tell me you like what I do to you better than staring at the damn mirror."

"How can I tell you that when you've not given me the chance to stare—" She suddenly sat upright as a thought occurred to her. "But it could be— It's not as if—" She jumped out of bed, jerked the sheet off him, and wound it around her naked body. "Come with me."

"Where the devil are you going?"

"The mirror..." She moved toward the door, stumbling over the folds of the sheet at her ankles. "I have to look at the mirror."

"In the middle of the night?"

"Come with me." She hurled the words over her shoulder as she ran down the hall to Brianne's room. A moment later she lit the lamp on the table under the mirror with trembling hands.

"This is nonsense." Kevin stood frowning in the doorway. "Come back to bed."

"Not yet." She took a step back and looked in the mirror. "Dear heaven, you have no clothing on. Cover yourself."

"For the mirror?" He snapped his fingers. "That's right, we wouldn't want it to remember anything shocking." He stepped behind her and put his hands on her bare shoulders. "I'll let you hide my shame."

"Hush, I'm concentrating." She closed her eyes, letting his touch and the strong sense of unity flow through her. So strong. Surely such strength would spark something, anything. Let it happen, she willed with all her strength. Please let it happen. She held her breath and opened her eyes.

Nothing. Just her own reflection and Kevin standing behind her, his gaze fixed on her face in the mirror.

The disappointment was overwhelming, and she had to blink rapidly to keep back the tears. "Do you see anything?"

"No." Kevin's hands tightened on her shoulders. "For Lord's sake, there's nothing to see, Zara."

"Yes, there is. I guess it's just not time yet," she said wearily. "I thought tonight might be different."

"Why?"

"The bonding. I felt so close to you...joined."

"Did you?" he asked thickly.

"I thought together we might make it happen. You have more

Delaney blood than I do, but I believe and you don't. That should count for something, shouldn't it?"

"Dammit, are you weeping?"

"No, of course not. I never weep." She swallowed. "I'm just trying to explain my reasoning. I thought the joining might—" Her voice broke, and she had to pause a moment before she could go on. "But it didn't and—"

"Oh, no, you never weep." He jerked her around into his arms. "Dammit, why does it mean so much to you?"

Comfort flowed into her, soothing the desperation and disappointment, warmer and sweeter than the passion that had gone before. How she needed that comfort. She buried her face in the springy triangle of hair matting his chest. She would stay for only a moment, take just a little strength from him.

"Why?" he asked again.

"Then they will all know it's true. They will know I'm—" What was she doing? Comfort was one thing, confidences would strip her of her defenses. She tried to back away from him. "Let me go."

"Be still." His tone was rough but his hand stroked her hair with exquisite gentleness. "If you raise your head I'll see your tears, and you wouldn't like that. It might prove you have a weakness or two."

"Everyone has weaknesses."

"Ah, an admission at last. Now, let's see if you can be equally honest about the mirror. Why was the blasted thing worth a journey across the world?"

"It would prove—" She stopped and then continued haltingly. "It would lift the *Malan*."

"*Malan?*"

"It's an ancient law that no member of our tribe can mate with an outsider, a gadjo. To do so is to instantly invoke *Malan*."

"And what the devil is *Malan?*"

"It means . . . the aloneness." She paused a moment. "A man is exiled from the tribe for such a transgression. A woman is still permitted to live under the tribe's protection but travels in a caravan marked with the sign of the *Malan*. She must remain always alone and is forbidden to join in the tribal festivals or be present at birthings or rites of the dead. The *Malan* affects not only the transgressor but her children and her children's children. They're also shunned and despised. If they're taken to wife or husband, their mate also lives under the *Malan*. It is . . . not a good life."

"I can see that." Kevin's tone was grim. "Your people don't appear to be very forgiving."

"No," she whispered. "But they're good people, wise people, *my* people."

"And your grandmother invoked this *Malan* on your head?"

"She mated with an outsider. She told the elders the man was Donal Delaney but he wanted no responsibility and denied her claim. The elders did not believe her and invoked—"

"The *Malan*."

"Yes, she still hoped she would be able to persuade him to go to the elders, but Donal was killed in a barroom fight a few months after the child was conceived. When the boy was born he had red hair like his father and she thought perhaps then the *Malan* would be lifted, but the elders wouldn't change their decision. They were sure she had lied to save herself and her child from shame."

"And why would the child having Delaney blood make a difference?"

"Because Shamus Delaney had done a great service for the tribe and had earned kinship. Why else would they have created the mirror for him? My grandmother went to find Shamus Delaney in Dublin, hoping he would tell the elders that his cousin was the child's father, but Shamus and Malvina had already left for America."

"And so she and her children were forced to live under this curse?"

"Not curse. *Malan*. There's a difference."

"Very little, in my opinion. Why didn't your mother and father try to break it?"

"They were not like me. They said it was their fate and we all must accept it. I could *not* accept it. It is not my nature. All my life

I've dreamed of lifting the *Malan* and having them tell me I'm one of them. That's why I wrote to Malvina. The magic of the mirror would work only for a Delaney, so if the mirror would work for me—"

"Then your grandmother would be vindicated and the *Malan* lifted from your family."

"Yes." She lifted her head to stare up at him. "That's why you must let me have the mirror."

"Stop looking at me like that," he said harshly. "Can't you see? The mirror doesn't work. The stories you've heard are all lies. You've even tried the mirror and seen nothing."

"It will happen soon," she said desperately. "It's only a matter of time."

"And I'm supposed to let you bandage up your feet and put on your old shawl and carry your treasure away from here?"

She smiled tremulously. "Consuelo gave me a fine, strong pair of shoes."

"You've not got a penny in your pocket. How will you get back to your tribe?"

"I'll find a way."

"Doing what? Telling fortunes at Garnet's?"

"It would not be so foolish an idea."

"No!" His grip tightened bruisingly on her shoulders. "You stay away from Garnet's. It's a wonder nothing happened to you when you went there before."

"The mirror?" she prompted him. "Will you give me the mirror?"

"Maybe."

Her heart leapt with hope. "Truly?"

He smiled sardonically. "Suppose we strike a deal. I'll give you the mirror when you come to me and tell me you've seen something in it besides your own reflection. That's fair, isn't it?"

She frowned. "I suppose so. But what if it doesn't happen right away?"

"Then I'll be graced by your company until it does."

"Or until you grow bored with me. I know you don't believe I'll ever see anything in the mirror."

He bowed. "I stand corrected. Until I grow bored with you." He turned away from her. "Under the circumstances I believe you'd better spend the night in this room. I'll see you at breakfast in the morning."

She gazed at him in astonishment. "You don't wish me to come to your bed?"

"Wish is not the word." He opened the door. "But I'm finding it too difficult to keep from wanting to murder the people who caused you so much hurt. I have to give myself time to reconcile the conflict." The desire and frustration in his glance shocked her. "And you can bet I'm going to make every effort to do it. This isn't what I had in mind at all. I don't want to feel like this, dammit."

Kevin was not in the dining room when Zara went down for breakfast the next morning and only one place was set at the table.

"He's in the study. He had his breakfast at six." Consuelo came into the room carrying a plate of pancakes. "Sit down and eat. He says he wishes to talk to you before he goes to town." She set the pancakes down on the table and stared coldly at Zara. "You did not do as I told you. Do you wish to see him die?"

Shock went through her. "No!"

"Then why did you leave his bed?"

Good God, did the woman know everything that went on in this house? "That's none of your concern."

"He is my concern," Consuelo said fiercely. "While he lives, my people have a chance to be treated with dignity and my daughter will have a fine education and grow strong. I will not have Kevin die because you decide to deny him and sleep alone."

"I *didn't* decide. Kevin was the one who—" She stopped. "And even if I had made that choice, you have no right to tell me what to do. I don't play the harlot at your command."

"You're saying he cast you from his bed?" She shook her head. "I do not believe you. I've never seen him in such a fever for a woman."

Zara tried to shrug nonchalantly. "Perhaps he had enough of me. Men are seldom constant."

"True." Consuelo appraised her critically. "And thin women are not to his taste. Sit down and eat."

"I won't be stuffed with food to make myself more pleasing."

"You're right, it would take too long. You must do something at once to change his mind." Consuelo turned to leave the dining room. "I will go tell Pepe to remove one of his horse's shoes. That will delay him for a while and give you time to act. Eat your breakfast quickly and then go to him."

"And what am I supposed to do?" Zara asked with exasperation. "I'm not versed in—" She stopped as she realized she was talking to the air. Consuelo was already gone.

She cast a baleful eye at the pancakes on the plate. She would not be fattened like a calf for the market by the woman. She was tired of being made to feel guilty and afraid because the stupid man was determined to get himself killed. She marched out of the dining room and down the hall and threw open the door of the study. "Why are you leaving Killara?"

"What?" He turned away from the window to stare at her.

"You heard me." She slammed the door and strode over to stand before him. "Last night you said—you know what you said. And now Consuelo tells me you're leaving."

"I did some thinking last night." He grimaced. "I was too uncomfortable to sleep and it kept me from coming to—"

"You don't have to leave Killara to get away from me. This is your home, not mine. I won't bother you anymore. I'll just take the mirror and go. It's not as if—"

"Will you be still?" He reached out and grasped her shoulders. "I'm trying to say something to you."

"Good-bye? There's no word for good-bye among my tribe. It's a stupid word anyway. It's much more intelligent to just go." Her voice was tremulous and she paused to get control. "But if you have to say it, go ahead."

"You're not letting me say much of anything. Dammit, stop putting words in my mouth. This is difficult enough as it is." He paused. "I want you to marry me."

She went rigid with shock. "What?"

"You're looking at me as if I'd suggested you break that blasted mirror," he said testily. "It's not such an outrageous idea."

"You're crazed. Why would you wed me?"

"Why not? We're both outcasts, we enjoy each other's bodies, and I believe we wouldn't find our time together out of bed too dull. Many marriages are founded on less."

She knew this was true, but she had never considered marriage for herself and certainly not with a man as rich and powerful as Kevin Delaney. "You've never wished to wed before, and we've known each other for only a few days. It's not reasonable that you would want to marry a stranger who had come to rob you. Why do—"

"I've not been behaving reasonably since the moment I met you," he interrupted. "I saw you, I wanted you, and I took you. I've been acting on instinct, rutting like an animal without considering the consequences."

"Consequences?"

He didn't speak for a moment, and then said slowly, "You might have a child."

Another ripple of shock. She wondered why she had not permitted herself to think of that possibility. Kevin's child ... "I suppose it could happen."

"Of course it could happen," he said harshly. "You could be carrying my child now. Do you think I'll let you wander away? Do you think I'll ignore my responsibility?"

Kevin will never ignore a responsibility even if it brings him pain.

She felt a sharp jolt of hurt as she remembered Consuelo's words. "You don't owe me anything. We have a bargain and there was nothing about—"

"To hell with the bargain," he said violently. "You've lived with a shame that wasn't your own all your life and now you expect me to saddle you with a child born on the wrong side of the blanket?"

Responsibility and pity. The hurt was growing until it seemed to fill her entire being. "I don't expect you to do anything except what you promised me," she said shakily. "If I have a child, I'll take it back to my tribe and raise it myself."

"And what about the *Malan?*"

"The child would be a Delaney. There will be no *Malan.*"

"If I remember correctly, that's what your grandmother said and the elders didn't believe her."

"But I'll have the mirror. The elders will know—"

"But you'd have to tell them you've seen nothing in the mirror. The elders will think you're lying about the child to save yourself just as your grandmother did."

"Stop *arguing* with me." Her hands clenched into fists. "I don't need either your protection or pity. I'll take care of myself."

"You haven't done very well so far. It's time I took over. I'll go back to town and send for Silver to come and chaperon you until I can arrange for the preacher to come out and perform the wedding."

She looked at him in disbelief. "Chaperon?"

"I know it's a little late, but I won't have my wife's name muddied."

"What nonsense. I'm no lady to be cosseted and guarded."

"I'll send for Silver until after the wedding," he repeated.

He wasn't listening to her and suddenly she couldn't stand any more. "There will be no wedding," she said. "And when you go to Hell's Bluff, I'll take the mirror and leave."

He went still. "The hell you will."

"The hell I will." She planted her hands on her hips and said defiantly, "No chaperons and no wedding."

"Listen, Zara, I can't stay here with you and not—it will happen again and again."

"Did I ask you to stop? A bargain is a bargain. If you no longer want me in your bed, then go visit your tribe in the valley. Go protect them. I have no need for it." She turned and left the study.

"Zara, dammit, come—"

She stalked out the door and almost collided with Consuelo in the hall.

"Well, is he going?" Consuelo asked.

"I don't know and I don't care. If you want him to stay, I suggest you shoot him in the leg."

She ran across the hall and up the steps.

"Would you care to tell me what she meant by that remark?" Kevin snapped at Consuelo as he came out of the study. "Since it's my leg that appears to be in jeopardy, I believe I have a right to know."

Consuelo avoided answering directly. "You have made her very angry. What did you say to her?"

"Nothing that should have made her want to shoot me." He headed for the stairs. "For God's sake, I was only trying to protect the woman."

"Ah, no wonder." Consuelo nodded understandingly. "You hurt her pride. She is not like most white women, who like to be cosseted."

"How would she know? I doubt if she's ever had the experience," he muttered. "And I wasn't trying to cosset her. I just don't want to see her hurt anymore."

"You cannot keep everyone from harm. I would have thought you'd have learned that by now."

"Well, I certainly haven't kept it away from her. I did my bit in inflicting it." He grimaced. "But I can set it right—and by God I will."

"Not by making her want to shoot you in the leg."

"And I suppose you have a suggestion as to how I can prevent that?"

"You could make her believe you need her. Not that you do, of course, but it would soothe the sting."

He noticed that Consuelo was smiling curiously as she watched him climb the steps.

"If that's what you wish to do," she added.

He didn't know what the hell he wanted to do. No, that wasn't true. He knew damn well he wanted to drag Zara back to bed and spend the next week exploring her small body with its power to obsess him.

He quickly tried to think of something else. It did no good. Dammit, why couldn't he control his lust for her as he did for other women?

Because it was a consuming lust unlike any he'd experienced before. And it was more.

In the past twenty-four hours he had actually begun to wonder if there really were spells. She had managed to touch him and amuse him and last night when he had listened to her story about that blasted *Malan*, he had wanted to hold and shelter her, to keep her from every threat. Why couldn't the idiotic woman realize she needed him? It was a cold, bitter world for a woman alone, and for a woman with an illegitimate child it could be a disaster. He had seen too much destruction in his life to risk being a destroyer himself.

He could not permit her to leave him. He would have to overcome her defenses and the barbs with which she surrounded herself and convince her to stay.

6

A POLITE KNOCK SOUNDED AT ZARA'S DOOR. "MAY I COME IN?" Kevin asked.

She stiffened. "It's your house. You can do anything you like." She knew how determined he could be and had expected him to come after her. She tried to stoke her fading anger. Anger was armor; she needed it.

Kevin opened the door. "I said, may I come in? I'd like an answer."

She nodded jerkily. "But it will do you no good. I'll not be forced to—"

"I'm not going to force you to do anything. That's all over."

She gazed at him suspiciously.

He closed the door and leaned against it. "I've been clumsy. I did it all wrong, didn't I?"

She didn't answer, her wariness increasing. He was different than he had been downstairs—gentler, less threatening.

He smiled coaxingly. "It's partly your fault, you know. I always feel that if I don't get in the first word I may never get another."

"You're saying I chatter?"

"Heaven forbid, but you must admit to having strong views and an eagerness to state them."

"I suppose I do." She was silent a moment. "When I was a child, the only way I could get anyone to listen to me was to talk fast and hard and keep on talking."

"And it was important they listen to you?"

"They wouldn't speak to me because of the *Malan*." She added fiercely, "But I made them listen."

"I bet you did. You don't have to do that here though. I'm listening, Zara."

"You don't if I'm saying something you don't want to hear."

"I can't promise to believe what you believe, but I'll listen." He straightened away from the door and came toward her. "If you'll promise to do the same." He smiled faintly. "Without blasting my leg off."

She smiled reluctantly. "It was only a passing thought. You made me angry."

"I noticed." He reached out and gently touched her cheek with his index finger. "And I hurt you. Forgive me."

"You didn't hurt me. I don't let anyone hurt me."

"No, of course not. My mistake." He cupped her face in his hands and looked down into her eyes. "I was the one who was hurting."

"You?" she asked, startled.

"I felt guilty and you wouldn't let me make things right with you."

"There was no reason for you to feel guilty."

His thumbs gently rubbed the curve of her jawline. "I disagree."

His eyes were night-dark and held hers with mesmerizing power. "Guilt doesn't enter into it. We had a bargain."

"Not exactly an honorable bargain to strike with a kinswoman."

"Kinswoman?"

"Why do you sound so surprised? You've been telling me you're a Delaney from the moment I met you."

"I *am* a Delaney." She added wonderingly, "But no one else has ever called me that."

"Kinswoman," Kevin repeated. "And a kinswoman should be treated with courtesy and respect. Let me make it right, Zara."

She tore her gaze away. "I won't wed you."

"No wedding, no chaperon." He added, "Yet."

"Never."

"We'll talk about that later. In the meantime, you'll stay here and I'll get to know my kinswoman." A brilliant smile full of mischief lit his face. "If you think you can tolerate living with a 'savage.'"

This wasn't the savage. No one could be more gentle, coaxing, or persuasive than Kevin at that moment. "I'm not going to change my mind."

"Stay," he urged softly. "Live here and see how you like it. Make a place for yourself. You say you're a Delaney, so be a Delaney. Wouldn't you like to know more about this magnificent clan you're so eager to join? I've had stories of their glory drummed into me from the time I was a lad. I'll gladly share them with you."

She did want to know more but she had not dared to ask. "You're not going back to Hell's Bluff?"

"And have you take off to Ireland with the mirror the minute my back is turned? We Delaneys are very possessive of our property."

She wasn't sure whether he was referring to the mirror or to herself, but the moment was too fragile, the prospect too tempting for her to challenge him. "Perhaps, I could stay . . . for a few days." She added hurriedly, "The mirror might be more likely to show me something while I'm here at Killara with so many Delaneys close by."

"Very sound reasoning," Kevin said solemnly. His hands dropped away from her face and he stepped back. "I'm sure that must make the magic stronger."

"You're making fun of me." But there was no sting for her because of his tone of gentle raillery. "But you'll see. Someday you'll know I'm right about the magic."

"Will I? Are you foretelling the future now?"

"I told you I couldn't— Oh, you're joking."

"Yes, I'm joking." He turned to go. "But if I don't get out of the room I'm not going to find the situation amusing for long. That bed over there is much too inviting. I'll see you downstairs in fifteen minutes."

Tingling sensuality abruptly disturbed the warm security in which he had wrapped her. "If you want me, it's quite all right. We do—"

"Don't say it," he broke in. "I'm already aware of your views on the subject of bargains." He darted her a rueful glance over his shoulder. "Unfortunately, the rules are different for a kinswoman. All bargains are null and void; there are only genteel agreements."

She suddenly smiled. "I don't believe you know the meaning of the word genteel."

"Then teach me." He winked. "And I'll teach you."

Kevin pointed to a large X just a little west of Tucson on the map spread before them on the hearth. "And Silver and Nicholas are here. Their estate is called Firebird Place."

"What a strange name." Zara's brow knotted in concentration as she crept closer to the map. "Why did they call it that?"

He shrugged. "I have no idea. Nicholas is Russian, and I think there's some kind of Russian fairy tale concerning a firebird."

"Fairy tale? From what you told me of Silver, she doesn't seem to be the kind of woman to believe in fairy tales."

"No, she's far more likely to create legends of her own." He pointed to a spot west of Killara. "Shamrock is here. My cousin Patrick and his wife, Etaine, run it as a horse farm."

"His wife helps him?"

"Help isn't the word. Etaine is a miracle worker with animals. I've seen her do some amazing things with those horses." He shot her a sly glance. "It's enough to make a man believe in magic."

She ignored the thrust. "She sounds like a very intelligent woman. I wonder if she's as good as Carlo."

Kevin pounced. "Would you like to meet her? We'll ride over tomorrow and—"

"No, thank you," she said. During the last week he had made many such suggestions and of late had grown increasingly persistent. She pointed to the tiny dot to the north. "And that's Hell's Bluff?"

"Yes." He refused to be diverted. "Why don't you want to go to Shamrock?"

"I just don't."

"All right. Then we'll start tomorrow for Silver's. It's a long trip, but I think you'll find it worthwhile. No one can say her household is boring."

"I'd rather stay here."

"Why?"

"Stop asking me questions. They are all strangers to me. Why should I wish to visit them?"

"Because for over a week you've been drinking in every word I've spoken about them as if you were dying of thirst."

"Naturally, I was interested."

"But you don't want to meet them."

He was not going to give up. "Have you ever thought that perhaps they wouldn't want to meet me?" She added quickly, "Not that I care."

"For Lord's sake, why wouldn't they want to meet you?" He grasped her shoulders. "Look at me."

She stared down at the map instead. "They must have a fondness for you. They wouldn't realize you feel nothing for me. It would worry them."

"And that's why you don't want to go?"

"It's reason enough." She said in a rush, "And, besides, it would make it too hard."

"Too hard for what?"

"To go," she whispered. "I mustn't get to like it too much here. I've been thinking lately that it was a mistake to stay so long. It's always harder to leave a place once you get to know it."

He lifted her chin on the arc of his fingers. "And you like it here at Killara?"

"Well enough." She closed her eyes, remembering the long rides, the spirited conversations, the other mornings like this one before the fire. Safety. Warmth. Sweetness. "Oh, yes, I like it here."

"Good. I'll ride to Hell's Bluff and bring back the preacher."

She could stay here and make a place for herself. She would have a home and children and everything she had always dreamed of. She could take advantage of Kevin's guilt and wrest this happiness for herself. He would not be too badly cheated. She would work and study until she was a fit mistress of Killara. If Malvina had done it, so could she. Then, too, she had seemed to bring Kevin pleasure in bed, and that was important to a man.

But he had not touched her for the last week. Perhaps his talk of genteel behavior was only an excuse, and he'd had enough of her body. Carlo had often grown quickly bored with his women; maybe Kevin was the same.

"Answer me," Kevin urged softly. "It would be a good marriage, Zara. You've not had such a bad time with me, have you?"

She opened her eyes to see his face close to her own. His expression tender and glowing, his eyes glittering with intensity, he almost swept her away. The time with him had been perilously sweet, their bond tightening imperceptibly until now she had trouble picturing life without him. Dear heaven, how had she come to this point?

She was not so weak as to grab a man who didn't really want her to complete her life. She didn't need either Kevin or Killara. Once the mirror spoke to her, she would have a place for herself with her own people, a goal she had worked toward all her life. Why did that goal now seem so far away and lacking in importance?

She moved back away from him. "I told you there would be no marriage."

The softness vanished from his expression. "Why not?"

"For the same reasons I gave you before. Nothing has changed."

"Something has changed. You *like* me, dammit."

"I like Consuelo too, but I have no intention of wedding her."

"The situation is not quite the same. Not quite?" He ran his fingers through his hair. "Lord, what the hell am I saying? I think you're driving me loco."

"You've been most kind," she said formally. "But you must realize you have no obligation toward me and stop trying to force me on your people."

"If I want to do it, I'll force you on the whole damn world." He glared at her. "Why shouldn't they want to know you? You're honest and clever and beneath those barbs you have a heart as mushy as Consuelo's oatmeal."

She suddenly chuckled. "That sounds very messy. Though I agree I'm a most worthy person." Her laughter faded and she said haltingly, "I'd like to stay a little longer, but if you mention this again, I'll have to go."

He studied her determined expression for a moment. "Lord, you're stubborn." He rose jerkily to his feet. "All right, blast you, I'll drop it for now."

The door of the study slammed behind him seconds later. She should have been relieved he had given up so easily, but she felt only an aching hollowness. He was angry with her. After the days of laughter and companionship, not to be in harmony with him was painful.

She couldn't stand it. She jumped up and ran toward the door and out into the hall. She could not give in to him, but perhaps she could find a way to rid him of anger and make it right.

"He's gone." Consuelo turned away from the open front door. "Rode away from here like a bat out of hell."

She joined Consuelo at the door. The sharp wind was sending the falling snowflakes spiraling, but she was able to catch a glimpse of Kevin just as he crested the hill. "It's snowing harder. Where did he go?"

Consuelo shrugged. "He didn't say and, from the look of him, I doubt if he's feeling the cold. He'll probably be back after he gets rid of the burr you planted on him." She met Zara's gaze. "But it can't happen again."

Zara frowned. "What do you mean?"

"He's heading south, so I'd say he's only going for a ride to let off steam. Next time he might decide to go back to Hell's Bluff." She paused. "Pepe went into town for supplies yesterday. Plainfield is up and about and talking nasty."

A cold chill rippled through Zara that had nothing to do with the wind. "Did Pepe tell Kevin?"

"No, because I told him I'd slice his gullet if he opened his mouth. But it's only a matter of time before someone else sends him word or Plainfield comes himself."

Panic rose in Zara, closing her throat, threatening to choke her. She had felt so safe and secure these last days that she had almost forgotten Plainfield and his threat to Kevin. Now it was here before her.

Kevin could die. His life could be snuffed out by that man whose face she had never seen.

"Keep him here," Consuelo said. "I've told the men to watch out for Plainfield. We can keep him safe if you don't drive him away."

Zara barely heard her as she numbly turned away and started up the stairs.

Kevin could die.

"Do you hear me?" Consuelo called impatiently. "We've got to keep him safe."

"Yes, I hear you," Zara whispered. "Don't worry. I'll keep him safe."

Nausea roiled in her stomach as she closed the door to her room. A few careless words might have driven him away from her and back to Hell's Bluff. He could die because she had been concerned with her own inner turmoil and forgotten his danger.

She automatically glanced at the mirror that, as usual, reflected only her own image. But it didn't take a magic mirror to reveal the truth she had been trying to hide from herself since she had met

Kevin Delaney, the truth that had come crashing down on her when she had thought she might lose him.

Why had she not realized she was beginning to love him so that she could have run away and saved herself before it was too late?

The snow continued to fall throughout the day and Zara grew increasingly anxious as the hours passed and Kevin did not return.

It was nearly midnight when she finally heard the front door open and close, then his step sound on the stairs. She breathed a sigh of relief and ran to the bedroom door she had left ajar. She hurried down the hall.

She met him as he reached the top of the stairs. His olive cheeks were reddened with cold, starlike flakes glinted frostlike in the dark hair of his queue, and he smelled of leather and horse. She wanted to reach out and touch him, brush away the snowflakes, share both the chill and the weariness. Her hands clenched into fists to keep herself from doing it. "You've been gone a long time."

"Kind of you to notice." His brows rose. "And surprising. I assumed you'd be too busy staring at your mirror to realize I was gone."

She detected a thread of bitterness beneath the mockery. It hurt her. "You were gone a long time," she repeated. "I thought you'd had an accident."

"What kind of accident?"

"Oh, I don't know...." She made a vague motion with her hand. "Fallen off your horse, bitten by a rattlesnake..."

"I haven't fallen off my horse since I was three years old." He smiled faintly. "And Consuelo would tell you no rattlesnake could hurt me. I'm too mean."

"It wasn't courteous of you to leave like that," she said haltingly. "I'd appreciate it if you didn't do it again."

"Good God, what a meek request. I believe you must be sick."

His mocking tone was too much after the hours of anxiety she had just gone through. "I'm sick all right. Sick of talking to a stupid man who has no better sense than to ride around in a snowstorm trying to freeze himself just because he didn't get his own way. But it's no more than I'd expect from you. Consuelo is right, a rattlesnake could do you no harm— Stop *laughing*."

"Yes, ma'am." His lips were still twitching. "Will it lessen your poor opinion of me to know I wasn't wandering around in the snow? After I cooled off in body and temper, I rode over to Shamrock and stayed for supper."

"Then you should have told Consuelo. She was worried."

"Only Consuelo?"

"Why did you go to Shamrock?"

"To invite them here for Christmas. It's next week, you know." A sudden thought occurred to him. "Or didn't your tribe celebrate Christmas?"

"Do you think we're heathens? We went to the cathedral in Dublin every year to give thanks." She frowned. "But there was no celebration. It was not our way."

"Well, it was Malvina's way. She spent days decorating the house and invited every Delaney within summoning distance to Killara for Christmas dinner."

"Why haven't you mentioned this tradition before?"

"I haven't celebrated Christmas since Malvina died."

"Why not?"

He shrugged. "I don't know. It was too much bother."

And by denying Malvina's rituals he could deny her importance in his life, she thought. "Sometimes bother is worthwhile."

"I'm glad you think so." He grinned. "Because I'm counting on your help."

"*My* help?"

"I can't do that decorating and folderol all alone."

"You have Consuelo and forty or more hands to help you."

"It's not the same."

Her eyes narrowed. "Why are you doing this? After six years it seems strange you'd suddenly change your mind."

He smiled coaxingly. "You wouldn't go to visit them, so I had to bring them to you. Will you help me?"

He was doing this to keep her there, to draw the bonds closer. "I know nothing about decorating a fine house like this."

"I do. Malvina made sure I knew the placement of every ornament as well as every tradition the Delaneys created. We'll do it together."

Together. The words warmed and comforted her. All evening she had told herself how dangerous it was to linger since she'd come to realize she loved him. Yet now that she had the chance to snatch a few more precious days to remember, she was overjoyed. She was not being totally selfish, she assured herself. If she could keep him busy making these Christmas preparations, he would be unable to give any time and thought to Plainfield or going back to Hell's Bluff. She smiled brilliantly. "Yes, I'll help you."

"You'll stay until after Christmas?"

She nodded. "And tomorrow we will go out and find a fine tree for you to chop down."

"Zara!"

"In the parlor," she called as she reached into the box and pulled out a wooden ornament. "This tree is so enormous we may not have enough decorations. What if—"

"What the devil is this?"

She turned to see Kevin holding out a small leather pouch. "I found it under my pillow."

She quickly looked back at the tree. "Really? I wonder how it got there. Consuelo must have gotten it mixed up with the linens." She hung the wooden ornament on the branch directly in front of her. "But I'm glad you found it. I've been looking for it."

"I don't know how you could lose it. I smelled the damn thing the moment I walked into the room." He frowned. "It smells suspiciously like that good luck talisman you made for your journey here."

"It's not a talisman for luck." At least that was not a lie. The talisman was fashioned to protect and guard, but he must not know that. She searched wildly for some purpose for the talisman he would accept. "It's—" She thought of something. "It's an ornament for the tree."

"*That's* an ornament?"

"Certainly. Don't you see the decorations on the side?"

"I thought those were some kind of written incantation."

That was exactly what it was. "How foolish of you." She snatched the pouch from him and hung it on one of the lower branches of the tree. "There."

Kevin wrinkled his nose. "Even the smell of the evergreen can't overpower that odor."

She lowered her lashes to hide her eyes and tried to make her tone wistful. "I'll take it off if you like. I know it's not a very fine ornament. I just thought I'd like something of my own on the tree."

"Oh, for Lord's sake, keep it there. If anyone doesn't like the stink, they can go outside for air."

She turned to smile happily at him. "I can get rid of the smell. I'll let it set in a jar of cinnamon for two days."

"I'd profoundly appreciate that." He didn't speak for a moment as he looked solemnly at her. "I thought you'd made it because you were going to leave."

"Did you? Then why would it be in your room instead of around my neck?"

"How the hell should I know? It ... worried me."

He had been concerned that she might leave him. A tiny hope sprang in the warmth of that realization. "I promised to stay until after Christmas. I wouldn't break my word."

"No, you wouldn't break your word." He gazed at her for another moment before he turned away and reached into a box of wooden ornaments. "Where do you want this?"

The moment of sweet, hopeful intimacy was gone, but she had another memory to store away. "On one of the top branches. I couldn't reach them...."

* * *

"Blast it, is this supposed to be an ornament too?" Kevin strode into the dining room and dangled a pouch in front of her face. "I found it underneath the girth of my saddle."

Zara swallowed hard. "I was wondering where you were. Why didn't you wait for me before you went for a ride? Shall I tell Consuelo you want supper now?"

"No, I want to know what this stinking talisman was doing underneath my saddle."

She had hoped the smell of horse would overpower the scent. "It's not stinking. I perfumed it with cinnamon, just like the ornament."

"Which is only minimally better than whatever noxious mixture you dipped it in before." He tossed it on the table in front of her. "What is it, Zara?"

She supposed she might as well tell him. "It's to keep you safe."

"What?"

"You heard me. It's a very strong spell. I prepared it at midnight in the full of the moon and gathered herbs and chicken droppings and—"

"Don't tell me any more." He grimaced. "I'd rather not know. What are you trying to help guard me from?"

She looked down in the depths of her coffee cup. "Oh, the usual things. Snowstorms, rattlesnake bites . . ."

"You've decided my nature isn't poisonous enough to protect me from the serpent's tongue?"

"It never hurts to have a little help. I've noticed you mellowing of late."

"I've noticed that too."

There was a note in his voice that made her lift her gaze to his face. She inhaled sharply, unable to look away.

"If you came back to my bed, it would be much easier for you to guard me," he said softly.

"It's you who didn't want me there. You had only to tell me."

"I don't want you!" He took a step forward and then stopped and drew a deep breath. "Not without the wedding, dammit. This time we're going to do it right."

Disappointment rushed over her. She had not known until this moment how much she had wanted him to claim that strongest of intimacies. "Then it's useless to discuss it."

"I could arrange a wedding on Christmas Day. We already have the guests invited."

She looked away from him. "No wedding."

She thought he was going to continue arguing, but instead he sat down across from her and reached for the coffeepot. "Very well."

She glanced at him in surprise.

"Oh, I'm not going to browbeat you." He poured coffee into a cup. "I'm not going to have to."

"No?" she asked warily.

"You've made two ghastly concoctions to keep me safe and haven't called me a fool or arched your back and spat at me for the last two days. Very promising signs." He smiled at her over the rim of his cup. "I believe you're mellowing too."

7

"THERE IS SOMETHING YOU SHOULD KNOW."

They turned to see Consuelo standing in the doorway of the dining room.

She frowned sternly at Kevin. "But you must promise not to do anything stupid."

"You sound like someone else I know." Kevin smiled. "What am I not supposed to be stupid about now?"

Consuelo hesitated. "The man, Plainfield, is on Killara."

Zara gasped in shock.

Kevin went still. "Indeed? Just how do you come to be privy to this information?"

"Lefty Corman saw him this afternoon at Diablo Springs. He was headed south toward the canyons."

"And why did Lefty come to you instead of to me?" Kevin asked with a distinct edge in his voice.

"Because I told him to."

"Six miles from here," Kevin said slowly. "You're sure he wasn't headed in this direction?"

Consuelo shook her head. "But that doesn't mean he couldn't double back."

"Not likely. Killara is too well protected. He wants a scalp, not a major battle. He'll wait until he can find me alone." He smiled. "After he's come all this way I'd be churlish not to accommodate him."

Rage tore through Zara. "Why did you tell him?" she spat at Consuelo. "You knew he would do this. You should have kept silent."

Consuelo shrugged. "We couldn't keep it from him forever. He had to know Plainfield's nearby. There are rumors that varmint would just as soon shoot a man in the back as face him."

"Then you should have told me, not him. I could have watched out for—"

"Wait a minute." Kevin's narrowed gaze shifted from Zara to Consuelo and back again. "What the hell is this?"

Neither of them answered.

"Consuelo?" Kevin demanded.

"Plainfield's arrival here was not unexpected. Pepe told me last week he was well again and shouting threats."

"And you didn't think it was worth my while to know," Kevin said with dangerous softness. "Yet I gather you discussed it with Zara."

"Because she knew you would do something foolish," Zara said. She crossed her arms across her chest to stop their trembling. "And she was right. The minute you hear Plainfield is near you must go search for him."

"I've always preferred to be the hunter, not the prey."

"And walk into a trap? Why not wait until he grows impatient and comes here, where you'll have a better chance?"

"No! I don't want him here."

Zara jumped to her feet. "Then you're an idiot."

"I'm getting a little tired of being called a fool and an idiot, and I'm sure as hell sick of having the two of you meddle in my concerns." He turned away. "I'll start out at daybreak."

Desperation sharpened Zara's tone. "I'm surprised you don't go now. The two of you could blunder around in the darkness like two blind donkeys until you stumble over each other."

"Are you calling me an ass?"

"Yes. And stupid and conceited and—" Her voice broke and she had to stop.

The hardness vanished from his expression as he looked at her. "Tears for me? I was right, you are mellowing, Zara."

"Nonsense." She blinked rapidly. "It's only charitable to try to talk a madman out of walking off a cliff. But you're so stubborn, I don't know why I bother with you."

"I wonder too. It would be interesting to find out," he murmured. "But I have to take care of this first."

She took a step forward. "Then take me with you."

He gazed at her, incredulous.

"Don't look at me like that. You have to find this man and I'm a fine tracker. We used to let the horses run free in the hills in the summer and then gather them for the trek to the north in the autumn. I became almost as good as Carlo at finding them."

"I don't need your help."

"You do, but you're too proud to admit it. You'd rather have Plainfield blow your brains out while you're trying to find him in those canyons."

"No, Zara."

She knew that note in his voice, and her desperation mounted. "But I have the power. Sometimes I can sense—"

"Stop arguing with me. You'd get in the way, dammit. I'd be too worried about you getting hurt to think about Plainfield."

He strode from the room.

"Not smart," Consuelo told her disapprovingly. "You handled him wrong. If you had goaded him much further, he might have gone after Plainfield tonight."

"You shouldn't have told him he was here," Zara countered fiercely.

"There was risk either way."

"Not if you'd let me—" She broke off. Recriminations were use-less now. She had to concentrate on repairing the damage. Dear Lord, she wished she could think more clearly, but the panic was making that impossible. "It was a mistake."

"I've told all the hands to look out for him. Kevin is a fine tracker and will not be careless. There comes a time when we can do no more."

"Well, that isn't the case." Zara moved toward the door.

"What are you going to do?"

"I don't know. I have to think." She glared at Consuelo over her shoulder. "But I'm not going to let him die. If you're not going to help me, then stay out of my way."

She ran up the stairs, her heart pounding as hard from fear as from the physical effort. She felt helpless, abandoned. Consuelo appeared to have accepted Kevin's demand to let him handle Plainfield alone. There was no one to—

The mirror.

She had forgotten the mirror! The mirror would not speak to her for her own sake, but it had been fashioned to protect Delaneys, and there was no question Kevin was a Delaney. Hope leapt within her as she took the rest of the stairs two at a time.

She was gasping for breath as she slammed the door of her room behind her and moved to stand before the mirror.

She braced herself. "All right, help me. Tell me what's going to happen. Tell me where Plainfield is now."

Only her own angry, fearful face stared back at her.

"Tell me how to save him."

No change in the mirror.

"He's a Delaney. You have to *do* something."

Nothing.

Didn't the blasted mirror know Kevin was worth saving? *"Help me!"* she demanded desperately. "What good are you if you can't save him?"

Glittering mystery, revealing nothing.

She closed her eyes against that terrible blankness. Kevin was right; there was no magic here. Surely if the mirror held any magic at all it would show itself at this moment of crisis. Perhaps there was no magic anywhere in the world. Desolation flooded her. She was alone. There was not going to be any mystical solution that would save Kevin. She could not place her faith in the mirror. She must get rid of this terror and count only on herself to keep him alive.

"Well, this is a surprise." Kevin sat up warily in the bed as she walked into his room. His gaze raked over the green velvet cloak enfolding her. "Where the hell are you going?"

"What a lot of questions you ask." She closed the door and strolled toward him. "It seems very clear to me. I'm here in your room, therefore that must be my destination. Since you appear to be overly sensitive about having your foolishness brought to your attention, I hesitate to—"

"Why are you wearing that cloak?"

"The hall is chilly." She unbuttoned the fastening at the neck. "I would have been cold without it."

She let the cloak fall from her shoulders to the floor.

He inhaled sharply as he took in the sight of her naked body. "Get out of here, Zara."

She pulled back the covers and got into bed. "No."

"I told you that there would be no—"

She tried to keep her face without expression. He must not see how uncertain she felt. Sweet Mary, how did she even know if he truly wanted her in his bed? "That was before you decided to go out and get yourself killed. I see no reason why I should not have one more enjoyable experience before Plainfield shoots you."

"What tender sentiment. I have no intention of letting Plainfield shoot me."

"Consuelo told me you would respond better to sweet words, but tenderness is difficult for me."

"What has Consuelo to do with this? Did she send you here?"

"No one sends me anywhere. It was my choice to come to you."

"Then it's the wrong one. Get out of here."

"I think not. At first I thought you were tired of me, but now I believe it's your tedious sense of honor that's kept you from bringing me to your bed. If I stay here, it will happen. Men are ever ruled by their lower parts."

"I'm not *men* and I'm ruled by my mind, not my body."

No, he was Kevin Delaney, the man she loved, and this flippancy was becoming more difficult with each passing second. She must vanquish him quickly or not at all. Her hand slid beneath the covers and grasped him. "There seems to be some conflict here. Your mind appears dormant while your body is not. Are you sure you—"

"Let—me—go."

"Why? I think you like me to touch you." She squeezed gently and a shudder went through him.

His hand closed on her wrist with bruising power, forcing her to release him. "Get out of here, Zara."

She hadn't expected his will to be this strong and the panic rose swiftly. It would spoil everything if he made her leave him. She raised herself on her elbow to look down at him. "This isn't easy. You could help me."

He laughed incredulously. "Maybe I'm not making myself clear. I have no intention of helping you."

She moistened her lips. "Please," she whispered.

"What did you say?"

"I'm not going to repeat it. It was hard enough the first time." Her voice was shaking with desperation. "I need this."

His gaze narrowed on her face. "I believe you do," he said slowly. "But I don't know why." He reached out and touched her cheek with gossamer gentleness. "Talk to me. What's wrong, Zara?"

He was all strength and tenderness and caring. She had never loved him so much. She had never been so afraid.

"You're usually verbose enough." He smiled coaxingly. "Why won't you talk to me now?"

"That's . . . different."

"Because it doesn't leave you open to—"

She turned her head and buried her lips in his palm.

He went still. "I wish you hadn't done that. I'm really trying to— Oh, what the hell!" He stripped off the sheet and moved over her, smiling recklessly down into her eyes. "To the devil with being ruled by the mind. This is a damn sight more rewarding."

"It was splendid, wasn't it?" Zara asked dreamily. "I knew it would be. It gets better and better with practice."

"Splendid," Kevin agreed as he gently stroked Zara's hair back from her temple. "Are you going to tell me why you came here?"

"Wasn't this enough?"

"Lord, yes," he said hoarsely. "More than enough."

She cuddled closer, nestling her cheek into the hollow of his shoulder. "I think so too."

Another silence.

"Why?" he asked again.

"I told you, I needed you."

"I suppose I should be content with that since you've never admitted before to needing anything except that damn magic mirror."

"It's not magic."

"What?" He looked down at her quizzically. "What brought you to that conclusion?"

She didn't answer.

"Zara?"

"It's stupid to believe in magic. It's just a mirror."

"Why this sudden loss of faith?"

"What difference does it make? You were right and I was wrong and that's the end of it. The only true magic is the pleasure we've just had together."

"I'm glad you've made me an exception to the rule." He frowned. "But I don't understand this. What about all those blasted talismans you fashioned?"

"When I was a child I needed to feel strong, and talismans are symbols of strength." She did not feel strong now. She felt more frightened and unsure than she ever had in her childhood. It was all very well to say sorcery didn't exist, but without it she was so alone. She nestled still closer to him. "It's time I gave up that blindness."

"And what about your own power?"

"How do I know it's magic? Maybe it's only a talent like that boy Mozart possessed."

"Don't throw my words back at me."

"Then why are you arguing with me? You've told me many times you don't believe in magic."

He thought about it. "I guess I don't like the idea of having anything taken away from you."

"Nothing has been taken away from me. I gave it up. Magic is only a silly superstition and the mirror is only a mirror."

"You said Malvina told you she saw something in it."

"Malvina was superstitious too. Sometimes our minds trick us."

"She was not one to—" He shook his head ruefully. "Why am I trying to convince you the blasted mirror works? If it doesn't, you can't go back to your tribe, which leaves you with one choice."

"A woman with a free will always has many choices." She scooted away from him and jumped out of bed. "I'm thirsty. I'm going downstairs to get a glass of cider." She scooped up her cloak from the floor and slipped it around her. "Would you like some?"

"If you're hoping to avoid a discussion, it's not going—"

"When I come back." Her promise trailed back to him as she left the room. "I'll bring you a glass too, and we'll talk."

Twenty minutes later Zara handed Kevin a tall glass of cider, cradling her own glass in both hands as she sat down on the bed beside him.

"You were gone a long time," he said grimly. "Did you think I'd fall asleep?"

"Oh, no, you're much too stubborn." She sipped the cider. "I couldn't find where Consuelo kept the jug. I've asked her to let me help her, but she refuses to permit me in her kitchen."

Kevin's expression suddenly lightened. "I can't say I blame her after smelling your foul talismans."

"Smell is not taste," she protested. "I cook quite well."

"In whose opinion?"

"Mine. You're not drinking your cider."

Kevin took a drink. "It's cold enough to numb the tongue."

"It was outside."

"I've been thinking about the mirror." He looked down at the glass in his hand. "I want you to have it."

She asked, startled, "You're giving it to me?"

He grimaced. "It's a little late. I seem to make a habit of giving gifts that prove worthless."

She realized he was speaking of the valley he had given to his mother's tribe. "The mirror isn't worthless. It's a treasure I've dreamed of having all my life."

"Because it was magic."

"I don't think I really wanted the magic." She looked away from him. "I guess I've never been certain I was a Delaney and I wanted to reassure myself as well as the elders." She forced a smile. "But even if it has no magic, it's very precious to me. It belonged to both my tribe and the Delaneys. A thing of double value. I thank you."

"You're welcome." He added deliberately, "I'm not really being all that generous. When you marry me, it will still be in the family."

She shook her head. "I shall leave Killara soon. There's nothing here for me now."

"The hell there's not. There's what we had in this bed tonight and what we have out of it."

Zara swallowed the last of the cider and set her glass on the nightstand before smothering a yawn with her hand. "Finish your cider. I want to blow out the candle and get to sleep. You were quite vigorous tonight."

"You're not going to avoid talking about this." He finished the cider and set his glass beside hers on the nightstand. "If you're not going to go back to your people, the sensible thing to do would be to stay here and marry me."

"I'll think about it." She blew out the candle and lay down, curling up spoon fashion to him. "If you'll think about not going after Plainfield in the morning."

He tensed against her. "I can't do that. It's not safe to leave him out there." His arms slid around her. "Two days and it will be over. I promise you."

In two days you could be dead, she wanted to tell him. In two days she could lose him. "You seem so concerned I may be with child. Didn't it occur to you that if Plainfield kills you, the babe would have no father?"

"Plainfield won't kill me." He yawned. "And this is a fine time for you to start worrying about the possibility of a child."

"I'm not worrying, but I thought since the weapon was there, I'd be foolish not to use it."

"Since you can no longer rely on magic?"

"Yes."

He nuzzled her neck, his words slightly slurred. "Why does that make me feel so damn sad?"

"Because, like most men, you have little reason?"

"No, I think it's because I don't know if you'll be the same woman if you give up your belief in magic mirrors and potions and talismans."

His arm was growing heavier over her body, a sweet, endearing weight. In another moment he'd be asleep.

She blinked rapidly to banish the threat of tears. Her words were barely audible in the darkness. "But I never said I no longer believed in potions. . . ."

8

LORD, HIS HEAD ACHED.

Kevin rolled over, opened his eyes, and then closed them quickly as the afternoon sunlight struck him like the butt of a rifle. Hangovers were always hell. Much easier to sleep this one off and get up later.

Afternoon sunlight?

Why should he have a hangover when the only thing he'd had to drink was that cider Zara had brought him?

His eyes flicked open again and his gaze flew to the empty pillow next to him and then to the two empty glasses on the nightstand.

There is nothing here for me now.

He threw the covers aside and was out of bed in an instant. He strode across the room and threw open the door. "Zara!"

She didn't answer. He hadn't expected her to be within hearing distance. She wouldn't have gone to the trouble of drugging him if she hadn't intended to be long gone when he awoke. He strode to the top of the stairs. "Consuelo, get the hell up here!" he bellowed.

He was dressed and sitting on the bed, pulling on his left boot when Consuelo came into the room a few minutes later. "You roar like a bull."

"Where is she?"

"I do not know. She was gone when I came this morning. I checked at the stable and she took the mare."

He jerked on his right boot. "And I'm supposed to believe you don't know where she went? You two have been close as two peas in a pod with all your little plots and secrets."

"Believe what you will. It's the truth." Consuelo's gaze went to the glasses on the nightstand. "She drugged you?"

"Yes." He stamped his left foot into the other boot. Consuelo always came to the house at six, and it was nearly two in the afternoon now. That meant Zara had been gone at least eight hours and could almost have reached Hell's Bluff by now. Dammit, why couldn't he remember what time the train left Hell's Bluff for Tucson? But she might not be able to afford the train; she didn't have any money. What was he thinking? He couldn't count on that lack stopping her. Zara had been resourceful enough to make her way from Ireland to Killara, and she'd get where she wanted to go if it meant riding the rails. "Why didn't you wake me, dammit?"

"I tried. But she must have given you pretty strong stuff." She suddenly grinned. "She's good, that one."

"I'm glad you're pleased." He stood up and reached for his gun belt. "I thought you liked her. I'm surprised you're glad to see the last of her."

"I do like her, but I had to choose. You are more important to me."

"What the hell is that supposed to mean? She's alone out there and when she gets back to her tribe she'll be even more alone. I'm bringing her back." He muttered, "If I can get to Hell's Bluff before she gets on that train."

Consuelo looked at him in surprise. "You think she left Killara?"

"Of course she left Killara. She's probably in Hell's Bluff by this time."

"And you are going after her?"

"Of course I'm going after her." He pulled on his suede jacket. "If I have to follow her all the way to Dublin."

Consuelo frowned. "I did not think you'd assume she—" She shook her head. "I cannot let you do that."

His head swiveled toward her with lethal swiftness. "Let?" he asked softly.

"She did not run away from Killara. She went after Plainfield."

He stiffened in shock. "What?"

"I thought it only fair she be given her chance. But it may prove dangerous, and you should be here if she—"

"Why should she go after Plainfield?"

"What a foolish question. To keep him from killing you. She told you she wanted to go with you."

He shook his head. "She wouldn't have gone without me. What could a woman alone do against a man like Plainfield?"

Consuelo snorted. "Male arrogance. No wonder she drugged you. She should have hit you on the head."

The mere idea of Zara near Plainfield filled him with such icy fear he quickly rejected it. "You're wrong. She as much as said she was leaving Killara."

"So you would believe as you do and not interfere. I'm not wrong."

Her tone was so positive, it sent the fear spiraling. "Did she tell you she was going after Plainfield?"

"No." Consuelo shrugged. "But she is much like me, and it is what I would do if I loved a man as she does you. It is natural to wish to protect those you love." She turned and walked toward the door. "Do not go to Hell's Bluff. She may need you."

Kevin's hands were shaking as he pulled on his leather gloves. Zara had never said she loved him and, even if she did, she wouldn't be mad enough to try to protect him from a killer like Plainfield. She was too shrewd and canny to risk her life.

But she was also driven by dreams and ideals and had proven time and time again she would venture wherever she had to go to reach her goals.

The talisman under his pillow, another under his saddle . . .

"All right," he muttered. He knew there was a possibility Consuelo was correct. How could he prove it one way or the other so he could take action?

The mirror.

Zara might have lost faith in the mirror's powers, but it still had value for her. If she had left Killara for good, she would have taken it with her.

He strode out of the room and down the corridor to Zara's room.

The mirror wouldn't be in her room, he assured himself. She would not have gone after Plainfield. The mirror would be—

The mirror was still in place, shining in the sunlight filtered by the white gauze drapes behind him.

He stood before the looking glass, feeling the muscles of his stomach tighten as he fought off sickness. "Oh, Lord, no."

She had an eight-hour head start on him. Plainfield had been heading for the canyons, but there were more passes and byways in those canyons than in an anthill. How was he to find her before Plainfield did? Or before she found Plainfield? What the hell did she think she could do if she did find him? Make one of her blasted spells or—

He turned and headed for the door. This was no time for idle wondering. There was no time for anything but scouring those canyons if he was to—

A whirling flash of movement in the mirror.

He had barely glimpsed the shifting swirl from the corner of his eye.

It must be the reflection of the white curtains across the room stirring from a draft, he thought.

But the house was drum-tight and strong; no drafts were allowed to force their way into its rooms.

He slowly turned his head and stared into the mirror.

He was just ahead of her.

Hatred and evil swept over her in a dark tide, and she had to
stop a moment on the trail to block it out before it overwhelmed
her. She had not expected Plainfield's hatred to be this strong, but
the closer she came to his camp, the more it affected her. It was
much worse than the sorrow she had felt at the Indian village.

She edged around the curve in the path. Plainfield was there below her, camped beside the lake. She had never seen him before but
knew there could be no mistake. Medium height, dark beard, hat
pulled down over his eyes. He looked quite ordinary . . . but what
she sensed inside him was not ordinary.

She steeled herself, her right hand tightening on the club she had
made from a tree branch. She started down the shale path toward the
lake. It was difficult keeping the stones from shifting beneath her feet,
but he must not hear her. If she could creep up behind him and—

A hand clamped over her mouth!

An arm encircled her throat from behind as she was jerked to the
side of the trail behind a boulder!

Plainfield must have brought someone with him. Her elbow shot
backward into a hard abdomen. She heard a *whump* as she made
contact and felt a surge of satisfaction. She opened her lips and
bared her teeth.

"Don't scream."

Kevin's low voice. Kevin's arm around her neck. Kevin's hand
falling away from her mouth to let her breathe. Relief made her
dizzy. "I wasn't going to scream," she hissed. "What good would
that have done? I *hate* having my mouth covered. I was going to bite
your hand."

She heard him mutter a curse, then he suddenly started to
chuckle. "Forgive me. I should have known you'd do nothing so

common as scream." He nodded to the wooden club that had dropped from her hand to the path. "And what did you intend to do with that?"

"What I still intend to do. Hit Plainfield on the head."

"And then?"

"Tie him up and starve him until he promises to leave you alone."

"What a charming plan."

"Kinder than shooting him. I considered taking one of your guns, but I have no experience with weapons."

"But you would have done it?"

She had not known whether she would have shot him or not until she had felt the waves of malice emitting from Plainfield. So much evil and all aimed at Kevin. "Oh, yes, I would have done it."

"Why?"

Because life would not be tolerable without Kevin in the same world. She looked away from him. "You've been kind to me. We are kin."

"Bull. It won't wash, Zara."

She stepped back from him. "How did you get here? I've been tracking him for hours and you weren't supposed to wake up until after noon."

"I didn't." He smiled curiously. "Maybe I'm a better tracker than you."

"Nonsense. You must have started earlier than noon." She frowned. "Maybe the potion wasn't strong enough. I should have put more— Oh, well, now that you're here you might as well make yourself useful. While I go back behind him, you circle around and— What are you doing?"

He drew taut the noose he had just slipped over her wrists. She started to struggle.

"Stop it." He wound the rope twice more around her wrists. "It's my fight, not yours. I don't need your help."

"Let me go!"

"Hush." He leaned forward and gave her a quick, hard kiss. "It should take you ten minutes to get loose. By that time it will all be over. Of course you could scream, but then Plainfield would hear you, and you don't want that, do you?"

"You're going to face him?"

"I don't shoot men in the back."

"Plainfield would have no such scruples."

"I'm not Plainfield." He drew his gun and started down the trail.

She wanted to call him back, to scream at him in frustration, but that would have warned Plainfield. It was maddening to feel this helpless.

She would *not* stay helpless. She would not stay trussed up while Kevin walked into danger. Whether he liked it or not, she was going to be there for him. She rose awkwardly to her knees. Her wrists were tied in front of her, but that didn't mean she couldn't find a way of helping him. After a quick search she found the club she had dropped. Kevin seized her and took it from her with both hands. She muttered a curse at Kevin's stubbornness as she started down the trail.

Dear Lord, he was already facing Plainfield, standing in a half crouch, a reckless smile touching his lips. They were speaking, but she couldn't make out the words from this distance.

But she could understand the icy malevolence Plainfield exuded, and it caused her pace to quicken until she was almost running, stumbling.

A slide of rocks tumbled down the path, the sound echoing off the canyon walls!

Blast it, she had forgotten about the loose shale.

Plainfield stiffened, drawing his gun as he turned to face her.

"No!" Kevin shouted.

She stopped on the trail, transfixed, her gaze on the barrel of Plainfield's Colt.

Dear Lord, he was going to shoot her. She was going to die! She instinctively threw herself to the side of the path even as pain streaked through her, agony so intense she could not tell where it originated.

More shots.

Was Plainfield still shooting at her? Something warm and damp trickled down her arm. She was bleeding, she realized dimly.

Kevin! Maybe he was firing at Kevin. She had to—

"Lord, I could strangle you." Relief poured through her as she saw Kevin kneeling beside her, his face ashen, his hands trembling as he pushed aside her cloak. "Why didn't you stay where—" He broke off, looking at the blood-soaked tunic. "Blood. Where?"

"I think..." It was difficult to concentrate, but the painful throbbing appeared to be centered on her arm. "Upper arm. Plainfield?"

"Dead." He took out his handkerchief and knotted it tightly around her arm. "What the devil were you trying to do?"

"I wanted to be there...for you." She closed her eyes as another wave of pain rippled over her.

"Did you?" he asked thickly. "You were there all right. You were almost—" He broke off as he cradled her in his arms, rose to his feet, and strode up the trail. "Lord, you're a madwoman."

"Poultice."

"What?"

"You must make a poultice for my arm. After you clean it, make a poultice of aloe and molded bread and—"

"Dear Lord in heaven." His laugh held a note of desperation. "Can't you even be sick without trying to run things? I'll take care of you. I'll send for a doctor as soon as I get you back to the house."

"But the poultice is—"

"Have you forgotten I'm Indian? If you want a poultice, we have poultices of our own."

"Not as good as mine."

"Zara, I promise..." He trailed off and drew a deep breath. "Don't do this to me. I can't stand it. I'm going to move heaven and earth to get you well." He looked down at her. "For Lord's sake, *trust* me."

"It's not that I don't trust you...." She did trust him. It was just difficult to feel this weak and not be able to do anything about it. Her eyes closed and she let her head fall to rest on his chest. His arms were strong and safe and she was too tired to fight anymore. "Make...sure the poultice is hot enough to...draw the infection...."

9

_____

KEVIN'S SKIN WAS TAUT OVER HIS CHEEKBONES, AND ITS USUALLY olive tint appeared oddly pale in the candlelight, Zara thought hazily. "You look terrible," she whispered. "Are you ill?"

"No." Kevin's hand tightened on her own on the coverlet. "You are."

The answer appeared entirely reasonable since she was the one on the bed looking up at him. "Well, I hope I don't look as bad as you do."

"You look beautiful," he said thickly.

She snorted. "I must be dying for you to tell such a lie." The thought frightened her, and her gaze flew to his face. "Am I dying?"

"Lord, no. The doctor said you'll be fine. It's only a flesh wound."

"Are you sure? I feel very weak."

"You lost a bit of blood."

"And I can't seem to remember anything."

"That's the laudanum he gave you when he sewed up your arm. He said you'd be muddled for a while."

But she wasn't muddled, she realized in surprise. It was like drifting on a lake in a fog that masked everything distant but magnified and clarified everything close by.

"Go back to sleep," Kevin said gently.

How handsome he was, she thought dreamily. No amount of strain could alter the superb perfection of his bone structure or those magnificent black eyes. Handsome and strong and...lonely. So lonely. She had never been more aware of that terrible isolation that was always with him. He'd be even more alone when she was gone. She would have to do something....

His hand reached out and covered her eyes. "Stop staring at me and close your eyes. You need to rest."

It didn't seem sensible to argue with him even though she didn't regard it good practice to let him order her about. "Very well."

His hand left her closed lids, but she could still see him sitting there, proud and splendid and lonely. Magic. No, she had forgotten there was no magic in the world; it was only memory.

"I'm going to get up and you're not going to stop me." Zara glared at Consuelo. "I've been lying in this bed too long already."

"You have no patience. Two days is not too long." Consuelo picked up Zara's lunch tray and moved toward the door. "A decade might be too long, a century is definitely too long, but two days is nothing."

Zara jumped out of bed and moved purposefully toward the armoire, ignoring the unsteadiness of her knees. "You haven't been the one lying here, watching the sun move across the ceiling. Two days is more than enough. I don't—"

"Get back in bed," Kevin said grimly from the doorway. "The doctor said at least a week's rest."

"For this scratch? The doctor is used to treating you puling gadjos. Gypsies pay no attention to such trifles."

"A gunshot wound is not a trifle." He studied her mutinous expression and then threw up his hands. "We'd have to tie her to the bedpost to keep her there, Consuelo. Help her dress and then bring her down to the parlor."

She turned to Consuelo as soon as the door shut behind him. "Have Pepe saddle the mare."

Consuelo's expression didn't change. "You're leaving Killara?"

"Not at once." She opened the armoire and pulled out the doeskin tunic. "I want you to give me ten minutes' head start and then tell Kevin to meet me at the Indian village."

"It's bitter cold outside. He won't like you out in this weather and especially going there." She studied Zara's face. "Why are you doing this?"

Zara pulled off her nightgown and reached for the tunic. "Because it's necessary. Will you do it?"

Consuelo smiled faintly. "I will go tell Pepe."

Zara studied Kevin's face as he rode toward where she waited at the crest of the hill overlooking the village. She could not determine whether there was more anxiety or exasperation in his expression.

"What the hell do you think you're doing?" he bit out as soon as he came within hearing distance. "Look at you, you're white as snow and can barely sit that saddle. It's not enough that you disobey the doctor about getting up, but you have to ride out here on some loco whim to—"

"I want you to go see them."

He stiffened, his gaze following hers to the village in the valley below. "The hell you do. Come on, I'll get you back to the house, where it's warm."

She shook her head. "Go down and see them, talk to them."

Kevin's hands tightened on his reins. "We've talked about this before. I thought I'd made it clear that I'm not welcome there."

"They can't continue to resent you just because you're half white." She met his gaze. "Besides, I'm not sure they do resent you."

"I assure you they do."

"I think you're too full of guilt to judge."

"Guilt?"

"Because you couldn't help them, because you had to spend your childhood watching them suffer defeat after defeat. I think you read resentment because you think it should be there."

"And if you're wrong?"

She shrugged. "Then you should still go to them. All resentments fade and, in time, they will stop seeing you as a conqueror and begin to realize you're the same as when you were a boy."

He shook his head.

"Very well. Maybe it won't happen at once," she said, exasperated. "But if you keep at them, you'll wear them down. It *will* happen."

He studied her thoughtfully. "Why is it so important to you?"

"We're kin. Naturally, I want—" She stopped as she met his gaze and said simply, "You care about these people. I don't want you to be alone anymore. Loneliness is a terrible thing." She smiled with an effort. "So we will make another bargain. You go down and see them and I'll go back to the house and rest."

"And if I don't?"

"Then I'll stay on this hill until you do. It's going to be a very cold night. In my weakened condition you might well have good reason to feel guilty by morning."

He frowned. "I don't want to do this, Zara."

"I know," she whispered. "But you must. I can't bear it if you don't." She kicked her mare and sent her galloping along the path to Killara. She was afraid he might follow her and she was over a mile away before she dared a glance back at the summit of the hill.

Kevin was no longer there.

Kevin was gone for over four hours, and darkness was beginning to fall when Zara saw him ride into the stable yard. She let the curtain swing back and drew a deep breath. He did not look angry or upset, but Kevin was a master at hiding his emotions when it suited him.

A soft knock sounded on her bedroom door. "He wishes to see you in the parlor," Consuelo said.

"I'll be there in a minute."

She heard Consuelo's retreating footsteps and took a moment to compose and prepare herself before going downstairs.

When Zara came into the parlor Kevin was standing before the Christmas tree looking up at the angel on the topmost branch. "Malvina got Shamus to carve that angel from a picture in a book she had on home management. I've never liked it."

He wasn't angry, she realized with a rush of relief. "I have to talk to you."

His gaze remained on the tree. "I've always thought golden-haired angels were very boring. I think I'll have to carve another one to suit myself. Would you care to donate a few strands of hair?"

"What?" She motioned impatiently. "Have you no sense of what is proper? Red hair is not at all angelic."

"But much more interesting. Who is to say what's proper and what's not in angels' hair? Maybe it's time we started a few of our own traditions. I think an angel with my wife's hair would be quite appropriate."

"You have no wife." She paused. "Well, are you going to tell me about your visit or keep mumbling about angels?"

"They were all polite and distant. It's not going to be easy."

"But you're going to go back?"

He nodded. "Toward the end I saw . . . I don't know . . . something. It's worth making the attempt anyway."

"I'm glad." She paused. "I'm leaving tomorrow morning for Hell's Bluff."

He shook his head. "You promised to stay until after Christmas."

"I've changed my mind. It's better that I go now."

"Why?"

"I'm becoming confused. Everything is . . . It's time I left."

"I'm afraid I can't let you go. You've spilled your blood for my sake and there's an old Delaney tradition that says I can't let you leave until I've given mine for you."

"You don't care a fig for Delaney traditions, and Malvina never mentioned that tradition in any of her letters."

"No? How curious." He stepped closer and gently touched her cheek. "But you're wrong. I can accept certain traditions if they suit my convenience."

"Well, this one doesn't suit mine." She stepped away from his touch. She wouldn't look at him now. "I know you're grateful to me for saving your life but—"

"Grateful?" He started to chuckle. "I wanted to murder you myself. You didn't save my life, you nearly got yourself killed."

"Well, I would have saved your life if you hadn't interfered."

"You certainly went to a great deal of trouble toward that end. It was a gallant effort but no more than I would have expected of you. If Geronimo had warriors like you, he would never have been defeated."

"Are you making fun of me?"

"If you'd look at me instead of the floor, you might be able to tell."

She glanced back at his face and felt a sudden weakening in her knees. Sweet heaven, she loved him. She swallowed. "Then I thank you for the compliment, but it doesn't change my mind. It's time I left."

"I can see how you might think that. What else is there for you to do here? You've sent my life into turmoil, disrupted my home, and set about arranging my future to suit yourself."

"I was right to make you go to the village," she protested.

"Oh, yes, you were right." He smiled lovingly. "And caring and completely magnificent."

Her eyes widened. "I was?"

"Absolutely." He stepped closer. "And that's why I'd be a fool to let you go. You should agree with that. You're always telling me I should curb my foolishness."

She stared helplessly up at him.

"Particularly when you've made it clear you love me."

"I've never said that. We're kin. I admit there's a certain affection, but I—"

"You love me."

"Why should I love you? You're stubborn and arrogant and always think you're right."

"I'm right about this. Say it."

She remained silent.

"I need you to tell me," he urged softly. "I need the words. Give me that gift, Zara."

He was not trying to blandish her; the need was there and she couldn't deny him. "Oh, very well, I love you," she burst out. "Does that make you content?"

"No, I doubt if I'll ever be content with you. It's much too mild a word for what's between us."

She should never have told him she loved him. She felt naked, vulnerable, and suddenly she couldn't bear it. She turned and ran from the parlor.

He caught up with her before she reached the staircase and whirled her around to face him. "For the Lord's sake, why can't you stop fighting me?"

She said fiercely, "I've spent my life battling and clawing for a place for myself with my people, trying to prove I was good enough to earn their love. I'll never do that again. You have no love for me. Do you think I'm going to live with you and meekly accept the crumbs of affection you choose to throw? I'm too good for that. I'd rather not be with you at all than know I was only—"

"Hush." His hand gently covered her lips. "Now, listen to me. Crumbs, hell, I'm offering you a feast."

She tried to shake her head to rid herself of his hand.

"No, you don't talk again until I'm through. What do you want me to do to prove I love you? Go to Ireland and fight all those people who hurt you? I'll do it. We'll start out tomorrow and catch the train from Tucson. I've been wanting to get a few licks at them anyway and I can— Ouch!" He jerked his hand away from her mouth as her teeth sank into his palm.

"I told you I don't like to have my mouth covered." She looked at him uncertainly. "I didn't hurt you, did I? I didn't bite that hard."

"Hard enough." He smiled down at her. "Does this sudden concern mean you want me to continue with my declaration?"

"Not if it's not true. You don't have to love me just because I love you. I understand it happens all the time that one person loves and the other does not. It's not as if I need—"

"If I weren't afraid you'd draw blood this time, I'd cover your mouth again," he interrupted. "Listen, I love you. I adore you. If you went away, my life would be a barren ruin. Is that clear?"

"You're joking," she said uncertainly.

His smile vanished. "I've never been more serious in my life."

Happiness burst through her in a radiant flow. "Truly?"

"Why can't you believe me?" He cupped her face in his hands. "You fill my life. You have strength and tenderness, honesty and passion. I'd be a fool not to love you."

"If I'm that exceptional, you certainly would." She hurled herself into his arms, buried her face in his shirtfront, and whispered gruffly, "You should have told me before."

"How was I to get around all those barbs and make you believe me? I'm not even sure you do now."

"I'm beginning to." Her arms tightened around him with desperate strength. "And I'm glad you have the good sense to realize what a treasure you have in me. I . . . feel a similar emotion for you."

"Then it behooves me to point out that if you want to keep me around, you'd better loosen your grip. You're breaking my ribs." He pushed her back and looked down into her face. "Tears?"

"It's not kind of you to notice." She blinked rapidly. "I understand it's common at such a moment to show a certain weakness."

"Yes, very common." He kissed her gently. "And you could never be weak."

She felt as light as air, exploding with happiness. "Since you understand me so well, I see no reason why I shouldn't stay here."

"No reason at all."

"And perhaps even wed you."

"I appreciate your condescension. Christmas?"

"The New Year. Good fortune always follows a New Year bride."

"Superstition? Are you back to believing in magic?"

A little of her joy faded. "I didn't say that. That foolishness is past for me."

"Too bad. It's very much in the present for me. I'm beginning to be extremely fond of your magic mirror."

"It's not magic."

"Then why did I see your exact location in the canyon in it when you were stalking Plainfield?"

Her shocked gaze flew to his face. "You saw me in the mirror?" Before he could answer she shook her head. "You're lying to me. You just want to make me believe—"

"It's the truth! And it scared the hell out of me. I didn't know what the devil was happening, but I didn't care as long as it gave me a chance to find you."

He was telling her the truth, or what he believed was the truth. She felt a stirring of hope. She hadn't realized until now how much she had missed those beliefs that had shaped her life. "You said once that when we believe in magic we see what we want to see."

"I wish you wouldn't keep throwing my words back in my face." He kissed her lightly on the nose. "Try the mirror again."

"Even if what you say is true, I probably wouldn't see anything."

"Try it anyway."

"But I don't need the mirror any longer to tell me I'm a Delaney. In the New Year I'll be one by marriage, if not blood."

"You need it," he said soberly. "All quests may not end with treasures, but they should at least yield some answers. I don't want you cheated."

She would have the man she loved, who gave her understanding as well as passion. She would have Killara and a home and the chance to make a fine life for herself and their family. She was tempted to tell him how absurd he was to believe she could be cheated by the past when the future was so bright. Perhaps he was right about her mellowing, for she magnanimously decided to forgo that criticism.

"Oh, very well, I'll give it another chance. Actually, I'm inclined to believe you did see something in the mirror." Mellow or not, she couldn't resist one mischievous jab. "For I knew you couldn't be a better tracker than me."

"No, you don't come with me tonight." Kevin stopped before Zara's room and handed her the candle in its copper holder. "And no arguments."

Zara was abruptly jarred from the haze of contentment that had surrounded her for the entire evening. "You don't want me to sleep with you?" she asked indignantly. "What foolishness is this?"

"You're still an invalid and that ride to the village had to be a strain on you." His lips set stubbornly. "I won't have you suffering a setback."

"The doctor said only that I should rest. Why should it not be with you?"

He smiled ruefully. "Because I don't know if I can keep from disturbing your rest if you're in the same bed with me." He opened the door and gently pushed her over the threshold. "So you sleep here tonight and every night until you're well."

Kevin, as usual, was trying to protect and guard her. Even through her frustration she felt a warm glow of love suffuse her. "Kevin, this is—"

He stopped her words with his lips on hers, and the next instant the door closed between them.

She made a face as she turned away and set the candle down on the table beneath the mirror. Kevin must learn he could not dictate to her even for her own good. But perhaps she would indulge him tonight. She was too happy to fight battles about small—

Three flames, not one, were reflected in the mirror.

She went rigid, and her breath left her body as she stared into the looking glass.

Three flames emerged from a swirling hazy mist. Then, as the mist cleared, she saw the three flames crown three thick white candles on a tall wrought-iron candlestick.

A young priest with carrot-colored hair stood by the candlestick.

A small, red-haired child huddled in the corner of a pew.

An ivory and mahogany crucifix shone above the altar.

The vision was there for only a moment and then vanished once more in the mist.

She stood, stunned, now gazing only at her own reflection and that of the single candle in its copper holder.

Joy exploded through her, dispersing her shock and bewilderment as she realized her grandmother had not lied. If she did not have Delaney blood, she would not have seen the vision. She had tried to deny the importance of proving that truth to herself, but Kevin had known what she had not.

She had needed this gift from the mirror, this gift from the past.

But why this particular gift? Why had the mirror shown her a scene of that Christmas Eve of long ago?

To remind her of a child who believed in magic.

To remind her of Father Timothy and the sacrifice he had been willing to make to see that child's miracle come true.

To remind her of other miracles, other magic, other sacrifices. . . .

Kevin's hands paused in unbuttoning his shirt, and he turned with a frown as she opened the door of his room. "Zara, I told you—" He stopped as he saw her face. "Zara?"

She felt as if she were glowing, brilliant as sunlight, bursting with happiness. She was not surprised he had seen that light. "I've not come to offer you my body. I was going to tolerate your foolishness, but I decided against it. Do you know why?"

"No."

She closed the door and came toward him. "Because there are wonders in this world."

He smiled gently. "Are there?"

She nodded. "Magic and miracles."

"I'm glad to hear it."

"Kindness is magic, and so are understanding and giving." She stopped before him. "And love is the greatest magic of all."

"I know."

"And tonight I'm full of magic, brimming with magic." She slipped into his embrace and felt his arms close around her with exquisite tenderness. She whispered, "Let me share it with you."

EPILOGUE

Killara

December 25, 1894

"WHAT ARE YOU DOING UP HERE?" ZARA TURNED TO SEE KEVIN standing at the head of the attic stairs. "I've been looking all over the house for you. The family is starting to arrive. Patrick and Etaine just rode in from Shamrock."

"I'll be down in a minute."

His expression softened as he looked at her crouched by the trunk. "There's no reason to hide. You'll see there's nothing to be nervous about once you meet them."

"Don't be ridiculous, I'm not hiding. You're too clever to care about anyone who would be so lacking in judgment as not to recognize what a superior wife I'll make you."

"You weren't so confident before."

"I am now." She turned the mirror to the wall. "I'll come down right away, but I have to do this first."

"The mirror?" He came toward her. "Why did you bring it back up here?" He knelt beside her, his gaze fixed intently on her face. "You were so happy the other night when you saw Father Timothy."

"I was very happy." She sat back on her heels. "So I looked in the mirror again."

"And?"

"I became . . . frightened."

His arm slipped around her shoulders. "What did you see?"

"It wasn't what I saw but what I realized I might see." She whispered, "I thought Malvina was a fool and a coward not to use the mirror, but it's easy to be brave when you have nothing to lose. I have so much to lose now, Kevin."

"It could be of value to us. It showed me where you were in the canyon."

"You saw me because it was destined you were going to be there, but it could just as well have shown you the death of our children, as it did to Malvina." She shivered. "It could have shown me your death. It's not a good thought."

"No, it's not a good thought." His arm tightened around her, his lips pressed her temple. "So don't dwell on it. We're going to live a long time and enjoy every minute of it."

"No, there will be moments of sorrow. No life is without pain." She smiled tremulously. "But I don't want to know about those moments ahead of time. If we live in dread and fear of the future, it will spoil the good times in the present." She draped the mirror with a fringed flowered shawl. "We cannot change our destiny, but we can enrich every step of the way toward it."

"With magic?"

"The best kind of magic." She brushed her lips against his cheek. "Now let's go downstairs and forget it. I wish to meet Patrick and Etaine."

He stood up and glanced at the shrouded mirror as he pulled her to her feet. "What if someone else in the family discovers it?"

"Oh, someone will." She led him toward the stairs. "That's what I saw in the mirror. A young woman dressed like a man in denim trousers and a blue and white woolen upper garment kneeling before the mirror. I think she must be our daughter. She had my ugly red mop of hair but your fine looks. It's pleasant to know she's going to turn out so well."

"Our daughter . . ." Kevin mused. "No son?"

"Not so far as I could see in the mirror." She frowned. "A daughter is just as good. Better. Why must all men feel the need to spawn a child in their own image? A woman can have as much intelligence and determination and— Put me down!"

Kevin had paused at the top of the steps to grab her under the armpits and hold her high over his head. "Do I have your attention? It's the only way I can shut you up long enough for me to get a word in. I only asked a question, dammit. A daughter is fine, a daughter is wonderful."

She looked down into his laughing face and was instantly mollified. "Well, I should hope you'd have the good sense to realize that. Let me down."

"Presently." He let her slide slowly down his body and then kissed her lingeringly. "I don't suppose you'd care to start this daughter here and now?"

The devil was making quite sure she wanted that very much indeed. "Patrick and Etaine," she said breathlessly. She reluctantly pushed away from him and started down the stairs. "I will not have your people thinking you're wedding me for lust alone. We will show restraint."

"Yes, ma'am." His lips twitched. "Unless I can catch you in the pantry in a weak moment."

"Kevin, you're being most unhelpful. I cannot do this alone. You must—" She suddenly frowned. "Are you particularly fond of the name Elizabeth?"

"Elizabeth? I don't care one way or the other. Why?"

"I've always disliked it." A frown knitted her brow. "Why should I name my daughter Elizabeth?"

"Are you sure you did—will?"

"Of course I'm sure. It was embroidered on the back pocket of her denim trousers. Liz Claiborne." She repeated the name experimentally, "Elizabeth Claiborne Delaney." She made a face and then shrugged. "Oh, well, perhaps she will be named for someone for whom we have a great fondness. Claiborne is clearly a family name. I will not worry about it. It's enough to know she will grow up strong and healthy."

"And will discover the mirror," he reminded her.

"When that happens, I will tell her its history and caution her, but she must make her own decisions. I'm certain they will be the right ones." She shot him a glance over her shoulder. "Even though she is only a mere woman."

"Your daughter could never be referred to as 'mere' in any context, my love."

"Sweet words." Her eyes narrowed suspiciously. "You're still thinking about luring me into that pantry."

"Exactly. I should have known I couldn't fool a woman with the power." His face was alight with loving mischief. "I'm definitely thinking about pantries . . . and magic."

FAYRENE PRESTON

Christmas Present

1

THE BOARDS OF THE FLOOR CREAKED BENEATH BRIA DELANEY'S feet. She was in the oldest part of Killara's attic, the part that stretched over the original homestead section of the sprawling house. She had never been in this section of the attic before, never had a reason to come, and, strictly speaking, she didn't now. The Christmas decorations her mother, Cara, had sent her up to find wouldn't be way back here, but it didn't occur to her to leave.

Since graduating from college five years before, she had lived in Tucson, working for her father and Delaney Enterprises. She had learned a great deal, but these had been the hardest years of her life. When for the fifth year running her mother had asked her to take some of her accumulated vacation time and come home early for Christmas, she had finally decided to agree. Her mother needed help in preparing the house for the upcoming festivities, and she needed some down time. That much was clear to her. But she didn't know why, today, she felt compelled to go farther back into the attic than she had ever gone before—except that she was intrigued and drawn.

As she turned another corner, darkness and a musty smell greeted her. Automatically she began to search for a light switch; she felt the faint tickle of cobwebs against her hand and brushed them away. She wiped her hands down the side of her Liz Claiborne jeans, then remembered that the oldest section of the attic had never been wired for electricity.

Carefully she picked her way through looming shapes, ghosts of a bygone era. Whatever was in this section had rested undisturbed for years. In an odd way she felt like an intruder, but in another way she felt a strong sense of belonging.

Reaching the window, she flung open the inner shutters. Sunlight poured in, revealing an assortment of trunks and boxes stacked in piles or sitting alone on the floor. A dressmaker's form stood in the corner. Dust motes danced in the air and a thick coat of dust clung to every surface.

She wrapped her arms around herself as a defense against the chill and continued to study the room. How long had it been since anyone had been here? Some of the things around her might have been placed here well over a hundred years ago.

"Amazing," she whispered. She felt as if she had entered a place that time had forgotten.

Excitement made the back of her neck tingle. This room held a part of Delaney history, and she was a Delaney through and through.

She knelt in front of a camelback trunk covered in a finely grained leather and fastened with straps. The brass hinges creaked in protest as she raised its lid. She reached in and pulled out a bundle of yellowed tissue paper that almost shredded as she removed it. Inside was a very old, very simply cut violet-colored dress. Any remaining thoughts of the misplaced Christmas ornaments fled from her mind.

Outside, the sun rose higher in the sky, and the sunlight crept across the dusty floor. But Bria was only vaguely aware of time passing. She discovered a Miss Beetle's book on home management and, to her delight, she saw Malvina Delaney's name inscribed on its inside front cover and notes written in the margins. Digging further, she found a silver-backed brush.

One of the most amazing items she uncovered was a picture made out of red hair. She had read about people of the Victorian era using hair to make pictures, and here was one before her. She turned it over and glanced at its back. Someone had written *Made from Brianne's hair.*

She gave a cry of delight. The hair was Brianne Delaney Lassiter's, the ancestor for whom she had been named.

Sometime later, a distant sound of a helicopter lifting off brought her back to the present. A glance at her watch told her several hours had passed since she had come up to the attic.

Carefully, reluctantly, she closed the trunk she had been delving through and rose to go, but when she got to her feet, her stiff muscles protested. She took a step backward for balance and bumped into something.

Curious, she studied the shawl-covered object about three feet high that rested against the wall. From its oval shape she guessed it was a picture frame. Her pulse quickened at the thought that she might have found a long-forgotten portrait of one of her ancestors. She knelt quickly, pulled the shawl away, and dropped it to the floor. The picture's face was to the wall.

Lifting and turning it, she found it was heavier than she had expected. She also discovered that it wasn't a portrait after all, but a mirror. And there was something very familiar about its frame.

Downstairs in the drawing room, a clock sat in the exact center of the drawing room's white marble mantel. Her ancestors, Shamus and his wife, Malvina, had brought the clock all the way from Ireland, then overland in their covered wagon to Arizona. Although the ornate carving of holly on the mirror differed from that of the clock, they were both made from the very same dark wood. Bogwood.

Thoughtfully she stared at the mirror, its surface dulled by a heavy layer of dust. Shamus and Malvina must have also brought the mirror with them, but something didn't make sense. For generations the clock had sat in a place of honor. Why had the mirror been left in the attic for so many years, its face to the wall?

She raised her forearm and rubbed the sleeve of her blue and white sweater over its dust-covered surface. Her image appeared. Green eyes, rich red hair, dirt-smudged cheek. She absently swiped a hand across her cheek.

Suddenly, out of nowhere, there was a flash of flame-hued color in the mirror. Then she saw a silver-haired girl riding a magnificent Arabian bareback across a meadow carpeted with wildflowers. As the girl rode, the crimson, tangerine, and gold skirts of her dress undulated like a flame in the wind.

The image vanished.

Bria rubbed her eyes and looked again, but only her own face with its utterly bewildered expression stared back at her.

The girl had been her mother, she realized, stunned. She recognized the dress. Shortly after her parents had married, her father had commissioned a portrait of her mother wearing that very dress. It had been the dress her mother had been wearing the first time her father had seen her as a young woman. And of course she recognized the scene because she had heard it described many times. Her father had flown over Killara and seen her mother beneath him, riding Shalimar across the meadow.

But why had the scene been in the mirror? Her head spun with confusion and astonishment.

She fit her fingertips into the hollows formed by the carving, lifted the mirror against her, and went downstairs.

Bria walked slowly into the drawing room. Her mother stood atop one of the two tall ladders placed on either side of a fifteen-foot-tall Christmas tree.

Cara, stringing lights, glanced down at her daughter and smiled.

"Where have you been? I thought I was going to have to send a search party for you."

"I've been up in the attic," she said, carefully placing the mirror in a nearby chair.

"I hope you found that box of ornaments."

"I couldn't find it. I'm sorry."

"Darn. The tree won't be complete without the red-haired angel Kevin made and the ornaments the original Patrick forged from gold they brought back from Kantalan."

"I'll look again later on this afternoon." She was stalling, reluctant to tell her mother about the scene she had witnessed in the mirror. Quite simply, seeing what she had seen was an impossibility. Mirrors weren't VCRs that could run tapes of events that had happened in the past. Still, she had seen it. Hadn't she?

"Don't worry about it, honey. I put that box in one of my safe places. I just have to remember where."

She gazed consideringly up at her mother. Cara's silver hair was pulled back into a ponytail, her face was free of makeup, and in Bria's opinion, she looked as if she could be her sister. Cara was, and had always been, an exceptionally loving and extremely supportive mother to both her and her twin brother, Patrick. That's why Bria couldn't understand why she felt an instinctive urge to keep to herself what she had seen in the mirror. She chalked the urge up to shock.

"I couldn't find the ornaments, but I found something else. Something rather remarkable."

Cara frowned at the colored lights she was weaving in and around the boughs at the top of the immense tree. "A string of lights that's not tangled?"

"No," she said slowly, "it's a mirror. And I saw you in it. Come down and look."

Cara came to the end of the string and reached for the next string that she had draped over the top rung of the ladder. "It's a picture of me? I wonder what it was doing in the attic."

"No, it's a mirror that I found, not a picture."

Standing on her tiptoes, she reached as far around the tree as she could, then flung the strand so that it fell on a bough at the back. "Oh, I'm sorry, I thought you said you saw me."

Bria shrugged. How could she explain what she didn't understand herself? "Yes, well, that's the tricky part. Just come down and see for yourself. Please."

Cara cast a last glance at the lights, then abandoned them and descended the ladder. As she crossed to her daughter, she gave her a motherly once-over. "Are you all right? You sound funny. You're not getting sick, are you?"

Bria forced a smile. "No, Mom. Just look in the mirror and tell me what you see."

Cara bent down, gazed briefly at her face in the mirror, smoothed a stray hair back into place, then turned her attention to the frame. "Why, this is *bog*wood." She gazed over her shoulder at the clock on the mantel, then back at the frame. "This is wonderful, darling. It's the same wood as the clock." She straightened. "Do you realize what this means? Shamus and Malvina probably brought this from Ireland with them."

"That's what I thought too." She hesitated. "What did you see?"

"See?" Cara frowned, uncertain what Bria was referring to. "You mean the frame?"

"No, in the mirror." She took a deep breath. "When I was up in the attic and looked into it, I saw you on Shalimar, riding across the meadow in your red chiffon dress."

Cara's frown deepened. "That's impossible, Bria. How could that be? It's only a mirror."

"You're right, but I'm telling you I saw you riding Shalimar in your red dress." She gnawed on her bottom lip for a moment. "At least that's what I *thought* I saw. It happened so quickly."

Cara stared at her daughter, concerned. Bria had never been given to fantasy. From the time she could talk, she had been strong-willed and self-assured, with both feet firmly on the ground. But now she seemed very confused and upset. Suddenly Cara snapped her fingers, and her expression lightened. "I know what must have happened. You fell asleep up there and had a dream."

"No—"

"Darling, it's the only explanation. Ever since you were a little girl, you've heard the story about when I came back to visit Killara and met your father again. And you've seen the portrait of me wearing that dress every day of your life until you left home to go to school. Your father refuses to take it down...." Her voice trailed off. "I wonder if Burke knows about the mirror. He's never mentioned it."

Bria slowly shook her head. "I don't know. It didn't seem like a dream. I looked in the mirror, saw myself, then *you*."

Cara responded to the distress in her daughter's eyes by reaching out and gently clasping her arms. "Oh, honey, I'm not doubting you. Sometimes dreams are so clear and vivid, they can seem almost real."

Bria sighed. Maybe her mother was right. After all, it was the only thing that made any sense. But she had felt too wide awake even to daydream.

Cara smiled at her. "Your dad is going to be thrilled about the mirror. If he ever knew of its existence, I bet he's forgotten about it. Otherwise, it would be hanging in a very prominent place. As soon as I have a minute, I'll clean it up."

Bria gazed broodingly at the mirror. For some unknown reason, she didn't want to relinquish possession of it just yet. "I'll do it. I'll help you finish the tree, then I'll take it up to my room and clean it."

"Okay. Get some lemon oil and glass cleaner from Mrs. Copeland. By the way," she said, returning to the ladder, "you do remember, don't you, that your dad is bringing Kells Braxton home with him this afternoon? He left a little while ago to pick him up at the airport."

"Sure," she murmured, her mind and her gaze on the mirror.

"Rather than having him stay in Tucson until the lawyers finish drawing up the agreement, we invited him here. We wanted to pay him back for his hospitality to Patrick in Brisbane. Hand me that next string of lights, will you, darling?"

Bria quickly pulled the brush through her long red hair, then stole a glance at her watch. Darn, if she didn't hurry, she was going to be late for dinner. It had taken all afternoon for her and her mother to finish the tree, and she had spent a long time oiling and polishing the old wood of the mirror's frame. Too much time, if she were honest. But it had seemed important.

Though she didn't have a clue why, the mirror was proving an irresistible draw to her. While she had worked on it, she had peered into its center more times than she could count and had seen nothing but her own reflection. But even now, knowing that she was running late, she paused before the mirror that she had propped against a chair's cushion. Her own face, flushed from hurrying, looked back at her. She felt an aberrant twinge of disappointment.

Then in a twinkling she was looking at a man's back. The width of his broad shoulders stretched against a black split-leather jacket, his long, muscular legs were gloved in faded jeans. He had brown hair with a hint of red that gleamed in the sunshine. And his attention was focused on the valley below him—and Killara.

Then he turned and looked at her—at someone—and she felt as if the air had been sucked from her lungs.

He had amazingly direct eyes that were the color of the blue sky behind him, and his face was strong with a wide, clean jawline and a scar that angled over his left brow.

He appeared hard, dangerous, and very angry.

Her heart thudded against the wall of her chest. A roaring filled her ears. He opened his mouth as if he were about to speak. But then before her eyes he vanished, and once again she was left staring at her own image.

She exhaled roughly, painfully. This morning she had viewed her mother as she had ridden Shalimar across a meadow on Killara, something she knew had already happened. But this scene was different. She had no past references to tell her who the man in the mirror could be, or why he was looking down on Killara. Or why he seemed so angry.

But she did know one thing: She wasn't dreaming.

Kells Braxton propped his arm on the gleaming white marble mantel, sipped at the scotch he'd just poured for himself, and surveyed the drawing room from beneath half-closed eyes. Fabulous works of art and one-of-a-kind pieces of furniture, collected from around the world, had been arranged into an elegant, graceful, and surprisingly comfortable room. From what little he had seen so far, Killara was everything he had expected and more.

Grimacing, he turned his attention to the Christmas tree. It was huge and dripped with ornaments, some of them obviously very expensive, some of them homemade, a great many of them very old. He wasn't surprised.

By all accounts the Delaneys were mired in tradition and family—two things he was in short supply of, two things he'd never felt a need for.

He took another sip of scotch and reflected. He'd thought long and hard before deciding to accept Burke Delaney's money. He had gone his way alone too long to be beholden in any way to anyone. But with the agreement he and Burke Delaney would sign at the end of his stay here, they both would get something they wanted. Burke would receive certain rights to use his patent for a next generation of microchip, and he would receive a much-welcomed infusion of money into his company. He was giving as good as he was getting. Hell, maybe even better. It made it easier for him to accept what he was doing.

It was a nice, clean agreement, free of entanglements or complications—just the way he liked it. He took another sip of scotch.

The door to the drawing room opened, and a young woman wearing a wine velvet dinner suit rushed in, her long red hair swinging and shining beguilingly. "Dad, are you in here?"

She came to an abrupt halt. Her green eyes widened in shock, and the color drained from her face.

It was him, the man in the mirror, Bria realized. The floor went soft beneath her feet; her legs lost their strength. She reached out for support but found nothing she could hang on to. Her surroundings receded, and the room darkened until finally she couldn't see anything but the man.

He was the same man, yet he didn't look the same. Instead of jeans and leather jacket, he wore a double-breasted midnight-blue suit. His eyes—they were still piercingly direct, but there was something different in their expression, something that had not been there in the mirror. And there was one other thing: He wasn't angry. His expression was curious and coolly assessing.

What was he doing here? Why had she seen him in the mirror?

"Who are you?" she asked, her voice a mere whisper.

He set his glass of scotch on the mantel. "I'm Kells Braxton."

"Kells Braxton." She repeated the name, trying to match it with a piece of information in her head, but she couldn't.

"Obviously I've startled you," he murmured. "I'm sorry." She had startled him too, he reflected, intrigued because he couldn't ever remember being startled by a woman. But she had an unusual beauty about her, the kind of beauty that wasn't conventional, in fact, was almost irregular. The kind of beauty that would never bore.

She looked very sleek, very sophisticated, very expensive, but beneath it all he thought he detected a hint of something untamed. Maybe it was her mouth, which was almost too wide, too full, or her jawline, which was sharply angular. Or maybe it was the dark auburn brows that feathered above her expressive green eyes. Then there was her body. Tall, slender, she had impossibly long legs and high breasts that pushed against the velvet jacket.

Whatever it was about her, the parts or the whole, she was unexpected and a definite shock to his system, making his mouth go dry. Instant attraction was foreign to him, but then, so was turning his back on something he wanted. Still, an unexpected, complexly fundamental, vastly annoying gut instinct told him to be cautious.

"What are you doing here?" she asked.

"I'm having a scotch. Would you care to join me?" She continued to stare at him. He had had a lot of interesting reactions over the years from women, he reflected wryly, but none as interesting as hers. "You're looking at me as if I were a ghost or a mass murderer. I assure you I'm neither."

Her silence, along with her vivid green eyes that still showed shock, propelled him across the room to her. He wanted to reassure her; he wanted to touch her. He lifted her hand and pressed its back to his lips. "If I were a ghost," he said, his voice pitched comfortingly low, "my lips would be cold. And if I were a mass murderer, you'd probably be dead by now."

She barely heard him. Her mind was too involved, trying to come up with a reason that would explain why she had seen him in the mirror. "Who are you?"

"I've already told you."

Her brow creased. "No, I mean who *are* you? What are you doing here?"

"I'm here as Burke Delaney's houseguest."

"Kells Braxton..." She *remembered*. And then something else happened. She slowly became aware of the still-warm imprint of his lips on the back of her hand, and for the first time it dawned on her that she was not dealing with an image in the mirror, but, rather, a flesh-and-blood man. She was stunned that it had taken her so long to notice. But now awareness came in a rush.

His eyes held her, making it impossible for her to look away from him. The heat of his body lapped and circled her, the power of his virility pulled. Suddenly she was extraordinarily conscious of her skin, her body, her sexuality. And that he still gripped her hand.

With his thumb he was outlining the area he had just kissed, as if he were embossing the kiss onto her skin. When she had seen him

in the mirror, she remembered, she had thought he appeared dangerous. He did now too, but she couldn't find the will to pull her hand
away. The mirror was a mystery, and he was part of the mystery.
"Have we ever met?"

"I'm sorry to say we haven't."

"But I've seen your picture somewhere."

It was a definite statement and delivered in a manner that was
meant to force him to agree with her. He smiled. "Have you?"

"I must have." It was the only answer. She had seen the picture,
and though she had forgotten about it, her subconscious had stored
away the memory. Then, for some unfathomable reason, her mind
had conjured him up as she had gazed into the mirror. She supposed
her theory made sense. But if it had happened according to her theory, she was more tired than she had originally thought, and her
subconscious was playing *major* tricks on her.

Her continued scrutiny prompted him to ask, "Do I look familiar to you?"

"More than you could possibly know."

His head tilted to one side as his regard turned curious. "That's
a strange way to put it."

"I'm sorry. I'm feeling a little strange."

"Well, I can assure you that we've never met before. Meeting
you would be something I wouldn't forget."

A small, disconcerting thrill darted through her. No, she
wouldn't have forgotten him either. And in reality she couldn't imagine having seen his picture and forgetting it. He wasn't a man one
could ignore, and she was sure that same magnetic quality would
come through even in a photograph. But there *had* to be an explanation. "Where could I have seen your picture?"

His smile widened, and he saw her gaze go to his lips. His stomach muscles tightened. Remaining cautious was growing more and
more difficult. "You know, if you were anyone else, I would say you
were using a pick-up line. But then, I'd be willing to wager that
you've never used one in your life." She certainly didn't need a line

with him. She already had one hundred and ten percent of his attention. He paused. "Who are *you?*"

"Bria Delaney."

He dropped her hand. His instincts that urged caution had been right on the mark. She was a Delaney, and that made for complications he didn't want. "Why couldn't you have been someone's secretary?" he muttered.

"I beg your pardon?"

"Never mind." He should never have had that glass of scotch, he reflected grimly. A person needed every one of his wits about him when he dealt with a Delaney, *any* Delaney. His father had taught him that lesson early in life. Adopting a casual, strictly social tone, he said, "I entertained your brother, Patrick, for several weeks in Brisbane."

"Yes, I know." Her mind raced. Patrick had spoken to her about Kells Braxton in phone conversations, but she couldn't recall that he had ever described him. "Wait a minute. You live in Australia, don't you?"

His lips twitched. "Last I checked, that's where Brisbane is."

She made an impatient sound. "I know where Brisbane is, Mr. Braxton. But you have a decidedly American accent."

"Call me Kells. And I have an American accent because I was born and raised in New Mexico."

She rubbed her forehead. Patrick had told her he was an American, but she had forgotten. What else had she forgotten?

Her hair lay in a silky slide against the velvet suit, flame against dark wine. But her face remained pale, and he couldn't stop the pang of concern he felt. "Are you all right?"

She was fine, she told herself, and tried to believe it. "Business publications," she said firmly. "Has your picture ever been published in any that I might have seen?"

The light in his eyes became more pronounced. "My picture has appeared from time to time in various publications, but I haven't the faintest idea whether you might have seen any of them."

"I must have. That's got to be the answer." She felt unsteady and unbalanced and wasn't sure whether it was because she thought she had seen him in the mirror or because being close to him was making it hard for her to think. She turned her back on him and walked to the Christmas tree, noticing with pleasure that the red-haired angel was in her place, high atop the tree, and that the ornaments made from the gold brought from Kantalan gleamed on the boughs.

"It's a beautiful tree," he said, following her but keeping several feet between them. He had made a mutually beneficial business deal with the Delaneys; to get further involved with them didn't fit into his plans.

"Thank you," she murmured, gazing with a troubled expression at the tree, as if it might offer an answer. And in a way it did. The tree held ornaments that had been made a century and a half before and called to mind the history of the Delaneys. Down through the years, time and time again, her family had overcome seemingly impossible odds. What were images in a mirror compared to what the generations of her family had been through? She felt comforted and inhaled the tree's fresh pine scent. "Nothing beats the smell of a real Christmas tree, does it?"

Not unless it was she, he thought. He remembered the sensual scent that emanated from her skin as he had lifted her hand to his mouth. Even now he would swear that her fragrance drifted in the air between and around them. He shifted his weight and, in the process, took a small, unnoticeable step backward. "Isn't it a little early for a tree?"

She smiled and he stilled at the sweetness of the curve of her lips. He definitely should not have had that scotch, he thought grimly.

"Mom always puts up our tree this early. She likes to get a head start on the Christmas season."

"Don't the trees die by Christmas?"

"They wouldn't dare. My mother has her own special way of keeping the trees fresh right through New Year's Day, and most of it is pure will on her part." She realized with gratitude that she was feeling calmer. As a child, Christmas had always been a magic time, and it had remained very special for her. During the Christmas season, all things, up to and including peace on earth, seemed possible. Maybe, she thought, she shouldn't question too closely what she had or hadn't seen in that mirror.

She smiled at herself. Her Irish blood was really showing. The superstitious Irish never questioned luck or fate, whether it was good or bad, and the mystical was left alone. Good policy. If there was an answer, she would find it. If there wasn't, she would forget it. "When do you put your tree up?"

"I don't."

She swung her head around so that she could look fully at him. "Why not?"

A lock of her hair had been caught by a branch of the tree. Before he could think about it and censor his actions, he stepped to her and freed the glistening red strands. "It's always seemed a lot of trouble to go to for one day."

"But it's a season, not just one day. You had Christmas trees as a child, didn't you?"

"Once or twice maybe. To tell you the truth, I can't remember." He smiled as he interpreted her expression. "Is that distress for me?"

"Distress?"

He reached out and smoothed a finger over the furrows that ridged her brow. "You and I come from different backgrounds, Bria. I don't have a family to celebrate Christmas with, so I see little point in putting up a tree. I don't even own any ornaments."

She didn't know of life without family, tradition, and Christmas trees. His way struck her as very sad. "I'm sorry."

"Don't be. I have everything I want." It was true, wasn't it? he asked himself even as he remembered that her skin had felt petal-soft beneath his finger. If it wasn't true, these few days on Killara were going to make it true. He slipped his hand into his pocket. "Who's Joshua?" he asked, deliberately changing the subject. "There's a wooden ornament behind your head that has *Joshua* written on it."

She glanced at the ornament. "He was one of Shamus and

Malvina's sons. Shamus and Malvina are the Delaneys who founded Killara, and they had nine sons. If I remember correctly, Joshua was their fourth son. Shamus carved nine Christmas ornaments, one for each of his sons. See." She picked out two more wooden ornaments that were nearby and pointed. "This one is Dominic's and that one over there is Falcon's. Somewhere on this tree there are six more."

"Nine sons," he said reflectively. "That's very impressive."

"Shamus and Malvina and their sons were all very impressive people. They were the start of the Delaney dynasty."

"From what I've observed, the modern-day Delaneys are no slouches."

She laughed. "There speaks a man who has just concluded a business deal with my father."

"Don't forget Patrick. He's the one who initiated the discussions, and he's an extremely sharp young man."

She never forgot Patrick; they were very close. At the moment, he was visiting with Nicholas and Sydney Charron, but he'd be home for Christmas and he'd be bringing Nicholas and Sydney with him, along with their son and daughter. "I was working on another project while Dad and Patrick were in negotiations with you, but from what little I've heard, you more than held your own."

The colored lights on the tree lit her skin with a soft glow. The sight made him want to touch her again. "I managed. By the way, you and your twin brother don't favor each other."

She nodded, noticing that his blue eyes had grown darker. Was it the lights or something else? "I know. Both of us have green eyes, but Patrick's are a darker shade than mine. He took after my father in coloring and looks, and I'm a throwback to another ancestor. Her name was Brianne too. She was Rory's daughter."

"Too?"

"Brianne is my full name."

"I like Bria," he said, his voice low and husky. He touched her. He hadn't meant to, but suddenly his fingers were sliding over her cheek, feeling the smooth velvet texture of her face, then curving along her jawline to the fullness of her mouth. They stopped on the softness of her bottom lip. Without wondering, he knew that she would taste like a flame—fiery, golden, consuming. *Damn, this wasn't in the plan.* Abruptly he lifted his hand, and his voice hardened. "I think I like everything about you, except for the fact that you're a Delaney."

Shaken, Bria blinked. What had just happened? His fingers had laid down a trail of sweet heat; she had almost gasped aloud at the sensation. And now his expression was cool and dispassionate, as if he had never touched her.

"Bria, what's this I hear about a mirror?" Burke Delaney asked, striding into the room. "*Kells!* Glad to see you've settled in all right."

Kells turned to his host with an extended hand and a pleasant but impersonal smile. "Hello, Burke."

2

BURKE DELANEY WAS AN IMPOSING MAN, TALL, DISTINGUISHED, HIS dark hair silvered at the temples. "Have you and Bria been getting acquainted?" he asked.

Kells glanced at Bria. The color had come back to her skin and it glowed golden-beige. Had it been her father's sudden appearance that had produced the color or had it been his touch? It was safer to believe it was her father. He looked back at Burke. "Yes. I was surprised to meet her. I knew you had a daughter who lived in Tucson, but for some reason it didn't occur to me that she and I would be here at the same time."

Burke smiled at his daughter and held out his arms. As she had countless times in her life, Bria walked to him to be embraced in a loving hug.

"Her mother and I finally got her to take a vacation. Since I don't spend as much time in Tucson at the office as I used to, we don't get to see her or her brother as often as we'd like. Besides, we thought she could use the rest."

Bria's lips twitched. "The story I heard was that Mom needed help with the house."

He chuckled. "That too. In about ten days our whole family will be here for Christmas."

"How many people are you expecting?" Kells asked.

Bria observed Kells as he talked to her father. He was perfectly at ease, being the polite houseguest, asking about the host's family, when in reality she sensed that he couldn't have cared less. If she were to strip away all his surface layers, what kind of person would she find? she wondered. Then in a flash of insight she realized she would never know; he would never reveal his innermost self. Kells Braxton was one of the most guarded people she had ever met.

"I'm not sure," Burke admitted with a grin. "My two brothers and their families will be coming in from Shamrock and Hell's Bluff, plus our three Australian cousins and their families. In addition, there'll be some old family friends." He glanced at Bria. "Cougar, Bridget, Kathleen, Deuce, and Mandarin. I guess we should do a head count once everyone gets here."

"They're all going to stay here?" Kells asked, his curiosity now genuinely pricked.

Burke's grin widened. "The day Killara can't hold all the Delaneys is the day we add on rooms."

Bria groaned. "If this house gets any larger or any more rambling, we're going to have to start wearing beepers to keep track of each other."

Burke laughed. "If we have to, we will. Now, we should go into dinner. Cara's waiting." A large emerald cut to the precise shape of a shamrock glinted on his finger as he gestured for Kells and Bria to precede him.

"Would you mind going on ahead, Kells?" she asked, laying a detaining hand on her dad's arm. "I'd like a quick word with my father."

Kells sent her a sharp look that, strangely, probed and nettled at Bria. But with a polite nod to her, he left the room. Her gaze followed him until he disappeared from sight.

"What is it, sweetheart?" Burke asked.

She made an effort to push Kells from her mind. "Do you know anything about the mirror I found today?"

"No, but I'm eager to see it. I can't imagine why it's been put away all these years. Where is it now?"

"In my room."

"As soon as dinner is over, we'll go up and see it. Okay?"

"Okay." Surely, she thought as she walked by his side into the baronial dining room, he would be able to explain the unusual power the mirror seemed to possess.

The dinner conversation flowed around Bria. She listened, but heard only part of what was said. Her thoughts constantly switched back and forth between Kells and the mirror.

She longed to dismiss Kells from her mind as just another business associate of her father's, but she found it impossible to do so. With his charisma and strength of personality, her father could easily overshadow another man; she had seen it all too often.

But Kells was a match for her father in every way. Where her father was polished steel, Kells was a hard-edged, jaggedly cut piece of granite. She was used to strong-willed, powerful men; they abounded in the family. But there was an unyielding force within Kells and an inherent self-confidence that against her will pulled at her and made him impossible to ignore.

Had she really seen him in the mirror? Had his touch really burned as much as she remembered . . . ?

"Bria? Bria?"

The sound of her name snapped her back to the present, and her gaze flew to her father. "Yes?"

"I just made the suggestion that it would be nice if you showed Kells around the place tomorrow." She stared at him blankly, and he frowned. "I have some things I need to attend to, or I would do it myself."

"Of course she'll do it," Cara prompted, breathtakingly lovely in a black chiffon dress. "You'll be happy to do it, won't you, darling?"

She glanced at Kells and saw him looking at her, his eyes enigmatic. "Maybe Kells would prefer to wait until you could take him, Dad."

"Not at all," Kells said, cutting in smoothly. "I'd really enjoy having you show me around."

"Really?" Her tone was skeptical.

He smiled. "Really."

"Do you ride?"

"Some."

"Some? Maybe we should take the Jeep."

"Whatever you think is best."

His overly polite responses grated on her nerves. She clenched her teeth. "Perhaps it would be better to wait until morning and see what the weather's like before we decide."

"That sounds good." He tossed his napkin down on the table, stood, and addressed Burke and Cara. "If you'll excuse me, I think my jet lag has finally caught up with me. I don't want to fall asleep in the middle of our tour tomorrow, so I believe I better go to bed."

Burke nodded. "Certainly. Get a good night's rest."

"If you need anything," Cara said, "press three on the phone, and you'll be connected with our housekeeper."

"I'm sure everything will be fine." He looked at Bria. In spite of himself, he hadn't been able to turn down the opportunity of being alone with her once again. His only comfort was that it would be without the influence of scotch or jet lag. "I'll see you in the morning."

His touch had flustered her and his appearance in the mirror had caused a major disturbance in her mind, and she fervently wished she would never have to see him again. But he was a guest of her father's, and she hadn't been raised to be rude to anyone. She searched for a neutral but courteous reply. "I'll be looking forward to it," she said. His answering grin told her she hadn't fooled him.

* * *

"I think your mother's right," Burke said, his tall frame bent as he studied the mirror. "I think Shamus and Malvina must have brought this over from Ireland. Wait until York and Rafe see it. The frame is extraordinary."

Bria clasped her hands together anxiously. "But what about the mirror?"

He gazed at the reflective surface. "It's held up extremely well over the years. There's not a scratch or a mark on it. Remarkable."

"Do you see anything in it?"

He straightened. "You mean did I see anything in it besides myself?" She nodded. "Honey, what's bothering you? Your mother told me that you fell asleep in the attic and dreamed that you saw her riding Shalimar."

She gnawed on her lower lip. "Dad, I'm not sure it was a dream."

He studied her. "What do you think it was?"

It was a question she would give anything to answer. "I don't know."

"What else could it be?"

"Again, I'm not sure. I was really hoping you would know something about the mirror's history that might explain..." She debated telling him about seeing Kells in the mirror, then for a reason she couldn't name decided against it. Maybe she didn't believe what she had seen herself. Or maybe she didn't want her father to think she was losing her mind.

He grasped her arms and placed a gentle kiss on her forehead. "Get some sleep, honey. When you've had some rest, you'll be able to put everything into perspective."

She smiled wearily. "Yeah, I guess you're right."

Once her dad had left, she changed into a nightgown and prepared for bed. But when she was ready, she didn't immediately climb between the sheets. Instead, she walked to the mirror.

Her own face looked back at her.

She wiped a hand over her eyes. She felt like a fool, an utter fool. Being in the attic this morning and finding the old section had apparently kicked her imagination into overdrive. She had discovered a book of Malvina's and a picture made from Brianne Delaney Lassiter's hair. And fantasy had taken flight in her mind. She had never known herself to conjure images out of air, but she certainly had today.

She lifted the mirror and carried it to her closet, where she placed it at the far back. It would stay there, she decided, until her parents decided where they wanted to hang it.

With the problem of the mirror settled in her mind, she went to bed. But as tired as she was, sleep didn't come right away.

Instead, Kells Braxton appeared in her head, his rugged countenance somber, his blue eyes mocking. And he stayed there all night, even after she finally fell asleep.

Bria dressed in jeans and an oversize moss-green sweater. Since she had put the mirror away, she felt as if a weight had been lifted from her, but she was still left with the problem of Kells Braxton.

As she pulled on her boots, she considered the situation. Actually, she supposed, there really wasn't a reason to try to fight the way he riveted her attention whenever he was near. She was unattached, and she couldn't remember hearing that he was married. Surely if he was, he would have brought his wife with him. No, he wasn't married. Maybe he had a girlfriend, though, someone he was serious about. Her spirits plummeted.

But he had kissed the back of her hand and touched her.... Not exactly a ravagement, but a definite sensual experience. And his touch hadn't been an accidental or casual gesture. He had wanted to touch her, she was sure of it.

She frowned as she remembered something else. He had dropped her hand when she had told him her name.

She had learned early that the name Delaney was a mixed blessing. The Delaneys had enemies; they always had, undoubtedly they always would. Then there were people who thought by becoming friends with them they could use the association to their advantage in some way. They soon learned differently.

But Kells...His whole demeanor had changed when he had found out who she was. He had said he wished she were someone's secretary. Why?

Her father was too smart to invite an enemy into his home. And Kells hadn't given her the impression he wanted to further their relationship. Even when he had said he would enjoy having her show him around, his eyes had been more challenging than inviting. No, for whatever reason, the man simply wasn't interested in her. So, fine. It was no big deal. This morning she would give him the quickest tour of Killara she had ever given. Then she'd find a project to keep herself busy for quite a while so she could ignore him for the rest of his stay.

Her frown still firmly in place, she walked to a window and gazed out. Her room faced the back of the house and overlooked the pool and garden area and gave her a clear view of her father and Kells walking side by side.

Kells was wearing a black split-leather jacket.

Her heart stopped, then started again with a hard thud.

He was wearing the *same* jacket she had seen him wearing in the images in the mirror.

Her peace of mind fled. There was no way she could have known that he owned a jacket like that one.

Slowly but with great purpose, she turned and made her way to the closet. She pulled the mirror out and carried it to a chair, then knelt before it.

Forcing herself, she looked into the mirror. For a brief moment she saw her own reflection, exactly what she had prayed she would see. Then suddenly she was gazing at something else, an image of her and Kells in a torrid embrace, clinging to each other, kissing passionately.

She stared, mesmerized, taking in everything about the scene before her—the way his mouth was crushing hers, the way his hands were beneath her sweater, caressing her breasts, the way her arms were wrapped tightly around his neck . . . and the extraordinary way she was responding.

The image vanished. She gave a small cry and sat back on her heels.

She had seen it; she hadn't imagined it; she hadn't dreamed it. She had seen Kells Braxton kissing her and her kissing him back. What should she do?

There was a school of thought stating that if you visualized something that you wanted to happen long and hard enough, it would eventually happen. Was that what was happening? Did she want so badly for Kells to kiss her that she had made the image appear in the mirror?

She passed a shaking hand over her face. No, she couldn't buy that theory. There was no doubt that Kells had had an effect on her, but not enough to send her imagination soaring so that she could clearly see each and every detail of a passionate kiss. No, no, no. Something else was going on here and she had to get to the bottom of it.

"You said you rode some," Bria said, watching Kells as he easily controlled the spirited Arabian beneath him. The supple lines of Kells's powerful body made him seem a part of the stallion. "You understand your ability."

"He's a beautiful animal," he said, as if that explained his riding prowess.

"He's a Delaney horse, bred and trained on Shamrock, just as mine is." She reached down and patted the sleek brown neck of her bay. "So where did you learn to ride?"

He shrugged. "I grew up on a ranch in New Mexico."

"Oh, yes. You did mention you were born and raised there." The day was clear and cool, and the sky was as deeply blue as his eyes. Suddenly she was fiercely glad she had agreed to take him on this tour.

"The ranch was nowhere as grand as Killara. Just a lot of brush and tumbleweed and a hundred or so head of cattle, but my grandfather loved it."

"It was your grandfather's place?"

He nodded and reflected with mild surprise that he couldn't remember the last time he had talked with someone about his childhood home. "He named it The Star because of all the stars that appeared over it every night. He pictured the ranch becoming a star among America's ranches, like Killara."

"I don't think I've ever heard of it. Did it become a star?"

"Not even close, but I honestly don't think he cared."

He smiled. She remembered the image of them kissing that she'd seen in the mirror, and she couldn't help but stare at his mouth. What would it be like to be kissed by him? His lips were firm and well shaped, and her instincts told her he was practiced in the art of kissing. How would those lips feel against hers? Would she feel a pleasant tingle as she had so many times in the past? Or would she feel something stronger?

She blew out a long breath. Lord, help her. She needed to think of something *other* than Kells's mouth.

"You said it was your grandfather's ranch and that you grew up there. Did your parents live there too?" To her astonishment, she saw him stiffen.

"Both my parents died when I was young," he said curtly. "My grandfather raised me."

"I see. I'm sorry. I didn't mean to bring up painful memories."

He glanced over at her. Her tight jeans delineated the long, enticing length of her legs, her open jacket exposed the swell of her firm breasts against the big sweater. Her hair swayed and rippled like a red banner in the wind, shimmering with every movement. Her skin was golden, and she was more desirable than he wanted to admit.

It had taken guts and grit to conquer this land, and she was part of the family who had done it. And seeing her set against the wild beauty of her land, his sense of something untamed in her was stronger than ever.

Hell, he thought. Rest and sobriety hadn't made any difference. He shouldn't have been so eager to come on this damn tour. "It's not painful, just something that happened a long time ago."

The tone of his voice told her he had no intention of saying more about the death of his parents. She stifled her curiosity on that subject, but gave vent to it in the other area that troubled her. "Have you ever been to Killara before?"

"No, but of course Killara's legend stretches far and wide. I've heard of it all my life." His eyes scanned the range they were riding across. Meadow rolled toward meadow, where cattle grazed and saguaros raised their arms toward heaven.

Her gaze followed his and she took in the stark beauty of the landscape that had always been her home. Kells Braxton's strength equaled that of the rugged land around him, Bria thought. He wasn't overwhelmed or overpowered by Killara, as so many people were.

But nothing changed the fact that she had seen his image in the mirror, or that there had been a sharp bite to his words as he had talked of Killara. . . .

"Do you see those mountains over there?" she asked, pointing to the craggy peaks in the distance.

"It would be hard to miss them," he said dryly.

"Those mountains are part of Killara."

His lips twisted into a wry grin. "That doesn't surprise me at all. An outsider's perception of the Delaneys is that they own most of the world."

"Do you think that?"

He glanced at her. "No. You probably own only a sizable part of it. But there isn't any doubting a Delaney's penchant for acquiring."

Again she heard the biting edge in his tone. "Does that penchant you just described bother you?"

"No. Why should it? Your dad didn't buy my company."

"But he tried, didn't he?" Kells smiled; her eyes went to his lips. He had beautiful lips, she thought. Sensual. Patrick had told her that Kells was a brilliant computer engineer and that a number of heads of corporations had been after him. She supposed that over the years a great many women must have also been after him—but not for business reasons.

"Burke tried all right. But when he realized there was no way I was going to sell him my company, no matter how much money he offered, he came up with another offer."

Those must have been some negotiations, she thought, regretting that she had missed them. "Another offer that was on your terms."

His eyes glinted with hard blue lights. "It's the only way I do business."

"That's usually the only way Dad does business, but you had something he wanted."

"And in the end he got it. I don't imagine there are too many things that Burke Delaney has wanted in his life that he hasn't gotten."

"I guess you're right," she said slowly, trying to analyze his words, his tone. There was something there; she just wished she knew what.

"And I imagine that trait has been passed down to his daughter. Tell me, Bria, what is it that you don't have that you want?"

Actually, there were things she wanted, normal things, like a man to love and to be loved by, and children to raise and adore. But she was shocked to realize that when he had asked the question, her gaze had gone straight to his lips. It was with relief that she saw they had reached a stream, a glistening, clear flow of cool water that came down from the mountains and cut a path across the meadow.

She dismounted and led her horse to the water. Kells followed suit, letting the silence hang loudly in the air with his still-unanswered question.

But she wasn't sure she wanted to bare her innermost desires to this hard man who could heat her skin and fog her mind. She pointed again toward the mountains. "There's a road up there that comes from Hell's Bluff. It leads down to the foothills and then on down to the valley. Have you ever driven in any of the mountains around here?"

"I told you, I've never been on Killara before."

"Yes," she said softly, "you did say that." The image in the mirror had shown him standing on that very mountain road, looking down on Killara. But then, the mirror had also shown her kissing him, and that hadn't happened either.

Would it? To her alarm, her pulse began to race.

Kells knelt upstream from the horses and scooped a handful of water into his mouth. When he stood, he was somehow closer to her. And his voice was a husky rasp. "You keep looking at my mouth."

"I . . ." She couldn't deny it.

"Do you want a taste? Is that what you want?"

"No, I'm sorry if I—"

"Do you want me to kiss you?"

His question struck her dumb, because she realized the answer was a heartfelt yes.

"To hell with it," he said roughly. "Let's both be sorry."

He reached for her and hauled her against him. But once he had her body against his, he paused. She was all softness and femininity, pressing into him, making his gut tighten and his mouth dry—and he had just had a drink of water.

Did he really want to do this? he asked himself. Hell, yes, he answered. But the urge for caution was still in him, causing him to go slow.

He bent his head and lightly brushed his lips back and forth across hers. Lord, he thought. He had been right. She did taste like a flame.

She had been braced for a hard, crushing kiss and was unprepared for the surprising featherlike strokes of his mouth over hers. It was as if he were sampling her, uncertain if he wanted to go further. But she knew he would; she had seen it happening in the mirror. And so she waited and was rewarded as a heated sweetness began to grow in the pit of her stomach and her lips started to burn. With a sigh that indicated surrender, she opened her mouth.

He knew what he was doing was madness, he knew that he never should have allowed himself that first fiery taste of her. And once he had, he knew he shouldn't be continuing it. But her lips were so soft, the sound she made so tantalizing. Without further thought he accepted the invitation she gave him and plunged his tongue deeply into her mouth. Raw need rushed to his head and down into his groin.

His hands tightened on her upper arms like iron bands, making it impossible for her to move. She was caught in a trap of desire, oblivious to the rhythmic music of the stream and the horses that had wandered a few feet away to graze. Sense of place or propriety was lost to her. She strained against him and groaned with pleasure when she felt the hard ridge of his sex press against her pelvis. His kiss was hot, urgent, all-consuming. And she was left bereft and confused when he abruptly pulled away from her.

His eyes glittered like dark sapphires as his chest heaved with the harsh intake and expulsion of air. He looked like a man who very much wanted a woman, but as she stared bewildered at him, he brought his hand up to his mouth and wiped it across his lips. "What's wrong, Kells? What happened?"

"Nothing is wrong," he said roughly. "You wanted me to kiss you. I kissed you."

"Yes, but—"

"You got what you wanted."

Anger surged in her. "And you didn't?"

"As a matter of fact, I enjoyed the hell out of it, but that's all there is to it. It's over. I came here to do business with your father, not seduce his daughter." He stalked over to his horse and lifted its reins.

Damn. He was right, she thought with chagrin. And after all, it had been just a kiss, one of countless she had received. Those kisses hadn't meant anything and neither had this one. She had even known he was going to kiss her, and in a very overt way had initiated it. So it had happened; now the thing to do was forget it.

Grappling for a hold on reality, she said, "We should be getting back. Lunch will be served soon." With a curt nod he mounted his horse.

For the most part their ride back to the house was made in silence. When they did speak, it was in a polite, stilted way and on subjects that didn't come close to touching what had happened between them.

They were nearly to the house before it hit Bria that the kiss she and Kells had shared *wasn't* the kiss she had "seen." No, in that kiss her arms had been around his neck and his hand had been beneath her sweater. Very passionate. Wild.

Dear God, what was happening to her?

3

WHEN BRIA AND KELLS REACHED THE STABLES, SHE QUICKLY EX-cused herself to race to the house, to her room, to the mirror.

"Come on," she muttered with frustration as she stared at her own reflection. "Do your stuff. Show me something."

Her own image continued to stare back at her.

"*Dammit.*" She hit the arm of the chair. "What in the hell is going on?"

She sat back on her heels and tried to come up with a meaning, an explanation for the things she had seen. First there had been her mother on Shalimar, something she knew had happened in the past. Then there had been Kells looking down on Killara, something that to her knowledge hadn't happened. Then she had seen the two of them kissing. It had happened, only not in the way she had seen it in the mirror.

"If you're supposed to be some sort of crystal ball, you're a complete failure," she said to the mirror.

She was gripping the arms of the chair to push herself up when the image in the mirror changed and she saw their housekeeper, Mrs. Copeland, carrying a crystal compote dish full of fruit into the dining room. Just as Mrs. Copeland reached the table, she turned suddenly and dropped the dish. It crashed on the floor. Then Bria was looking at her own reflection again.

"This is crazy," she whispered to herself, shaken. "Crazy."

She sat where she was, waiting until she thought her legs would hold her weight without giving way beneath her. In the bathroom she repeatedly splashed cool water on her face. Then she went in search of Mrs. Copeland and the compote dish.

Downstairs, she reached the doorway of the dining room just as Mrs. Copeland, carrying the fruit-filled compote dish, came into the room, using the door that led from the kitchen. The scene was exactly as it had been moments before when she had seen it in the mirror. Even the fruit was the same.

Something in Bria wanted to cry out to the woman to be careful, to hold on tightly to the dish, but reason prevailed. She didn't want to do anything that might influence the outcome of the tableau unfolding before her.

Mrs. Copeland walked briskly toward the dining table and was nearly to it when someone called to her from the kitchen. She turned suddenly and the compote dish slipped from her hands. Giving a cry of distress, she gazed down at the shattered glass and fruit that now lay at her feet.

Bria eased away from the door and fell back against the wall. Panic rose in her until it was a scream in her throat, trying to escape. In desperation she sought something normal to focus on. She was in Killara's stately entry hall, with its Italian marble floor and magnificent Waterford chandelier. Against a curved wall the stairway swept gracefully downward from the second floor. As always, her mother had decorated the banister with greenery, ropes of luminescent pearls, tiny clear lights, and red velvet bows. Pots of red poinsettias adorned each step.

Bria ran shaking fingers through her hair. Seeking out the normal wasn't helping. The normal had ceased to exist the moment she had found the mirror and then met Kells.

With great effort she attempted to will her panic away. When Kells walked up a minute later, she had been only partially successful.

He took one look at her nearly colorless face and closed his hand around her upper arm. "What's wrong, Bria? What's happened? Are you all right?"

What was happening between the two of them might be confusing to her, but the things she saw in the mirror made her think she was losing her mind. Kells, at least, made things happen in her that felt good. Without thinking she spread her fingers over his chest, unconsciously trying to absorb some of his strength and warmth. "I'm fine."

With his free hand he cupped the side of her face. "Then why do you look so pale?"

His touch was working its magic, heating her blood, sending it rushing hotly through her veins. But she didn't feel she could tell him the truth, at least not until she could reasonably explain the phenomenon of the mirror. She had to keep in mind that he was a stranger—a stranger she had seen looking down on Killara with an angry expression on his face. It was bred into her bones to protect Killara. She improvised. "I'm just hungry, that's all."

His brows drew together. "Are you sure that's all it is? You looked like this when I first saw you."

"I was probably hungry then too. Really, it's no big deal. I'm just hungry."

"Your dad said you needed to rest, that it was the reason they asked you to take some time off."

She passed a hand over her eyes. "I haven't had a vacation in five years, but I've been doing something I love, learning the business. It's been an exciting, fun time."

"But now you're tired."

He actually sounded concerned, she thought. She had to be wrong; she was probably still in shock. "I told you. I'm okay. You know how parents worry."

"No, actually, I don't."

Remembering that his parents had died when he was young, she sighed. "I'm sorry. I shouldn't have said that."

"Forget it. Didn't you have any breakfast?"

"No, but then, I rarely eat breakfast."

He pulled her away from the wall and kept his hand on her. "Let's go see how near to serving lunch they are."

As it happened, lunch was ready. And as soon as Mrs. Copeland had cleaned up the glass and the fruit, the meal was served.

Bria felt Kells's gaze on her all through lunch, so much so that she barely ate. His presence and his gaze were a tangible force. She had known him less than twenty-four hours, yet she couldn't remember a time when he hadn't loomed large in her life. It didn't make sense that he could affect her so, but then, at the moment so little did.

Immediately after lunch she asked her mother and father to meet her in her bedroom.

"What's up?" Cara asked, perching on the edge of the bed. Burke stood a few feet away.

"It's about the mirror."

Burke nodded, gazing at it. "We need to find somewhere to hang it."

"This isn't about hanging it, Dad. It's about the things I see when I look into the mirror."

"Did you have another dream, honey?" Cara asked, a flicker of worry in her lovely gray eyes.

"What I'm seeing couldn't be a dream. For one thing, I'm wide awake when I see these things; I'm sure I am. For another, the details are too real, and I'm seeing things that have either happened or are about to happen."

"What do you mean?"

She made a quick decision to withhold the times she had seen Kells, and she chose the latest episode to tell them about. "Right before lunch I looked into the mirror and saw Mrs. Copeland drop the compote dish. Then I came downstairs, stood in the dining room doorway, and actually saw her do it. It happened just as it did in the mirror, detail for detail."

Cara threw a worried glance at Burke; he returned it.

Her frustration built as Bria looked from one to the other. "I'm *not* making this up."

Cara slid off the bed and crossed to her. "Don't you think it's possible that you fell asleep for a brief period of time—you know, a little catnap—and dreamed it?"

Bria shook her head. "No, I don't. Not anymore. I was wide awake. Look into the mirror, both of you. Go on. Look, really *look*."

With a glance at each other that plainly said humor her, they did as she asked, first one, then the other. Several minutes later neither of them had seen anything other than their own reflection. And Bria was ready to scream.

Burke put his arm around her. "We believe you, honey," he said in a particularly gentle voice he had always reserved for when she was hurt or sick. "We believe that you *think* you are seeing scenes in the mirror. But we can also see a broader picture than you can. Like how you've worn yourself out these last five years, learning the business and—"

"I'm *not* that tired, Dad—"

"No, Bria, your father's right. You're worn down. We shouldn't have asked you to take Kells out today. You need to kick back for a few days and do nothing."

"I enjoyed spending the morning with Kells." She really had, she realized, and was certain she didn't want to explore what that said about her. "Besides, I'd go crazy doing nothing." Crazier than she obviously already was, she silently added.

"Then at least try to take things a little easier, be kinder to yourself," Cara said. "Rest as much as possible. Sleep late. Read a good book."

Burke walked to her and put his arm around her. "Take your mother's advice, honey. And I'll get the mirror out of your room. I'll keep it in my study until we decide where to hang it."

Cara nodded in agreement. "That's a good idea."

"*No.*"

Burke exchanged another worried glance with Cara. "It's for the best, Bria. The mirror obviously disturbs you."

"No—that is, I'd like to keep it here in my room for a while. And I promise I won't let it bother me. Please, Dad."

Burke's dark brows drew together. Cara shrugged. "Okay," he said, "if that's what you want. But promise me you'll get plenty of rest."

"I will," she murmured.

Her parents' gentle, reasonable, consoling manner was like a knife across her nerves. They didn't believe her. And after all, why should they? What she was telling them was positively ludicrous. And unless the mirror decided to show them something, there would be no basis for them to believe. From now on she would keep whatever she saw to herself. And one way or another, she was going to solve the mystery of the mirror.

I hate to be entertained, Kells thought later that evening, prowling his room, restless, unable to sleep. The afternoon and evening had seemed endless. Burke and his wife were the consummate host and hostess, making certain he had everything he needed, ensuring that he wasn't bored for a moment. The truth was, though, he didn't want to spend time with either of them. He would much rather have had the contracts expressed to him in Australia, signed them there, then expressed them back.

He must be among a minority of businessmen who weren't pleased when the Delaneys came courting. First Patrick Delaney had come, then Burke. Initially he had resisted, but eventually they had offered him a deal on his own terms too good to turn down. What a Delaney wanted, a Delaney got.

But again, he must be one of the few people in the world who would consider turning down an invitation to Killara. His first impulse had been to refuse when Burke had insisted he let him return the hospitality to Patrick. Kells's reasons for not wanting to visit Killara were vague, even to him. In the end, he had grudgingly given in.

He wished he hadn't. He was uncomfortable being on Killara, and he had no intention of staying a minute longer than necessary. He didn't want to become involved with Burke and Cara Delaney, or their home—or, heaven help him, their daughter. He ran his hand around the back of his neck as he realized he had reached the crux of his agitation.

Bria.

He sure as hell hadn't counted on Bria. Unconsciously he had kept track of her today. When he had been with Burke, he had fed him seemingly irrelevant questions until Burke had divulged his daughter's whereabouts. He had done the same with Cara.

His need to know Bria's movements and activities didn't make sense. But then, neither did any of the emotions currently bombarding him.

He wanted Bria, there was no question about it. He had made the mistake of kissing her, getting a sample of her taste, and he had been hard-pressed not to take her right there by the stream. Where was his caution? His common sense? Dammit, why was he letting her get to him?

There was something bothering her; something had spooked her—and badly. Twice now he had seen her pale and shaken, and he didn't like it one bit. He shouldn't care, but much to his disgust, he realized he did.

He walked to the window and stared down. The garden and pool were a pale shade of moonglow. He and Burke had walked there that morning before he and Bria had gone riding, had kissed. *Dammit.*

He turned back to the room and glanced at the bedside clock. Two A.M. Lord, why couldn't he sleep?

A knock at the door drew a frown from him. Curious about who else was up at this hour, he went to answer it.

"Hello, Kells."

"Bria?" She was wearing an ivory satin robe, and her long hair tumbled over the rich material like a river of fire. Her skin was scrubbed clean, and appeared to be as smooth and soft as a child's, but her eyes were shadowed with fatigue. Protectiveness confusingly mixed with desire and took him by surprise.

"May I come in?"

He stepped aside so that she could enter and closed the door behind him. "What's wrong?"

"Nothing's wrong." She glanced around the large room, but the room with its king-size bed and comfortable sitting area barely made an impression. His image remained with her, an incredibly sexy image. He was wearing trousers; his chest and feet were bare. "I was surprised to see your lights still on. Isn't the bed comfortable?"

"It's very comfortable. Do you want to try it?"

"What?" She jerked around to face him. He was eyeing her broodingly.

He slipped his hands into his trouser pockets. "Apparently you can't sleep either. Why are you wandering the halls this late at night?"

"I wasn't wandering. I said I was surprised to see your lights still on, but I came here hoping that you'd be up."

"Really?" He stared at her. "You're remarkably candid, some people might say dangerously so."

She clasped her hands in front of her. "I'm sorry. I know how this must look, but—"

"It's not how it looks, Bria, it's how it *feels*."

She wasn't so stupid that she didn't know what he meant. The air between them fairly crackled with heat and electricity. Beneath the satin of her robe she could feel her nipples hardening and a dull ache beginning low in her body. She combed stiff fingers through her hair, pulling a portion of it back behind her shoulder as she did. "Look, let me just ask you what I came here to ask, and then I'll leave."

"That would probably be a good idea," he said softly.

She silently agreed. Everything feminine in her was responding to the blatantly masculine picture he made. Her fingers itched to stroke across his broad chest, to feel the softly curling dark hairs there and the strength beneath. "Remember those mountains I showed you today?" At his nod she went on. "I'd like to take you up there tomorrow in the Jeep."

"Why?"

"There's a spot that offers a great view of Killara. I thought you'd enjoy seeing it."

"You did?"

His question, devoid of intonation, threw her. It wasn't as if she had expected him to jump at the invitation, but she also hadn't expected this utterly cool indifference. She persevered. "Yes, I did."

"Are you really interested in what I enjoy?"

"Yes, of course—"

"Then maybe I should tell you again—I enjoyed the hell out of our kiss today."

"Yet you ended it."

"Guilty. I didn't see much point in continuing, and I told you why." He studied her for a moment. "But because I did end the kiss, you feel safe enough to ask me to drive up into the mountains with you."

She met his gaze with a directness that matched his. "A person would be a fool to feel safe with you, ever."

"Funny, I feel the very same way about you."

"Why? I'm completely harmless."

"It's been my experience that no Delaney is harmless."

"Yes, or no, Kells?"

"Why, Bria?"

"I told you—"

"That's not the reason. There's something else. A minute ago I said you were remarkably candid. Prove me right and tell me the real reason."

For one wild moment she wished with all her heart she could. But after the reaction she had gotten from her mother and father, she didn't dare. She didn't want Kells to think that she was foolish, or, worse, mad. "The truth is, I can't tell you the reason right now. All I can say is that it's terribly important to me."

There wasn't a doubt in his mind that he was going to go, he thought. She could ask him to go to hell with her and he probably would. He could only hope that a few hours' sleep would bring a return of his caution. "Your father may have something planned for tomorrow."

"I'll clear it with him. Will you come with me?"

He stared at her for a long moment. "I wouldn't miss it."

She exhaled and realized she had been holding her breath. "Good. I'm sure you'll enjoy it."

He *knew* he would, and that was what was troubling him. He was positive he was doing the wrong thing by agreeing to go with her, but only the promise of being alone with her again gave him the strength to open the door and let her leave.

Clouds scudded across the gray sky; wind glided through the mountain passes, carrying the promise of rain. "Don't worry about the weather," Bria said, guiding the Jeep up the twisting gravel road. "We should be back before the storm breaks."

"I'm not worried."

"I guess you're used to our Southwest storms."

"I've seen a few."

She looked over at him. He was dressed in jeans, a royal blue sweater, and his black leather jacket. He looked overwhelmingly masculine and smelled of leather, musk, and a tantalizing hint of citrus. When she had come up with the idea of taking him to the place where, in the mirror, she had seen him standing, she hadn't considered the hazards of being closed up in a Jeep with him. "What happened to The Star?"

"I own it. My grandfather left it to me. It was his dream. You don't sell someone's dream."

"Yet you moved away from it."

"Yes."

"You don't like to talk about yourself, do you?"

"I know everything there is to know about myself; the subject bores me. Besides, why talk about myself when I'm enjoying our little trip so much?"

His sardonic tone drew a smile from her. "Yes, well, I told you I thought you would."

"Yes, you did. You gave it as a reason for inviting me."

"We're nearly there."

She glanced at him again and saw him looking at her with such concentration, her breath caught in her throat. She wrenched her gaze back to the road. It was with gratitude that she saw the lay-by up ahead and was able to pull off and park.

The wind had died down for the moment, but the sky was low and the clouds rushing by were increasingly darker.

At the sight, his mouth curved wryly. "Looks like your weather forecast might be wrong."

"Then we'd better hurry." Too impatient to put on her jacket, she got out of the Jeep and walked to the cliff's edge.

He didn't give a damn about the impending storm, Kells thought, following her. But he was extremely curious to find out what she was up to.

Killara spread as far as the eye could see—north, south, east, and west. In the valley below, the huge, rambling, red-tiled house sat—Killara's heart.

"Is this what you wanted to show me?" he asked.

She nodded, observing him closely. "I know you said you've never been on Killara before, but does this view seem at all familiar to you?"

"Should it?"

"I'm asking you."

"It's an impressive view," he said, "but no, it's not familiar to me."

"Stay where you are," she said, and moved behind him. He turned, watching her with a frown. "Don't look at me. Look at Killara."

"Killara doesn't interest me half as much as you do. What the hell are we doing here, Bria?"

"Please, just look down at Killara."

With a shrug he turned back to gaze down on the land.

It *was* the same, she thought, feeling a little jump of excitement. His broad shoulders stretched against his leather jacket, his long, muscular legs were gloved in faded jeans. Her mental survey abruptly stopped. His hair wasn't gleaming in the sunshine as it had in the mirror because today was gray and overcast. Disappointment scored through her.

"Okay," she said, "you can turn around." He did look very hard, very dangerous, just as he had in the mirror. But he wasn't angry. His expression was one of puzzlement and growing frustration.

"Are you going to tell me what this is about?"

"I can't," she said, feeling both stupid and helpless. Whatever the powers of the mirror were, she didn't have similar powers. She couldn't re-create an image she had seen in it.

"What kind of game are we playing, Bria?" he asked, walking to her. "If I know the rules, I'll have a lot more fun."

She eyed him warily, for the first time noticing a dark tension etched into the lines of his body. "It's not a game."

"Oh, yeah? Then what is it? You bring me up here, ask me to face one way, then another. Excuse me if I think that's a little odd."

She nodded. "You're right. It is."

"Then tell me."

"I'm sorry. I can't."

He stepped closer. "Don't you think you owe me an explanation?"

His nearness, not the question, caused a tightness in her stomach. "Maybe. Probably. But if I did, you'd think I was crazy."

His teeth ground together. "I'd love to think you were crazy, Bria. At least then I might have some sort of defense against you. But I don't. I came up here all too willingly because you asked me, and I'm pretty damned unhappy about the fact."

There was a distant boom of thunder; it could have been the sound of the heavy pounding of her heart. "Why?"

The wind picked back up and sent her hair flying in wild streamers. His hands shot out and clamped on either side of her head, holding the silky strands prisoner. And her. She had no will to move.

"Because you're all wrong for me," he muttered, gazing down into her wide green eyes.

They were suddenly onto another subject, the subject of the two of them, but she had no trouble following his train of thought. Out of the corner of her eye she caught a glimpse of lightning streak from heaven to earth as around them the elements intensified. "You mean because I'm Burke Delaney's daughter? Because you don't want your precious deal ruined?"

He was beginning to care less and less about the deal. "Those are pretty solid reasons in my book."

"Nothing is going to ruin the deal. You're in the final stages."

"So you're saying it's all right for me to feel defenseless against you? To want to kiss you again and this time not stop?"

She wrapped her arms around herself. "No, of course not—"

"There's something going on with you, Bria. Something besides what's between the two of us. I can feel it as surely as I'm feeling you right now. Tell me. Let me help you."

A cold, misty rain had begun to fall; she barely felt it. She was totally focused on the heat in his eyes. Mutely she shook her head.

He uttered a curse. "Then help *me*, because right now, at this exact moment in time, I don't think it matters who or what you are. I'm damned well going to come apart if I don't kiss you." His lips ground down on hers, his tongue drove into her mouth.

With a moan of desire Bria surrendered. She wound her arms around his neck, absorbing the raw sexuality of the kiss with a need that caught her off guard and left her weak. It seemed as if his hands were everywhere on her body, skimming up her back, down her sides to her bottom, then sliding beneath her sweater to her breasts.

She was wearing a silk and lace bra, but the material didn't deter him. He kneaded the soft mounds with an authority and possessiveness that left her trembling. She clung tightly to him and returned the kiss with a passionate intensity.

The rain fell harder and the wind picked up, but she didn't notice. Her entire body was radiating heat. She pressed into him, trying to ease the heavy ache that was growing in her lower belly.

A growl rumbled up from Kells's chest. Yesterday's kiss had been only a prelude to this. He was so damned hungry for her, he wasn't sure he'd ever be able to stop kissing her. He wanted to glide his tongue over every inch of her; he wanted to bury himself inside her. She was wild and hot in his arms, but he knew he was getting only a hint of what she could be like. In bed, he was sure, she would reveal untamed layer upon layer, like veins of gold in her being.

His thumbs flicked back and forth across the hardened tips of her nipples, then with barely conscious thought he closed his hands over her buttocks, lifted her against his throbbing arousal, and carried her to the hood of the vehicle. He bent her back across it and laid his body over hers. He had nothing in mind other than getting as close to her as possible. He kept kissing her because he couldn't do anything else. He was being driven by something that had nothing to do with rational thought or cautious emotion. It was something that had taken possession of him and wouldn't let go. It was her—*Bria*.

He reached for the waistband of her jeans.

The Jeep's horn blared sharp and loud and shocking. He stilled, and beneath him he felt her do the same. The horn sounded again.

"What in the *hell?*"

She put her hand to her forehead, vaguely surprised to find it cold and wet. "It's the phone," she murmured, her words short and breathless. "It's rigged so that when the Jeep is turned off and the phone rings, the horn honks. If you're on the range, you can hear it."

"No kidding." He muttered a string of succinct and colorful curses and pushed upright with an action that bordered on violence.

She moved slower, each blare of the horn activating jangling nerves. Pulling her sweater down, she made her way unsteadily around the Jeep. She opened the passenger door, sat down, and punched the speaker button on the phone. "Hello?"

Burke's concerned voice greeted her. "Hi, honey. Where are you?"

Kells opened the other door, dropped down on the seat beside her, and pulled the door closed after him. She strove to keep her voice normal. "We're still up in the mountains."

"I was afraid you got caught up there. Ever since the storm broke, I've been worried."

Storm? She glanced around her; the rain was coming down in sheets. Lord, how could she have not noticed before? She closed the door to keep the rain out. Kells took a handkerchief from an inside pocket of his jacket and wiped his face. The action drew her attention. His hair was plastered to his skull. His skin was pulled taut against his bones so that he looked as fiercely primitive as the storm sounded. Her blood heated. "There's nothing to worry about. We're fine."

"What took you so long to answer the phone?"

Kells was staring at her with eyes that held glints as hard as steel and hot as fire. She had never seen him look more dangerous. "We, uh, we were walking back to the Jeep."

"Did you get wet?"

"A little. Listen, Dad, don't worry about us. We're just about to head back."

"Well, be careful, honey. You know how treacherous that road can be when it's wet. Use your own judgement, but it might be worthwhile to wait until the storm dies down."

"I'm not sure this storm is going to die down anytime soon," she said, and wondered if she was talking about the weather. "But we'll be careful. See you soon. Bye." She punched the button, disconnecting her father. And for the first time she began to feel the cold. "That was Dad," she said unnecessarily.

"You're trembling."

He was right, she realized. "I'm okay. Let's change seats and get out of here."

"No," he said with a decisiveness that carried over to the forceful way he turned on the ignition. "I'll drive back." His body was tensed for action, and he couldn't simply sit and do nothing but be a passenger.

"But you don't know the road."

"What's to know? I'll just follow it down." But he didn't move.

He couldn't tear his gaze away from her mouth. Her lips were red, swollen, made that way by his hard kisses, and he felt absolutely no remorse. He wanted to kiss them again and then again. "You're soaked," he said curtly, and flicked the heater to high.

"So are you."

"Not as bad. I had on my jacket. Where's yours?"

"In the backseat."

"Take off your sweater and put it on." He pushed the gearshift into first.

"That's not necessary."

He slammed the gearshift back to neutral and applied the emergency brake. "Dammit, it *is* necessary. Look at you, you can't stop trembling."

The trembling didn't bother her as much as not knowing if she was trembling out of reaction to what had just happened between them or because she was wet and cold. One thing was certain, she wouldn't like to place any bets on the reason.

She gazed down at her soggy sweater; it was icy against her skin and felt as if it weighed ten pounds. Why not take it off? she thought dazedly. It wasn't as if she had too many secrets left from Kells. He had held her breasts in his hands, shaping and reshaping them through the material of her bra until she had caught fire.

"Well?" he asked impatiently.

She peeled the soggy sweater up her torso and off her head and tossed it into the backseat.

"The bra too."

Her head came up. "No."

"It's wet, Bria. Take it off, and you'll be warmer." His voice was rough, the color of his eyes so dark there was very little blue left in them.

"I—" Her hands automatically went to the front opening of the bra, but her fingers were stiff with cold and nerves and she fumbled with the clasp.

He brushed her hands away and undid the bra himself.

She almost stopped breathing. Everyplace his fingers touched her, heat replaced the cold. Her pulse, temporarily normal, now began to race again.

He threw the bra into the back, then grabbed her jacket and pulled it around her, intending to help her into it. But suddenly he stopped. He had gotten too close to her—a huge mistake. He could see crystal droplets clinging to her long lashes, smell the rain in her hair and on her skin, see the desire that still simmered in her eyes.

He groaned. "Lord, Bria. What is it that you do to me?"

"I don't know," she whispered, and wondered the same thing about him. The cold and chill of the elements had done little to dampen down the heat inside her. She found that she couldn't sit upright one more second. Leaning back against the door, she allowed the softness of her fleece-lined jacket to shield her from its curves and knobs.

"What are you doing?" he asked raggedly. Her high, firm breasts were completely exposed to him, and the rose pink of her nipples had hardened into tight buds.

"I don't know." She had never felt less in charge of herself or her emotions.

The storm continued to lash around them—wind, rain, thunder, lightning. The heater was blowing warm air into the interior of the Jeep, but it had little to do with the heat that was crawling over her skin. Neither the storm nor the heater air was touching her. She felt battered by a need she couldn't even begin to understand. Then she saw him slowly reach toward her, and she held her breath.

He cupped one breast with a gentleness that was in marked contrast to the fierce way he had kissed and caressed her before. But it seemed right. Outside, the storm might be savage, but in the Jeep a sensual languor reigned. He had no idea what would happen next, but he couldn't leave this place without feeling her, tasting her, one more time.

Time stood still; the windows fogged. Her breast was warm and full in his hand; her nipples were irresistible. He lowered his head and drew one into his mouth. A hard shudder shook his body.

He sucked and pulled at the tip with a concentration that implied he was empty and only she could fill him. He could actually feel the heat rising from her skin, smell her deeply feminine scent, taste the sweetness. His arousal pressed against his jeans, his control was in danger of dissolving.

His brain sent scrambled messages. Take her. Leave her alone. *Take* her.

Her pelvis lifted and undulated, trying to ease its aching heaviness. Threading her fingers through his damp hair, she held his head to her breast. Sensation after searing sensation scored through her body. She wanted out of her jeans; she wanted to wrap her legs around his hips and have him thrust into her, she wanted...

Take her. Leave her alone. Take her. Burke Delaney...

With an almost inhuman effort he jerked away from her. And for a few moments all he could do was lay his head against the steering wheel and pull in deep, gasping breaths.

Bria closed her eyes. She was in pain and didn't know how to deal with it. She lay against the door and tried to fight the impulse to reach out for Kells. He had made a sound as he had pushed away from her; it rang in her ears. The sound had been filled with anger and a strange kind of agony. Her body was throbbing for him, and she had to believe that had they continued, she would have welcomed him into her body. But he didn't want her.

"Bria?"

She opened her eyes and looked at him. His expression was harsh, dark, forbidding. "What?"

"Put on your jacket. Your dad is going to be worried if we don't get back."

She nodded. "Whatever you say."

A muscle in his jaw moved. "Whatever *I* say? You don't think we should leave?"

She straightened, put on her jacket, and zipped it up. "I think we should leave," she said woodenly.

He drove his fingers through his hair. "Dammit, Bria. Why did you ask me to come up here with you?"

What an excellent question, she thought. Had it really been an experiment to check out the veracity of the mirror? Or had she unconsciously used the mirror as an excuse to be alone with him again? Was it possible she had wanted what had just happened between them? Lord help her, she was beginning to think it was.

When she didn't answer, Kells shoved the gearshift into first and started the Jeep down the mountain.

The storm continued on into the night, hurling its fury against the big house, pounding Killara with its strength. In her bedroom Bria sat in front of a roaring fire.

In spite of the fire, she was chilled. Because in remembering what had happened between her and Kells on that storm-blown mountain, she had suddenly been struck by the thought that the first kiss they had exchanged there had been the kiss she had seen in the mirror. When she had looked into the mirror she hadn't seen the surroundings, only herself in his arms, his hand beneath her sweater, her arms around his neck.

She drew two conclusions: Sooner or later the things she saw in the mirror came true.

And if the mirror didn't drive her crazy, Kells Braxton surely would.

In his room Kells paced in front of the fire that burned brightly in the fireplace, cursing, and thanking the gods that he didn't know where Bria's bedroom was. Because if he did, there was no doubt in his mind that he would go there and finish what had been started between them in the mountains.

4

BRIA TOSSED AND TURNED MOST OF THE NIGHT, AND WHEN SHE FI-
nally fell asleep, she dreamed of Kells. It was as if he had slipped under her skin and was becoming a part of her. She couldn't escape
him. She could feel his touch on her breasts, his mouth on her lips.
She could almost feel him inside her. . . .

She awoke to a clear, cold day. And the first thing she did was to
place a call to Shamrock.

"Hi, Uncle Rafe."

"Mornin'. How's my favorite niece?"

The laughter that was natural in his voice warmed her. "I'm
your *only* niece, Uncle Rafe."

"Oh, that's right. Why do I always forget that?"

Bria grinned at the running gag between them. "Senility?"

He sighed. "When are you going to learn respect for your
elders?"

"Any day now. I feel it coming."

"We'll all celebrate, I'm sure."

"I'll let you know when to set off the fireworks. And switching right away to another subject, has Dad told you about the mirror?"

"Sure has. I can't wait to get there and see it."

Bria had never hesitated to ask her uncle a question before, but now she found she was stalling, afraid of his answer.

"Bria?"

"Yes, I'm here. I was just wondering..."

"What?"

"You've read all our family journals, haven't you?"

"Why are you asking me a question you already know the answer to, darlin'? You know I have."

Even though he didn't have an accent, there was a rhythm in his speech that made a person think of Ireland. Bria smiled.

"Yes, well, I was wondering if there was any mention in any of them about the mirror."

"Not a thing. Why?"

She had been afraid it was too much to hope that one of the journals would hold a clue to the mirror. "Just curious. Do you think you have all the family journals? I mean, could there be more journals somewhere else?"

"I have all that we know about."

"That's what I thought. I was only wondering. Well, I'll let you go."

"Are you sure you don't want to talk to me for a little while longer? I could give you a few clues about your Christmas present."

She giggled. Her uncle Rafe had always had the ability to make her giggle. "And, if I guessed correctly, Aunt Maggie would shoot us both."

"Naw. I'm not that good a clue giver, and you're not that good a guesser."

She giggled again. "What you really mean is that you'd lie if I guessed correctly. Thanks for the offer, but I really do need to go now."

"You were a lot more fun when you were a little girl, Bria Delaney. Whoever it was who told you there was no Santa Claus did you a grave injustice."

Right, she thought. Now she believed in a mirror. "Bye, Uncle Rafe."

"Bye, darlin'."

She stared at the phone for a few minutes, considering.

Okay, so all of the known Delaney family journals were at Shamrock. But she had found a magic mirror in the old part of Killara's attic, a mirror no one had known existed. Maybe she could also find a letter or a note up there that would give her the explanation she needed. It was certainly worth a try.

Several hours later Bria had found a great many interesting things, but not what she was looking for. She checked her watch and discovered it was almost lunchtime. She uttered a mild oath. If she didn't show up, her mother would come looking for her. Reluctantly she left the attic and went to her room to change out of her dusty clothes.

She slipped into a fresh pair of jeans and an ivory silk blouse, all the while telling herself that she wasn't going to look in the mirror.

But the mirror held a strong fascination for her. For some reason, she was the only person it showed anything to. It was wreaking havoc with her life, but . . .

The mirror, still resting on the chair seat, teased, beckoned—and infuriated her. Taking a defensive stance in front of it, she put her hands on her hips and glared down at the mirror. Her own image glared back at her.

"Oh, come on. Is that the best you can do? Surely you have a surprise for me today. Something that will push me that much closer to complete craziness. Come on. Where's your spirit? Do your worst."

Almost immediately another image appeared.

It was her, with Kells standing behind her. His arm was fastened around her waist, his mouth was at her neck, licking, kissing, biting.

She was naked from the waist up, and his hand was squeezing one breast in an erotic caress. Her head fell back against his chest and ecstasy suffused her expression.

She was shocked and utterly riveted. The images she had seen until then had been short flashes; this one seemed to last and last. In the mirror she suddenly turned to Kells and he lifted her into his arms. Then the two of them disappeared, and the mirror's surface was once again smooth, reflective.

She dropped to the edge of her bed, hot, shaken, and breathing hard. She had challenged the mirror, and it had responded with a knockout. The scene couldn't have been more clear—she and Kells were about to make love.

Bria forked a bite of something she had found on her plate and brought it to her mouth. For a brief moment she wondered what she was eating, then her mind quickly returned to the searing image she had seen in the mirror. The memory had her nerves strung so tight, they were almost shrieking in protest.

She couldn't meet Kells's eyes, but she could feel him willing her to look at him. Beneath her lashes she saw his long fingers close around a water goblet, and she remembered how those same fingers had made her feel the day before in the mountains and how they had looked in the mirror as they had caressed her breast. Where touching her was concerned, he was a magician. He could make her feel sensations she hadn't known were available in the entire universe.

She pulled her gaze from his hand and switched it to the low, elegant arrangement of creamy-white poinsettias, glittery gold pinecones, and gold pearl sprays that graced the center of the table. No matter what Kells had made her feel up to this point, he had made it abundantly clear he wasn't interested in anything else happening between them. But she had already learned that what she saw in the mirror came true, and she had seen him lifting her into his arms as if he were about to carry her to bed.

What would it be like to have his powerful body drive into her, she wondered. Immediately the answer came to her. It would be like having undiluted ecstasy pumped straight into her veins.

The conversation whirled around her, but she could focus only on the image of what their two bodies would look like writhing naked on a bed. Desire crept through her body. And all the while, Kells's will pulled at her. In the end she had no choice. She gave in and looked at him.

His face was hard, his expression questioning, his eyes dark with growing anger. She knew she was acting peculiarly and that he wanted to know why. Desperately she searched her mind for something that would help her.

"Bria? Darling?"

Startled at hearing her name called, she turned to her mother. "Yes?"

"Don't you like the fish?"

She glanced at her plate. So *that* was what she was eating.

She pushed her plate away and sat back in the chair. "Mom, do you have anything you need in Tucson? I think I'll fly back there for a few days."

Burke's dark brows rose. "You don't plan to return to work, do you?"

"No, of course not. It's just that Mom doesn't seem to need my help with the house—"

"Honey, I didn't invite you home early to work here. That was just an excuse."

"I know, but I really need to finish up my Christmas shopping." An ever-increasing tension emanated from Kells, and she could see objections forming on her parents' faces. She told herself that she didn't care about Kells's tension. And she was old enough not to need her parents' permission, but she loved them and didn't want to cause them any concern. She hurried to play her ace. "I had planned to wait until Patrick gets back so that we could do our shopping together, as we usually do, but you know how he enjoys buying everything in one long marathon session. I've decided if I stretch my shopping out over a few days, I won't get so tired."

"Will you be able to rest there?" Burke asked, obviously still unconvinced.

"Oh, absolutely." She had no doubt that being away from Kells would increase both her appetite and the number of hours that she slept.

"Maybe it would be a good idea," Cara said slowly, gazing at Burke. "And there are a few last-minute things I do need."

Bria could almost read her mother's silent message to her father. In Tucson, Bria would be away from the mirror.

She envied her parents the strength of their love that allowed them to read each other's minds. She knew true love existed because her parents were such shining examples of it. Their love was deep, complete, and without reserve. She had always hoped for the same kind of love for herself, but so far true love remained out of reach.

Burke slowly nodded his head. "Okay, then, if that's what you want to do. When are you thinking of leaving?"

"This afternoon. The sooner I can get the shopping done, the sooner I can get back. In fact, I think I'll get ready now." With a smile for both her mother and father and a nod in Kells's general direction that barely satisfied propriety, she left the table.

It was all Kells could do during the hour that followed lunch to be civil to Burke. His host was being most congenial, showing him the two-level Baroque-style library. It was a large room, and the thousands of bound volumes it contained were extremely interesting, but slowly, surely, Kells began to feel suffocated.

Maybe being on Killara was getting to him more than he had thought it would, he reflected. Spending time with Burke Delaney was proving to be an irritant, provoking Kells's impatience and anger. And the muscles in his jaw were beginning to ache, a result of his continually clenching them.

He smiled pleasantly at Burke, but didn't hear the man's words. Bria was leaving on some trumped-up excuse; she hadn't even been able to meet his eyes at lunch. What in the hell was going on?

There was a pressure building inside him, strengthening, intensifying, becoming rapidly unbearable. Suddenly he opened his mouth and words he had given no thought to came out. "You know, Burke, Bria has given me an idea."

"Oh?"

"It might not be a bad notion for me to do a little shopping while I'm here." The statement astonished him, but the minute he said it, he knew it was absolutely the right thing to do. "I have several people on my Christmas list who would love a uniquely southwestern gift." He laughed. "Actually anything from the States would go over big."

Burke nodded his understanding. "It doesn't matter what kind of great things you can buy where you live, gifts from other places always seem more special."

"Exactly. And since it will be a while longer until the lawyers have our papers ready—"

"I told the lawyers to take their time. I wanted this to be a social visit instead of a business trip."

"I know, and I appreciate that, but would you mind very much if I interrupt the visit for a few days?"

It *was* the right decision. The feeling flowed through Kells with an ever-growing strength that formed into a single-minded determination to follow through with it, no matter what Burke's objections. Kells wasn't sure what would happen once he got to Tucson. He just knew he had to go. Because Tucson was where Bria would be.

Burke eyed him speculatively. "I didn't realize you were talking about going in for more than a day. I have made plans for us—"

"I know, and I'm sorry if I'm fouling anything up. But like I said, when Bria mentioned Christmas shopping, it gave me the idea. I hope you don't mind."

Burke hesitated for only a moment. "Of course I don't mind, if that's what you really want to do. My plans will wait until you get back. You can hitch a ride with Bria. She'll be flying one of our helicopters in."

"She's a pilot?"

"She learned to fly almost before she learned to drive. You can also stay in our apartment there."

"I don't want to put anyone out. I can check into a hotel."

"I won't hear of it. You're still our guest, and you'll be much more comfortable in our place than you will be in a hotel. Our apartment is in Delaney Towers. Bria's apartment is on the same floor, and I'm sure she'll be happy to recommend places for you to shop."

It was right. "If you're sure..."

Burke clapped him on the back. "I'm positive. You'd better hurry and pack. I'll call Bria. Shall I tell her you'll meet her in thirty minutes out by the landing pad?"

"Thirty minutes."

It was right.

It felt good to be back in her own apartment, Bria thought later that evening, trying to soak away her tension in a tub of scented bubbles and hot water. She loved Killara; it was part of her, a piece of her heart that never left her no matter where she went. But when she had moved into her own place, she had taken great pleasure in decorating it herself in styles, textures, and colors that she loved. The basic color she'd chosen was cream, to which she'd added the vibrant, rich accent colors of purple, crimson, and gold. And the furniture, paintings, and ornaments reflected her need for things casually elegant and sensually comfortable.

So she was home. It wasn't in her makeup to run from anything, but the situation had made it seem necessary. But unfortunately the problem she had tried to leave behind had come with her.

At first she had been furious when her dad had told her that Kells was coming along. She had considered her plan foolproof.

But Kells's reasons for wanting to make the trip had made as much sense as her reasons had, and she hadn't been able to protest without making a scene. Besides, she figured she had only herself to blame for bringing up the trip in his presence.

She and Kells had barely spoken on the flight into Tucson, and her anger had slowly given way to a new tension. Kells was like no man she had ever known. Even his silence seemed to be filled with words, and at times his stillness could be more volatile than his movements.

Danger. Danger. Danger. The words flashed in her mind like a lit-up road sign, but other than proceed with extreme caution, she couldn't think of a thing to do.

When they had reached the twentieth floor of Delaney Towers, she had given Kells the key to her parents' penthouse, pointed down the long hall toward the front door, then left him. At least they were in different apartments, instead of living in the same house, she thought—but it gave her little comfort. Delaney Towers was a big building, however. If she worked it right and was lucky, she wouldn't have to see him.

She climbed from the tub, dried herself off, and wrapped herself in an emerald-green satin robe. The material against her skin further soothed her nerves.

In the kitchen she set chicken breasts simmering in white wine and started to make a salad. She was slicing a tomato when the doorbell rang. The knife blade slipped and barely missed her fingers. So much for soothed nerves, she reflected ruefully.

Her living room, dining room, and kitchen was one very large area, with the kitchen separated from the other two rooms by a wraparound East Indian satinwood bar. She stared across the vast expanse of polished wood floor to her front door, wondering who it could be. None of her friends knew she was back in town. She supposed one of them might have called Killara and been told she was here. But . . .

She wiped her hands on a dishtowel and went to open the door.

"Hello, Bria." Without waiting for an invitation, Kells walked past her and into the apartment. He did a quick scan of his surroundings, then turned and fixed her with a penetrating gaze. "Nice place."

She pushed the door shut, using more force than was strictly necessary. "It's not as nice as my parents' apartment," she said pointedly. "What's wrong? Do you need something? Towels? Soap? A cup of sugar?"

"As a matter of fact, I do need something."

His husky tone made her swallow and led to the discovery that her throat had constricted. "What?"

He almost smiled. At this moment, barefoot and dressed in a robe, she somehow managed to look very regal, very imperious. But he felt much too tightly wound to smile.

"I need an answer. Why did you decide to leave Killara to fly here?"

She blinked. "You came here to ask me that?"

"I think it's important." After hours of unrelenting self-interrogation, he knew the answer to why he had come. Quite simply, he couldn't stand her being out of his sight. And because no matter what reasons he gave himself for doing the opposite, he wasn't going to rest until they had come together in hours of hot, steamy sex.

She shrugged. "I came here to do the same thing as you. Shop. Anyway, why are you asking? You were there at lunch. You heard."

"What I saw was more interesting than what I heard. You couldn't look at me."

Between the time the doorbell had rung and now, Bria's tension had come back full force. She had nothing on beneath the robe, and she was sure he knew it. Naked, unprotected, she felt in danger of baring everything to him, both physically and emotionally. She jerked the robe's satin belt tighter around her waist. "I was preoccupied."

"With what?"

"None of your damned business."

His eyes narrowed. "I'm beginning to wonder."

His gaze was too sharp, too piercing. She crossed her arms over her breasts. "I don't understand, Kells. Why should you care what my reasons are or were?"

"Because I think by coming here you were trying to run away from me."

"If that was the case," she said, biting off each word, "my plan failed, didn't it? Quite miserably actually. Anyway, why should I run? As far as I can see, there's nothing to run from." Her last statement was true as far as it went, but on some level of consciousness she hadn't allowed herself to explore until now, she was afraid she had tried to run from her own feelings. The truth unsettled her, but she went on, hoping for a nonchalant tone. "You've made yourself perfectly clear. I have nothing to fear from you. Every time we've been together, you've pulled away from me."

"You brought that up before. It must bother you."

She turned from him, red hair and green satin whirling. "Why in the world wouldn't it? You blow hot one minute and cold the next. You asked me what kind of game I was playing. I could turn around and ask you the same thing."

If he was playing a game with her, he thought grimly, then he was also playing one with himself. And by coming to Tucson, he had lost both games. He circled her until he was again standing in front of her and could see every nuance of her expression. "It's not because I'm rejecting you, Bria. Believe me." It was as hard on his system as it was on hers, probably harder. His body had come to crave her, and the craving was beyond his experience, almost beyond what his body could endure. "Besides, we only shared a few kisses. Nothing more."

Only. A *few* kisses. Funny, it seemed so much more. She exhaled a long breath. "Okay, Kells, you're right. I ran. Whatever we have or haven't shared, I decided I had had enough, and so I removed myself from your path."

"Yet here we are again, together."

The softness of his voice danced across her skin, and the jangle of her nerves increased to a clamor. "This time it's not my fault."

"Isn't it?" He reached out, touched one finger to her cheek, but then quickly withdrew his hand. The softness of her skin was too delightful to bear with equanimity. "No, you're right. This time it's my fault. I came with you. Maybe not entirely willingly, but nevertheless I'm here because I wanted very much to be here."

Maybe it was her overworked imagination, but his words seemed to carry one meaning on the surface and another beneath it, and she felt the need for clarification. "You wanted to be here to do your Christmas shopping, right?"

"Of course." He looked away, out a large window, toward the lights of Tucson that spread below them. What in the hell did he think he was doing? She was a Delaney. Worse, she was Burke Delaney's daughter. On some deep-seated level, the fact still bothered him slightly. But on another, stronger, more potent, body-involving, mind-controlling level, he didn't give a damn anymore. "I was wondering if you could recommend a good restaurant. I was also going to ask if you'd like to go with me, but I see you've already started dinner." He nodded toward the kitchen.

"Yes."

"It smells wonderful." In reality, he hadn't been able to smell anything else but her for days. "Did you make enough for two?"

"Now, why would I do that?" She had, thinking that she could eat the rest for lunch tomorrow, at least that's why she *thought* she had done it. And now all she could do was stare at him and try very hard not to believe that she was actually going to ask him to stay.

"I hate eating alone, don't you?" He did it all the time, and it had never bothered him.

She rubbed between her eyes, experiencing a feeling of inevitability. She had tried to get away from him, and it had done her no good. The really scary thing was, she had seen them kissing in the mirror and had wanted it to happen in real life. Next, she had seen them about to make love, and, Lord help her, she was very much afraid she wanted it also to happen.

There, she had admitted it. But not by so much as a word would she initiate a thing. Not if she could help herself. It was her problem to work out, hers and hers alone.

"The dishes are in the top cabinet to the left of the sink. Set the table. I'll change clothes."

"Please don't." His words were velvet-soft and caused heat to skim through her veins. She turned on her heel and walked to her bedroom. In her enormous walk-in closet she hurriedly slipped on panties and a strapless bra then reached for one of her favorite dresses, a comfortable purple cashmere sweater dress.

She checked herself in a mirror, a *normal* mirror, and fretted at what she saw. The neckline rested off her shoulders; the cashmere knit clung to the curves of her body. Too provocative? The hell with it, she thought, irritated with herself and the situation.

She marched back to the kitchen, where Kells had set the table.

"Can I do anything else?" he asked, his gaze following the lines of the dress with an engineer's precision.

She randomly picked a job and pointed toward her wine rack. "You can select the wine."

Silently she set about finishing the dinner. Kells studied the rows of bottles, chose one, and opened the wine, then walked into the living room and decided upon several jazz compact discs from her collection. She had a specially designed sound system that had come with complicated instructions, but within seconds Kells had figured out how to work it, and soft mood music drifted through the air. A minute later he had a fire blazing in the fireplace.

His efficiency further agitated her. She felt as if a powerful tide were rushing toward her, and there was nothing she could do to turn it or fight it.

Dinner passed, if not easily, at least with some semblance of cordiality. They managed to have a civilized conversation, though Bria couldn't imagine how they were doing so. The emotions they provoked in each other were anything but civilized.

She was relieved when the meal was over.

While Kells cleared the table, she poured them each a cup of coffee. When he returned to his seat, she asked a question that had been flitting around her mind for some time. "So, who's on your gift list?"

He shrugged. "Friends, several employees."

"Men or women or both?" His raised eyebrows prompted her to add, "It would make a difference where you go to shop."

"How about helping me?"

"Sorry. I don't have one Southwest item on my list. My friends and family are saturated with the stuff."

"So? You could still come with me. It would be for only a few hours. It doesn't take me long to know whether I like or don't like something." One look at her had been sufficient.

She shook her head. "I don't think so, but I'll give you the names of several stores I'm sure you'll like."

He studied her for a moment. "Would it make any difference if I told you the only women on my list are my secretary, who is fifty-five years old, and the wives of friends of mine? In the latter instance, the gifts will be given to the couples."

A weight lifted from her, a weight she hadn't known she had been carrying. But nothing was changed.

"I think it's best we go our separate ways."

His eyes narrowed intently on her. "I wish I knew what went on in your head."

"Nothing very interesting." He had implied he had no girl-friends. A man as passionate, as virile as Kells with no woman in his life?

Her scepticism must have shown, because Kells suddenly cursed and pushed his coffee cup away. "I don't believe you for a minute," he said vehemently.

"What's wrong?"

"*You*, dammit. You're all wrong for me."

She sighed. She was beginning to feel as if the two of them were in a cage, created by the other, and neither could break free. They kept circling the same subjects over and over. "So you've said. But what's the problem? You told me you're not here to seduce Burke

Delaney's daughter, and you haven't. I don't see anything for you to be upset about."

"I do," he said quietly. "Because I'm very much afraid that Burke Delaney's daughter has seduced me."

She looked up in surprise. "I haven't done a thing."

"No, you haven't. Nothing other than respond in my arms like you were made of fire."

"I couldn't help it," she whispered.

"*Exactly.*" He leaned forward in his chair. "Do you have any idea what I feel like when I taste your nipples in my mouth? It drives me wild. It makes my brain close down. And your breasts, they feel so damned good, I've reached the point where I can't stand the thought of anything or anyone else touching them. You have a bra on, don't you? I wish you'd left it off."

The color washed from her face, then flared back with increased intensity. "Stop it! I can't *take* any more of this."

"Neither can I, Bria. Don't you understand? That's the whole point."

A cry rose in her throat. "What do you want from me?"

"I'm almost afraid to start exploring the possibilities."

She leapt to her feet. "And I don't think you should. What's more, you need to go now. Let yourself out."

5

BRIA HURRIED THROUGH HER BEDROOM TO HER BATHROOM. THERE, in the coolness of the blue marble room, she splashed water on the blazing skin of her face and neck, but it did no good. She felt as though a mist of heat had closed around her.

She reached for a hand towel and held it to her face. But the soft velour offered no comfort. Every nerve in her body tingled painfully.

Slowly she straightened and looked into the mirror. Kells was behind her. His eyes were a dark midnight blue, his stance aggressive and vibrating with tension.

"I can't leave," he said in a rough whisper.

Unable to move, to even turn around, she watched his mouth in the mirror as it formed the words. His lips were sensual and beautifully shaped, she thought yet again. And they could make her feel things she had never felt before.

"I'm sorry," he said, "but I just can't leave."

Desperately needing support, she gripped the edge of the marble counter. "You don't want this, Kells. You told me so."

"I know."

He sounded calmly resigned but very determined.

"This is madness," she said.

"Yes."

She should do something, she thought hazily. Leave. Or at the very least try to talk him out of what was about to happen. But her feet were rooted to the spot, and the ability to reason seemed to have deserted her. She could only watch him in the mirror. Watch, wait, and tremble with anticipation.

Holding her eyes with his, he unbuttoned his shirt, baring his broad chest and the dark hair that softly curled there. Then he skimmed his hand along her waist and pulled her back against him until her body was locked to his. The other hand slipped inside the top of her dress and beneath her bra. Reaction swelled and surged through her.

"Tell me you don't want me to go. Tell me."

"I don't." Two words. It was all she could manage to speak, but it was enough.

He swept the long length of her hair to one side and placed kisses, one after the other, down the side of her neck until his mouth came to rest on the wildly beating pulse at the base of her throat. "I want you so much," he muttered thickly. "I *need* you."

An empty ache began in her belly; a fire ignited between her thighs. He nipped the tender flesh of her shoulder with his strong white teeth and left a line of tingling points behind.

Something rent asunder inside her: Her resistance, her pride—until nothing remained but the need to have him make love to her. Hungrily she reached behind her for him, but at that moment he took a step away from her. In a quick, sure motion, he slid the off-the-shoulder dress downward until her arms were free and cashmere folds encircled her waist. Pressing featherlike kisses down her spine, he seared a trail to the edge of her bra. Each touch of his mouth burned, and she wasn't certain how much longer she could remain upright. He unclasped her bra and tossed it aside. Then he pulled her back against him and took a breast into his hand.

She gasped. The *mirror*. Lord help her, this was the exact scene she had seen in the mirror at Killara.

She slumped back against him and stared into the big, wide bathroom mirror, transfixed by the view of his long, lean fingers kneading her breast, molding the soft mound until her nipples tightened into taut, aching points. Her breathing became erratic; her trembling increased.

The sight of him caressing her, added to the sight of her physical response, was unbearably erotic. Fire drove straight to her brain as she viewed the musculature of his arm holding her tightly to him, the strong elegance of his hands and fingers as they stroked and shaped her, the darker beige of his skin against her lighter golden-toned skin. She was captivated. The edges of the mirror blurred until she could see only the two of them in its center.

His actions became even slower. He wanted her with a fierceness that was frightening to him, but he couldn't make himself hasten. She raised emotions in him that demanded care and thoroughness. And so he took his time, touching and fondling her, reveling in the satin feel of her skin, the fullness of her breasts, the hard nubs of her nipples. She was unlike any woman he had ever known. She made him want more, to know an ultimate satisfaction, a supreme fulfillment, things he sensed only she could give him.

His mouth once more went to her neck and the pulse point. He counted the beats of her heart against his lips, then softly bit. She moaned and moved her hips against his pelvis, wrenching a groan from deep in his chest.

He wanted to learn more of her, and where she was concerned his curiosity and need were apparently insatiable. But the pain of wanting was becoming unbearable.

His hand stroked downward and disappeared inside her dress at the waist, into her panties. She inhaled sharply, no longer able to see his hand, but, heaven help her, she could feel it.

The *feelings*. Like liquid ecstasy. Like distilled rapture.

His fingers delved into the soft folds of her sex with a sure gentleness and knowledge that had an out-of-control firestorm of pleasure twisting through her. A cry strangled in her throat and turned to a moan. She gave herself up to the feelings, closing her eyes and undulating against his fingers. With each movement backward, his hot hardness pushed against her soft, increasingly sensitized bottom. With each thrust forward, his fingers rubbed and manipulated. The combined pressures were indescribable. She felt caught in an erotic vise. Everything she was feeling was multiplied by two. Inside her, a burning urgency swelled and inexorably expanded. Her breathing quickened, then suddenly a powerful, unbelievable pleasure shook her from head to toe.

Slowly she opened her eyes and wordlessly stared at him in the mirror. What was he doing to her? He had taken control of her mind and body. She had never felt more vulnerable in her life—nor more alive.

She turned to him. He shifted his stance, lifted her into his arms, and carried her into the darkened bedroom. There he lay her against a mound of pillows. Though she had had sex before, she couldn't imagine what was left to happen between them. It was as if he had taken full and complete possession of her and there was no need for anything more. Except—she still wanted, hungered, longed for him. It was like a compulsion.

He leaned over her and pulled the cashmere dress and silk panties from her. And then she was naked, and soon after so was he.

He lay down beside her. Slowly he laved her breast with his tongue, scorching a path of concentric circles that drew ever closer to her nipple. Then he pulled the pulsating bud into his mouth and sucked and nibbled.

She hadn't thought any new feelings possible. She was sure she had experienced them all. But with his tongue and his hands he turned her into a wild thing. Her body writhed, feverish with need for him. She pulled and tugged at his sweat-slicked shoulders with a desperation that was unfamiliar to her. "I want you inside me. *Now*."

"Not yet." His pain was intense, but so was his need to prolong the sweet agony. It was as if he were in both heaven and hell at the same time. Fire threatened to consume him, but the ecstasy of learning her beckoned him into the flames.

He moved his mouth downward, across the flatness of her stomach, through the soft thatch of red curly hair between her legs. And his mouth took up where his fingers had left off.

His kiss devoured her, sweeping her up into the deep, dark velvet center of a full-fledged, raging, frenzied passion. She was in a world where she had never been before, a world she had never even imagined might exist. She wanted to explore him, do all the things to him that he was doing to her. But she wanted something else. Release. And she was convinced she would die if it didn't come soon.

She clawed at his back and cried out her need, using words she couldn't hear, words he couldn't ignore. Suddenly he was inside her, and it was as if they had been born already linked together. She arched her hips high to meet him, inviting him deeper, and he complied, driving into her with a power that was ferocious. He wanted her to be his. He wanted to take her, heart, mind, and soul.

He felt her reach her peak almost immediately, but he wasn't through with her. He had no idea from where he was drawing his superhuman endurance, except that it was all tied up with her. What he was doing to her went beyond sating a sexual appetite. And he didn't want it to stop.

She was everything he had known she would be, untamed, wild, scratching, and fighting for more. He loved the feel of her hands as they clutched frantically at his buttocks; he loved the way her nails scored his back; he loved the cries she made that told him how much she wanted him.

And, Lord help him, he loved her.

Her body shuddered as she reached yet another climax. He felt her contract around him, massaging and squeezing him until something inside him snapped. Violent convulsions took control of his body. He pumped into her, his lungs almost bursting with the effort, and didn't stop until he had emptied himself into her.

* * *

Bria rolled over and clicked on the bedside lamp.

Kells threw a forearm across his eyes to shield them from the sudden glare. But whether the room was light or dark, the reality wasn't changed. He was in love with Bria Delaney.

He wanted to curse and shake his fists at the gods. He wanted to scream at himself for allowing himself to fall so hard and so completely. But most of all he wanted to take her back into his arms and make love to her again and then again.

"What just happened?" she asked quietly.

Slowly he lowered his arm and gazed at her from beneath half-opened lids. One arm propped up her head so that she was looking down at him. The lamp backlit her, making her skin and hair appear luminous. Her body had a well-loved glow about it, as well it should. He didn't think there was a place on her he hadn't sought out and given attention to. But if there was, he would soon rectify his omission.

And he knew exactly what she was asking. What had just occurred between them had been beyond extraordinary. He had never had a lovemaking experience remotely like it, and from her question and the softly bewildered expression in her eyes, he guessed she hadn't either.

The answer was simple: The love he felt for her was what had happened.

That love had made him fanatical about holding himself back, putting her pleasure before his, and had ensured a depth of emotion that had lifted them both to an elevated plane of glory.

But for many reasons he didn't feel he could tell her of his love at the present time. The discovery was an astounding revelation to him that had shaken him deeply. He needed to think and assess and get his feet back under him; he needed to make sure he had dealt with the past once and for all. There was only one thing he didn't have to think about: He was going to try very hard to make sure that she didn't get away from him.

"Kells? What happened?"

"Fireworks." With a gentle smile he reached toward her and entangled his fingers in her hair. "Fireworks happened. I know you felt them. I also know you weren't afraid of them."

"No. But—"

"What's bothering you, Bria? The fact that you enjoyed it?"

"No." She had loved every minute of the experience. But something was definitely bothering her, and she would feel a lot easier if she knew what it was.

"Some people are just combustible together. You and I, Bria, went up in flames."

That they had, she thought, staring into his eyes. But did he really believe it was so simple? Could she?

She didn't have a lot of experience, but she did know that the intensity with which they had come together was very rare. Had what just happened been the result of days of pent-up emotions? Now that those emotions were spent, would the fire die down? Or had it been a chemical process that had to do with their makeup, separately and together, and that would happen again?

"It'll happen again," he said softly, as if he'd read her mind. "It will, at least, if I have anything to say about it."

Color tinged her cheeks. "I didn't ask."

"No, but the thought was in your head. I know the thought was in your head because it was and is very much in mine."

She caught her bottom lip with her teeth. "But why did it happen? I can't deny anything you're saying, and I'm certainly not complaining, but—"

He released her hair and freed her bottom lip with gentle pressure from his finger. "But?"

"You're the one who told me you didn't want things to go any further between us. What changed?"

His hand dropped back to his chest, but his gaze stayed on her. "You happened. You're a walking temptation—and you managed somehow to trample over every objection and protest I could muster."

"I can't recall us ever arguing about it."

His lips twitched. "Not aloud, at any rate. No, you wore me down just by *being*. I lost the argument with myself, Bria."

"Are you sorry?"

He laughed. "No way. I'm not crazy." The expression of amusement slowly faded from his face. He slid his hand around her neck and pulled her to him until she half lay over him and her mouth was mere inches from his. He could feel the softness of her breast pressing into his side, smell the sweetness of her skin. "No, Bria, I'm not crazy. I've never been less sorry in my life." He paused and his voice turned husky. "Did you really think I would be?"

"I wasn't sure." With Kells there was nothing she was sure of. She drew away from him and lay down again.

He rolled over and into her and immediately felt satisfaction in every cell of his body as he was sheathed by her warmth. "Be very certain," he whispered. "Let me show you how much I don't regret our lovemaking." Then he proceeded to lose himself once more in her.

When Bria awoke, she was alone in the bed. But the tantalizing breakfast smells that were wafting from the kitchen told her that Kells hadn't left. She was pleased . . . and she was troubled.

It was morning; outside, the sun was shining. But in the night she and Kells had done shatteringly intimate things to each other.

She didn't know how to face him. Or herself.

She hadn't recognized the wanton creature she had become beneath the ministration of his hands and mouth. She had utterly given herself up to him. He had said they were combustible together, and she certainly agreed. Yet though he had been an incredibly sensuous, inventive, and demanding lover, giving everything his body was capable of, Kells ultimately remained a mystery to her. She felt she should be on guard with him, censor what she said and did, shield herself from a yet-to-be-defined hurt. The problem was, she didn't want to supervise her every action or word. There was a happiness in her, bubbling and brewing, refusing to be contained. She wanted to feel free to kiss him if she got the urge, or to run her hands over his strongly muscled body.

Heaven help her, he moved her in so many ways. Yet, unfortunately, he also confused her.

She hated to be confused. She also hated to lie in bed on a perfectly beautiful day.

"I'm not solving anything by lying here," she muttered, getting out of bed.

She took a hot shower and dressed in a lightweight wool kelly green skirt and a matching silk blouse. After weaving her hair into a single thick braid that hung halfway down her back, she added a long green cashmere cardigan and brown boots to her outfit, then went to find Kells.

Sometime between the shower and the brown boots she had made a decision. The way he behaved would govern how she behaved.

"Good morning," she said as soon as she saw him. He was standing by the stove, staring broodingly down at a pan of sizzling bacon, looking dynamic and very sexy.

He turned and watched her as she walked to him. "Good morning. Green is a wonderful color on you."

"Thank you." She searched his face for some sign of what he was feeling—unsuccessfully. Those eyes that were so direct, paradoxically, could also hide more than they revealed.

"But I like you better with nothing at all on."

In a sudden move that took her completely by surprise, he closed his hands around her buttocks and lifted her up and against him. Her legs automatically wrapped around his waist, her arms around his neck. Then he turned and pressed her back against the large refrigerator and kissed her.

Immediately her senses awakened, her heart pounded, her blood sang through her veins. With utter abandon she tightened her legs around his waist and delved her tongue into his mouth, thrilling at the raspy feel of his tongue. This was the way she wanted it to be between them, she thought—free, spontaneous, wild.

Parts of him might remain an enigma to her, but at least they could communicate on a physical level. For now she would accept the combustion and wait and see what happened next.

"I like the way you say good morning," she said softly after the kiss ended.

He threw back his head and laughed. "Did I say good morning? I don't remember."

"You did, but that wasn't what I was referring to."

"I know, and so far I'd say it's a *great* morning." He gave her another kiss and set her on her feet. "I hope you're hungry, because I've made a big breakfast for us."

She glanced around the kitchen with only vague interest. "Where did you get the food? I never keep anything for breakfast here."

"I didn't even bother looking. I walked down the hall to your parents' apartment. The housekeeper was very helpful."

"But I don't eat breakfast."

"You will this morning." His look dared her.

She burst out laughing. "You know, now that you mention it, I think I am hungry."

"Good. Go sit down and I'll bring it to you."

Several minutes later Bria was happily munching on a piece of toast. There was an intimacy to sharing breakfast with a man with whom you had just spent a night of unrestrained passion, she reflected, an intimacy that was warm and oddly comfortable. And she liked it, liked it very much. "How did you get that?" With her toast she indicated the scar that angled over his left brow.

"I fell out a door."

She smiled. "I've heard of people running into doors, but not falling *out* of them."

"It was the loft door of the barn. I was trying to toss hay out the door to my grandfather, who was below in a wagon. Even though I was only eight, I had convinced him I could do the job, and I was determined to prove myself. But I found out right away how heavy those bales were and that there was no way I could actually *toss* one of them down, as I had seen my grandfather do so many times. So I started pushing and dragging the first bale, thinking it wasn't going to be a big deal after all. And I was pretty proud of myself for figuring out a way to do it." He grinned. "About then I overbalanced and went out the door with the hay."

Her eyes widened with alarm. "You fell from a second-story level to the ground?"

"No, I fell into the wagon, but I landed on hay that was already there, so I wasn't hurt."

"But the scar—"

"It happened when I pushed myself up. My face grazed the side of the wagon where there was a nail sticking out."

She grimaced. "*Ouch*. You poor kid."

"Yeah. The stitches weren't fun. But the next week I was up in the loft trying the same thing all over again. I succeeded, and I never fell out again."

She dropped her toast back to the plate and lifted her coffee for a sip. "Sounds as if you were one tough little boy."

"I had to be."

She eyed him thoughtfully. "Any reason in particular?"

He gave a noncommittal shrug.

"Did you enjoy growing up on a ranch?"

"Sure. What boy wouldn't? All that space. My own horse. A swimming hole that I sometimes shared with the cows. But I shouldn't have to tell you. You grew up on a ranch yourself."

"I know, it's just that I was wondering why you left The Star."

"It's simple. I didn't want to be a rancher, so I hired someone to run it who did want to be."

"And went to Australia."

He nodded. "Yes."

She leaned forward, placing her forearms on the table. "Why? I mean, why did you feel the need to leave the country in which you were born to go live in another? You could do what you're doing in Australia right here in America. For that matter, in the Southwest."

"I could do it anywhere. But Australia appealed to me for a lot of reasons. Australia has only a fraction of the population of the United States, yet the size is comparable. There's room for people to spread out, and a great part of Australia remains untouched."

"Brisbane is very touched," she said with sweet sarcasm. "I've been there."

His laugh held an edge. "Okay, you got me. Besides the reasons I listed, I simply felt the need to make a completely fresh start."

"Why?"

He tilted his head and viewed her through a thicket of dark lashes. "You're not eating. Are you using these questions as a smoke screen to get out of eating breakfast?"

"No. Did you just use that question as a smoke screen to hide the fact you don't want to answer me?"

He exhaled. "I didn't know your questions were anything more than idle conversation. What is it exactly that you want to know, Bria?"

Instinct told her she was treading into a sensitive area, but that same instinct also made her persevere. "What was it here that you wanted so badly to leave behind?"

He made a sound of exasperation. "Memories. Okay? Memories. But in the end, my plan didn't work." She opened her mouth to speak again, but he held up his hand. "Eat, Bria. You're going to need your strength."

If he had wanted to divert her, he had succeeded. Besides, she knew she would have another opportunity to try to get him to talk about the memories that had driven him from the place where he had been raised. "Why am I going to need my strength?"

"You're going to need your strength for *shopping*. What else did you think I meant?"

"I—" His eyes were alight with mischievous sparks of humor, something she had never seen in them before. She was captivated. "Shopping. Of course. The reason we both came here." She hesitated, her eyes twinkling. "Would you like me to go with you and help you?"

He relaxed back in his chair and folded his hands across his lean waist. "If you'll remember, I asked you to last night. I haven't changed my mind. Have you?"

She smiled. "Yes."

His answering smile was slow and held more than humor. "I'm glad. Now, are you going to eat or am I going to have to come over there and help you?"

"I think I need some help."

Bria held up an elaborate turquoise and silver necklace for Kells's consideration. "What do you think? Would your secretary like this?"

He looked doubtful. "I'm not sure. She seems to favor pearls."

Bria reconsidered her suggestion, and as she did, the memory of how the two of them had looked last night in the mirror as his mouth had kissed her neck momentarily paralyzed her. Then she saw the twinkle in his eye and knew he was remembering the same thing. She gave him a stern look that failed miserably. "The thing is, Kells, if she loves jewelry—and what woman doesn't?—she'll love this necklace. It's not only beautiful, it's unusual, and most definitely Southwest."

"Then it's settled. Let's get it."

She handed the necklace along with a pair of matching earrings to the clerk, then turned to a magnificent sculpture of a coyote. But the sculpture failed to hold her attention. Instead, her mind detoured back to that morning and how it had been several hours before she and Kells were ready to leave the apartment. And she had never gotten much of a breakfast. The memory drew a smile from her.

"Do you really like the coyote that much?" Kells asked, obviously having observed her expression.

She jerked back to the present. "No, I don't."

"Then why were you smiling?"

"I was just thinking how hungry I am."

His expression changed, tightened, and his voice dropped to a husky rasp. "Let's go back to the apartment and I'll feed you."

Her eyes wide, she slowly shook her head. "I *can't* be that easy to read."

"You're right. You're not. Except for when your mind is on certain subjects." He brushed the back of his knuckles down the tender curve of her cheek. "By the way, you blush beautifully."

"That's impossible," she said firmly, "because I never, under any circumstances, blush."

The sensuality of his lips held a tinge of amusement. "If you say so."

"I do. Now, who's left on your list? As soon as we're through here, we'll go eat at a great restaurant I know."

"Restaurant? Why not at your apartment? I like the menu there much better."

His voice was full of meaning that had her blood heating. If she wasn't careful, she reflected, she was going to throw herself into his arms. Desperate to maintain at least a semblance of decorum, she repeated her question. "Who's left?"

"Two couples, and we can get them the same thing, because one lives in Alice Springs and the other in Melbourne."

She glanced almost blindly around the shop. "How about an Indian blanket for each of them?"

"Perfect. Now, about that hunger of yours..."

She sighed, defeated. "You're a dangerous man, Kells Braxton. I knew it the minute I saw you."

"Why? All I was doing was sipping scotch."

"No, you were—" She stopped, realizing she had never told him about the mirror, and now certainly wasn't the time. "You were also looking at our Christmas tree as if it might bite you."

He grinned. "Not at all. I was merely in awe of all the Delaney tradition."

She laughed huskily. "I've known you only a short time, but I think I can safely say there's not much that awes you. In fact, I'd be interested to know if there's *anything* that awes you."

"Oh, yes," he said, his eyes darkening. "You. I'm in absolute awe of you and how you make me feel."

He bent his head and kissed her, pressing his mouth hard against hers and plunging his tongue deeply into her warmth. And regardless of the fact that they were standing in the middle of one of Tucson's most exclusive shops, he didn't end the kiss until he was good and ready, which was many long, passionate seconds later.

6

BRIA LAY IN THE CROOK OF KELLS'S SHOULDER AND LIGHTLY TRACED a nail around his nipple. He clamped a hand over hers, stopping her. "I can't concentrate when you do that."

"What is it you're trying to concentrate on?" she asked, mildly curious how he could concentrate on anything when they had just made love to each other with an intensity that had her totally spent. The afternoon shadows were deepening. She still hadn't eaten anything, but food was the last thing on her mind. Kells had a way of filling up all her senses, satiating her until there was nothing else she wanted, nothing else she could think of.

"I'm trying to concentrate on anything but you and the way your naked body feels pressed against me."

"Why?"

Lightly he stroked the tips of his fingers up and down her arm. "It seems a sensible thing to do." His lips curved upward in pleasure at the silky smooth feel of her skin. "It's even sort of an experiment."

"An experiment?"

"To see if I can get through an hour without wanting you." His voice roughened. "I still don't know how we ever managed to pick out those Indian blankets and pay for everything without my taking you right there on the shop floor. I came so close. . . ."

She laughed softly, thrilled and comforted that she wasn't caught up in this sensual storm alone. "We would have shocked several very nice clerks if we had."

"Maybe, but after the money I spent in there, they wouldn't have said much. And knowing that made it twice as hard for me." He angled his head so that he could look down at her. "Would you have objected if right there and then I had taken you down to that pile of Indian blankets and made love to you?"

She hoped, she prayed, she would have objected, but she couldn't say with any degree of certainty that she would have. The responses he could draw from her constantly amazed and surprised her. "Of course I would have. For one thing, it wouldn't have been polite."

"And for another?"

"It would have been . . . uncivilized." She heard laughter rumble in his chest.

"Bria, you don't give a damn about being civilized."

"Maybe not, but I try to care about being considerate of others."

"In this case, I think *try* is the operative word." He shifted over her and gazed deeply into her eyes. "You would have let me, wouldn't you?"

There was a possessiveness in his voice and expression that stole her breath away. "The truth is, I don't know. I'm positive I wanted you as much as you wanted me. But I'm glad we waited until we got back here. It not only made the anticipation greater, it saved those poor clerks a great deal of embarrassment."

He was still for a moment, then he bent his head and pressed a kiss to her lips. "You are truly a wonder, Bria Delaney. Since I've met you, I don't know which way is up and which way is down."

She listened carefully for some clue as to whether he considered the way he felt to be good or bad. But all she could hear was amazement. "How do you think your friends will like their gifts?"

He lay back down. "They'll be crazy about them. Thank you for helping me."

What were they like, she wondered, those friends of his? It was both depressing and somewhat astounding for her to remember that he had a whole other life that didn't include her. Astounding because another life for either of them didn't seem possible. The powerful ecstasy they shared tended to black out everything but each other. How could either of them exist outside this magical, exciting world they had created together?

But the reality was that on Christmas Day he would be back in Australia with his friends, and she would be in Arizona, not alone by any means, but definitely without him.

"Tell me about your home," she said on impulse. "What's it like? What do you see when you look out its windows?"

"My home sits on a hill, and when I gaze out my front windows or sit out on the veranda, I can look down on the Brisbane River."

"It sounds wonderful."

"I like it."

"Tell me more."

"Okay, well...from every window I can see palm trees, bougainvillea, and frangipani. Exotic birds are everywhere. I have a sailboat, and some days I get into it and sail down the river to the sea. Other days I get in my car and drive to the coast and surf."

"You know how to surf?"

He chuckled at her amazement. "I learned when I moved there."

"It sounds as if you couldn't have chosen a place any more different from New Mexico," she said somewhat wistfully. His life there seemed full and complete.

"You're right about that."

"Do you ever think of moving back here?"

"Here?"

"The Southwest."

Strange, he thought. He had always viewed the Southwest as Delaney country. And he had left. Then the Delaneys had come to Australia to him. "Not really. But I do love it here, and actually I visit The Star quite often. I go back to The Star to be recharged."

His words struck a familiar chord in her. "Killara is the same kind of sanctuary for me."

"I know it is, and I understand."

But he had left his sanctuary. "Where are your parents buried?"

"The Star." He was silent for a moment. "That's a funny question to ask."

"I know. Sorry. I guess I was thinking about roots and under what circumstances I would consider moving to another country."

It was an issue he should address too. Bria was so much a part of Killara and the land the Delaneys had tamed, he was uncertain she could ever be happy in Australia or anywhere else. Ultimately, taking everything into account, if he asked her, would she even want to come with him?

"People move for a variety of reasons, Bria, and Australia is a wonderful country."

"I know, but you said you moved there to escape memories, but that it hadn't worked. What did you mean?"

He absently smoothed a hand up and down her arm. He had discovered he loved her, but love was so new to him, such an unfamiliar emotion, that he was floundering. And he wasn't sure he could explain what she wanted to hear. He certainly didn't feel as if he could explain everything to her—maybe one day, but not now. He even wondered if he was capable of explaining part of it.

He had been too alone for too long. It was easy for him to give his body to her without reserve. But he was finding that revealing parts of his heart was excruciating and painful. He could try though.

"When I was five, my mother died in an automobile accident, one of those stupid, senseless accidents that never should have happened. When I was nine, my father died."

"How?"

For a moment he was silent. "He committed suicide."

With a cry of distress she came up on her elbow. "Kells, I am so sorry. You were so young. That must have been very hard on you."

He nodded. "Yes, but fortunately for me I had my grandfather. He wasn't much for shows of affection, but he was a genuinely good man. He was also a smart man, and he taught me to go after what I wanted. When he died, I buried him beside my mother and father. Afterward, I would go out to the graveyard and sit for hours, staring at those three graves."

She almost wept as she visualized the scene. Kells, all alone, sitting by the graves of his family. She had been surrounded by her family her entire life, and she couldn't even begin to imagine the pain he must have felt with every member of his family gone. "I wish I'd known you then. I could have tried to make it easier for you somehow."

Yes, he thought. Once he had let her past his guard, she would have made him feel better simply by being with him. "I got through it all right. In their individual ways, each of them played an important part in my life, but they weren't with me any longer. And what I wanted wasn't on that ranch. So I decided to go somewhere completely new and different."

"You decided to follow your own dream."

He nodded again. "I'm in an incredibly exciting business. No matter how far computers have come today, they are going to go even further in the future. The technology will have continuing surprises. We've only scraped the surface. I have so many ideas...."

"And you can make those ideas a reality."

"Yes, with Burke's money." He had already laid out to himself the reasons he had agreed to accept that money, but another reason suddenly came to him, a reason that shocked him. *He had grown to admire Burke.*

"I wish you well, Kells. I really do."

Her soft voice drew his attention back to her. Her green eyes stared solemnly at him. "Why are you talking like we're about to part?"

"Because in a few days we will."

The idea was so abhorrent to him that it was almost impossible to make himself think about it. He didn't want to leave her, but he didn't know if he could make her come with him. It had always been hard for him to face the fact that there was anything beyond his ability. He had no intention of giving up on making her his. But . . . dammit, why did this have to be so hard for him, so complicated?

He linked his fingers with hers. "When we get to that point we'll face it, but not now. Now I want to make love to you again."

"Again?"

"And again."

In the midnight, moonlit darkness of the bedroom, Kells lay with Bria in his arms. Her face was pressed to his chest, her leg and arm thrown over him, her hair a silken spill that fell over her shoulders and onto his chest.

This was their last night in Tucson, and because it was, he couldn't sleep.

By nature and circumstances he had always been a loner. He lived alone, traveled alone, had always accomplished everything that was important to him alone. But now Bria burned in his blood, a permanent passion, a forever love. He had overcome a lot of things in his life, but he wasn't sure he'd be able to make it from now on without her.

He would do anything to keep her. Anything.

Bria awoke before Kells, and to her delight she was able to watch him while he slept. His hard face didn't soften much in sleep; only his lips showed a relaxation—those lips . . . His breathing was strong and even, and his skin showed a night's growth of dark beard that she longed to touch.

She was in love with him.

The realization had dawned slowly, but once she had admitted the knowledge to herself, she had been struck hard.

By happiness. By doubt.

The earth had shifted beneath her; the center of her gravity seemed to have altered.

After this time in Tucson she felt she understood him better, but he remained a man of granite. She wasn't intimidated by him, nor was she afraid of him. But the happiness she felt about being in love with him was shadowed. He didn't love her.

She could worry and speculate over the situation until the end of time and it wouldn't matter. There was nothing she could do about her feelings. She had been in love with him since before she had met him. She had looked into the mirror and into his eyes and felt the air leave her body. And over time his effect on her hadn't lessened one iota.

She was in love with him.

Cara perched on the end of Bria's bed and watched as her daughter unpacked a small bag. "Did you have a good time in Tucson?"

"Shopping is shopping," she said carefully, knowing how intuitive and sharp her mother was, "but I'm really pleased with the presents I chose. They're being gift-wrapped, and they'll be sent out tomorrow or the next day."

"The space beneath the tree is really getting filled up. The presents from Hell's Bluff and Shamrock have arrived, plus a shipment from Australia that included Patrick's."

"He's already done his shopping?"

"Apparently." Cara studied her daughter. "Did you see much of Kells while you were in town?"

"Some."

"Just some?"

Bria turned and looked fully at her mother. Cara was smiling. Apparently her mother was sharper than even she had suspected. "You know."

"Honey, I would have to be blind not to see the electricity between the two of you. Before you left for Tucson, you and Kells were so absorbed in each other, it was all your father and I could do to keep the conversation going at mealtimes."

"Dad noticed too?"

"It was obvious to everyone, Bria, except maybe the two of you. Your dad wasn't surprised when Kells decided to spend a couple of days in town. Because of his high regard for Kells and his desire for you to be happy, he didn't object."

Bria sank down onto the bed beside her mother. "I love Kells, Mom."

A smile spread across Cara's lovely face, and she put her arm around Bria. "I am so happy for you."

"No, you don't understand. He doesn't love me."

Cara's smile faded as her expression turned skeptical. "I'm not sure I believe that. What man in his right mind wouldn't love you?"

"*Mom.*"

"Well, anyway, maybe he loves you but just hasn't admitted it to himself. Sometimes men have things they need to work through."

"Well, whatever it is, it's not simple. He's a difficult man."

Cara made a dismissive sound. "Darling, you've been surrounded all your life by difficult men, and you've had no trouble wrapping any of them around your little finger."

"They're my family. There's a difference."

"Listen to me. If you love Kells and think that you want to spend the rest of your life with him, then don't give up hope. It will happen. True love has a way of winning in the end. I know, because it happened to me and your father."

Bria gave her a hug. "Thanks for being my mom."

Cara solemnly nodded her head. "You're entirely welcome. Except for the labor pains, it's been my great pleasure."

Bria burst into laughter, and Cara joined her.

Late that night Bria made her way to Kells's room.

There was an expression of relief on his face when he opened the door. "I thought you'd never get here." He took her hand, pulled her into the room, and shut the door behind her.

"I wanted to wait until everyone was settled."

He gathered her into his arms. "Do you think your parents would be shocked by the idea of you sleeping in my bed?"

She frowned at his faintly mocking tone. "No. They're not prudes by any stretch of the imagination. It's just that I don't think it would be in good taste for us to flaunt our—" She hesitated, briefly panicking when she couldn't think of a word to describe their relationship.

"Affair?"

She nodded, wishing with all her heart he had said *love* affair. "Yes. Our affair."

"I understand." He rubbed her back through the satin of the robe. "Forgive me. I'm not used to having to consider a family."

"I know, and it's all right. It's no big deal, just my preference." She stood on tiptoe and placed a light kiss on his lips.

He laughed huskily. "I got used to being with you all the time when we were in Tucson. It's been damned hard on me this afternoon and evening having to pretend a polite friendliness when it wasn't what I was feeling at all."

"No?" she asked playfully. "What were you feeling?"

"Well, first of all," he said, smoothing his hands down her spine to her firmly rounded bottom, "I wasn't feeling at all polite. I kept wanting to leap across the room or the table or wherever we were at the time and grab you up against me so that I could feel you, pretty much like I'm doing now."

His hands kneaded her buttocks, sending the now-all-too-familiar heat skidding and sliding through her. "What kept you from it?"

"You. I knew it wasn't what you wanted."

"I very much wanted to be with you like this," she said softly.

"I know. You just didn't want to embarrass your parents any more than you wanted to embarrass those clerks back in town."

She lightly laughed. "Those clerks will never know how close they came to being embarrassed."

He pulled her pelvis against his. "Lord, do you have any idea how it makes me feel to hear you say that? Tomorrow is going to be twice as difficult for me."

She wrapped her arms around his neck and kissed him again. "We'll find some time to be alone together. I'll take you up to the Norman keep."

He growled. "Promise?"

"Absolutely."

He swept her up into his arms and carried her to bed.

Once comfortably settled among the pillows, Bria watched with unabashed enjoyment as Kells undressed. "How does a man who does nothing but sit and design computers all day get to have such a great body?"

He grinned as he stripped out of his shirt. "A great body, huh? Thanks."

"You're welcome."

"Well, I swim, play handball, and ride whenever I can."

"You have horses on your property in Brisbane?"

"Sure. And I already told you I surf."

"Sounds like you have a busy life."

He nodded. "Just as you do in Tucson."

"Yes." They each had their own worlds, worlds that were far apart and different. But when you got right down to it, she didn't think their worlds were so different in basic values. "By the way, I believe it's only fair to tell you that Mom and Dad have noticed the attraction between us."

His hands froze on the waistband of his trousers. "Did they give you a bad time about it?"

"No. Why should they? I'm a grown woman. And they both like you very much."

"Do they?"

"Yes. Mom said Dad holds you in high regard."

Kells continued undressing. "I've come to admire your dad too. And it's funny, because I didn't think I would."

"Why not?"

"His reputation."

"If Dad has a bad reputation, it's not deserved."

Her loyalty drew a grin from him. "He doesn't have a bad reputation. But I'm sure it isn't any surprise to you that because of his wealth and power, he is feared in many quarters." He finished taking off his clothes, then lay down beside her and felt an immediate contentment and peace he hadn't felt since they had left Tucson. She was beside him once again, his to touch, to kiss, to make love to. At least for now.

Bria turned her head along the pillow to look at him. "You're not afraid of him. As a matter of fact, you bested him."

"It was a good fight, and we both won." He thought for a moment. "I suppose your dad and I are alike in some ways, but we're also very different. He fights from a position of power, and he never has to fight alone."

"Whereas you always fight alone."

He nodded. "I've had to. Besides, there's never been anyone I trusted enough to let him fight by my side."

She lay her hand on his chest, wondering if she heard sadness in his voice or if that was simply her interpretation of his remarks. He continued.

"And where your father inherited an empire and a rich heritage, I didn't inherit anything but The Star, which, some years, is more of a financial liability than an asset."

"You also inherited a philosophy from your grandfather that seems to have held you in good stead."

He rolled onto his side to face her. "That's right. He taught me to go after what I want." He tugged open the satin cloth belt of her robe. "Guess what I want right now."

"You can have it without a fight," she said softly, closing her arms around his neck.

Bria drummed her fingers on her bedroom windowsill. Kells and her dad had been closeted all morning in her dad's study. And waiting for them to finish, she felt exactly as Kells had yesterday, she thought ruefully. Neither polite nor friendly.

At breakfast she had casually mentioned to her parents that she would like to show Kells Killara's twelfth-century Norman keep. She had been grateful when they had agreed that it was a good idea, grateful but not surprised at their understanding.

She stared broodingly out the window. Lord, she had it bad. She was finding that being away from Kells for just a few hours was torture. What was she going to do when he left for good?

The *mirror*. Her gaze was drawn to her closet door. She didn't know what had made her suddenly remember the mirror. She had thought of it only once in Tucson and not at all since she had returned home. Kells had permeated and pervaded every part of her and her life.

A small smile curved her lips. Wouldn't it be wonderful if the mirror showed her a scene that would reassure her about her and Kells's future? A scene that might show them standing at an altar, exchanging vows? Perhaps a scene with them surrounded by laughing children, *their* children?

She knew the blasted thing could be capricious, but still . . .

She pulled the mirror from the closet. Once she had it propped on a chair, she knelt before it, her heart beating fast with anticipation. Several minutes passed while she waited, and she began to think the mirror wasn't going to show her anything.

She was about to give up and return it to the closet when suddenly she was looking at another scene, a scene that for an instant her mind refused to accept. But the scene wouldn't go away. It glittered at her from the mirror's shining surface, its colors vivid, its content a nightmare.

Her dad was lying on the ground, colorless, lifeless, blood spreading across the front of his shirt. And Kells was standing over him, looking down at him, a gun in his hand.

Dear Lord, Kells was going to kill her father.

7

THE MAN SHE LOVED WAS GOING TO KILL HER FATHER!

No. Bria sank back on her heels and put her hands to her head. Her heart was pounding loudly and she could barely think. The awful image she had seen in the mirror remained in her mind. The blood, the blood...

Why would Kells want to kill her father? The business deal the two men had struck was weighted in Kells's favor. But from the first there had been something of an edge in Kells's voice when he spoke of Killara and her dad. And the first time she had seen Kells in the mirror, he had been looking down on Killara with an angry expression on his face. It was the only scene so far that hadn't come true, but from her experience with the mirror, she had to believe the scene would happen in the future, as the one she had just witnessed would.

No. It couldn't be true. She wouldn't *let* it be true.

But what could she do to stop it? Going to her dad and telling him about what she had seen wouldn't work. He had no basis to believe her, and she had nothing to show him that would corroborate her conclusions. Plus, he would immediately begin to worry about her again. The last thing she needed was her parents clicking into their protective mode and hovering over her, watching her closely for signs that she had snapped. At the moment going crazy was the least of her worries.

Kells. She couldn't, wouldn't, believe he was capable of killing anyone in cold blood. During the time they had spent in Tucson together, she had never detected the slightest thing that would lead her to believe he could be violent. The only violence she had seen had been contained in his need for her, but even that had been controlled. In the fiercest heat of passion he had been utterly unselfish and had taken great care with her.

On the other hand, based on her experience with the mirror, she had to believe what she had seen would happen.

Her heart, her mind, her soul, were in agony. She thought she could actually feel tissue inside her tearing and ripping. She loved both her father and Kells, and with everything that was in her she wanted to protect them both. Somehow she had to find a way to do just that.

When she had flown from Killara to Tucson, it had been a half-hearted attempt on her part to stop the lovemaking scene she had witnessed between her and Kells from happening, and she hadn't been successful. She was glad she hadn't.

But *this* time she would change fate. She had to.

Bria and Kells climbed the stairway that spiraled tightly upward inside one corner of the Norman keep. Since only one person at a time could fit on the stairs, Bria was ahead of Kells.

When Kells stepped into the large, completely round room on the top floor, Bria was placing a match to wood already laid in the stone fireplace.

She straightened. "The walls are six feet thick and hold the heat well."

"I'm not worried about us being cold," he murmured, studying her with narrowed eyes. "Bria, is something wrong? You seem preoccupied."

"Do I? I'm sorry." She shoved her hands into the pockets of her skirt and gazed at him. He was wearing jeans that clung to the muscles of his calves and thighs and a sweater whose dark blue color was picked up in the depths of his eyes. He looked strong, reliable, and incredibly wonderful, and she wanted nothing more than to run into his arms, have him tell her everything would be all right—and believe him. But some quirk of fate had made it appear he was an enemy, and until she could prove otherwise, she had to put some distance between them. Doing that, however, was going to be difficult. "I do have something on my mind, and I'd like to talk with you about it."

"Okay." He motioned toward a long sofa. "Do you want to sit down?"

She shook her head. "Not yet." She wasn't ready for the repercussions that would come once she had said what she had to say. She wanted a few more minutes of peace before the storm hit and perhaps changed forever everything between them. "Let me show you around. This was Patrick's and my playroom, game room, hideaway—you name it." She pointed toward two toy boxes labeled PATRICK and BRIA, then gestured toward three more toy boxes labeled BURKE, YORK, and RAFE. "Before it was our playroom, it was Dad's and his brothers'."

He came up behind her and slipped his arms around her waist. "This is a great place for kids. But I also think it's an inspired place for us."

She had thought so too when she had suggested it earlier this morning. She had pictured the two of them making love before the fire while the December winds blew outside. But with one look into the mirror, everything had changed. Nevertheless, she gave herself the luxury of leaning back against him for a moment. "Patrick and I spent long hours up here."

"It must have been nice to have someone your own age to play with."

The almost undetectable thread of wistfulness in his voice touched her heart. His life on The Star must have been a lonely one, especially after the death of his parents. He had said his grandfather hadn't been one to show affection. She ached to shower him with all the love and tenderness that was in her, but never by so much as a word had he indicated he would want her to. And besides, even if he had, the scene in the mirror made it impossible. "One of our favorite games was one our dad taught us, a Delaney version of cowboys and Indians—Delaneys and Indians. Patrick played a Delaney and I played an Indian."

"If I had been guessing, I would have guessed that," he said, his words slightly muffled because his mouth was against her hair.

"Why?"

"Because there's a strong streak of something not quite tame in you. I sensed it when we first met, and I benefit from it every time we make love."

Heat swept through her so strongly, she had to close her eyes.

"Your hair always smells so damned good," he whispered. "But then, I haven't found a place on you that doesn't. Do you want to know my favorite place on you?"

She broke free of his arms and circled until she had put a table between them. "Let's go up to the battlements. There's a breathtaking three-hundred-and-sixty-degree view of the Sulphur Springs Valley and Killara."

He shook his head and a little smile played around his mouth. "It's cold out there, and I can see the only part of Killara I'm interested in right here. You."

She had hoped to give herself a little time, but it was fast running out.

"Come here," he said, his words an erotic command.

The sensual huskiness of his tone nearly had her moving back to him, but she firmly shook her head.

"Then I'll come to you."

She held up her hand, stopping him halfway to her. "Kells, I'm going to ask you to do something for me, and it's not going to make any sense to you, but I'm hoping you'll do it anyway."

His gaze turned thoughtful. "I can't imagine I wouldn't. In case you haven't noticed, you've become very important to me."

She nodded, hard-pressed to keep the despondency from her voice. "I know. You said we are a combustible combination."

"Yes, and that's part of it, but only part."

Her head jerked up and her heart skipped a beat. It was the first time she had received even a hint of what he was thinking or feeling about her. Under any other circumstances she would have rejoiced and pushed for clarification. And even taking the circumstances into account, her mind raced. Was it possible that he could fall in love with her? *No.* She brought herself up short. She couldn't allow herself to think about his loving her, couldn't because it would make what she needed to do doubly hard. She was about to attempt a tightrope act, and she couldn't allow her concentration to be broken.

"Kells . . . I want you to leave Killara. Today. Within the next few hours if possible."

He sucked in his breath. He felt as if she had hit him in the stomach with a baseball bat. "What?"

The utter incredulity on his face caused a faint pounding to start at her temples. "I'm sure you heard. I want you to leave Killara."

"I did hear, but I don't even come close to understanding."

"I told you it wouldn't make sense to you, but please, Kells, do it anyway. I'll have someone fly you into Tucson, and you can catch a flight to Dallas or New York or San Francisco, and then to Australia. Or anywhere . . ."

"You mean, it doesn't matter where I go as long as I leave here?"

"That's right."

His brow pleated as he fought to find reason in something that seemed so insane. "Did Burke ask you to—"

"No, no. Dad doesn't know anything about this. I'm asking you because it's what *I* want."

She had blindsided him without warning, without explanation.

His expression slowly hardened until his face was a mask of anger. "Sorry, sweetheart. I'm not going anywhere."

She clasped her trembling hands together. "If it's about the business deal you have with my father, don't worry. It won't fall through."

"To *hell* with the deal."

She had known getting him to leave wouldn't be easy, but she hadn't known how much asking him would hurt her. "I'm trying to negotiate myself some time so that I can sort some things out, find some answers—"

"Well, that's certainly a master statement of vagueness. Would you care to be more specific?"

"It's as specific as I can get. I want you to leave."

"Because I'm in your way?" His eyes held dark lights.

She hesitated. "Yes."

"Tough. I'm not leaving." He felt as if he were bleeding inside, and it was a strange, unique sensation for him. He had known the odds were against him with her. She was a damned Delaney, for God's sake. But for the first time in his life he had allowed himself thoughts, hopes, of inviting someone else into his world to share it with him and to banish his aloneness.

She linked her hands together, tightly entwining her fingers. "Isn't there anything I can do or say to change your mind?"

"Yes, dammit. You can explain in detail *why* you're asking me to leave. Have you gotten tired of sharing my bed? Is that it?"

"No—"

"Because if it is, I can assure you I won't be bothering you again."

Tears threatened, and she almost faltered. But a picture came to her, a picture of her father lying on the ground, his life's blood seeping out of him. This madness had to be stopped. She couldn't let her father's or Kells's life be destroyed. "I can't explain this to you, at least not now. You wouldn't understand."

"You're not playing fair, Bria. Somehow I thought better of you."

His stare was ice cold and froze her to the bone. What was there left for her to say? "I'm sorry, Kells. I really am."

"Save your apologies. They don't help."

No, she thought, they didn't. But then, when you were trying to change fate, there wasn't too much that did help.

"Dad? Have you got a minute?"

Burke looked up from his desk and smiled. "For you, two minutes. Come on in. I've been wanting a chance to talk to you alone."

She closed the door to his study and crossed the room to one of the chairs that stood in front of his desk. She sank down into it, angling her body so that she could hang her long legs over the arm. It was a position she had taken more times than she could count in her life. Her dad had always put everything aside to listen to her confidences. He had given her his complete attention and addressed her problems with a seriousness he reserved for major business decisions and a special love he reserved for his children. It wasn't until she was older that she realized how strenuous the demands of his empire were on him and how great a gift he had given her all her life. "What have you been wanting to talk to me about, Dad?"

"Kells. Your mother tells me you're in love with him, but I have to say you don't look too happy."

She sighed, knowing she had never in her life been so unhappy. But she wasn't dismayed that he was privy to her secret. She knew her parents never kept anything from each other. "I am in love with him, but it's not simple."

Burke chuckled. "Unfortunately love never is. I wasn't completely happy until I had made your mother unconditionally and unequivocally mine."

His phraseology drew a small smile from her. The wonderful thing was, he was still head over heels in love with her mother. Her hope that she would know that kind of love was growing dimmer and dimmer. "Dad, how much do you know about Kells?"

"I know enough to trust him with my money, and enough that I can easily say I admire him very much. The things that he has accomplished, he has accomplished on his own, and there aren't too many people who can say that."

"No," she said with thoughtful agreement. "By the way, he has said that he admires you too."

Burke chuckled. "He's still wary of me, but the wariness has lessened since he's been here."

There wasn't much her dad missed. She swung one leg, thinking. "When is the signing set for?"

"Day after tomorrow."

"And then Kells is scheduled to leave?"

"Yes...."

Her logic told her the day after tomorrow wasn't soon enough. Her emotions told her it was too soon.

"Unless you'd like to ask him to stay. The whole family will be here, and you know they're all going to want to meet the man you're going to marry."

Her eyes widened with shock. "No one's mentioned marriage, Dad. We're not even close to marriage."

Smiling, Burke leaned back in his chair. "It'll happen if you want it to."

"You sound just like Mom."

"That's because we understand how turbulent love can be when it's in its first tender stages."

Turbulent didn't even begin to describe what she was going through, Bria thought sadly.

The attic was cold, and, in the old part, completely dark. Bria flashed the battery-packed lantern she had brought up with her around the section. Everything was just as she had left it several days before, but maybe this time she could find a diary, a letter, something that would explain the mirror and its powers. Not only would it make everyone believe her, it might enable her to deal with and stop the scene in the mirror from happening.

She set the lantern on one large travel trunk and aimed its beam at another. As she knelt to open the second trunk's lid, she thought about Kells. He and her parents should be starting dinner right about now. She had called her mother on the internal telephone system, pleaded a headache, and told her she was going to sleep. Her mother had been understanding, bid her good night, and said she would make sure no one bothered her.

Kells was probably still furious with her, and she didn't blame him. But asking him to leave had been the only way she could think of to protect both her father and him. Now she had to come up with another way, and she was hoping more knowledge of the mirror would provide that way.

She set to work. Hours later she was tired, dirty, had a real headache, and had not found a thing.

"What in the *hell* are you doing?"

She jumped at the sound of Kells's voice and peered through the darkness. He stood there, pointing a strong beam of light directly at her.

Startled by his sudden appearance, she instinctively went on the offensive. "What are *you* doing up here? How did you find me? Why are you yelling?"

"I asked a maid where your room was. She told me, but she also told me she had seen you heading up here several hours ago. And I'm not yelling."

No, he wasn't, she thought, rubbing her head. "Why did you want to know where my room was? I didn't want to be disturbed tonight. I told Mom I was going to sleep."

He walked closer to her. "You lie well. She bought it. Now tell me what you're doing up here and leave out the lies."

She began to fold articles of clothing back into the trunk she had been searching. "I'm looking for some information. I thought it might be up here."

"Why?"

"Because it isn't anywhere else." She slammed the lid down and then coughed as dust flew into her face.

"I gather you didn't find it."

"No. And will you please get that light out of my eyes?"

The light swept away to scan the area. "This stuff looks pretty old."

She had been trying to fight off the weariness and the headache, but suddenly she was overcome by both. She placed both hands on the top of the trunk and pushed herself to her feet. "Very perceptive."

She started to brush past him, but he caught her arm. "What information?"

His face was in shadows and his hand was only lightly circling her arm, but his tone was unyielding. "It's none of your concern, Kells. It's family business, that's all."

"I thought I told you to leave out the lies. If it was family business, you wouldn't have told your mother you have a headache."

"I *do* have a headache."

"That you got after you came up here, right?"

He *was* perceptive. "Let go of me. I'm tired, and I want to go downstairs and try to sleep this headache away."

His hand dropped from her arm, but for a moment he stayed where he was, blocking her path. "What you're doing up here does concern me, doesn't it? This morning you asked me to leave. You said you needed time to find some answers. I have no choice but to figure that the two are connected. What I *can't* figure out is why you'd be searching in the damned attic for something about me."

"I'm not searching for information about you." It was true as far as it went; she was searching for information about the mirror. "Please, Kells, my head is pounding. Leave it alone. You didn't agree to go; you got your way. Now—"

"I didn't get my way, Bria, not by a long shot. But I will let it drop. For now." He took her hand and led the way back out of the attic.

With a distant part of her mind Bria had to admire the fact that although this was the first time Kells had negotiated the twists and turns of the attic, he never once lost his way. With another part she realized she was enjoying the feel of her hand in his too much. As soon as she could, she drew it away.

When they reached the second floor and her room, she said, "Good night, Kells."

"Do you have any aspirin in your room?"

She looked at him blankly. "Yes, why?"

"Because you obviously need a couple." He took her elbow and steered her inside.

She jerked away from him as soon as she crossed the threshold. "What are you *doing?*"

His stance was so tense that for a minute she thought he was about to do something violent. Instead, much to her surprise, she saw his eyes soften, and when he spoke his voice was very gentle. "Helping you, Bria. You look like your head is hurting so badly it's about to come off, and all I want to do is make sure you take some aspirin and go to bed. Okay? Will you let me help you?"

She exhaled a long breath and nodded. "The aspirin is in the medicine cabinet."

He left her where she was standing, and a minute later was back with two tablets and a glass of water. "Do you want to take a shower before you get into bed?"

She put a hand to her head. "I'd like to, but I don't know if I can—"

"I'll help you." Before she could protest, he went on. "No strings, Bria. No pressure. No hidden agenda. All I want to do is help."

She nodded wearily, unable, unwilling, to object any longer. "All right."

The next minutes flew by. With his assistance she undressed, and before she knew it she was standing beneath a hot, steaming shower. Fortunately for her peace of mind, he didn't get into the shower with her, and he also kept to his word and didn't touch her unless she needed help with something.

She was extremely grateful. Tired and with a headache, she still wanted him. But loving him as she did, she had to keep an emotional distance from him until she could unravel the mystery she was trying to solve and avert tragedy.

When she stepped out of the shower, he was there, holding a large, fluffy towel for her to wrap herself in.

"What do you want to put on?" he asked, his voice without emotion.

She gestured vaguely toward a closet door. "There are night-gowns hanging in there."

His expression remained stony as he found a lace and be-ribboned silk nightgown and slipped it over her head. In the bed-room she saw that he had already turned back the covers. She climbed in.

He stared down at her, his hands on his hips. "Has the aspirin taken effect yet?"

"No." She sat up and frowned at her pillow before lying back down again. "And I don't think I'm going to be able to sleep until it does." If then, she thought. Weariness pulled at her, but there were so many things going on in her mind. She felt as if she needed to stay awake around the clock. In fact, she needed more than twenty-four hours in the day, because what she needed to accomplish seemed, at this point, so impossible. And then there was Kells....

He seemed to hesitate, then without a word he lay down beside her and drew her into his arms.

"What are—"

"Shhh. Close your eyes, relax...." He nestled her head into his shoulders and began to lightly massage her temple, exerting a sooth-ing pressure with his fingers. "Tomorrow you can start again with whatever it is that you're doing."

She should protest, she thought. She really should. But already his nearness and touch were beginning to work their magic. "What about you? You can't hold me all night."

"Why not? I've done it before."

"What I mean is," she said softly, slowly, almost thinking one word at a time now, "you're dressed and lying on the outside of the covers. You won't be comfortable like that; you won't be able to get any rest."

"Trust me, Bria. This is probably the *only* way I'd be able to get any sleep. Taking off my clothes and getting under the covers with you sure as hell wouldn't work. Don't mistake my wanting to help you with a sudden elevation to sainthood. The way my body responds to you, it would take me about ten seconds flat to forget your headache. And going back to my room wouldn't work either. I'd only worry about you and get angry all over again about how absolutely stupid you're acting."

She believed the part about his anger, but she didn't believe that he would forget about her headache. What he was doing spoke of a caring person.

She started to protest, but he went on. "Close your eyes. Relax. You'll feel better when you wake up. And if I won't, it's nothing for you to be concerned about. I'm doing this because, for better or worse, it seems to be what I want to do."

He was right, she thought. Even though they had slept only a few nights together, she was certain she would now find sleeping without him close to impossible. She might as well try to stack the deck in favor of a good rest. "Thank you, Kells."

"There's nothing to thank me for. We'll resume our battles tomorrow."

She had no doubt they would. Days before she had likened him to a hard-edged, jaggedly cut piece of granite. And what she had learned since bore out her conclusion. It wasn't in his nature to yield to anyone. She should have known he wouldn't simply leave because she asked. No, whatever it was that he wanted, he would keep trying to get. That's why she had no time to waste in finding an answer to the puzzle created by the vision in the mirror.

But he was right; she couldn't do anything more tonight. Already she could feel the aspirin working, dimming her pain. Or maybe it was his fingers as he gently massaged her temples and occasionally stroked her hair.

Whatever it was, she began to relax and soon drifted off to sleep.

8

His shoes were off, Kells thought, still half asleep. And someone had pulled a cover over him. His hand automatically went to the other side of the bed. It was empty. *Bria.* His eyes flew open and searched the room until he found her.

She sat cross-legged on the floor in the slant of the early morning sun, staring into a mirror she had propped against a chair leg. Her long lace and beribboned nightgown skimmed her body and lay in silky folds around her bare feet. Her hair was a shining fall down her back. Her profile showed an expression set in concentration and a beauty that still tended to stop him cold every time he saw her.

When she had asked him to leave Killara, he had been hurt beyond what he had believed was his capacity to be hurt. Like a wounded animal, he had retreated to his room to pace, to exercise, to do anything he could think of to rid himself of the pain of her rejection. But his anger and hurt had gotten so bad, he had been driven to seek her out the previous night. Even now, the more awake he became, the higher his anger climbed. And the more he wanted to fight for what he wanted.

"How's your headache?"

She jumped. She hadn't known he was awake, hadn't expected his softly husky morning voice to scrape across her nerve endings like the serrated edge of a knife. She looked over her shoulder at him. "It's gone."

"Good. When did you cover me up?"

"I woke up briefly sometime in the night. I thought you'd sleep better if you were warm."

"How kind." She returned her gaze to the mirror, and he silently cursed himself for being unable to keep the sarcasm from his voice. But he had never loved like this before, never been hurt like this. He tossed the cover aside and sat up. "What are you doing?"

"Nothing." She shifted to her knees and lifted the mirror into the chair's seat.

"You must have been doing something. You were concentrating pretty hard. If it's the way you look that's bothering you, let me be the first to tell you, there's something seriously wrong with that mirror."

"I wasn't looking at myself." She knew the minute the words were out of her mouth, it had been the wrong thing to say.

"Then what *were* you looking at?"

She surged to her feet. "Nothing." She had been staring into the mirror for over an hour, looking *for* something. Unfortunately, or perhaps fortunately, it hadn't showed her anything. "Why don't you go back to your room now?"

"Still trying to get rid of me?" He walked slowly to her. "It's not going to work, you know, not until I know the reason why."

As he approached, the musky male scent of his body grew tantalizingly stronger. She sought to counter its effect on her by injecting her words with coldness. "Everyone will be awake soon, if they're not already, and I don't want anyone to know you spent the night in here."

"You came to *my* room the night before, Bria."

"Yes, and if you'll recall, I said then I didn't want to *flaunt* our affair."

"There's nothing wrong with my memory. The way you cried out while we were making love is burned into my mind. You didn't seem too concerned about your parents then."

"Don't be cruel, Kells."

"Baby, you don't even have a clue about how cruel I can be. And stating a fact is not being cruel. Not explaining what has changed between the night before last and now most definitely is."

"I told you I needed time—"

"You used a bunch of words that were full of nothing but air, Bria. I want to know what changed, and I want to know it now."

Involuntarily her gaze flew to the mirror. "Nothing."

He followed her gaze. "What is so damned fascinating about that mirror?"

"Nothing."

He grabbed her arm and hauled her against him. "I have a very sure feeling," he said softly, "that if you say the word *nothing* to me one more time, I won't be responsible for my actions."

She wrenched her arm from his hold, and for one wild moment was tempted to tell him about the mirror. But she immediately backed away from the idea. He wouldn't believe her any more than her parents had.

His expression sharpened. "Wait a minute. The first night I arrived, Burke asked you about a mirror, but then got sidetracked to something else. Me, I think. Is this the mirror he was talking about?"

She nodded, deciding there wouldn't be any harm in at least sketching in what little she knew of the mirror's background. Hopefully it would appease him. "I had found it in the old part of the attic earlier that day, but I haven't found any documentation on it yet. That's what I was doing up in the attic last night, looking for something that might fill me in on its background."

His eyes narrowed. "Really? Well, then suppose you tell me what's so damned important about a mirror that it would make you lie to your mother and stay up in a cold attic until you were exhausted and in pain?"

She should have known he wouldn't be satisfied with tidbits. "I—I'm interested in its history, that's all."

"Why don't I believe you?"

Because she was telling him only half truths, she thought guiltily. She turned on her heel. "I'm going to get dressed and—"

He caught her by the arm and swung her around. "You're not going anywhere until I understand why you want me to leave Killara. Now, it's damned hard for me to believe that it's because of a stupid mirror, but at the moment it's all I have to go on. So explain, Bria, and make me believe it, because, dammit, you owe me that much."

Maybe she did, she thought, suddenly weary of shouldering her fears alone. And after all, he was one of the two people most directly affected. He wouldn't believe her either, but she supposed she should at least try to make him understand. She exhaled a long, ragged breath. "All right, Kells. I'll tell you everything, I promise. But I'm warning you, it may make things worse, not better."

He released her and crossed his arms over his chest. "I'm waiting."

"Look into the mirror."

"What?"

"Gaze into the mirror for at least a minute, then tell me what you see."

His expression was clearly dubious, but he did as she asked.

"What did you see?" she asked after a minute.

He straightened away from the mirror and faced her, his hands on his hips. "That I need a shave."

She sighed. At least the mirror was being consistent. So far, she was the only person it responded to. "When I look into it I see scenes of things that I know have happened or are about to happen."

"*What?*"

"When I first found it, I looked into it and saw my mother riding my dad's horse across a meadow. I knew that was something that had happened. Since then, I've seen various scenes which have come true, up to and including the two of us making love. That particular scene was behind my sudden decision to fly to Tucson."

"Why? Because you didn't want it to happen?"

"No, because I did."

He uttered a long string of oaths. "Lord, Bria, you're really a piece of work."

"Yeah, well, wait, there's more. Yesterday I saw a scene in the mirror that has me more frightened than I've ever been in my life."

His expression darkened. "*Why*, for God's sake? Bria, you can't believe what you're saying, that you actually see things in a mirror that come true. You've got to be joking. Tell me you're joking!"

She shook her head, her lips tight. "Look, you wanted to know. Just listen and let me finish. The scene I saw was of you and Dad. He was lying on the ground, dead. You were standing over him, holding a gun. *That's* why I asked you to leave Killara. I'm trying in every way I know to keep that scene from coming true."

He stayed very still for long moments. When he finally spoke, his voice was vibrating with quiet fury. "Do you honestly believe I would kill Burke?"

"No. That is, I don't think you would want to, but sometimes people do things they never planned on doing. Fate can take sharp turns without warning, without our permission."

"*Fate?*"

She threw out her arms. "Don't you realize that I know how preposterous what I'm saying sounds? I wish I'd never found that damned mirror. But I did, and I'm telling you, almost everything that I've seen in there has come true."

"*Almost* everything?"

"I've seen five scenes, not counting the scene with you and Dad. So far, four have come true. Based on the mirror's track record, I'm convinced that what hasn't yet come true will."

He stared at her. "I know you're not crazy. . . ."

"Thank you for—"

"But you must be pretty damned desperate to get rid of me to come up with this cock-and-bull story."

"Kells, it's all *true*."

"It *can't* be, Bria."

"It is."

He jabbed long, stiffened fingers through his hair. He felt as if she were killing him part by part. If anyone but Bria had asked him to leave, had told him an absurd story about a mirror, he'd be gone in a heartbeat. But here he was.... "You leave me speechless, Bria."

"Please—"

"No. Stop. Don't say another word." His eyes blazed with fury. "I've figured it out. *I'm* the one who's crazy, because it doesn't seem to matter what you say. Despite everything, I'm still here, and I can't help but want you."

"Kells, don't."

"Why not? At least my need for you makes sense. Nothing else appears to."

At her sides, her hands curled inward. "Damn you, Kells, take me *seriously*. If you even try to kill my father, there won't be a place on earth where you'll be safe. If the law doesn't get you, a Delaney will."

He swirled and hit the wall with his fist. A painting fell to the floor. A chip of wood flew off its frame. He never once looked at it. "I have *no* intention, no matter *what* the circumstances, of *killing* your dad. *Believe* me."

His anger was hitting her in waves, but she didn't even flinch. She couldn't. Too much was riding on the outcome. "I do believe you. Now *you* believe me. It's going to happen, just like I saw in the—"

"Impossible." He flung up his hands. "Absolutely impossible."

She briefly closed her eyes as pain swept through her. She knew he was talking about her and them and whatever future they might have together. "Listen to me. Try to understand. Something is going to happen in the future to cause you to kill my father, something you and I can't foresee, something over which you're not going to have any control."

He muttered a crude oath. "You mean like a crime of passion? Forget it, Bria. It'll never happen. For better or worse, all my passion is reserved for you."

"Kells, please, help me. Leave. Go back to Australia until I can find some information on the mirror. If I can keep you and Dad separated—"

"Forget it. I won't leave unless you come with me."

The air between them was charged with raw emotion. The emotion made him want her, but it couldn't make him love or believe her. "I can't come with you. Don't you see?"

"*No*, Bria, I don't. Not even a little bit." Frustration had tightened the tendons in his neck until they were clearly defined. "And there doesn't seem to be a damn thing I can do about it."

"Yes, you can—"

"No. I can't. There's *nothing* I can do about it. And now that I reconsider, you may *be* certifiable, but oddly enough, I don't give a damn. I want you. And since I don't have the willpower to leave you, I guess the only thing I can do, the *only* damn thing that makes sense, is to make you want me as much as I want you. At least that way the present will be bearable and, for a little while, the future will seem less important."

He reached for her and pulled her against him.

"Kells, don't—"

"Save your breath, sweetheart. Save it for something that will make us both feel good."

Already the heat was beginning inside her. "Kells, I can't."

"Yes, you can," he said, his voice almost a growl, "because you need it as much as I do. Afterward you can go back to believing in mirrors and smoke or crystal balls and magic for all I care. But, for now, believe in the way we can make each other feel. It's the only real, important thing anyway."

He drew her to the bed and pulled her down on it with him. Thoughts of resistance were fleeting. He wouldn't listen, and she didn't think she could say any more. The passion was there, around them and in them. It was basic, elemental, and impossible to fight. And she wanted him, oh, how she wanted him!

He unfastened and adjusted his slacks and lifted her gown. Then he stabbed deep within her. Incredible waves of pleasure rolled throughout her entire body, and she arched up to him, trying to take him deeper.

"You see," he said through gritted teeth. "You *see*. You want me as much as I want you." As he spoke, he drove in and out of her. Fire raged in his brain and in his loins. Each time he thrust into her, she closed tightly around him, so tightly he didn't think he'd ever be able to, ever want to, pull free. But then, in the next heartbeat, he would; the urge to plunge into her again was too primitive, too all-consuming. "We can never stop, you and I . . . because we'll never get enough of each other." His breath was hot and harsh, the rhythm of his speech broken. "Tell me you understand. Tell me."

"Yes . . ."

It had been destined for them to come together like this, though this might very well be the last time.

He flexed his hips and thrust into her powerfully, deeply, piercing to her very center. She lost control. She wrapped her legs around his frantically undulating hips, dug her fingers into his shoulders, and hung on. Cries ripped from her throat to mingle with his cries.

The pressure inside her became more intense, the coiled tension more acute. She felt hot, feral, and soaked to her bones with desire. Then suddenly her head went back, her body tensed, and she exploded, and at the same time she felt his forceful spasms begin. A sound of utter satisfaction that was almost a scream tore up from her chest. And she came apart in his arms.

When Bria woke up, the light of the sun had lowered and she was alone. She wasn't surprised that Kells had left. She had delivered two major blows to him: one, that she believed in something as crazy as a mirror that showed her the future, and two, that she believed he would kill her father. By turns he had been angry, passionate, furious. But beneath each emotion there had been pain for which she was totally responsible. And she hadn't escaped the pain either. She felt as if her insides were in shreds.

Traumatized to the extent she felt almost physically injured, she moved slowly as she went to take a shower and dress. Then she returned to her room and sat down in an easy chair by the window. She pulled her feet up onto the cushion and propped her arms on her knees. It was the position she took whenever she had a problem to work out, only she had never had a problem as pivotal, as monumentally important, as this one.

Kells might still want her, but he would never be able to love her now. He thought she didn't have any faith in him, and he viewed that lack of faith as a betrayal. In reality, her faith in him was strong. She just had some weird Irish, fatalistic streak in her that was equally as strong.

But she wasn't one hundred percent Irish. Among other kinds, Apache blood also ran through her veins, giving her strength and a certain fierceness. She was determined that some way, somehow, she would overcome the mirror and the awful scene it had shown her.

Her heart was full of sorrow. For Kells. For what would never be. Earlier, when he had taken her in his arms, she hadn't been able to refuse him, just as she hadn't been able to hold back. And she didn't regret it for one second. How could she? She loved him with her whole being.

She was fighting *for* him and she was fighting for her father. Her love for both men wouldn't allow her do anything less.

But at the end of it all, after she was through fighting, she was going to look around and find Kells gone.

She *had* to do something. She raked her fingers through her hair, closed them tightly around a thick section, and twisted until she felt a pull. *Think. Think.*

She had seen Kells standing over her father, holding a gun.

A gun.

She mulled over that particular problem, finally deciding there was no help there. Attempting to rid Killara of all guns and ammunition would be an impossibility. The number of guns was countless, and she wouldn't even begin to know where to look for them all. They were a part of Killara's history, and though her father's rules regarding their use were strict, they remained a very practical part of everyday life around the ranch, especially out on the range.

Suddenly she snapped her fingers. *"Motive."*

As far as she knew, Kells didn't have a motive to kill her father. It was true that something unforeseen could occur between them, but if she could prove to herself without a doubt that Kells didn't presently have a motive, it might buy her precious time with him while she worked on unraveling this mystery foretold by the mirror.

She wiped her hands over her eyes. She was rationalizing, she knew, stretching to create an excuse to continue being with Kells. But she couldn't help herself. She had tried pushing him away and her still-tingling body attested to her failure. She would never be able to deny him, never again be able to ask him to leave.

She levered herself out of the chair and strode toward a double set of doors set into one wall. She opened them, revealing a closet-like room that held a desk, a set of bookshelves, and a computer.

She sat down and switched on the computer. Computers were incapable of holding emotions, she thought, but they could hold patterns of behavior which in turn might shed the light she needed. With that in mind, she punched in a combination of commands that linked her to the extensive network of information that was available to her through the Delaney computer system, including the New Mexico libraries.

Thirty minutes later she sat back in her chair, stunned.

Kells had a motive.

His father's suicide.

Through various records and newspaper clippings, she had been able to build a picture of Kells's father, and it wasn't pretty. His business had begun to decline a year or so after his wife's death. By the time Kells was eight, the business was in serious trouble. His father tried successively more desperate maneuvers to save the business, but it wasn't long before his credit rating was shot to hell. Then *her* father stepped in and bought him out. Eight months later Kells's father committed suicide.

If Kells did want to kill her father, the motive was revenge. And if she understood anything in her life, it was family loyalty. It was the way a Delaney thought. If someone hurt one of them, that person got hurt in return. No exceptions.

Kells had a definite motive. Worse, she could completely empathize with that motive.

She found Kells on the roof of the Norman keep. The day was crisp and cold, and the air held a breathtaking clarity. The view extended for miles, but she had seen it many times. Besides, the sky could be made exclusively of one large sapphire and she would still be able to look only at Kells.

He was superimposed against the brilliant blue sky, a hard, angry man in his black leather jacket and form-fitting jeans. And to her amazement, she realized his expression was very close to what it had been when she had first seen him in the mirror. The anger was there, plus another emotion she couldn't decipher. But this wasn't the scene; they were in the wrong place.

"What are you doing up here?"

He stared at her with those eyes of his that could hold her so effortlessly. "I thought a little air might help to clear my head."

"Has it?"

"Not really. You're still there." Anger filled his every word. "Tell me, Bria. When you come up here and everything you see belongs to the Delaneys, does it make you feel like God?"

"No," she said slowly, "but the view does engender feelings. What I see when I look out over the land, what any Delaney would see, is our heritage. And we would fight to the very last man to keep it." She paused. "Just as your father fought to keep his business."

His brows drew together and his eyes darkened. "My *father?* What brought that up?"

"You told me that your father committed suicide, but you didn't tell me he did it mere months after my father bought out his business."

He moved his head, jerking it back as if she had hit him. "How did you find that out?"

"I spent about thirty minutes on the computer."

His eyes glittered dangerously. "Invading my family's privacy?"

"Protecting *my* family. Besides, it was all a matter of public record. Why didn't you tell me?"

"It didn't seem important." He was lying. As soon as he had realized he was in love with her, he had known the moment would come when he would have to tell her. But he had put it off. As much as he loved her, he still found it hard to reveal his heart. But here she was, beautiful, strong, demanding that he do so. And the time had come when he couldn't do less.

"Kells, you told me your father committed suicide. Why didn't you go that one step further and tell me why?"

His lips drew into a tight line as he braced himself to open up that portion of his heart he had always felt better having closed. But Bria deserved the truth. "Because Burke buying the company wasn't the reason he killed himself."

The wind whipped her long hair across her eyes. With a toss of her head she sent her hair streaming away from her face. "Maybe Dad's buying him out wasn't the whole of it, but it looks to me as if it was the final straw."

"What do you want me to say, Bria? That I've held a grudge all these years, waiting for an opportunity to kill Burke? Forget it. Life is rarely that simple or easy. I was only nine when my father shot his brains out, and of *course* I was deeply affected. But I knew my dad pretty well. I had seen what my mother's death had done to him. I had watched as he started drinking more and more. I didn't know anything about what was happening to the business, but it didn't escape my attention that he was spending more and more time at home because he was incapable of going in to work. My grandfather and I both tried to help him in our own ways, but there came a time when we could no longer reach him. That's when it happened."

She stared down at her clasped hands. "I'm sorry. I know this must be hard for you."

"Yeah, it is. And it was at the time. But the thing I'm currently finding damn near impossible to bear is that you actually believe I would kill your father because of it."

"The facts—"

His growl cut her off. "The facts don't measure my intelligence, Bria—not now or when I was nine years old. Yeah, Burke's buying out of the company probably pushed my dad over the edge. But if it hadn't been Burke, it would have been someone else. And if it hadn't been the buyout that pushed him over the edge, it would have been the company's bankruptcy, or something, anything, else. I knew that then, and I know it now."

"But—"

He held up his hand, forestalling her words. "I'll admit that when Burke invited me to come here, my first instinct was to turn him down. I had made the decision to take his money, but deep down inside there was still something left of that nine-year-old little boy's hurt, and I didn't want to have anything more to do with him than was necessary. In my defense, I think a little of that feeling, however much I was or wasn't aware of it, was natural. When I first got here, I was edgy and wishing like hell I was back home. I didn't want to be friends with Burke or Cara. And I sure as hell didn't want to become involved with their daughter. But things rapidly jumped beyond my control. More and more I became aware that I was getting tangled up with you. At one point it dawned on me that I wouldn't have accepted Burke's money if I hadn't come to like and admire him. It was a shock to me, but it was true. Then everything else but you faded in importance."

"Kells..." She wasn't sure what she wanted to say to him. She was caught up in something that made her feel totally helpless. And though her instinct was to protect him and her father, she had only ended up hurting him more.

"Damn you, Bria. Have I ever given you any reason to think I would lie?"

She shook her head. "No." She sighed and rubbed her forehead. "No, you haven't." She walked to the battlement, but turned so that she could see him. "So far, four out of six of the scenes I've seen have come true. I guess you think I should latch on to the mirror's inaccuracy and not dwell on its accuracy."

"I wish like hell you would, because, Bria, I'm promising you, there's nothing on earth, *nothing* that would make me kill Burke."

It was a huge gamble in a deadly serious game, she thought. But over the years Delaneys had certainly played worse odds and won. "I'm still going to continue searching for an answer to the mirror. I have to."

His jaw clenched, his body stiffened. He had given her every assurance he was capable of, and it wasn't enough. "Break the damn mirror, Bria. Throw it away. Put it back in the attic. But whatever you do, *get it out of your life.*"

She shook her head. "I can't."

Frustration and anger etched his features. "Why in the hell not?"

"For a lot of reasons. It's obviously part of the Delaney history, but for some reason its history has been lost. I have to find it."

"Why? Why do you have to be the one Delaney out of all your family that is worried about this damn mirror?"

She shook her head again. "I don't know. But for some reason, at this time I'm the only one it shows anything to." She didn't need an interpreter for his dark expression. His fury was climbing to an all-time high. "I know it doesn't make any sense, Kells. I've said that right from the beginning. But no matter what, I can't put the mirror away until I understand it."

He uttered a long string of oaths. "It's resting squarely between us, you know that, don't you? And it's creating one hell of a barrier."

She knew the answer, but she had to ask anyway. "Against what?"

"Whatever might have happened next between us."

She swallowed and felt pain. "The mirror's important, Kells. How could I not think it was? It's shown me too many things."

His expression turned implacable. "Tomorrow morning Burke and I will sign our agreement. Tomorrow afternoon I'll be leaving here."

"*No.*" Her response was instinctive, without thought.

"I already have my tickets, Bria. Besides, isn't that what you wanted? Me back in Australia or anywhere besides here. Cheer up, sweetheart. Your dad will be safe, and you'll have all the time in the world to search for that documentation you want so badly."

"Kells—"

The urge to either yell at her or make love to her was impossibly strong. But he had done both and neither had helped. He turned his back on her and left the rooftop.

She laid her hand on the cold stone of the battlement and stared unseeingly out over the land.

That damned mirror. Had other Delaneys struggled with it as she was? Had they cursed it and then put it away?

Whatever they had done, it wasn't in her to give up. She couldn't leave the problem of the mirror alone, not now. Nor could she bear to lose Kells.

Time was of the essence. If she could find her answers before he left tomorrow, maybe he would be able to understand. *Maybe.*

But where were the answers? She had no idea, but since nothing she had tried so far had worked, she had no choice but to return to square one.

9

DUST MOTES DANCED IN THE SUNLIGHT THAT STREAMED THROUGH the window. Bria sat on the attic floor not too far from where she had found the mirror. It seemed to her that she had searched every trunk and box in this old section, and she wasn't sure what else she could do. But there had to be something, something she hadn't yet thought of.

Her gaze went to the place where she had found the mirror. Long ago a member of her family had put it there, placing it face to the wall and covering it with a shawl. And the mirror had remained there, undisturbed for decades.

It didn't make sense that whoever placed the mirror against the wall would have done so without leaving some record for the generations to come, something that would explain the powers of the mirror and perhaps tell why they had returned it to the attic. They wouldn't have simply draped the mirror with a shawl and—

The *shawl*. Her eyes flew to the aged silk material that lay crumpled on the floor where she had dropped it. She shifted, and picked it up with care and deference. The shawl's background must have been white at one time, she guessed, and the flowers vivid, but now faded flowers bloomed against an ecru background. As she brought it closer to her, something fell into her lap. A yellowed envelope.

With barely contained excitement she pulled out three sheets of paper and began to read.

My dear Elizabeth,

So you found the mirror at last. It's about time.

How well I feel I know you. Even as I write this letter I can see you as clearly as I did that day over forty years ago when I looked in the mirror and the magic showed me the young woman I thought was to be my daughter. There you were, kneeling before the mirror in your blue and white sweater and men's trousers, your face as pretty as my Kevin's was handsome, and with my red hair. I felt very lucky in you, Elizabeth, and very lucky in my vision of my future.

But I had only one child, Brendan, and he only one son, Patrick. So it seems you may not appear in my lifetime. Too bad. I would have liked to have known you. Of course, it's possible that you may pop up from some unknown branch of the family as I did, but I cannot chance leaving you in ignorance of the mirror.

I have chronicled all I know of the history of the mirror on the following pages. Read them and make your own decision about whether or not you should leave the mirror where you found it. As for myself, I've never regretted my own choice. My life has been full and rich, but there have been many moments I would not choose to have had foretold—and, thus, to have lived through twice. A terrible world war has claimed the lives of friends and loved ones. I would never have wanted to see those dark shadows approaching. Whatever your decision, good fortune and God's blessing on you.

Affectionately,
Zara Delaney

Bria's head spun. Zara had described *her* right down to the clothes she had been wearing the day she had found the mirror. Zara must have looked into the mirror and seen her discovering it. Yet she called her Elizabeth. Why?

Her mind quickly switched to something of more importance. The tone of Zara's letter seemed to indicate that whatever was seen in the mirror came true.

Impatiently Bria turned to the following pages and once again began to read. When she put down the last page, she had her answer. The history of the mirror confirmed her worst fear: What was seen in it always came true.

Sweet heaven, she had to find Kells. And she had to show the letter to her father right away.

She rushed downstairs. The first person she encountered was her mother, discussing menus for the upcoming Christmas festivities with Mrs. Copeland.

"Mom, have you seen Kells?"

In an instant Cara's motherly gaze took in Bria's flushed complexion and anxious expression. "He and your dad went riding a little while ago. Why? What's wrong?"

"Oh, Lord."

"Darling, what's wrong?"

"Nothing, I hope. Where did they go?"

"I think I heard Burke say something about the west range. You know how proud your dad is of that new bull—"

Bria's mind worked fast as she ran to the two massive hand-carved wooden front doors.

"Bria."

"I'll tell you all about it as soon as I get back," she shouted over her shoulder.

Her dad and Kells had a head start, she thought, but they were on horseback and wouldn't be riding fast. If she took one of the four-wheel-drive vehicles, she would have a chance of catching them. And luckily the keys were always left in all the cars at Killara.

She jumped into the first one she saw. A second later the engine roared to life, and the vehicle's tires burned rubber as she headed toward the west range.

Please, God, let me be in time. The refrain played over and over in her head as her gaze stayed glued to the horizon, looking for her father and Burke. The problem was, men on horseback were common on Killara, and several times she raced toward two riders only to find it was a pair of ranch hands. But one cowboy was able to tell her that he had seen Kells and Burke riding toward the mountains.

Bria pushed the accelerator to the floorboard and sent the Jeep hurtling across the range. Her heart pounded as she drove for what seemed like hours but in reality was probably less than thirty minutes. All she could think of was that she couldn't lose either her dad or Kells. The importance of each to her was without measure, without definition.

Two riderless horses came into her view. They were standing up ahead by an outcropping of boulders. She willed the Jeep to go even faster. She didn't spot the men at first, then she saw one man straighten from a kneeling position and look over his shoulder at her.

It was Kells. But where was her dad?

Her fear heightened until she felt encased from head to foot in ice. She brought the car to a skidding stop and bolted from it. She rounded the hood and came to a shocked halt.

The scene in the mirror.

Her father, pale and lifeless, was lying on the ground, his jacket open, blood staining the entire front of his shirt. And Kells was standing over him, a gun in his hand.

"My God, Kells. You *killed* him."

Kells's expression was taut and scored with anguish, but all he said was, "Do you know how to handle a gun?"

Tears stung her eyes as she looked at him in disbelief. "A gun? A *gun?* What difference does that make? I'm not going to try to kill you." The horror of her father's death was suffocating her, blinding her, numbing her. She stumbled to her father and fell to her knees by his side. "Damn you, Kells," she cried. "Why didn't you listen to me?"

Kells bent down and pressed the gun into her hand. "Get hold of yourself, Bria. We've got to act fast. I'm going to assume that you do know how to handle a gun. Keep him covered while I call for help."

"Help? Have you lost your mind? He's dead." She swatted the tears from her eyes, feeling the pain ripping her apart. Strangely, though, a part of her that operated on a level beyond awareness began to act to protect the one she loved that still lived. "Take the Jeep and leave," she said, tears streaming down her face. "Drive straight to Mexico. I'll be all right. Quite a few people saw me heading this way. If I'm not back by nightfall, they'll come find me."

"Bria—"

"*Listen* to me. By that time you'll be very close to the border. You should be able to make it over with no trouble at all." She had no idea if her words had made any impact on Kells. His eyes were darker than midnight and completely unreadable.

With a curse and a quick glance over his shoulder at something he ran toward the Jeep.

She fought back sobs as she turned to her dad. He had always been so strong, so all-powerful. She hadn't been able to keep him from being killed, but she could hold him and stay with him so that he wouldn't be alone until someone came to find them.

Without regard for the blood she slid her hands beneath his shoulders so that she could cradle him against her.

He groaned. Her breath caught in her throat. *"Dad?"*

He didn't say anything; his eyes remained closed.

She glanced back at the Jeep. It was still there and so was Kells. He looked as though he was delving for something in the backseat.

"Kells. Dad's alive!"

He raced back to her. With another look over his shoulder he jerked off his jacket, then his shirt. "I tried to find something for a compress, but this will have to do." Kneeling, he folded his shirt, then pressed it against Burke's shoulder. "Hold this to his wound. I've called for help. They should be scrambling a copter within the minute."

She hurriedly wiped the tears from her eyes and did as he said, willing the compress to work. And all the while her head filled with questions. "You knew he wasn't dead?"

"I didn't kill him, Bria," he said grimly. "I told you I wouldn't." He lay his black leather jacket across Burke, leaving his own upper body bare to the December cold. "The bullet got him in the shoulder, but it must have nicked an artery. He'll be okay, though, if we can stop the flow of blood and get him to a hospital."

"But—"

"Later." He jerked to his feet and strode to one of the horses. Quickly, expertly, he untied the rope from her dad's saddle and carried it toward another body, a body she hadn't seen until this moment because it was half hidden by brush and boulders.

"Who is that?"

"The man who shot your father," he said, tying the unconscious man's hands together, then his feet.

"Kells . . . saved my life."

Her dad's voice sent relief pouring through her. "Thank God you're alive. I thought—"

"I know. Kells . . . told me about the mirror."

She fought back sobs of happiness. "You're weak. Please don't talk. Help is on the way."

"I'm all right, and I . . . I want you to know something. I knew everything."

"Bria's right, Burke," Kells called. "You've already lost consciousness once. Try to stay awake this time, but don't use up your energy trying to talk."

Even wounded and bleeding Burke didn't take orders. He concentrated on his daughter. "I knew when . . . Kells's dad committed suicide, and though I knew I wasn't responsible . . . I've kept an eye on Kells all these years."

"Dad, please be quiet. There'll be plenty of time—"

"I wouldn't have invited him here if I hadn't known he was a good man . . . and that I could trust him."

Tears continued to stream down Bria's face. She remembered thinking that her father was too smart to invite an enemy to Killara. Why hadn't she trusted her father's instincts and left the damn mirror alone?

She heard the whir of helicopters and saw three approaching, no doubt one of them carrying her mother. In the distance she could see the dust whirls that meant several Jeeps were driving toward them, accelerators jammed to the floor. There was a faint reverberation beneath the ground, indicating horsemen riding flat out to reach them.

Burke Delaney was down. The alarm would have been sounded throughout Killara, including Hell's Bluff and Shamrock. There wasn't a man, woman, or child on Killara who would draw an easy breath until they knew he would be all right.

She smiled down at him and pressed a kiss to his forehead. "I love you, Dad."

A faint smile touched his lips, and having said what he wanted to, he closed his eyes. In the next minutes it seemed as if half of Killara converged on them. But there was no confusion. Everyone worked single-mindedly to help Burke.

After he was carefully loaded onto the helicopter, Cara climbed in after him, then glanced back at Bria. "York and Rafe are meeting us at the hospital. You're coming too, aren't you?"

She hesitated as her gaze went back to Kells. Someone had returned his jacket to him and had wrapped it around his shoulders, leaving his chest still bare. But he looked as if the cold wasn't touching him, as if nothing could. "Kells?"

"You go with your dad," he said tonelessly, his eyes bleak. "Someone is seeing to the horses. The sheriff will be flying in here any minute to pick up the man who shot Burke. As soon as he does, I'll drive the Jeep back."

There were so many things unresolved between them, so many

things that she wasn't certain could be resolved or forgotten. She certainly couldn't forget her first words to him when she had leapt from the Jeep. *You killed him.* "Are you sure you don't want to come with us?"

For an answer he silently turned and walked toward his prisoner. With one last look at him, Bria climbed into the copter with her parents.

As soon as the doctors assured Bria that her dad was going to be fine, she flew back to Killara. Her mother had her uncles, York and Rafe, plus her aunts, Sierra and Maggie, to stay with her, but Kells had no one.

And by this time she had heard the whole story from her dad and from the sheriff. An escaped prisoner from a local jail had jumped out from behind the boulders and demanded not only money from her dad and Kells, but also their clothes, boots, and horses. Her dad had been trying to reason with the man, who panicked and shot him. Her dad had fallen from his horse but managed to remain conscious long enough to see Kells launch himself off his horse at the man. A fight ensued. Then, apparently, once Kells had managed to knock the man out, he had run back to Burke. It was at that point that Bria had arrived and immediately jumped to the wrong conclusion.

He would never be able to forgive her, she thought sadly, and she wasn't sure she blamed him.

What she had seen in the mirror *had* come true, but while it had shown her a truth, it hadn't interpreted that truth. The scene also hadn't included the man lying on the ground behind Kells.

She had tried to change fate and failed. Her father had been shot, but not by Kells, and thankfully her father was still very much alive.

Ironically, ultimately it had turned out that she hadn't really needed to change fate after all.

* * *

As soon as Bria landed on Killara, she went in search of Kells. She knew she was probably the last person he wanted to see, but at the very least she owed him an apology. Before he returned to Australia, she wanted him to know how sorry she was that she had believed in the mirror instead of in him. She also wanted to tell him that she loved him. The knowledge wouldn't make any difference to him, but somehow, in some way, it would to her.

But she couldn't find him. He had returned, someone said, put on a fresh shirt, and then left again. For a split second she panicked, but then she forced her mind to clear.

And suddenly she knew exactly where Kells was.

She jumped into another Jeep and headed for the mountains.

She pulled the Jeep off the gravel mountain road and onto the lay-by and parked it by the vehicle that Kells had driven.

He was standing at the edge of the cliff, his back to her. And it was the same scene she had seen that first night in the mirror.

The width of his broad shoulders stretched against his black split-leather jacket, his long, muscular legs were gloved in faded jeans. His brown hair gleamed with a hint of red in the sunshine. And his attention was focused on the valley below him—on Killara.

Then he turned and looked at her with those amazingly direct eyes of his that were the color of the sky behind him. He appeared hard, dangerous, and very angry. And his eyes held the expression she had never been able to interpret.

Then just as he had in the mirror, he opened his mouth to speak. "I'm sorry, Bria."

The breath left her lungs. She had imagined many things that he might say, but his apology had taken her totally off guard. "What?"

"I'm sorry I didn't believe you about the mirror. Can you ever forgive me? If I had, maybe I could have done something—"

"Why on *earth* should you have believed me? The idea of a mirror that shows the past, present, and future is totally irrational. My own parents didn't believe me."

"Yeah, but you asked me to believe you and I didn't. I should have."

She stared at him for a moment, having a hard time absorbing what he was saying. "You're angry. Why?"

"Because I didn't jump that guy *before* he had a chance to shoot Burke. But most of all I'm angry because I didn't believe you. Like I said, if I had, maybe—"

"I didn't believe you when you said you would never shoot my dad."

"You had reason not to believe me."

She could hardly believe her ears. Hope was beginning to build where before there had been nothing but despair. "Dad's going to be all right."

He nodded. "I know. I telephoned from the Jeep and checked."

She chose her next words carefully. "Dad will want you to stay until he's released from the hospital. Knowing him, he'll stay there only as long as is absolutely necessary."

He slipped his hands into his jeans pockets. "What about you? Do you want me to stay?"

She nodded slowly, afraid to hope, almost afraid to breathe. "Very much."

"Christmas is less than a week away. Your family will be coming in. I'll be in the way."

"I want you to stay, Kells, but only if you'll feel comfortable." She smiled nervously. "And before you make your decision, there's something you should know, something Mom and Dad already know."

"What?"

She shrugged, feeling more uncertain and vulnerable than she ever had in her life. "I love you."

The hard lines of his face transformed until his lips were curved with the biggest smile she had ever seen. And it was then she understood the hard-to-define expression in his eyes. It was *love.*

"Thank God," he said softly. He walked to her, drew her into his arms, and gazed tenderly down at her. "I love you, Bria Delaney.

More than I can say, more than I will ever be able to show you in a hundred years of living together. But—"

"There's a but?" She laughed shakily.

"A very big one. Could you be happy in Australia, away from Killara? Because if you can't, I'll move."

Her eyes misted with tears at what he was willing to do for her, but she shook her head. "You love Australia. You've made your home there, built your business there. We'll come back often to visit both The Star and Killara. We have to, Killara is as much a part of me as my breath. But *you're* my heart, and wherever you are will be my home."

He looked as if he were almost afraid to believe her. "Really?"

"Oh, yes," she said fervently. "I'm going to love working by your side, helping you in your business, making us a home together, raising a family—"

He threw back his head and laughed with sheer happiness. "A *family?*"

She nodded, smiling. "And Kells, I promise you, you'll never have to fight alone again."

He tightened his arms around her and lowered his mouth to hers. And there in the windy mountain pass, they kissed, clinging together, their love as wild and unrestrained as the land below them.

EPILOGUE

A snow fell Christmas Eve, blanketing Killara in a pristine cover of white. The frozen crystals whispered down on the land that the Delaneys had fought and died for through the years, coating the sagebrush and cactus until they looked like glistening Christmas ornaments.

The Delaneys and their own were gathered inside Killara's Gothic chapel. Candles offered soft, golden illumination. Shamrocks, flown in from Ireland, had been entwined with white lilacs, white orchid sprays, and white roses, and were all tied together with golden ribbons to decorate the Spanish olivewood altar railing.

A radiant Bria walked slowly down the aisle on her father's arm, wearing the dress in which her mother had married her father. The long skirt of the ivory satin gown was embroidered with shamrocks that were sewn from shimmering threads spun from gold. Her floor-length veil trailed behind her. Made of yards of antique lace, it was strewn with diamonds brought from Kantalan and worn by many Delaney brides before her.

Love surrounded Bria as she walked toward Kells. There was her uncle Rafe, his arm around the woman he would forever call his lass, her aunt Maggie. Beside them was her beautiful uncle York, holding hands with the love of his life, her aunt Sierra.

The three women the family had always called the Australian girls and their husbands lined other rows. There was the exquisite Sydney and the darkly handsome Nicholas Charron. Behind them was Manda, alight with exuberance, and Roman Gallagher who had somehow managed to grow more interesting looking with age. And then there was Addie, as always deceptively delicate looking, and her husband Shane Marston, every inch the aristocrat.

Cougar, his hair completely white now, but still full and hanging to his waist, sat beside Bridget, her hair amazingly fiery red and bound into a regal coronet for the occasion. Kathleen was beaming as if she had orchestrated the whole romance. And Deuce Moran tenderly held the hand of his lady, the exotic Mandarin.

Scattered around the chapel were her cousins, Dominic, Erin, and all the others.

Beneath his tuxedo, Burke's shoulder was bandaged, but he stood proud, straight, and strong as he linked his daughter's hand with Kells's and uttered the words that for all time would give his beloved daughter to the man she loved. Then he turned and went to join Cara, the silver-haired, silver-eyed, quicksilver woman who had captured his love so many years before and who still controlled his every heartbeat.

Patrick, tall and handsome, a picture of Burke when he had been the same age, was the couple's only attendant. With a special smile for him, Bria handed him her bouquet. Then she turned to Kells and, directed by the priest, they repeated the vows that joined them as husband and wife.

When Kells slipped a diamond and gold band on her finger, Bria's eyes brimmed with tears of pure joy. And when she and Kells sank to their knees on the aged silk and gold-threaded petit point kneeling cushions, she whispered a prayer of thanksgiving that the Delaney luck had held and that she was going to spend the rest of her life with a man she loved without limit and who loved her without reservation.

"Don't worry about the other clothing and furniture and all that, darling," Cara said to Bria the day after Christmas as she helped her finish packing. "Your dad and I will oversee the shipping of your things to Brisbane."

"Thank you, Mom," Bria said with a loving smile. "You've been wonderful. I don't know anyone but you who could have put together such a beautiful wedding in such a short time."

"I had a lot of help. Besides, there's nothing to thank me for. I'm just so grateful you've found a love that is as strong as the love your dad and I have for each other. My only question is how long do we have to wait before we can visit you?"

Bria laughed. "You can come tomorrow as far as I'm concerned. Kells too."

"I don't know about that. I don't want to get off on the wrong foot with my new son-in-law. We'll wait a bit, but not too long." She strolled to the closet, checking for anything Bria might have forgotten, and saw the mirror. "What do you want me to do about this?" she asked, pointing.

Bria barely glanced at it. "Put it back up in the attic. I don't need to look at it again. I know my future is going to be filled with joy."

Smiling, Cara nodded and shut the closet doors.

Bria reached for her Liz Claiborne jeans, folded them, and put them into her suitcase. Suddenly she stilled.

Elizabeth.

Zara had seen her in these jeans and thought her name was Elizabeth, a natural mistake. She wished she had known Zara. What an interesting and wonderful woman she must have been.

With a warm smile of affection for her ancestress, she closed her suitcase. And with a final hug for her mother, she went downstairs to Kells and to her future.

Kells and Bria were pelted with shamrocks as they ran to the helicopter that would take them on the first leg of their trip to their home in Australia.

Bria slid into her seat beside Kells and reached to take his hand. The helicopter lifted off, and the pilot circled the homestead before heading for Tucson.

Bria waved to the laughing, happy crowd that was her family, then turned to her husband, her expression one of undiluted love.

He leaned toward her and kissed her with a tenderness and passion that she returned. She was secure in his love and secure in a future that she knew without a doubt was going to be filled with ecstasy and happiness.

The next morning Cara climbed the steps to the attic, the mirror in her arms. Zara Delaney's letter was locked away in the safe for future generations.

In the old section of the attic Cara knelt to place the mirror against the wall as Bria had directed. She reached for the shawl, but then hesitated, and an impish smile appeared on her lovely face. Unable to resist, she turned the mirror to her and gazed into its brilliant depths.

And in a twinkling she saw Bria and Kells, plus Patrick and a beautiful young woman she didn't know, sitting on Killara's lawn, watching over children who were running and tumbling and laughing happily. Her *grandchildren*, she realized. And she and Burke were there too, his arm around her, as together they watched with loving indulgence.

With a gentle smile she turned the mirror to the wall, draped it with the shawl, then went downstairs to Burke.

KAY HOOPER

Christmas Future

1

KILLARA WAS BURNING.

Brett Delaney closed his eyes. He could almost hear the thunder of his heartbeat, and his entire body felt cold, leaden. If he had received a mortal wound, if his flesh had been laid open to the bone with a single vicious blow, he couldn't have felt more shock or pain.

He didn't want to look again. But he was compelled to look, just as he'd been compelled to open the crate, knowing what it contained. He'd been compelled to look into the mirror for only the second time in his life, even though he expected to see something devastating, as he had the first time.

When he opened his eyes, the scene was still there, as clear as if he were gazing through a window. The outline of Killara was unmistakable and achingly familiar, from the ancient Norman keep and adobe homestead built so long ago to the more modern additions to the sprawling house. Brett could easily make out the glass-walled study his own father had constructed more than fifteen years before, and there was an addition to the kitchen he'd never seen that must have been built during his absence from the place these last ten years.

There was snow on the ground, on the roof. The entire scene was lit with a hellish glow, and flames licked hungrily at timbers even as they shattered glass and blackened stone. He would have sworn he could hear the roar of the fire as it consumed the house, feel the dreadful heat, and his imagination—surely it was merely that—conjured in his mind a sound of inhuman anguish that could only be the death throes of a home so old and solidly rooted in its place it had taken on a life of its own.

Unable to bear any more, Brett turned jerkily away from the mirror and stared out his office window. But he couldn't see the beauty of Sydney Harbor visible from that window; all he could see was what the mirror had shown him.

God, he hadn't wanted to look. For days the crate had sat unopened in a corner of his office, ignored by him despite the curious glances of visitors. He had tried to not even think about it, but the very presence of the crate had drawn his attention again and again. He had wondered briefly why she had sent it to his office rather than his apartment, but had refused to let the question trouble him very much. He had known too well what the crate contained. From the moment he'd received her telegram about his father's death more than a year before, he had known the mirror would come eventually. It was the one promise his father had kept.

"You'll have it when I'm gone, boy. And that's when you'll learn fate can't be changed."

For the first time, Brett began to understand the source of his father's bitterness. If he had seen some tragedy in the mirror—the death of his first wife, Brett's mother, in a car accident, for instance—perhaps that had caused the corrosive bitterness. He'd been a strong man, and strong men are often unable to handle the realization that control of their lives is an illusion.

Brett wondered if that was a realization he himself would have to accept. Because he had to try. He had run away from the question before, unwilling to put his own strength of will to the test. Or simply unable to risk failure, because some part of him *had* believed in fate. This time he couldn't run from the mirror's promise. He had to challenge it. Running away hadn't changed anything ten years ago—and he was no longer that intense, volatile young man. This time he had to fight. He had to try to change what the mirror proclaimed was fated to be.

The future. He was certain the mirror had shown him that, even though he knew Killara had burned in the past. He was sure because of what he had seen: his father's glass-walled study and the other new addition. He was also sure because there had been a car parked in the drive and it was next year's model; they had only just become available in the last month or so, he knew. And he was sure because, unless all his father's traditions had died with him, the huge family Christmas tree was always brought into the house and trimmed no earlier than a week before Christmas Eve; the mirror had plainly shown the gaily decorated tree in one of the front windows.

Christmas was only a few weeks away.

Of course, the mirror could have been showing him what was happening now, in the present, but Brett knew that wasn't the case. He knew beyond any shadow of a doubt that despite everything he had thought and believed for most of his life, he could no longer deny his own roots lay deeply planted in that place. Killara was so much a part of him that he would feel its death even on the other side of the world, with no need of a phone call, or a telegram—or a mirror—to tell him it was happening.

No, it was the future he'd seen. And the compulsion he felt to hurry back there with all speed told him that the threat was both powerful and immediate. He didn't want to go back to the States. To Arizona. To Killara. He had scorned and reviled every symbol of his heritage, abandoning all of it ten years before and swearing he would never return.

He hadn't returned, not even for his father's funeral. But now Killara was calling him, not with a father's unwelcome demands or the enticing call of a lover, but with a summons he could never deny with his mind, his heart, or his soul. He had to go back. He had to do everything in his power to protect Killara. It was an instinct programmed into his very genes, a need so basic and absolute, it was beyond question.

He was dimly aware of going to his desk and punching up the code of the shuttle service; he hardly heard his voice as he booked a seat on the next morning's shuttle to the States. Then, reluctantly, he turned to the mirror again, his shoulders braced against another vision.

But the window into time was closed. The mirror, two feet wide and three feet tall, its dark oval bogwood frame carved intricately with holly, looked old, and lovely, and perfectly innocent. And the glass itself was brilliant with unusual clarity. This time all he saw was the reflection of himself, a tall, athletic man in his early thirties with black hair and dark eyes. A man who was unusually pale and held himself stiffly, as if all his bones hurt.

Slowly he moved toward the mirror to repack it in its crate. He would ship it back to Killara tonight, he decided, using the overnight service. That way it would get there before he would and announce his arrival.

The last of the Delaneys was coming home.

The efficient shuttle service required no more than an hour to transport a passenger halfway around the world. Brett left Sydney at eight A.M. on Friday and arrived in Tucson at four P.M. on Thursday. He'd left with little preparation and had only one small worry: his business partner. Gideon Paige's reaction to his announcing his plan had surprised Brett who'd never seen him display so much anger and distress. He'd calmed Gideon and put the scene out of his mind.

The speed of modern technology had made the Earth seem very small, turning it into a true global village, but the human body still clung to its ancient rhythms that were based on light and darkness and the phases of the moon.

Brett had arranged for a car at the shuttle station in Tucson, and paused only to buy a newspaper before going directly to the rental counter. Glancing at the headlines, he noted that the terraforming of Mars was proceeding on schedule; a few more decades and the people there would be breathing home-grown air instead of canned. Ironic, Brett thought, not for the first time. After all the science-fiction stories, the real Martians turned out to be transplanted Earth people.

He used his debit card to pay for the car and stepped through the doorway to the garage where his luggage had already been taken. He'd managed to keep his mind fairly blank during the trip, resisting thoughts about the mirror's prophesy, but when the valet pulled up in front of him with his rental, Brett felt a coldness creep up his spine.

From the sleek design all the way down to the gleaming hubcaps, this was the car he'd seen in the mirror, the car parked at Killara while the house was being engulfed by flames.

"Sir," the valet asked, "is anything wrong?"

Brett looked at the kid a little blindly, then shook his head. "No. No, nothing's wrong. Thank you." His voice sounded normal enough, he thought. He got into the car and programmed his destination into the onboard computer, then settled back with his newspaper.

After no more than five minutes he stopped trying to convince himself that the paper could hold his interest. He tossed it onto the seat beside him and gazed out at the passing scenery. Tucson was little changed, still sprawling lazily within a ring of sun-baked mountains. The city was soon left behind, and Brett was unnerved to realize how eagerly he scanned the arid landscape of Sulphur Springs Valley.

God, it was so familiar, even after ten years. The car was on Delaney land now, land that the Delaney family had chosen to keep basically unchanged for two hundred years. Cattle and horses still roamed, herded by men and women on horseback. Fences were still few and far between, and even though irrigation had turned the valley greener than it had been in its past, it remained a windswept place subject to the sometimes violent whims of nature. It would never be a tame land, no matter what technology was used to attempt to master it, and he thought the Delaneys had always taken a somewhat perverse pleasure in that.

They'd been like this land for much of their colorful history, basically untamed but curiously stable for all of that, and with a proud awareness of their faults as well as their virtues. While other great families had set their mark on their land, molding it to their will, the Delaneys had settled here and changed the land only as much as necessary for survival. They had formed a partnership with their piece of the earth.

And they had survived. They'd survived summer droughts, flash floods, and winter blizzards. They had survived attacks by Indians, wars, famines, outbreaks of disease, financial setbacks, and internal strife. They had survived—but they had paid for the family's survival with real blood at times, and always with sheer effort, strength, and will.

But time fought them, just as it fought every living thing. And great families seemed to struggle to maintain their greatness. For the second time in two centuries there was only a single direct descendant of old Shamus, one lone male to carry on the name.

If he carried on the name.

Brett thought of all that as the car carried him swiftly toward Killara. And he could feel the spell of this place winding itself around his heart again, tugging at him with a feeling so intense it was almost pain. He fought the emotions as hard as he could, refusing to give in, to let himself be seduced. No matter what instincts had drawn him back, he rejected even the idea that any place could hold him against his will.

Even so, the first glimpse of the house made his heart beat faster, and he half-consciously let out a rough breath of relief to see it whole and unharmed. He'd been sure nothing had happened to it yet, but the living proof before him was like a calming touch to his soul. And there was no Christmas tree up in any of the front rooms;

he could see that even before the car drifted to a halt near the steps. There was no snow on the ground.

With the relief of knowing he had time to find the threat against Killara, some of his tension eased. But its going wasn't a very pleasant thing, because it made room for the other emotions he'd pushed to a dark corner within himself. He couldn't ignore them, couldn't avoid facing the tangle of feelings now that he was here.

They said when you came back to a place after years away, it always seemed smaller. But not Killara. Killara was big and grand and somehow magnificent. Larger than life could ever be.

He got out of the car slowly, his gaze still fixed on the house. The sun, low in the sky, painted the house with a golden glow that was warm and inviting, but nonetheless he half zipped his casual black leather jacket. He felt chilly, and told himself it was only the early December cold he felt; it was unusually biting, and there was moisture in the air.

Still, it wasn't only the outward cold that touched him with a wintry brush, and he had to admit that to himself.

With the practice of ten years as a hard-driving businessman, he controlled his features, molding them into an expression of rocklike calm. He was, he reminded himself, no longer twenty-two and hotheaded; he was perfectly capable of being polite and neutral for as long as he had to. It shouldn't be long, he thought. He wasn't here for good, no matter how strongly he felt about the place. This was no longer his home. He would return to Australia as soon as he'd handled the threat against Killara.

But he could feel himself stiffen when the front door opened.

"Welcome home, Brett."

His tension eased a bit as he watched the heavyset middle-aged woman come down the steps toward him. "Thanks, Moira." His tone was carefully matter-of-fact, just like the expression on the housekeeper's calm face. There was no welcoming smile from the woman who had practically raised him, merely neutrality. Brett was surprised to feel a pang of regret when he realized that Moira hadn't forgiven him for leaving Killara; her family had served his for so long that all she lacked in being a Delaney herself was the name, and it had wounded her deeply that he had turned his back and walked away from everything his family had built.

"You go on inside," she was saying briskly, her vigorous attitude unchanged by the years. "Hank'll be here in a minute to help me with your bags." Facing him with her hands braced on wide hips, she held his eyes deliberately. "Cassie's in your father's study, working on the accounts."

Without replying, Brett turned away from the housekeeper and made his way into the house, moving without haste. He passed through a number of rooms and hallways, only half noticing the eclectic mix of styles and decorations that had filled the place in more than two centuries; the Delaneys never threw anything away, that had been a family joke for generations. He didn't feel like laughing now, however. His hands felt cold, and his heart was beating with a slow, heavy rhythm, and a part of him wanted to yell or tear something to shreds just to dissipate the tension building inside him.

But he walked on steadily, halting only when he reached the French doors opening into his father's study. The room was large, bright, uncluttered. Except for narrow bookcases flanking the windows and a corner fireplace made entirely of river rock, the exterior walls were almost all glass, and half a dozen skylights provided even more daylight.

So the woman seated at the big glass-and-oak desk didn't need any artificial light even this late in the afternoon. She was working at a computer, her slender fingers moving rapidly over the keyboard.

The old-fashioned way, Brett reflected absently; many people still disliked talking to machines.

As he stood in the doorway watching her, he realized slowly that Moira hadn't announced his arrival. Cassie didn't know he was there. Was she even expecting him? He'd seen no sign of the mirror, but its delivery had been confirmed before he'd left Australia.

He slid his hands into the pockets of his slacks, settled his shoulders, and spoke coolly. "Hello, Cassie."

The computer beeped indignantly as her competent fingers tangled to strike several keys at once, and she looked up slowly to see him standing only a few feet away from the desk. After a long, still moment, she rose to her feet and attempted a slight smile that didn't quite come off. Her eyes were shuttered, unreadable.

"Hello, Brett. Welcome home."

She sounded nervous, he thought, and wondered if the irony of her welcome had struck her as forcibly as it did him. Did she believe he'd come back to take the ranch and everything else away from her? It was his, after all; his father's will, a copy of which had been delivered to him at the same time as the mirror, had made that very clear. She had the right to live there if she wanted, and the estate would pay her a small allowance as long as she did, but beyond that she was entitled to nothing.

"Didn't you expect me to come back when you sent the mirror?" he asked, taking a few steps into the room and looking casually past her through the windows at the rolling land.

A little stiffly she replied, "When the mirror came back this morning, I didn't know what to expect. In any case, I was merely following Kane's wishes, the directions in his will. You must know that; you were sent a copy of the will."

Global village or not, some things still took a ridiculous amount of time, Brett thought; it had required fourteen months after his father's death for the admittedly large estate to be probated.

Almost to himself he muttered, "What do you call a hundred lawyers on the bottom of the ocean?"

"A good beginning."

He looked to see her smiling, but her expression settled back into a polite mask when he didn't respond.

Cassie sat down at the desk again, but turned away from the waiting computer and folded her hands on the neat blotter. "Since you sent no instructions or otherwise made your wishes known," she said evenly, "I've made decisions based on my own experience. The board supervises the corporation, of course; all the reports are available for you. I began running the ranch more than two years before Kane became ill, and he trusted me to continue. All the records are here in the computer, and all financial records were audited before probate. I'm sure you'll want to get a manager in—"

"No," Brett said.

"Then you mean to run the place yourself?" she asked in the same steady tone.

He hesitated, feeling suddenly and unexpectedly torn. Everything inside him rebelled at the thought of an outsider coming in to manage Killara, even though he certainly had no intention of remaining to do so himself. Cassie? He knew without looking at the records that she'd done well with the ranch; she'd lived on Delaney land all her life and undoubtedly knew more about the workings of the place than he did.

But it was obvious that she expected the responsibility to be taken out of her hands now that he was home. And why not? Why should she work for something that would never be hers?

"Brett? Do you mean to run the place yourself?"

He took a few more steps past the desk until he was at one of the windows. In the distance was a sparkling lake, a Delaney-made structure of fifty years before, one of the very few changes the family had wrought on this land.

"No," Brett said at last without looking at her. "I'm not here to stay. By the first of the year I should be back in Sydney. I'll decide about a manager before I go. In the meantime, just go on as you have."

"There are some decisions you should make—"

"I said no." He turned his head and found her watching him intently and frowning slightly. Even wearing a frown she was incredibly beautiful, and he felt something in his chest tighten painfully as he remembered the way she'd looked that summer. He had thought there was nothing on earth as beautiful as Cassie. The memory brought with it a rush of feelings, physical as well as emotional, and the combination suddenly made him absolutely furious.

His raw denial of all his ragged feelings about her and Killara spilled out before he could stop them. "I don't want anything to do with the running of this place, you understand? I don't want to look at the records, and I don't want to make any decisions."

She flinched at the harshness of his tone, and her face paled. The expression in her big gray eyes was bewilderment. "This is your home," she said softly.

He smiled thinly. "In case you haven't noticed, it's been ten years since I called this place home."

"I know you and Kane never got along," she said, her voice hesitant. "But I thought...after you came back from college, things would be better." She looked down at her folded hands, and he could see a pulse beating rapidly under the creamy flesh of her neck. "I thought they *were* better that summer. Until you left."

Brett wished the room weren't so brightly lit, or that he'd chosen to stand farther away from her, because he could see her too clearly and he could smell the unutterably sweet scent of her perfume. He wished he'd never come back, or that he'd never left in the first place. He wished the mirror had shown him nothing but his own reflection instead of twice disrupting his life.

Wrenching his gaze away from the gleaming gold of her bent head, he stared out through the window again. "No, things weren't better," he said, his voice still harsh. "They just seemed that way because I was...distracted."

She'd been eighteen then, as leggy and unruly as any Thoroughbred yearling and just as heartbreaking. Her haunting smoke-gray eyes had drawn him like a siren's song, and desire had exploded between them with all the heat of an Arizona summer. He had forgotten his troubled relationship with his father, or at least had not given it much consideration, because she had filled his time, his thoughts, and his senses.

Cassie cleared her throat. "No matter what happened in the past, this *is* your home. You're the last of the Delaneys."

Unemotionally, he said, "Trent still manages Shamrock, doesn't he? He's a Delaney."

"He's a distant cousin. He doesn't even have the name. You're the only direct descendant of Shamus."

Brett fixed his gaze on the distant lake, watching as the setting sun turned the water to silver. "I'm sure you tried to remedy that." He kept his voice detached with an immense effort. "You should have known better though, Cassie. Dad was past sixty when you married him, and all he had to show for a twenty-year first marriage—and quite a bit of whoring around since my mother's death—was me. He wasn't likely to sire another son, no matter how fertile his child-bride was."

"Is that what you believe?" Her voice was a little shaky, and so quiet he barely heard it. "That I married Kane to try and have a child to disinherit you?"

He shrugged. "It doesn't matter what I believe, since it didn't happen." He waited for some response from her, then finally turned his head when the silence dragged on. The chair behind the desk was empty; she had left the room without making a sound.

Brett stood where he was for a long time, concentrating on regaining control of the bitterness that had momentarily escaped him. He tried to make his thoughts matter-of-fact and businesslike, centering on why he had come back here. He reminded himself that of course he had to look at Killara's accounts and read the corporate reports whether he wanted to or not, because that was the only place he could start to find out who wanted to destroy Killara.

But in the midst of these analytical thoughts, a chilling question struck him. Cassie? The question no sooner emerged than he dismissed it. He even shook his head unconsciously as he stood staring outside. No, not Cassie. She'd taken her first unsteady steps on Delaney land, and since her father had been foreman of the ranch, her entire life had been spent here. Brett would have had trouble believing Cassie wanted to destroy Killara even if he'd caught her with gasoline and a match.

She wasn't the girl he had known though. She could hardly have failed to change in ten years—especially since marrying Kane Delaney. Brett felt his hands curl into fists in his pockets, and forced himself to relax. Blanking his mind, he checked his watch, which had automatically reset itself to local time, and realized that he had about half an hour in which to change for dinner.

Cassie had left the computer on, but Brett didn't do anything about that. He hurried out of the study, making his way back through the sprawling house to the front stairs. Moira was just coming down when he reached the foyer. She gave him a level look that told him she knew he had upset Cassie. He returned the look without batting an eye, half-consciously assuming a little of the authority that was rightfully his.

Moira didn't back down, but she didn't challenge him. Instead, in the same neutral voice of before she said, "Your bags have been unpacked. You're in the master suite."

Brett stopped with one foot on the bottom tread. The house-keeper's statement was a surprise. His father's rooms. Slowly, he said, "I assumed Cassie was there."

"No." Moira didn't amplify her answer, merely adding, "Dinner's at seven-thirty, as usual." Then she went to the kitchen, leaving him alone with his thoughts.

He went up the stairs and toward the second-floor master suite that his great-grandfather had personally designed by knocking out a few walls and rearranging floor space. Until that time, the "master suite" of Killara had been whichever room was the current master's—or mistress's—preference, an approach to the question that had begun as the house had grown away from the original adobe homestead of old Shamus and his brood.

Brett didn't hurry as he passed through two corridors on his way to the suite. The house was huge. He looked at some of the paintings on the walls and gazed into a few unoccupied bedrooms, realizing as he did so that no part of Killara had been closed up, even though only Cassie and the servants had been here for over a year.

It was another peculiarity of the family, he remembered, that even a room left unoccupied for years was kept ready in case it was needed—despite the fact that at various points of its history, Killara had boasted only a few inhabitants to fill a ridiculous number of rooms. There were never Holland covers over the furniture, or rooms closed off just for the sake of convenience, or even beds stripped of their coverings to save on linen.

"We're an extravagant bunch," Brett muttered to himself, wondering if Moira still had the daily help of half a dozen girls from the ranch families. It required that many people merely to keep the house up, especially since Moira did all the cooking herself.

At least, he thought she did. That had been the way things worked ten years ago, and he doubted it had changed. If Cassie had been running the ranch for the better part of five years, she certainly hadn't had the time to take over any of the housework, even assuming she'd wanted to.

He realized his steps had slowed as he neared the master suite, and swore softly. What was he worried about? Ghosts? In all their long history, the Delaneys had never been troubled by ghosts. At least not to his knowledge.

He unzipped his jacket and began shrugging it off as he reached the door, striding into the lamplit room with the businesslike pace that had been characteristic of him for the past ten years. He quite deliberately didn't look around, didn't take note of changes, or lack of them, in his father's rooms. He noticed only cursorily that the crated mirror sat in a corner of the bedroom, just as it had sat in his office, to mock him.

He didn't think about it. He just kept moving. Like a defiant boy whistling in the dark to give himself the determination to get past a difficult place, he hummed a brisk tune he couldn't have named as he tossed his jacket onto the custom-made bed, laid out what he meant to wear at dinner, and went into the huge bathroom for a fast shower.

He shaved and began dressing with the same single-minded preoccupation. It was only as he was arranging his tie before the Regency gent's dressing mirror in one corner of the bedroom that he stopped moving and realized what he was doing.

He was dressing for dinner. Another old habit stamped in his very genes, it seemed, one that went back generations. The Delaneys always dressed for dinner at Killara, no matter what.

Growing up, Brett had hated that custom, and once he'd left home he had dropped it. He had been stubbornly casual for the evening meal whenever possible, almost to the point of obsession. Yet he had only to enter Killara again for the old habit to resurrect itself.

After a long moment, during which he stared into the reflection of his own eyes, he finished his tie. Slowly, reluctantly, he turned toward the gleaming oak dresser across the room. There was a man's jewelry case on the dresser, a case he recognized because it was very old; he'd seen it first in this room as a child, when his grandfather had slept there.

It wasn't locked; he hadn't expected it to be. And despite its almost priceless value, the ring was inside the case awaiting him, a ring passed from father to eldest son in the Delaney family for centuries. All the other Delaney jewelry would be in bank vaults or the safe downstairs, Brett knew; there had been an insurance inventory with the will. But this ring had been placed here when he'd arrived, by Moira or by Cassie, because it was his now and belonged in his room.

The ring was exquisite with its large emerald of exceptional color and clarity that had been cut in the shape of a shamrock and put into a heavy gold setting. Brett could vividly remember it on his grandfather's hand, and his father's. He could remember as a child being fascinated by the way the emerald captured light and reflected it in brilliant shards of green fire.

And he could remember, as he'd grown older, how the ring had come to symbolize everything about his heritage that had smothered him. Passed down through the generations, it represented a gleaming chain, binding past, present, and future with unbreakable links.

Delaney. It was more than merely a family name. While other great families had gradually died out in power or in truth, the Delaney clan had continued to thrive and the name had grown even more renowned. Each generation had left a legacy of its own, adding more branches to the family tree and more color to the legend.

Delaney. A family of wealth that had never forgotten their own humble beginnings. A family of power that had seldom used force ruthlessly. A family whose history always had been very important, and always preserved for future generations. A family that always had been conscious of itself *as* a family, bound together by blood.

That was his heritage. He had gone halfway around the world to escape it, believing he could make a life for himself that had nothing to do with his ancestors or his name. Believing he wasn't bound by blood ties. Believing there was nothing stamped in his genes except the tendency toward black hair and stubbornness. And what had he done? He'd begun building an empire of his own, using innate business acumen to amass a fortune in only a few short years.

The Delaney name, as always, meant success.

He turned his head slowly and looked at the crate in the corner of the room. The mirror had sent him away in bitterness, and brought him back a decade later; it was another chain binding him to his heritage. Only a Delaney could see more than his own reflection in the mirror. Only a Delaney could be master of Killara.

As if someone else were doing it, Brett watched as the gleaming emerald ring slipped over the third finger of his right hand. It was a big, heavy ring, designed for an unusually large and powerful hand. In centuries it had never been too large for the hand intended to wear it.

It fit Brett perfectly.

He heard his own voice, hushed in the stillness of the bedroom, and the sound held the acceptance of a reluctant truth he could no longer deny.

"I *am* home."

2

WHEN BRETT WENT DOWNSTAIRS TO THE DINING ROOM, HE HALF expected to find himself alone at the table. But Cassie was there, standing by the big bay window and gazing out into a moonlit night. She was wearing a silky dress in a pale gray that matched her eyes, the material clinging to her slender body, and her golden hair was piled atop her head in an elegant style that gave her height as well as dignity.

The table was set for two, the extra leaves gone so that they wouldn't be forced to look at each other across acres of polished wood. Though the place settings were made up of good china, it wasn't the best china.

Brett felt a faint flicker of reluctant amusement, realizing that Moira's welcome for his return was tempered more than a little. The entree wasn't on the table yet, but he had a sudden intuition that it would consist of some kind of chicken—simply because it had never been a favorite of his.

He opened his mouth to share the idea with Cassie, but then remembered the last words that had passed between them. Considering what he'd said to her, he doubted she would be in the mood to be amused. After a slight hesitation he went to the sideboard and silently poured himself a glass of wine. It was rare that he drank the real stuff; synthetic alcohol was much better for the body and certainly less hazardous for the brain, besides being much more common and substantially less expensive. But Killara had always had a well-stocked cellar, and it was one family perk he appreciated.

He sipped the wine, and as the heat of it began spreading through him, heard himself say, "You look lovely."

Cassie turned from the window to meet his steady gaze. She had a glass of wine, and lifted it slightly in a gesture that seemed to him mocking. "Thanks." Her face was very still. Her eyes focused on his hand for a moment, and he realized she was looking at the ring.

"I was out of line before," he said, unwilling to make the situation between them worse than it already was. "I apologize, Cassie."

"For saying it, or thinking it?"

He didn't have a ready answer for that one, and shrugged. "Whichever you prefer."

"I prefer the truth."

Before he could stop himself, Brett said, "Be careful what you ask for, you might get it."

She drew a quick breath, as if she'd been kicked or hurt in some way, then smiled brightly. "I see."

His earlier tension in her presence had returned, only this time it was growing stronger. "What do you see?"

Her gray eyes were as enigmatic as mountain fog. "I see a lot of Kane in you," she said softly.

Brett didn't like hearing that, and he knew the reaction showed on his face. "My father," he said, every word spaced precisely for emphasis, "was a stubborn, bitter, self-righteous bastard. Any dispute never had two sides, only one. Only his side."

With a precision of her own Cassie lifted her glass and one eyebrow in a slight toast that said, more clearly than words, *exactly*.

Whatever retort Brett might have made was lost as Moira came into the room with a platter. "Sit down now," she ordered casually after a quick glance at the stiff posture of the two. "I don't want this to get cold."

They avoided getting near each other as they took their places at the table, and Brett was so angry he barely noticed that the entree *was* chicken. He also barely tasted it. The silence in the room grew more and more strained, broken only by the muted sounds of silverware clicking against china.

He would have gotten up to get more wine when the first glass was emptied, but he didn't want Cassie to think he needed it. It occurred to him that he didn't seem to have much more control around her now than he'd had ten years ago, and he didn't like that at all. Whatever Cassie said to him or thought about him, he had no intention of letting her get under his skin.

So he remained silent, eating without tasting a thing, and when Cassie rose after the meal and left the room, he followed her. His tension hadn't abated one bit, and even though he had put a rein on his anger, it was still there.

She went into one of several dens the house boasted, where a fire blazed in a big rock fireplace. The furnishings in the room were casual and comfortable; like most rooms of the house, the style here was eclectic, and covered a broad range from early American to one extremely modern piece, a sensory chair.

It was obvious to Brett that this was the room Cassie had chosen for relaxing in the evenings. There were magazines stacked untidily in a basket beside an old wing-back reading chair near the hearth, a good audio system with an assortment of tapes and discs, and the latest thing in video systems surrounded by shelves holding an impressive videotape collection.

Cassie went to the fireplace as though drawn by the warmth, her body rigid and her face closed. Brett went to the wing-back chair but didn't sit down; instead, he leaned against the back of it and watched her. He didn't realize his stare was so intense until she shifted restlessly and jerked her head around to meet his gaze.

"Will you *stop* watching me like a cat at a mousehole," she demanded in a very quiet, brittle voice.

"Sorry." He didn't sound it, and for the first time he wondered what he was trying to do. Force a confrontation of some kind? No, he didn't want that, he thought. He didn't want to hear what she would undoubtedly tell him if he forced her to drop the polite mask. So what was he trying to do? He didn't know. He couldn't think.

Cassie half closed her eyes for an instant, then spoke in a very steady voice. "Well, this is obviously not going to work, is it?"

"What isn't going to work?"

"The two of us in the same house. In this house. I should have known, but I'd hoped...Anyway, since you'll be staying, I should—"

Brett interrupted her flatly. "I said I was going back to Sydney."

Her eyes flicked to the ring he wore, then returned to his face. "No, I don't think so. I don't know why you decided to come back here, but the instant you set foot on this place, it got into your blood again. You're home, Brett. And you'll stay."

This time he couldn't deny it. Instead, he merely said, "We'll see."

Cassie shook her head. "As I said, it's obvious this won't work. I'll leave."

"No." It was an instant refusal, an instinctive one; he didn't even realize he was going to say it until he uttered the flat, hard words.

Her chin lifted slightly. "If you'd gone back to Sydney, I would have stayed on to manage the place. If you'd asked me to, of course. That's why Kane—" She broke off for an instant, then continued evenly, "That's why Kane left me in charge. So there'd be someone who cared about Killara living here. But since you're going to stay—"

"I don't know that I am going to stay," he told her brusquely. "But whether I decide to or not, you have a responsibility here, Cassie. I've been gone ten years. Whatever I once knew about running this place was forgotten a long time ago. You don't want to see me ruin the ranch just for the satisfaction of watching me fail, do you?"

She stared at him, her arms crossed at her waist, almost hugging herself. There was a strange look in her eyes; he could have sworn it was pain. Then a little sigh escaped her, and her shoulders seemed to slump.

Almost inaudibly she said, "Maybe I'm as much a prisoner of Killara as you are. This place is in my blood, even though I'm not a Delaney."

Brett had been leaning against the chair but straightened at her soft words. His own voice was as hard as before. "But you are a Delaney. By marriage."

There was a long, taut silence, their eyes locked together as if in some unspoken struggle. Then Cassie looked away and gave a ragged little sigh. She was very pale. "Never mind," she murmured, and it seemed to Brett that she was talking to herself. "It doesn't matter now, I guess." She flicked him a glance as she began walking toward the door. "I've had a long day. Good night, Brett."

He waited until she was at the door before he asked a question that he was half afraid to have answered. "Cassie? Am I really so much like him?"

"Yes," she said, and walked out without looking back.

What had brought him back here? Cassie didn't know, and she was afraid to ask him. She was afraid he'd seen something in the mirror, something so terrible that it had brought him back for the first time in ten years. But if he had, it was clear he wasn't ready to tell her about it.

She made herself think about that, because it hurt too much to think about him.

Cassie knew the history of the mirror, just as she knew the history of the Delaney family. The family history was fairly well documented in public sources for anyone who cared to look them up, especially as the Delaneys had always made news. The mirror, on the other hand, was a more private thing, and Cassie had learned its story only after Brett had left and no more than a few months before her wedding to Kane Delaney.

She had practically haunted the house after Brett had gone, hoping for some word of him, and Kane had eventually put her to work on the household accounts to occupy her mind, he'd said, and because he could use the help. That was how it had started, their odd relationship. It wasn't long after when he'd begun telling her some of the more private bits of family history. And, finally, about the mirror.

When the crate had arrived back at Killara that day, she had been tempted to look into the mirror again. Even after she'd had it sent up to the master suite and ordered it to remain crated, she had considered going up there.

You are a Delaney. By marriage.

It seemed the mirror agreed with Brett. It had shown her something other than her reflection when she had looked into it more than eight years ago, even though she hadn't married Kane until months after.

Was the mirror always right? Kane had believed it was. Most of his ancestors, she was sure, had also believed in the mirror. There was a fatalistic strain in the Delaney family, going far back to their Irish roots. For all their famed strength of will, not even the Delaneys had dared to take on fate.

But was the mirror always right? *Was* it a window into time, what it revealed of the future destined to be truth no matter what? It was a mocking thing, Kane had once said to her, revealing only what it chose, to whom it chose. He had looked in it often, she knew; it had hung in his dressing room, and he'd kept the key to that small room on a gold chain around his neck. He had wanted to see more than his own reflection, but the mirror had shown him the future only once, more than thirty years before.

Then it had shown him the death of Brett's mother.

That was really why Cassie had not looked into the mirror a second time in all the years since her marriage. She didn't want to see a tragedy. She didn't even want to see the future, no matter what it held—because she had seen it once. She had seen her wedding to Kane. And there must have been a fatalistic strain in her own blood, she thought, because that as much as anything else had prompted her to accept when Kane had asked her to marry him.

Cassie thought about that as she slowly climbed the stairs and made her way to her room. It was on the same corridor as the master suite, but at the opposite end, a bedroom/bathroom/sitting area that was very roomy and comfortable. Even if she did still sometimes feel like a guest in this house, these rooms were her sanctuary.

She went in and changed into a long nightgown and robe, and took her hair down. It was still fairly early, but a lifetime on a ranch had trained her to be up with the dawn, so she was usually in bed well before midnight.

Tonight, however, she was wide awake and restless. Her thoughts were tangled, and she was grateful when a soft knock on her door interrupted them.

"I wanted to make sure you were all right," Moira said a bit gruffly when Cassie opened the door. "I saw you leave him downstairs, and you looked upset again."

She managed a faint smile for the housekeeper. "You'd think I could stay calm, as much practice as I had with Kane."

"It's not the same," Moira said. "Kane taunted everybody around him for the pleasure of it, but Brett taunts you because he's hurting."

Cassie didn't ask Moira to come into the bedroom, because she knew the older woman wouldn't. Instead, she leaned against the doorjamb and sighed tiredly. "Maybe. Or maybe he inherited more than devil-black eyes from his father."

"Do you really believe that?"

"I don't know what I believe. All I know is that he didn't want to come home—and he sure as hell didn't want to see me. He thinks my motive for marrying Kane was to get my hands on the Delaney fortune."

Somewhat dryly Moira said, "Well, to be fair about the matter, it's a safe bet no one's told him anything different. I suppose it was the only reason he could come up with for a twenty-year-old girl to marry a man of sixty-four."

"I don't care what he believes." Then Cassie belied that fierce statement by adding, "If he could think that about me, it's obvious he never knew me at all ten years ago. Besides, why am I being punished for something that was his fault?"

Moira's voice was mild. "Why don't you ask him?"

After a moment Cassie looked away. "Maybe I will. I'm all right, Moira, really. I just need a good night's sleep, and everything will be clearer tomorrow."

"Then I'll see you in the morning," the housekeeper said, obviously aware that Cassie was through confiding for the time being. "Good night. Sleep well."

But that last, Cassie reflected later, was much easier said than done. Her mind wouldn't shut itself off, and this time it wasn't occupied with thoughts of the Delaney family in general, or of a strange mirror. This time all she could think of as she paced restlessly was Brett.

He was back, back in her life after ten long years without him. He hadn't changed very much physically. He was more powerful at thirty-two, his shoulders broader and heavier with muscle, and he seemed taller than she remembered. His face was harder, she thought, and his black eyes were shuttered.

Had he been cruel ten years ago? No—except when he'd left without a word. But she thought he was capable of cruelty now, even if he didn't enjoy it the way Kane had sometimes enjoyed it. Though Moira had remarked on the difference between father and son, Cassie wasn't so sure. She thought Brett was becoming very much like his father, and that hurt her.

It had shocked him to hear her say so, shocked him and angered him, she thought. Maybe it wasn't too late for Brett, maybe the best traits of the Delaneys would shine in him as they hadn't in his father. Cassie hoped so, for his sake. She hoped so, because she had fallen in love with his smile when she was thirteen years old, and had felt the first astonishing heat of passion at the touch of his kisses five years later.

She found herself standing by the window in her bedroom, staring blindly out at the night.

What had happened? Even now the only answer she had was a conclusion she'd reached on her own, arrived at through too many long hours of painfully repeating that question and sorting through her memories.

The passion between them had grown hotter and hotter as the summer had worn on, until finally it had exploded and had nearly consumed both of them. She had been lost, mindless with desire, whispering her love with all the aching intensity of the very young, and offering up everything she was to him. But Brett had stopped, tearing himself away from her with obvious reluctance. He'd muttered something about her being too young, and he'd left her there.

The next day he was gone.

I asked too much of him, Cassie thought as she gazed bleakly out the window at the dark, cold landscape of Killara in winter. *I demanded, like Kane. And he ran from both of us.*

Brett wasn't that volatile young man now. He was a man who had spent a decade working to build his own life, his own success, to make a name for himself independent of his ancestors, especially his father. He was older, undoubtedly wiser, certainly more secure in himself.

And he hated her because she'd married his father.

Cassie turned away from the window, trying to escape her thoughts. She looked at the clock on her nightstand and swore softly when she saw it was after midnight. She'd wrestled with her thoughts for hours. At this rate she'd never get to sleep, and she could hardly afford to lose any more. Ever since she'd shipped the mirror to Brett, she'd spent her nights tossing and turning restlessly, torn between the hope that he'd come home—and the dread that he'd come home.

She debated silently, then left her room. Because of a bend in the hallway, she couldn't see the master suite from her doorway, so she didn't know if Brett had gone to bed. Still, it was a big house, and all she wanted was to slip down to the kitchen and fix a little cocoa to help her sleep. Surely she could manage that without a problem.

The house was quiet, a few scattered lamps burning, as they always did, to hold back the darkness. Cassie knew that Moira and her husband, Hank, would have gone to bed hours before, since both would rise early. Hank was a sort of caretaker at Killara, overseeing everything not covered by his wife in the house and the ranch foreman outside; his duties extended from occasional head gardener and handyman to chauffeur and bellman.

Until Brett had come home, it had been just the two of them and Cassie in the house.

With every year that passed, Cassie had become more and more conscious of the emptiness of the house. Even when Kane had been alive and making his presence felt, Killara had an air of emptiness. Now it was worse. This place had been intended for a large family, she thought again as she made her way silently downstairs. The house had sprawled as the Delaney family had grown. And in the future? Would this great house ever again hold a large family?

Or was Brett truly the last of the Delaneys?

Cassie heard the wind pick up outside, and shivered as she heated the cocoa. Morbid thoughts—and only because of the strange weather, she assured herself. It had been an unusual winter so far, threatening snow half a dozen times in November, and the remaining winter months were likely to make good on the threat. She had ordered all the stock brought in from the outlying ranges and had laid in a large supply of feed and hay, but she was still worried about the weather.

This far south, the stock was rarely forced to endure rough winters, which meant that a really bad turn in the weather could kill even strong and healthy animals unaccustomed to freezing winds and snow.

Brooding over that possibility, Cassie took her cocoa and absently wandered toward one of her favorite rooms in the house, a two-level Baroque-style library filled with thousands of volumes on mahogany shelves. Cassie had often found peace in the room, even if in the end she had found nothing in particular that she wanted to read.

This time, however, she found neither peace nor an interesting book. She found Brett.

He was sprawled in an easy chair, his long legs stretched out before him. He'd discarded his coat and tie, his sleeves were rolled up over his forearms, and his shirt was unbuttoned partway down his chest. He was awake, but there was something about his eyes she didn't like. Then she saw the empty wine bottle and glass on the floor by his chair.

"Don't go," he said.

She had taken a step back toward the door, but hesitated when he spoke. Whether he was accustomed to raw alcohol or not, she thought he'd probably inherited the traditional Delaney hard head, and he certainly didn't sound drunk.

"I didn't know you were in here," she said. "Sorry. I was just going to find something to read."

Brett leaned his head back against the chair, watching her with hooded eyes. "Don't mind me." His voice was low, a bit raspy.

After a slight hesitation she moved to the shelves nearest the door and began scanning titles. Or tried to, at least. She felt nervous, and it showed when she started to pull a book from a shelf at random, only to have it fall loudly to the floor. Cassie knelt to pick up the book, cursing silently because she seemed to be all thumbs.

It was because he was watching her, but she didn't want to admit that to herself. She was able to deny it for another few minutes, until she reached the shelves nearest his chair. Then she looked at him without meaning to, and something about the way he gazed at her stole her breath. She couldn't seem to move; she just stood there holding her mug in front of her almost as if it were a shield that would protect her.

Cassie was vividly conscious of his stare, just as she was aware of the growing heat inside her. This wasn't the cool stranger who had frozen her with his unreadable glances and flat voice. There was something unnervingly primitive about him, as if the wine or something else had torn away layers of protection between him and the world.

His night-black eyes were sleepy yet hot, burning her as they wandered leisurely down over her clinging nightgown and robe. His thick black hair looked as if he'd run his fingers through it carelessly, a lock falling onto his forehead in a way that made her fingers itch to touch it. He was slouched in the chair, his arms resting loosely so that his powerful hands were relaxed, the long fingers slack. The emerald shamrock caught the light and gleamed, the ring fitting him so perfectly, it was as if it had been designed for him.

He was so still.

Clearing her throat, Cassie said, "I don't think I want to read after all. It's too late to start a book anyway."

His mouth curved in a faint smile. "Afraid, Cassie?"

"Of course not."

Brett made a little sound that might have been satisfaction. "I think you are. Why? Don't you think I'd respect my father's widow?" There was an added emphasis on the last two words, and a muscle tightened in his jaw.

She kept her voice even. "I think you're drunk, Brett."

He shook his head slowly, his eyes never leaving her face. "No. Oh, I tried—but it's in the genes, you know, like so many other things. All the Delaneys could hold their whiskey, so I can sure as hell hold my wine. I've got a dead soldier, though, and I don't feel much like going down into the wine cellar right now. I don't suppose you've anything interesting in that mug?"

"Cocoa."

One of his eyebrows rose, and the sensual curve of his lips went a little lopsided with amusement. "I don't think I believe you. Cocoa? No, that'd be too tame for the Cassie I remember." The smile faded. "Or did my father do the taming?"

She took two quick steps toward him, then halted. Her heart was thudding, and the quick anger his words had brought almost choked her. Would he believe the truth? No, she didn't think he would. He was too bitter. And she was too angry suddenly to go on skirting the subject warily. She was *not* going to just stand there and let him taunt her.

In a soft voice she said, "I didn't leave, Brett. Do you hear me? *I* didn't leave. My relationship with your father is none of your business."

He came up out of the chair in the swift, fluid motion of a striking cobra, and was standing an arm's length in front of her before she could do more than gasp. His eyes, still hooded, were burning yet curiously blind, and his lean face was so hard, it was like a stone mask. He didn't touch her.

"It is my business," he said, deadly quiet. "You loved me. Or was that a lie?"

Cassie had to tilt her head back to meet those dangerous eyes. She was still angry, and her voice shook with it when she answered him. "No, it wasn't a lie. But that hardly matters now, does it? Whatever I felt then, you're the one who left—without even saying good-bye."

Brett didn't seem to hear her. "You loved me. How could you marry him when you loved me?"

She caught her breath with what was almost a sob. "He was *here*, Brett. Not on the other side of the world trying to prove he wasn't a Delaney."

His unfocused gaze sharpened, and his mouth twisted as if it hurt him to look at her. "And since I wasn't around, any Delaney would do, huh?"

Cassie's mug fell to the floor, staining the rug between them with cocoa, and her slender hand cracked across his cheek with all the strength she could muster. As delicate as she was, her fury jarred him; if he'd had a little less wine, it might have even sobered him. In any case, it wasn't her slap but her words that triggered his own eruption.

"At least Kane didn't run away in a panic when a woman told him she loved him," she said unsteadily.

Brett reached out and yanked her against him, his arms closing around her like iron bands. His mouth covered hers with almost bruising force, and one hand tangled in her long hair to hold her steady as he took what he wanted.

For the space of a few heartbeats Cassie was rigid in his powerful embrace. Her arms strained to push him away from her, and her lips were tight beneath the pressure of his. But then her body recognized his touch, even though it had been years, and a wave of hot need swept over her. She felt herself soften and then helplessly melt against him.

The force of him eased just a little when she responded, but his intensity only increased. He plundered her mouth, his tongue stroking deeply in an act of possession, and his arms gathered her even closer.

Cassie felt the hard thighs against her own part slightly, and when he curved a hand over her bottom to press her into the hollow of his body, she almost cried out in shock and desire.

But even in that moment of utter longing she realized something. And this time it wasn't Brett who stopped. This time it was she.

The suddenness of Cassie's retreat caught Brett off guard. One moment she was in his arms, burning him with her searing response to his need, the next moment she was pushing him away. Her haunting eyes glittered almost silver, wet with tears, and her voice was ragged.

"Stop it! I won't let you use me to get even with him. He's *dead*, Brett. We buried him in the old cemetery, the way he wanted. You can't hurt each other anymore. It doesn't matter now which one of you was stronger, or which one was right."

"Cassie—"

"*No*. You might not be able to stomach the idea that I married your father, but you damn well have to accept it, because I did. And you have no right—*no right*—to act as if I betrayed you! You didn't ask me to marry you; you didn't ask me to go with you; you didn't even say good-bye. You just left. And for ten years I didn't hear a single word from you. If Kane hadn't kept track of you, I wouldn't have known whether you were alive or dead. So don't you *dare* come back here and start making noises like a jealous lover. And don't think for one minute that I'll lay down for you just because I'm the only weapon left that you can use against your father's memory!"

Brett lifted a hand almost instinctively, reaching out to her, but she whirled without another word and hurried from the room. He was left staring at the doorway, alone with all the painful realizations she'd flung in his face.

At Killara one stepped back into the past, Brett thought as he saddled a horse. The early morning air was bitterly cold. The ranch hands had already ridden out, so there'd been no one in the barn except a couple of maintenance people. Brett had ignored their covert glances; they knew who he was because he looked too much like his father, and he was in no mood for polite chitchat. He had remembered both where the pleasure horses were kept stabled and where the tack was stored; it seemed he couldn't escape his knowledge or memories.

He swung up into the saddle while still inside the barn hall, and used automatic skill to urge the muscled chestnut to move. The horse obeyed, striding out of the barn in a swift walk. Brett absently adjusted his hat, blinking as the wind stung his hot, tired eyes.

He had stopped in the kitchen for coffee on his way out of the house after having paced his room until dawn. Moira had looked up from making biscuits, but hadn't said anything beyond a polite good morning until he'd set his cup down and started for the door.

"There's an old hat of your father's still hanging in the closet by the door. You'd better take it. Hank went out earlier, and said it's bitter cold."

For a brief instant Brett had resisted the idea of wearing anything that had belonged to his father. But then he'd glanced down at the ring on his finger, reminded himself that he was in a house where

Kane Delaney had spent more than seventy years, and finally accepted the futility of mulish gestures.

So he got the hat from the closet and put it on, unsurprised when it fit him perfectly.

Now, riding slowly away from the outbuildings and toward a windswept hill that overlooked both the ranch house and a rolling valley beyond, Brett drew the cold air into his lungs in deep breaths. His body instinctively adapted to the movements of the horse as those memories came back to him, and he signaled the animal to lope with the same involuntary skill.

His eyes blurred a little from the strength and chill of the wind, but he nonetheless saw the weathered headstones long before he drew his horse to a halt at the cemetery. He sat for a moment, looking at the final resting place of most of his ancestors, then dismounted. The chestnut, as well trained as all Delaney horses were, obediently stood ground-tied and rested a back hoof as he waited patiently for the ride to continue.

Brett knew where his father was buried because of the newness of the marble headstone and because there was an arrangement of artificial flowers at its base, but he didn't go directly there. Instead, he wandered among the other graves, reading the names and dates. The long-denied family history came flooding into his mind, and this time he didn't try to avoid thinking about it.

The old stories were so familiar. Had he listened so well as a child, or was even that stamped into his genes because he was a Delaney? A kind of racial memory, perhaps? He didn't know.

Shamus and Malvina. Joshua and Rising Star. The first Patrick. All the Patricks. And the others. Most of them had come home to Killara, if only to rest for good. Most had led long and colorful lives. It seemed most had been happy. Certainly they had been proud of their family and its name. If any had found the weight of being a Delaney onerous or unbearable, the chronicles of the family had made no mention of it.

Brett stood there for a long time, hands in the pockets of his thick jacket, his head bowed, while the cold wind whistled all around him. How many men, he wondered, could stand in one place as he stood there and see all the branches of his family from the spread of centuries? What man in this day and age could have so clear an idea of his own beginnings?

Curse or blessing? Had he fought against being a Delaney all these years because that was what he hated, or had there been a deeper, far more complex reason?

He turned slowly and made his way across the cemetery to his father's grave. The headstone was plain, in keeping with all the others, and the inscription was brief. Just his father's name, the dates of his birth and death—and a single line.

It was his nature.

Brett murmured the words aloud, a dim memory tapping away at the back of his mind.

"Do you remember that story?"

He turned his head to find Cassie standing only a couple of feet away from him. Wrapped in a quilted jacket and with her golden hair tucked up underneath a woolen cap, she was so lovely it made his throat ache. But her eyes were shuttered, and her voice had been impersonal.

"No," he said finally. "I don't remember."

"It's an old fable, actually. But Kane had his own version. He told it often. I think he used it to explain himself, or maybe as an excuse for being the way he was."

"Tell me."

Cassie's voice remained dispassionate. "A turtle and a scorpion found themselves on one side of a wide river. The scorpion wanted to cross it, and so he asked the turtle to carry him over. The turtle refused, saying that the scorpion would sting him to death. But the scorpion pleaded, because he really wanted to cross the river, and he promised the turtle that he'd be completely safe. Finally, the turtle gave in. The scorpion climbed up on his back, and the turtle began swimming the wide river. Halfway across, the scorpion stung the turtle.

"As he began to sink, the turtle said, 'Now we'll both die. Why did you do it?' And the scorpion said, 'Because it's my nature.' "

After a moment Brett returned his gaze to the headstone. "Was the inscription your idea?"

"No. His. It's as close to an apology as you'll ever get, Brett. You Delaney men are so damned stubborn, you'd rather die than say you're sorry."

"Was he sorry?"

She drew a quick breath and released it impatiently, fogging the air for a brief moment. "Sorry you left? I think so, especially since you were the only one on Killara who was equal to his weight."

"He never asked me to come home."

"To Delaney stubbornness, add pride. He wouldn't let me call you when he found out he was dying."

Brett turned to face her. "I would have come if I'd known."

"I know. So did Kane. But he just couldn't bring himself to ask you. Maybe...because it was his nature. Is it your nature, Brett? Do you wound for the pleasure of it, willing even to destroy yourself in the process?"

"No," he said roughly.

Cassie's smile held disbelief. "Really? I was under the impression that was why you came back here. Because you felt like punishing someone, and you decided I was a good target."

Brett stiffened, but he could hardly blame her for thinking as she did. Not after some of the things he'd said to her. He turned his head slowly and gazed down on Killara. The smoke curling peacefully from several chimneys reminded him of the mirror's prophesy.

Looking back at Cassie's beautiful face, he sighed heavily. "I came back because I had to. Because I saw Killara burning, and I have to find a way to stop it."

3

_____

CASSIE INSTANTLY LOOKED TOWARD KILLARA, AS IF TO SEARCH FOR signs of flames, then returned her gaze to Brett's face. Her own face was suddenly very pale, her eyes clouded. "You saw the house burning? In—in the mirror?"

"So you know about it. I wondered."

She hesitated for only a second. "Kane told me. The mirror sometimes shows the past, present, or future...for the Delaneys. Are you sure it was the future you saw?"

"Yes, I'm sure. The near future. Sometime between now and the new year."

She took a few steps toward him, her cloudy eyes searching his face. Then, slowly, she said, "Kane believed that what the mirror revealed of the future couldn't be altered, that it was destined to happen no matter what anyone did."

"I can't believe that's true. Not this time. Everything inside me— all the feelings I've denied about this place for so long—tells me that

I *can* protect Killara, that I can save it. I may have been a lousy Delaney up to this point, but I fight when my back's to the wall, just like old Shamus and all the others . . . and I'll die a bloody death before I'll let anyone destroy Killara."

Cassie glanced at Kane's grave, half expecting to hear a satisfied chuckle. And maybe she did—or maybe it was only the wind.

She cleared her throat and nodded as she looked back up at Brett. "I see. Well, I can't really say I'm surprised. I think I always had a hunch you'd come back here one day."

"Did you?"

"As I said—this place gets into the blood, whether you want it to or not." She kept her voice deliberately dispassionate. "Besides, sooner or later you were bound to see that it was Kane and his expectations you were trying to escape, not being a Delaney."

Her perception surprised him, but he wondered if it should have. After what she'd said to him the night before, he had the somewhat unsettling idea that Cassie understood him far better than he ever could have imagined.

Naturally, he shied away from thinking about that, however, and kept the conversation firmly on the threat against Killara rather than on more personal matters. Focusing on that shut out all the other things he didn't want to think about . . . or feel about. Like Cassie and the effect she had on him. Like the grave at his feet, and the relationship with his father that had been denied a resolution.

"Whatever I may or may not have been trying to escape, it seems I'm back here at least for the time being," he said evenly. "And I have to find a way to protect Killara. I'm not interested in anything else. Just Killara. That means I have to know everything you know about any enemy."

Cassie felt colder than she had before, and it wasn't because the chill wind had picked up to whistle frigidly around them, or because of the threat against Killara—frightening as that was. Something else frightened her more. It was obvious to her that Brett had no intention of letting her get close to him. Last night he'd had too much wine, which, combined with his uneasiness and ambivalence at being back home after so long, had temporarily lowered some of his barriers to intimacy.

He had wanted her. Over and above his anger and bitterness, he had wanted her, she knew. She had felt his honest desire. But now, in the wintry chill of day, he behaved as if nothing had happened between them, as if that scene had never taken place. Brett's walls were back up.

Even the brief conversation about his father had been devoid of emotion. Damn these Delaney men! They felt so much, yet it seemed from the evidence she had that expressing feelings was easy for them only when the feelings were negative. Make a Delaney man angry, and he'd tell you more than you wanted to hear, she reflected bitterly; move him in any other way, and he'd turn to stone.

At least that was true of the two Delaney men she had known well.

"Cassie?"

She blinked, then glanced around them at the windswept hill. "It's cold," she said finally. And lonely. "Why don't we finish this back at the house? Moira'll have breakfast ready. Then we can talk."

Brett stayed silent as they mounted their horses and rode back down the hill to the barns. In a way, he would have preferred to remain at the cemetery, because the cold wind had made his face tingle and his eyes water, and had kept his thoughts sharply focused away from Cassie. He wasn't sure he could manage the feat without the help of the elements or a barren landscape.

He had realized, in the dark predawn hours, that too many of her accusations had been on target. He *did* feel like a betrayed lover, hurt and bitter that she had married another man—especially because that man was his father. And he had had some wild thoughts of punishing either Cassie or Kane when he had looked at her and felt desire.

He had to master the corrosive emotions, he knew, before they mastered him. In the first place, Cassie had been right—he *had* left, and without a word to tell her that he had cared. Despite her hunch that he might return, there was no way she could have expected him to come back, not really. And she'd certainly had no reason to expect him to come back to *her;* he had walked out of her life without a backward glance. So her marriage was none of his business, just as she'd said, and he had no right to feel betrayed or to be jealous of his father's place in her life.

That was the rational way to look at it, of course, and he'd been struggling to do so ever since she had left him in the library.

Rational. That was a laugh. His mind couldn't control his emotions. Every time he thought of Cassie with his father, it was like some awful wound inside him throbbed in raw pain. The pain led him to make harsh accusations, such as saying that she had married his father only to cut him out of his inheritance.

He had to *control* this, he told himself fiercely as they unsaddled the horses in the barn. Whatever was between him and Cassie, he couldn't afford the time or the energy to thrash it out now, not while Killara was threatened.

He silently wrestled with that problem all through breakfast. Cassie was just as silent, and didn't seem to have much of an appetite even though she didn't forget to compliment Moira on her cooking. Brett followed suit, but to his sincere appreciation the housekeeper responded with only a brief smile.

"She hasn't forgiven me," he noted a few minutes later as he and Cassie went into his father's study.

Cassie sat down at the desk and turned on the computer before she replied. "Did you expect all to be forgiven just because you came home, Brett?"

"No, I suppose not." Brett thought that perhaps he had, though. Another famed Delaney trait that might have been unconscious arrogance or simply a cockeyed optimism. By and large, most of the Delaneys, especially the men, had been forgiven a great deal in their lives. That black-Irish charm, some said. Or just the famed Delaney luck.

But Brett couldn't pick up where he'd left off and pretend that ten years hadn't passed, charm or luck notwithstanding. Too much had happened with him and at Killara for that to be possible.

Cassie didn't continue with the subject. Instead, she keyed a command into the computer and then leaned back as she looked across the desk at Brett. "I've asked that all the corporate files be dumped into the mainframe here; I was given the access code a long time before Kane died."

Hearing or sensing something a little defensive in that last statement, Brett heard himself say, "I wasn't going to accuse you of anything, Cassie."

Her face was expressionless. "I just wanted you to know that I haven't had anything to do with running the corporation. Kane deeded a few shares of his family stock over to me, but it certainly isn't enough for any kind of control, as you well know. He always trusted the board to run the company, and I haven't interfered in any way since his death."

"All right," Brett said finally in a level voice. "Duly noted." Having inherited his father's stock to add to that which had been his since birth, Brett was now far and away the majority stockholder of Delaney Enterprises.

She pushed back her chair and rose to her feet. "I don't know what you might find in all these files," she said, gesturing to the quietly humming computer, "but if you're looking for an enemy of the Delaney family, I suppose it's as good a place as any to start."

"You don't know of an enemy?" he asked.

"No. That is, no particular enemy. Kane seldom made friends in business, of course, but he spent most of his time these last few years here at the ranch. I'm not aware of any decision he made that could have angered someone so much they'd be prepared to destroy this place. Especially after his death. I mean, what would be the point?"

It occurred to Brett for the first time that for someone who had married the man, Cassie quite obviously had a negative view of his late father—and made no attempt to hide it. He wanted to ask about that, but felt reluctant to do so since he'd lost control last night.

What was between him and Cassie seemed to be Pandora's box, and he didn't want to open the lid again. The first time had left him raw and hurting.

Pushing that thought aside, he said, "It'll take days at least, probably weeks, for me to sort through the company and ranch records, and there's no guarantee I'll find anything. I need your help, Cassie."

"I told you, I don't know of an enemy. My responsibility was to run the ranch. And that's all I did. As far as I know, *I* never made an enemy while I was doing it. There haven't been any threats. No letters, no calls, no odd packages delivered here at the house. I haven't fired a ranch hand in more than two years—and the last one I did promptly signed aboard a shuttle for Mars. We haven't lost a worker to an accident in twelve years, which makes it unlikely that any of our people have distraught relatives out to burn Killara. And I can't recall anything unusual happening here recently. Kane may have made the enemy, but if he did, I don't know anything about it. Someone involved in Delaney Enterprises may have made an enemy. But I don't know anything about that either. So I don't think I can help you, Brett."

With every impersonal, matter-of-fact word she uttered, Brett felt himself grow more tense. She was talking, he thought, as if Killara meant nothing to her. She'd thought about the threat—that was obvious from her rundown of possible reasons someone might want to torch the place—but her expressionless face and remote voice declared that she didn't give a damn.

He didn't believe that, not for a minute. What he did believe was that Cassie was very carefully distancing herself—not from the threat so much as from Killara itself and from him. She was trying to make leaving less painful for her. Despite what he'd said the previous evening, and despite her own words about having Killara in her blood, Cassie meant to go.

There was a desk between them, a solid object of oak and glass that was more than a physical barrier. Kane Delaney's desk. In a very real sense it was a symbol of everything between them. And Brett realized as he stood there that Pandora's box or no, he couldn't afford *not* to at least try to settle things with Cassie. Whatever she said about not knowing who an enemy might be, he was all too aware that she knew this place, its day-to-day workings and most recent history, and the enemy had to be somewhere in the recent past of Killara—or of Kane Delaney.

Unwilling to keep that symbol between them, Brett moved slowly around the desk, lifting a hand to stop her when she would have given up her place to him. She watched him warily, visibly tense, but didn't move. He stopped a couple of feet away from her and rested a hip on the corner of the desk. Since she was standing, neither of them had to look up or down to meet the other's eyes, and though they were near each other, there was no invasion of personal space.

So their positions were as unthreatening as possible, and Brett tried to keep his voice pleasant and low-key when he spoke. He had learned a great deal in various business ventures over the years, not the least of which was the importance of finding something to trade for what he wanted. A good deal always began with a clear understanding of what the other side wanted.

"Cassie, I know you have no reason to want to help me. I've been something of a bastard since I got back, and I wouldn't win any prizes for the way I acted before I left. And even though you were raised here, I realize you don't feel any obligation to Killara, especially after the way Dad treated you. He should have left you something; you'd earned that for running the ranch all those years. Tell me what you want. Tell me what I can give you to keep you here."

She had the strangest expression on her face, he thought. A sort of amazed, wondering look, like someone who couldn't believe what they'd heard. And an odd sound left her, a sound that might have been a laugh except that there was no amusement to define it as such.

"My God," she said in a numb voice to match her expression, "you're Kane all over."

Brett stiffened, and his polished, businesslike facade shattered like so much glass. "Dammit, stop saying that," he snapped.

Her eyes narrowed, the incredulity fading, and a tinge of color stole into her cheeks as anger followed. "Why not? You sounded so much like him just now, like him when there was something he wanted. His solution was always the same, no matter what it was he was after. Buy it. Find out what they want and pay the price. The Delaneys can always spare a few dollars—or a few acres of land, or a few head of cattle or horses, or a few shares of stock. They can always spare the material things. That's the price they expect to pay. Nice and businesslike."

Had he really learned his tactics from his own experiences, Brett wondered, or had his father's teachings sunk in despite his resistance? It was a sobering thought. Cassie seemed adept at making him face sobering realizations, and he didn't like it one bit. He felt . . . exposed with her, as if she could see all of him no matter how he tried to hide.

Stiffly, he said, "What do you want me to offer you, Cassie?"

She tilted her head to one side briefly, as if she were studying something almost unbelievable. "That's the sad thing. You don't even realize what you're doing. Pay me something and I'll do what you want? Find my price and you've bought yourself something else? For God's sake, Brett, this place is the only home I've ever known! Do you really believe I need to be paid to stay here?"

"Then why are you planning to leave?" he demanded, ignoring most of what she'd said.

"Because it's time for me to leave. Because you're here now, and you'll stay. Because *you* are a Delaney. I am not. You obviously haven't noticed, but I didn't take your father's name."

Perhaps oddly, Brett hadn't noticed that. It was another bit of information he filed away for later because he wasn't ready to tackle the subject of his father's marriage head-on. Not now. Not yet.

"So far," he said, "I haven't heard a good reason why you should leave. You said it yourself, Cassie—this place is your home." He tried to control his voice. "Maybe my offer sounded a little cold-blooded, but it wasn't meant that way. I need you here, and there must be something I can do to persuade you to stay. For the sake of Killara, if nothing else."

She stared at him for a long moment, then seemed to brace her shoulders. "All right. I do have a price after all, Brett," she said in the carefully even tone of someone who didn't entirely trust their voice.

He nodded. "Then what can I do?" He warily avoided the word *pay*.

"You can tell me why."

"Why? You mean, why I want you to stay?"

"No." She drew a quick breath, and her voice shook as she spoke faster. "Why you left. I want to know what happened, Brett. I want to know if I did something wrong, something that drove you to the other side of the world. I want to know whose fault it was, mine or Kane's." She closed her eyes briefly, and swallowed before she finished in a near whisper, "Just tell me that so I can finally put it behind me."

He was silent for a moment, grappling with feelings that jabbed like poison thorns. He wanted to reach out and pull her into his arms, and fought the urge because he'd faced yet another bitter realization: if Cassie didn't hate him, it would be a miracle.

"Is that what you thought all this time?" he asked huskily. "What you believed? That I left because you said or did something to drive me away?" He remembered then what she'd said the previous night about Kane not running from a woman who said she loved him, and he realized that her words hadn't been intended as a stab at his ego but as the literal truth.

"What else could I think?" she said, her voice still unsteady. "Everything seemed fine, until . . . until that night. I've been over and over it in my mind. Kane said you two didn't fight that night, and I believed him. So it had to be because of me. What I said or what we almost did . . . something."

After so many years spent learning to protect himself from his father's skilled barbs, and then the years spent cultivating a polished business facade that was equally protective, Brett's instinct was to draw back, to retreat so that he wouldn't expose any part of himself to possible injury. For the first time in his life he fought that learned response to strong emotions. The need to heal what he'd done to Cassie was more important to him than his own vulnerability.

He eased off the desk and pushed the chair back out of the way, then took one of her cold hands and led her across the room to the sofa where Kane Delaney had preferred to relax and read his business reports. Brett released her hand when she drew it back, but sat beside her with no more than a foot of space between them. He half turned to face her.

"I'm sorry," he said, his voice low and a little rough.

Cassie looked briefly surprised, and he knew why. There was a difference between saying *I apologize*, and saying, *I'm sorry*, a difference the two Delaney men in her life had made clear. The former was easy and without emotion, less an acknowledgment of fault than a means to pour oil on troubled waters; the latter was a sincere admission of fault with all the regret and remorse that entailed—and it was the first time she'd ever heard it from Brett Delaney.

Even so, her face remained stiff and her eyes were both guarded and shadowed with old pain, and she didn't say anything in response. So he went on quietly, searching for the words to make her understand.

"Cassie, you were so young—and not just in years. I know eighteen's the brink of adulthood in a lot of ways, but you really were young. And so innocent. God, I was the first man to kiss you."

When she looked down suddenly, color stealing into her cheeks, he added huskily, "Do you think I didn't know that? You were so lovely, I could hardly believe it...but I knew. It was as if you'd waited just for me."

"I had," she said almost inaudibly, and lifted her eyes slowly to meet his. They were nakedly honest.

Brett caught his breath and tried to keep his thoughts straight. It was becoming more and more difficult. The way she looked at him made him feel unnervingly primitive. "I was arrogant, but not that conceited," he said with a short laugh. "I just told myself I was lucky you'd been cooped up on the ranch all your life. And I . . . I intended to take advantage of that, Cassie. At first. I couldn't believe that your feelings for me would outlast the summer. What happened between us was so sudden and explosive."

"What about your feelings?" she asked.

Brett hesitated, then sighed roughly. "I didn't think very much about what I felt. I was fascinated by you, maybe even obsessed. When I was with you, I couldn't see anything else. That last night I told myself you were taking things too seriously. That was why I stopped. But by the time I got back to the house, when I could think straight again, I knew. I knew that I was the one taking things too seriously."

"Then that's why you left?"

The pain in her voice cut at him, and he reached out instinctively to touch her cheek. "No. Cassie, I didn't leave because you told me you loved me. I didn't leave because I was afraid of loving you. And I sure as hell didn't leave because we almost made love. It wasn't your fault, I swear. Nothing you did sent me away from here."

"Why, then?" She was bewildered. "Brett, I don't understand. Did you and Kane have a fight?"

He wanted to go on stroking the velvety softness of her cheek, but the little caress was having a peculiar effect on his breathing and blood pressure. Reluctantly, he let his hand fall to rest on the cushion between them.

"No. The old man couldn't have picked a fight with me that night—all I was thinking of was you."

"Kane really never knew why you left?"

Brett hesitated. "He knew, in a way. He must have had a pretty good idea, at least. He saw me coming out of his bedroom, and the dressing room door was open, and I have a feeling I looked . . . upset. He didn't ask, but he must have guessed I'd seen something in the mirror."

Cassie shook her head slowly. "The mirror? Something you saw in the mirror sent you away from here? But Kane kept that door locked. Always. He wore the key on a chain around his neck."

For the first time, Brett looked away from her. He stared at nothing. Or at the past. And he spoke slowly, as if every word were heavy and had to be handled with caution.

"There were several strange things about what happened that night, now that I think back on it. The master suite was at the end of the hall; I'd no business down that far, and I still can't explain what I was doing there. But I found myself standing in the doorway and looking toward the dressing room. The door was open, which surprised me. It was always closed and locked; of course I knew why, but I'd always scoffed at the stories Dad told about the mirror. Even as a kid I hadn't been tempted to try to see into the thing. It was no more than another one of those boring Delaney stories I'd heard all my life, I thought. Something made-up so we'd sound better than we were.

"Anyway, Dad had been downstairs when I'd come up, so I knew he wasn't in his dressing room. I was somehow sure no one was. I walked across the bedroom and went into the dressing room. I knew that was where he kept the mirror, and with everything I was feeling about you, I suddenly wanted to look into it. I wanted to test the famous Delaney magic."

"You really didn't believe in it, did you?" Cassie said.

"No, I didn't believe. But that night I was . . . hell, drifting above the ground. Delighted and scared and feeling like the whole world had turned upside down. If there was any night when magic seemed possible, that was it. So I stood in front of the mirror and looked."

Cassie waited a moment, but he continued to gaze into the past with curiously blank eyes. She was afraid to ask, more afraid not to. "Brett? What was it? What did you see?"

He looked at her slowly, and in the liquid-black depths of his eyes was something hot and raw. But his voice remained quiet, almost conversational. "I saw you, Cassie. I saw you marry my father."

She felt cold as she stared at him, and her thoughts moved sluggishly. For the first time she wondered if the mirror possessed a life of its own, at best impish and at worst diabolical. Because if what he had seen had driven Brett away, and what she had seen had prompted her to accept Kane, then the mirror had not simply foretold events, it had created them.

Hadn't it?

While she wrestled with that intensely unnerving thought, Brett was going on in the same conversational voice.

"I didn't believe—until I saw that. It was so clear. You were marrying my father here at Killara in the chapel. And it wasn't far in the future, because you didn't look different. He slid a plain gold band on your finger, and you smiled up at him, and . . . it was over. The scene vanished. I was looking at myself, one fist raised to smash the damned thing."

Cassie swallowed hard. "But you didn't."

Brett smiled an odd smile. "No, of course not. In all these centuries, no Delaney's ever had the nerve to smash that mirror, even though I'm sure plenty of us have wanted to. As I understand it, the visions have held more pain than pleasure. For me, it was like—well, never mind. Let's just say that leaving was sort of a blind response."

He ran fingers through his hair and sighed heavily. "Until then, I would have said I didn't believe in fate. But when I saw you marrying my father in the mirror, I knew without a shadow of a doubt that it would happen. I couldn't change it. And if I tried to change it, it would be worse, more painful, I was absolutely certain. Remember, I already had doubts that what you'd said you felt for me was real. And Dad was still a handsome man, even charming when he set his mind to it. So the idea was more than possible, I believed. I thought of you, living in the house, married to my father . . . and I left."

"Without a word to Kane?"

"If I had tried to talk to him, I probably would have lost control and I knew it."

Cassie hesitated. "Brett, didn't you even think about asking me to go with you?"

It was his turn to hesitate as he wondered if he could make her understand. "I think there was a moment, an instant when I felt a blind urge to just grab you and run. But then all my doubts and uncertainties came flooding in. You were so damned young. You'd lost your father the year before, and I knew you hadn't gotten over the loss, so how could you really know what you felt about me? My own feelings for you were confused, and I think I was a little afraid of them."

He shrugged in a jerky motion. "Aside from all the emotional uncertainties, a streak of hardheaded practicality reminded me that I didn't even know where I would go, much less what I would do to support myself when I got there. I wasn't about to sell family stock or touch my trust fund—or any other Delaney money. I had a few thousand dollars in a bank account, money I'd earned over the years, and that was it. I couldn't ask you to leave the only home you'd ever known, especially when I had no idea what kind of future I could carve for myself."

Cassie waited for a moment, then said quietly, "There was another reason, wasn't there?"

With all the reluctance of a man of logic and reason facing something his mind told him was impossible, Brett nodded. "Yeah. The mirror. I'd spent most of my life scoffing at the thing, but like so much of my heritage, it seems that when it came to the point, I accepted. The mirror was right, always, and nothing I did could change the fate it predicted. It had shown me a vision of the future that would come true no matter what. I believed that. You were going to marry my father. I couldn't remain here and watch it happen. So I left."

Cassie continued to look at him steadily, even though her vision was blurring a little. So simple, really, but it had never occurred to her that he might have seen something in the mirror to drive him away. Because he had left so suddenly the night they'd almost made love, she had always felt she was somehow to blame for his leaving.

The ironic thing was that if she *hadn't* felt guilty, she probably would have learned to hate him in ten years. He had shut her out of his life so completely that only her agonizing about his reasons had protected her feelings for him.

"Cassie?"

She blinked, feeling her eyes and the tip of her nose sting to warn that tears weren't far off. "What?" she asked huskily.

"I never meant to hurt you. It never occurred to me that you'd blame yourself for my leaving. I thought—or, at least, I convinced myself—that what you felt for me was nothing more than a teenage crush. And with the mirror's promise haunting me, it seemed clear you wouldn't pine for me, at least not for long. I honestly believed whatever you felt for me wouldn't outlast the summer."

If there was an implied question there, Cassie chose to ignore it. "I guess that makes it all right, then," she said, unable to completely suppress a surge of bitterness, though she wasn't sure if it was directed at him or at that damned mirror.

Something flickered in the darkness of his eyes. "No, we both know that isn't true. I just want you to understand my viewpoint, Cassie. My reasons might have been confused and lousy ones, but at the time they seemed insurmountable. I wasn't much more than a kid myself, remember, at least in some ways. Yes, I ran away, and maybe that was a cowardly thing to do." He paused, then continued in a rougher tone. "Maybe if we'd made love that night, I would have found the courage to stay and fight the prophecy. Then again, if we had made love I might have gone anyway. And I might have left you pregnant. I wasn't very responsible in those days."

It was a possibility she'd considered more than once in the years since, but all her agonizing had at least taught her a painful truth. "Mights and maybes don't really mean much, do they?" she murmured. But she couldn't resist adding, "Have you ever thought that if we had made love, you might never have looked in the mirror?"

"Once or twice," he admitted in the same rough tone. "But as you said, mights and maybes don't mean a whole lot. We don't have the luxury of repeating critical moments in our lives, and I can't change what was. Besides that, you were meant to marry *my father*, not me, so—"

Cassie held up a hand to stop him, and saw that it was shaking. Returning it to her lap and clasping it tightly with the other one, she spoke as steadily as she could.

"Brett, since you mean to fight the mirror's prophecy this time, there's something you'd better consider about that other so-called prediction."

His black eyes narrowed. "What do you mean *so-called*?"

"I mean just what I said." She drew a deep breath. "As surely as I know my heart's beating, I know that I would never, *ever* have married Kane as long as you were here. Whatever did or didn't happen between us, marriage to him wasn't even a possibility. I know that. I am sure beyond any shadow of a doubt."

A sudden frown and visible tension made Brett look dangerous. "You're saying you married him only *because* I wasn't here? You must have felt something for him."

Cassie's smile was twisted. "You think so? Well, to be fair, I did feel a number of emotions for Kane. Anger, mostly. Pain sometimes, because he was as liable to sting me as anyone else. There were a few times I even thought I hated him. But that was after we were married." She shrugged. "Not that I went into it with my eyes closed, you understand. I knew what he was."

"Then why in hell did you marry him?" Brett demanded, his voice harsh.

For the first time, Cassie looked away. She stared across the room at a window she didn't really see, because what she saw was the past. "The simple answer? Because you weren't here. Because you'd been gone a long time by then, and even if you eventually came home, it was obvious you hadn't cared for me. You'd shut me out of your life without even a good-bye. I thought you'd probably get married on the other side of the world and bring a wife home to Killara."

"So you did it to get back at me?"

The question didn't surprise her. Cassie shook her head, still gazing at years in the past. "It wasn't about you, Brett. As far as I knew, you couldn't be hurt by anything I did, because I meant nothing to you. It was mostly about me. Mother had remarried and left Killara just a couple of months before Kane proposed, and the only reason I was still here was that he'd hired me to help him with the accounts. I had to make a decision about my future."

"You didn't have to marry him."

She pulled her gaze from the past and back to Brett's lean face. She thought she caught a glimpse of pain in his eyes, but it was fleeting and probably, she decided, her imagination, because his face was expressionless now, and his black eyes were unreadable. "No, I didn't have to. I had resources. An inheritance from Dad as well as an offer of any kind of help from Mom's new husband. I could have gone off to college, or found a job somewhere away from Killara."

Once again a humorless smile twisted her lips. "You said something about not being able to repeat critical moments in our lives. Well, I'd reached a critical moment just before Kane asked me to marry him. I was trying to plan a future when all I knew for certain was that my heart was here, in this place—where I'd offered it to you...and where you had left it."

Brett moved slightly, jerkily, the way a man will when he feels an anticipated blow. He didn't say a word.

Cassie looked at him steadily. "Even then, I doubt I would have accepted Kane's proposal just because I felt tied to this place. Part of me wanted to walk away and never look back, and that was the part I probably would have listened to eventually. But I was in a kind of limbo, so I stayed. Then one day Kane told me about the mirror. He told me the history, all the stories. He said only a Delaney could see anything except his own reflection. Then he gave me the key to his dressing room, and more or less dared me to go look into the mirror."

Hoarsely, Brett said, "What did you see?"

"I saw what you saw," she told him quietly. "My wedding to Kane. It tipped the balance, really, that prophecy. When Kane asked me to marry him, I said yes. After all, when a thing's fated to be, what's the use of fighting? I shouldn't have been able to see anything except my reflection, unless I was—or was going to be—a Delaney."

Brett cleared his throat. "But you said you didn't take his name."

She frowned. "I didn't. I guess a technicality doesn't mean much to the mirror. Besides, it was hell-bent to have its way."

He felt his earlier tension return. "Are we back to the so-called prophecy? What're you talking about, Cassie?"

"Don't you see?" She searched his hard face and shuttered eyes, and realized that he probably didn't. He was a Delaney born, and some things really were as inherent to a Delaney man as a tendency to black hair and a temper. Like an unshakable belief in fate, something he intended consciously to fight even though he still believed, deep down, that he couldn't win.

Cassie was worried about that for several reasons. There was Killara, of course. The mirror had predicted its destruction, and the thing was always right—even if it sometimes caused rather than simply foretold an event. How could Brett save Killara if he didn't *really* believe he could?

And there was Brett himself. She couldn't begin to think of what it would do to him to lose Killara, but if his own blind spot made him unable to fight for it with all his strength and will, then the enemy who destroyed Killara would destroy the last Delaney with the same blow.

4

"CASSIE?"

She felt more than a little helpless. Generations of his family had believed in fate, and had believed that the mirror always foretold what was fated to happen. How could she hope to change his mind about either? She spoke slowly, fumbling for words.

"Brett, if you hadn't looked into the mirror that night, would you have left? I mean, had there been any thought in your mind of leaving before you saw that scene?"

"No." He hesitated. "I had thought of leaving before I finished college—all the time I was away, in fact. But when I came home that summer . . . well, you were here, and I couldn't take my eyes off you. I didn't think beyond being with you. No, I had no intention of leaving until that night."

"Then, it was the mirror. You looked into it, and what you saw caused you to leave."

He nodded. "Yes, like I told you. What's your point?"

"My point is that if you hadn't left, what the mirror showed you would never have happened. I wouldn't have married Kane."

Brett didn't say anything for a moment, but then he shrugged. "You can't be sure of that, Cassie. If things between us had fallen apart naturally, if I had hurt you in some way, badly enough to destroy your feelings for me, if I had left Killara to work in Tucson, and just wasn't around anymore..." He shrugged again. "Who's to say? My leaving might have pushed you toward Dad, but if I'd stayed, something else might have achieved the same end. Fate. It will have its way, no matter what we do."

Cassie wanted to argue with him because she was utterly *certain* she was right about this, but she didn't know how to convince him. Logically—if logic could be applied in such a bizarre situation— what he said made sense. Every action caused a reaction of some kind; if he had not left Killara so abruptly, he might well have done something else to alter their relationship. Or she might have, or Kane might have. There was no way to prove what she knew was true.

Frustrated, she said, "If you're so sure of that, then why bother to fight for Killara? It's doomed, Brett. You might as well just concentrate on plans to rebuild."

He stiffened, his expression going hard, and something dangerous flashed in his eyes. She had never seen that expression before, not in him, but she recognized it. It was sheer, implacable determination, the kind that would never be deterred by any kind of logic or reason, or even his own inborn convictions.

Deeper than instinct in Brett—in all the Delaneys—was something far more solidly rooted even than the unshakable belief in fate. It was Killara. Home. And it would be defended by every possible means, even from fate.

That was what she saw in his eyes. When Brett had said he'd die a bloody death before letting anyone destroy Killara, he hadn't been indulging in a melodramatic boast. It was simple fact to him. He wouldn't hesitate to die defending this place.

"I won't let that happen," he said flatly, proving her silent realizations. "Mirror or no mirror, and fate be damned, I'll let no one destroy Killara."

Cassie felt emotionally wrung-out, and when she considered what had been discussed during this eternal morning, she was hardly surprised. It wasn't even noon yet, for God's sake. She had a great deal to think about, but she didn't have the energy for it now. She wasn't sure she ever would.

She felt a little stiff when she rose to her feet, and realized vaguely that her muscles had been tensed against a lot of things—like unbearable truths—for most of the morning. She looked down at Brett, and held her voice steady with a concerted effort.

"Then I guess the question is—which is stronger, your fatalism or your love for Killara? If I were a betting woman, I'd put my money on this place; it's always been the life blood of your family. So maybe you'll win after all. If I can help, I will. You can be sure of that. In the meantime, I have to go check on a sick horse, and you probably should get started on the company records."

She was halfway to the door before he spoke.

"You're staying, then?"

Cassie paused to glance back at him over her shoulder. "It looks that way. For the time being, at least."

He seemed to hear only the last sentence. "Is that a threat, Cassie? Things don't go your way, and you'll leave?"

She tilted her head as she looked at him, conscious of an ache inside her. Would he always be so suspicious of her? "No, it isn't a threat. I had a price, remember? You paid it. I'll stay here until the first of the year. You said it would be over by then, Killara's fate decided one way or the other, so I'll stay that long."

When she walked slowly from the room, Brett gazed after her. A hint of motion caught his eye. A fine, powdery snow was beginning to blow about outside.

It was three weeks until Christmas.

*　*　*

He kept his mind occupied for the next few hours. Lunchtime came and went as he worked at the desk; Moira brought him a tray, and when he asked, she told him that Cassie had already eaten and had returned to the barn and the sick horse. The snow stopped, except for an occasional flurry, leaving the frozen ground outside virtually unchanged.

From time to time he heard the wind whistling and moaning as it swept around the big house. It was a lonely sound. He concentrated on the records and reports of Delaney Enterprises, forced to read everything because he didn't know what might be important.

It was a little after two in the afternoon when the computer interrupted its scrolling of material to inform him there was an incoming call requesting a video linkup. When he looked at the origin of the call, Brett was tempted to instruct his system to hang out the high-tech equivalent of a Do Not Disturb sign, but his sense of responsibility overcame the impulse. He had the company records put on standby, okayed the video linkup, and accepted the call.

On the computer's screen a familiar face formed instantly. It was a thin, somewhat intense face with pale blue eyes which seemed even more pale due to fair hair and a receding hairline. Even though it was very early Saturday morning in Australia, Gideon Paige was wearing a business suit.

"Hello, Gideon," Brett said, leaning back in his chair but still within range of the video pickup so he remained visible to his business partner.

"Brett, sorry to bother you, but Rankin wants a decision this weekened on that option or he's going to hand off to Sutton and MacAfee—"

Brett held up a hand. "Gideon, I've been gone less than twenty-four hours, and it's Saturday in Sydney. Rankin plays golf on Saturday. What's the real reason you called?"

After a moment Gideon smiled sourly. "Okay, so he said by next week. I just wanted you to remember you have business on this side of the world."

"I'm not likely to forget." Brett managed a smile of his own and forced himself to concentrate on Gideon and the problems he presented. "We don't want the option at Rankin's price. And Sutton and MacAfee can't raise the money. So we stand pat. Rankin will come down within sixty days, and then we'll make the deal."

Gideon scowled, but his eyes gleamed with amusement. "You got spies in other companies, or what? For five years I've been trying to figure out how you always know what's going on with the competition."

Mildly, Brett said, "I keep my ears open, that's all. Now, if you don't mind, I'd like to get back to work here. The sooner I finish with this..." He let the sentence trail off, implying something he was no longer so sure of.

"Right, right. Say hello to Cassie for me." The screen went dark, then returned to display the Shamrock records.

Brett stared at the screen but didn't signal the computer to continue. He felt very odd.

Say hello to Cassie for me.

If anyone had asked him yesterday, or even an hour ago, Brett would have sworn he had never mentioned Cassie or Killara to Gideon Paige. But his partner's casual words had opened up a floodgate of memory in Brett's mind. He *had* mentioned both to Gideon. He had talked of Cassie and Killara for years without even being aware he was doing it.

He allowed the realization to settle in his mind but didn't examine it too closely. Instead, he returned to his work, forcing himself to concentrate. It was after three o'clock that afternoon when he finally sat back in his chair and wearily rubbed his burning eyes. The lack of sleep was beginning to tell on him, and his solitary wine party the previous night hadn't helped. Add to that the strain of facing too much of his past and too many emotional truths during a rather crowded twenty-four-hour period, and it was no wonder he felt so drained.

He put the computer into a standby mode and rose from the desk, wandering around the room aimlessly to stretch his legs. Without consciously planning it, he found himself leaving the room and making his way toward a rear door. When he realized where he was going, he almost tried to stop himself, but the impulse was too strong.

He donned his coat and Kane Delaney's hat, ignoring the curious glance from Moira as he passed through the kitchen. It was even colder outside than it had been that morning. The wind, sharp and gusty, was really beginning to wail as it swept about the house and outbuildings.

Turning his collar up and pulling the hat low, Brett walked quickly down to the barns. He went directly to the only fully heated barn; it had been designed for the winter needs of late foals and calves or sick animals, when cold or bad weather would have struck a killing blow. It was not the largest of the barns, nor the newest, but it was so solidly built that when Brett slipped inside and closed the door behind him, the sounds of the wind fell to silence.

It was comfortable inside, the temperature maintained precisely by a computerized system. The fairly narrow hall, thickly carpeted with wood shavings, ran the length of the barn, with numerous roomy stalls opening to either side and an insulated hayloft above. The lighting of the hallway was good without being overly bright. Except for a single one at the opposite end of the barn, all the stalls were dark. It was very quiet.

Brett heard her before he saw her. He had walked softly down the hall, moving toward the lighted stall, and tried to be even quieter as he reached it. Her coat hung on a peg beside the stall door, and she was inside. She was speaking in a low, soothing voice that was steady and rhythmic, talking to the old gray horse she was gently brushing.

"Remember how Killara looks in the spring? When the wild-flowers bloom wherever there's water, and even the cactus shows off with a blossom or two? Remember the sweet smell of the wind, and the colors of sunset? That's why you're holding on, girl. To see another spring. It's worth holding on, I promise you. There's nothing on earth as beautiful as Killara in the spring."

Her sweet, velvety voice was almost hypnotic, affecting him as strongly as it did the animal that stood relaxed with an ear cocked back to catch her every word. He listened, hearing her love for the old horse and for this land, and it reminded him of the journal entries he'd read and the stories about his family's love for Killara and all it contained.

Whether she'd taken the name or not, Cassie was, he thought, as much a Delaney as he was, and in many ways probably more. She belonged here. And she had, God knew, earned the right to stay. For one thing, running a ranch the size of Killara was difficult, exhausting work in the best of times—and both backbreaking and heartbreaking when times were bad. She had kept this place going, building it up even more so that it was extraordinarily successful in a time when working ranches were few and far between; the reputation of Killara was better than it had ever been.

"Stay," he said suddenly, obeying an urge as impossible to ignore as the one that had brought him out there.

Cassie started, then whirled around, though her hands remained gentle and steady on the mare. After a moment she gave the horse a final pat and crossed the few steps to the open stall door. Since Brett stood to one side, she was able to close the bottom half of the Dutch door, then set the dandy brush very carefully on the ledge before meeting his intense gaze.

"I said I would," she said in a level voice.

"Not just until the first of the year, until the threat against Killara no longer exists. I mean stay for good. You belong here, Cassie."

She spoke as if he hadn't, talking about the gray horse contentedly munching hay in the stall. "This week the vet's at Shamrock, but I had him over a little while ago. He says the only thing really wrong with Ladama is old age. Nothing much to be done about it. She's stiffened up, but she isn't in pain. By keeping her in here through the winter, she'll probably last till spring, maybe midsummer. A waste of time to try to prolong her life so briefly, some would say. But she's the oldest horse on Killara, older than half the people here, and that deserves a lot of respect, I think." She shrugged.

"Anyway, she'll be comfortable in here. Is the wind still building outside?"

"Seems to be. And it's colder than it was this morning." He found it curiously painful that the only words that seemed to come easily between them concerned a horse and the weather.

Frowning a bit, Cassie said, "Maybe we'd better go in and check the weather reports. It sounds like that storm front is moving faster than expected. I might need to bring the hands in early today so we can batten down and get ready to ride out the storm."

Brett watched her as she walked across the hall to the tack room. He felt tired, yet at the same time being around Cassie brought all his emotions almost painfully alive and alert, as if he were at the brink of something overwhelming.

"Brett? We should go back to the house."

He watched her as she returned from the tack room, and all the chaotic emotions of the past twenty-four hours jabbed at him like a tangle of brambles. When he heard himself speak, he wasn't at all surprised at the worn, strained sound of his own voice.

"You didn't answer me, you know. Will you stay here for good?"

"I don't want to talk about it." Her voice was unnaturally steady, and her face was very still. "Right now I'm not thinking past Christmas. I'm not even thinking past this minute."

"Cassie—"

She held up a hand. "Brett, you're tired, and I feel kind of numb, and there's a storm coming. All I want to do is go up to the house and check the weather reports, so I can make the decisions I have to about the ranch. That's what I've done all these years, what Kane trained me to do. Manage the ranch." She reached for her coat and shrugged into it quickly before he could help. "Right now that's all I'm thinking about."

Brett caught her shoulders when she would have moved away from him. He knew she was right, knew he was too tired for this, that his timing was all wrong, but he could no more fight these urges than he'd been able to fight the one that had driven him to find her.

"This isn't about the ranch," he said roughly. "It isn't about my father—"

"I think it is." She stared up at him, a little pale and rigidly controlled, her eyes shuttered.

Even through the thickness of her quilted coat Brett believed he could feel the deceptive frailty of her small-boned shoulders. He could smell her perfume, something both elusive and haunting and uniquely Cassie. Her gray eyes were dark in the low light of the barn hall, seemingly bottomless. Just looking at her made his heart ache, and kindled a need more fierce than he had ever felt for any other woman.

"Let go of me, Brett," she said, unsteady now.

"I can't." His hands tightened gently on her shoulders. "Don't you see? That's the problem, Cassie. I can't let go. I couldn't, even on the other side of the world. You're wrong if you think this is about Dad or the ranch. It's about us. I didn't take much with me when I left this place, but the memory of you was something I couldn't escape."

"That sounds like a curse," she said huskily, and her eyes were shining with sudden wetness.

"I used to think it was." His own voice was low and raspy. "I'd wake up from dreams so vivid, I could never get them out of my mind no matter how hard I tried. I even tried to hate you because I thought it would cure the ache. But I couldn't hate you."

Cassie sighed. "And now?" She didn't really expect an answer because she could see his inner struggle in the tightness of his face and the burning of his eyes. For the second time since he'd come home, Brett's guard was down, this time probably because he was just plain tired. It was truth he was telling her, showing her, but the truth was his struggle against his emotions for her, for his father, and for Killara.

Nothing had changed.

He might have felt her begin to draw away, or he might simply have felt the natural anger of a man in the grip of a painful struggle—in any case, it was anger she saw in him when he suddenly pulled her against him and covered her mouth with his.

Cassie wanted to struggle herself. She didn't want his passion like this, offered reluctantly and angrily with nothing resolved between them. But her body was instantly seduced by his, and the pure pleasure of his touch swamped reason.

How could she fight what she had longed for half her life?

His mouth was hot and hard on hers, so urgent that his touch could never be called anything so simple as a kiss. It was something primitive, compulsive, like a drowning man's desperate need for air. Everything inside Cassie responded to that need. She felt herself shrug out of her coat when he pushed it off her shoulders, and her own hands fumbled at his coat until it fell away from him.

She thought she was drowning, all her senses battered by shock waves of pleasure. The force of him, of his need, was far greater than it had been that last summer, and her own pent-up feelings had grown stronger over the years, more intense, like a storm trapped within a glass dome. Her arms rose to slide around his neck, her body molded itself to his, and her mouth answered his hunger.

Brett held her tightly against him, both his arms wrapped around her slender body. Even with the bulky sweater she wore, she felt delicate to him, her strength hidden somewhere beneath silky skin and small bones. He could feel her strength, a vitality and spirit far more potent than muscle could ever be, and that enticed him every bit as much as her golden hair and haunting gray eyes.

As innocently seductive and giving as she had been on that summer night ten years ago, and as precious as that memory was to him, it was this Cassie he wanted, this woman with the wary eyes and careful control and hard-won strength.

One of his hands slipped under the bottom of her sweater to find the warm, silky skin of her side, and he felt a faint tremor go through her. He lifted his head, reluctant to give up the burning pleasure of her mouth but driven to satisfy an equally powerful need just to look at her. God, she was so lovely! Especially like this, her face softened, eyes sleepy and dazed, her lips reddened and a little swollen from his kisses.

Brett had forgotten where they were. He had forgotten the approaching storm, the threat against Killara. All he could see was Cassie.

"I want you," he said, his voice barely more than a raspy whisper.

Her sleepy eyes widened slightly, and the dazed expression cleared as she seemed to search his face. He had the feeling she didn't find what she was looking for, or didn't like what she found, because the mask of control slipped back over her features. Her mask was imperfect now, strained, but there. She didn't draw away, and her body didn't stiffen against his, but he had the sudden awareness of great distance between them.

"There's something you have to know," she said huskily.

"All I have to know is if you want me too," he said. One of his hands slid down to curve over her bottom, pressing her lower body even closer against him, and a smile that was a little hard curved his lips when she gasped. "And I know you do, Cassie. Say it. Tell me you want me."

For a moment Cassie almost gave in because she had a pretty good idea of what would happen when she told him what he needed to know. But she didn't have a choice. Maybe Brett could accept a relationship between them with nothing resolved, but she couldn't. She wanted more than his passion, and he would never offer more until they had put the past behind them once and for all.

"Tell me, Cassie."

"There's something you have to know," she repeated, her voice steady now. "My marriage to Kane wasn't what it seemed. I never slept with him."

Cassie had thought she'd been prepared for his withdrawal since it was what she expected, but when he pulled her arms from around his neck and stepped back abruptly, she almost unbalanced. She felt cold, but not merely because the seductive heat of his body had been taken away. And the disbelief on his hard face hurt her more than she had expected it to.

"Nice try," he said flatly. "But my old man used sex to unwind the way another man might use a hot shower or a glass of wine. No way could he have kept his hands off you once you moved into the house."

After a moment Cassie slowly bent to get her coat. She brushed off the wood shavings clinging to the material, fixing her attention on the task because she didn't want to look at Brett's face. She kept her voice steady with an effort. "Why would I lie about it? So I could sleep with you without guilt? It was just a business arrangement, Brett, that's all. To protect Killara."

He had bent to get his own coat, shaking it out and putting it on somewhat jerkily. His thoughts were in turmoil and he couldn't begin to define his emotions. Why *would* she lie? He wanted to believe her, wanted to feel sure she had never spent a night in his father's bed, but he couldn't fight his way through a tangle of doubts.

Cassie looked at him a moment as she shrugged into her coat, then sighed. She was completely in control again, only the slightly swollen redness of her lips hinting that she had ever lost her self-command. He had no idea what she was thinking or feeling, no idea at all.

"Well, I don't suppose it matters," she said in a very calm voice. "You don't want me enough to believe I wouldn't lie to you—and we're both old enough to know that what we want isn't always good for us." She shrugged, apparently dismissing the matter as unimportant. "I'm going up to the house to check on the weather reports. I have a responsibility to Killara, and to the people who work here."

Ironic, Brett thought as he nodded an acceptance and followed her silently from the barn. He'd come back home to save Killara, yet it and the ghost of his father seemed to come between him and Cassie at every turn. He had the odd notion that making peace with this place was as important as resolving his relationship with Cassie, that the two were inextricably connected in his life—and that he would lose both of them if he wasn't very, very careful.

* * *

Instead of joining Cassie in the den to see the weather reports, Brett returned to the study. But after no more than ten minutes he put the computer on standby again and leaned back in his chair. The problem was, he needed to be doing something physical. With so much of his mind on Cassie, a warning printed in bright red on the screen would likely escape his notice.

Three weeks until Christmas—but the danger increased with every day that passed, and when the tree was up and decorated the clock would really be ticking. He had to *do* something, something constructive that would help Killara and something that would occupy his body as well as his mind.

Once he faced the problem, it didn't take Brett long to make up his mind. He had come back to protect Killara, and even though his instincts told him to look for an enemy from outside, he had to make sure the true threat wasn't something very simple—like the antique wiring still remaining in parts of the big house, or an overlooked can of some flammable liquid tucked away in a forgotten closet or storage room.

He shut down the computer system for the day, found a laser-powered light in a storage room off the kitchen, and flipped a mental coin. It came up heads, so he climbed the stairs to the attic.

Considering the "keep everything" philosophy of generations of Delaneys, Brett was surprised the attic was in such good shape. There was an amazing number of boxes, trunks, and crates, but most were labeled and even the clutter was rather neatly arranged. He was able to move with ease around all the stored items, and resisted the temptation to study paintings and look through trunks filled with old clothing and household items. Instead, keeping his mind on the threat to Killara, he carefully examined the exposed wiring in the attic, made sure all the electric lamps stored there were unplugged, and that the half-dozen antique oil lanterns were empty. He checked to see that no batteries from decades past had been left to corrode dangerously, and he moved a few items placed too close to electrical outlets and to the two lone hot air jets.

As the house had expanded in all directions, so had the attic. Brett had to bend low to get through doors that were little more than crawlways, and he was astonished by the sheer space. Because all the space was used solely for storage, there was a minimum of heating, so it was chilly as well as dusty.

He spent hours in the attic, and by the time he came back downstairs he felt he had at least achieved something. He had the peace of mind of knowing there was at least no danger of fire up there. He came all the way to the first floor, then glanced down at his clothes and realized he needed to change, and probably to shower, considering all the dust. As he turned to go back up the stairs, however, Cassie's voice stopped him.

"Going gray so young?"

He was too surprised by the question to remember immediately how things had been left between them. "What?"

She came slowly across the foyer from the direction of the kitchen until she stood a couple of steps away. Without touching him, she pointed. "Your hair."

Brett reached up, and found his hair liberally coated with dust and cobwebs. He had to laugh, thinking of how he must look, and was rewarded by a slight smile from Cassie. He sat down on the fourth stair, shaking his head. "I was up in the attic. Moira's a great housekeeper, but nobody's been worried about dusting that place in a long, *long* time."

"What were you doing there?"

It was then that Brett remembered how tense the interlude in the barn had been, but he refused to allow that earlier strain to come between them. No matter what the future held for them, they had to find some kind of peace in the present, and he concentrated carefully on holding that thought.

He kept his voice as light as before. "I wanted to check for fire hazards."

Cassie frowned slightly. "I thought you believed the threat came from outside Killara. The way you talked about it—"

"I do believe that. When I looked into the mirror and saw the fire, something inside me said it had been deliberately set by an enemy out to destroy Killara. But I can't be certain of that, Cassie, not absolutely. So I decided to check for the easy, obvious ways a fire could start. The attic was first. And, despite the dust, I can tell you it's clean. There's no fire hazard in that part of the house."

"Glad to hear it. Do you mean to check the rest of the house?"

"Of course. If nothing else, it'll keep me busy if we get snowed in here. Is that likely to happen?"

"According to the weather reports, yes. Tomorrow's going to be a very busy day. By the way, Moira sent me to find you. Dinner's almost ready."

Brett glanced at his watch and was startled to see how late it was. "I was up there longer than I thought. I'd better get cleaned up."

"Yes." Cassie turned away but threw a last dry remark over her shoulder. "You *are* too young to go gray."

He watched her until she was out of his sight, and only then rose and went up to his room to change for dinner. He thought fleetingly that it was no wonder he felt as if he were on an emotional roller coaster; it would have been a chaotic enough experience returning to Killara to face his complex feelings about Cassie, let alone everything else.

But there *was* everything else.

It hung over his head like a sword, his certainty that there was some faceless enemy who was even now plotting the destruction of Killara. It was an unnerving feeling, an itching between his shoulder blades that kept his senses on constant alert, as if he walked down a dark alley and knew an enemy lurked in the shadows, unseen and deadly.

Brett showered and dressed for dinner, his actions as automatic as they had been the night before. He really didn't want to think about anything, but as he was adjusting his tie, he eyed the still-crated mirror and then glanced across the room at the dressing room door. It was closed; he hadn't felt the need to use the room. But he could still remember precisely where the mirror had been placed in there.

He couldn't leave the thing crated, not if it was going to remain in this suite. The damned crate took up too much room, for one thing. He could order it hauled up to the attic, of course, where it wouldn't be visible to taunt and tempt him. Or . . . he could uncrate it and return it to its wall in the dressing room.

It was an unexpectedly difficult choice, and Brett realized only then that he *was* tempted to look into the mirror again. Despite everything. The thought was enough to send him immediately from the room, angry at his own perverse nature. That mirror had disrupted his life *twice*—and he still felt the lure of it?

"Who are you mad at?" Cassie asked lightly but somewhat warily the moment he walked into the dining room.

Brett made a conscious effort to stop scowling. "Just myself," he replied, helping himself to a glass of wine.

"Why?"

"Because I can't bring myself to drop that damned mirror into the deepest hole I can find." He looked at her, trying to distract himself—and succeeding all too well. Her simple dress was plain silk, unadorned, but it was a rich red color and did amazing things for her golden hair and fair skin. She was breathtaking. Heartbreaking. He wanted her, the desire so sudden and fierce, it was like a blow.

Had she been with his father? *Why would she lie?*

"If you were to do that," she murmured still lightly, as if nothing had happened between them earlier, "generations of Delaneys would be spinning in their graves."

"Do you really think that would bother me?" he asked absently, his interest in the mirror fading as he looked at her. There was absolutely no sign, now, of those heated minutes in the barn. She was cool and composed, face still and eyes unreadable. But he couldn't help wondering if her surface calm was as deceptive as his own was.

"Don't bite me, but yes, I think it would bother you," she said.

For an instant he couldn't remember what he had asked her. When he did remember, he realized she was right; it would bother him to do something that would have appalled and offended his ancestors. An unsettling realization. Brett decided to change the subject. "What's the plan for tomorrow?"

Cassie followed his lead without protest. "I met with the foreman and ranch hands. Most of the stock had already been moved to the inner ranges, but I want them in even closer; the hands will take care of that first thing in the morning. The rest of us will do what's needed around the house and barns. I've directed the computer to pump extra water into the reserve troughs and release extra feed for the stock. The men will rig rope guidelines between the buildings in case it gets really bad. We'll also raise emergency shelters here in the valley to protect as much of the stock as possible."

It was clear Cassie intended to be ready for the worst. From his own years on the ranch, Brett knew what some of those measures were. Though quite a few of the unmarried ranch hands lived in the comfortable bunkhouse year-round, most lived either off the ranch in homes of their own or occupied snug bungalows about a mile from the main house. During severe weather, however, every employee without family responsibilities elsewhere was expected to stay in the roomy bunkhouse for the duration.

And since the Delaneys had always believed that hard work and loyalty should be rewarded, all hands were paid triple time for the hazardous duty and were provided with the very best of everything, including their own cook, supplies, and numerous forms of entertainment to make the bunkhouse completely self-contained and as pleasant as possible.

The kitchens were kept so well-stocked with food supplies that every person on the ranch could be fed for weeks in the unlikely event that the delivery shuttles weren't operating. There were also emergency generators and liquid fuel in the event that all the stored power from the solar collectors and batteries was depleted.

But with all that, Brett was still very much aware of the dangers of a severe winter storm—especially so early in the season when neither the stock nor the people had been granted time to fully adjust to cold weather. With thousands of head of stock on the ranch, there

was no way all could be protected with shelters, and the animals
would need the help of people to survive; both would be vulnerable
to the destructive elements mankind was still unable to control.

"By noon tomorrow," Cassie said, "we should be as ready as we
can be for a storm."

Before Brett could respond, Moira came into the room bearing a
heavy soup tureen. "And I've got the perfect meal for the night before the storm," she said in a satisfied tone.

"Which is?" Cassie asked.

"Salmon stew."

"My favorite," Brett commented.

"I'd forgotten that," Moira said immediately. "Would have
made something else if I'd remembered. You two sit down and eat
while it's hot." She served the stew as Brett sighed and took his seat.
When she'd barreled back to the kitchen, he said, "She's still punishing me."

"You've been here barely twenty-four hours," Cassie pointed
out. "Give her time to get it out of her system. Besides, you know as
well as I do that so far she's been pretty tame about it. She could
have done worse. Like starched the sheets on your bed or put something awful in your coffee this morning."

"True. She always did have the knack for revenge."

Fixing her attention on her stew as she began to eat, Cassie said
lightly, "Tell her you mean to stay, and that'll go a long way toward
earning forgiveness."

Brett opened his mouth to say he didn't mean to stay, but decided to stop denying it when he wasn't sure. With every hour he'd
spent back on Killara, Australia seemed farther and farther away,
his business there less important—even after Gideon had called to
remind him of it.

Perceptively, Cassie said, "Not so sure anymore?"

He met her eyes. "No. But that doesn't mean I'll stay. Like you,
I don't want to think beyond this storm. I'm not ready to make a decision."

She nodded, accepting that, and the remainder of the meal was more or less silent. Afterward, Cassie immediately excused herself and went to her room, saying that since she planned to be up by four A.M. she was turning in early.

Brett didn't try to stop her. He debated whether he should work a couple of hours on the computer, but it didn't take long for him to decide to turn in himself. The immediate threat against the ranch was the coming storm, and that was what he needed to be ready for.

He had to go past Cassie's suite to reach his own, and found himself hesitating as he looked at the closed door. But he didn't stop, of course, going on with no more than the pause. He blanked his mind as well as he was able and got ready for bed. And, thanks to sheer exhaustion, he was asleep minutes after he closed his eyes.

5

_____

HE WOKE AT PRECISELY THE TIME HE'D SET FOR HIMSELF, FOUR A.M., feeling considerably less weary and much more in sync with both the time zone and the ranch itself. In fact, he found himself instinctively using all his senses to try to take the pulse of Killara.

It was very dark, and very, very quiet. Unnaturally quiet. Brett listened intently but heard absolutely nothing. With so many of the cattle in so close, and the rest probably being moved even now, he should have been able to hear at least an occasional bawling or the stamping of restless hooves, but he didn't. Silence. Even the whine of the wind, so audible the night before, was absent. It didn't reassure him; every instinct he could lay claim to told him this was literally the calm before the storm.

He was up and dressed in only a few minutes, wasting no time even to shave. Without thinking about it, he put on his warmest clothes and pulled on sturdy boots over thermal socks. Hat, coat, and gloves were downstairs, along with anything else he might need—like a thermal mask if conditions threatened the danger of frostbite and he had to spend a lot of time outside.

Brett hadn't thought much about what part he would play in readying the ranch for a storm, but as he went downstairs to the kitchen he found himself mentally going over all the things that needed to be checked as well as the various precautions taken to protect people, stock, and buildings.

"The coffee's hot, and breakfast will be ready in about fifteen minutes," Moira said when he entered her domain. She was wide awake and calm, a veteran of many winters on Killara. "Nobody goes outside this morning without a hot meal, so don't let me catch you trying."

Brett smiled as he fixed his coffee. "No, I know better than that. Where's Cassie?" Her door had been open when he'd passed, her rooms empty.

"In the study, setting up the tracking system. Go on. I'll call you both when breakfast is ready."

He went, carrying his coffee, and it didn't occur to him until he'd nearly reached Cassie that Moira hadn't called it his father's study. Now, he thought wryly, when she started calling it *his* study, he'd know he was more or less forgiven, his return accepted. He'd be master of Killara.

For the first time, that idea didn't unnerve him, but it did give him a lot of food for thought.

When he walked into the study, Cassie almost had finished setting up the tracking system. She was at the desk, the computer humming quietly, and from the ceiling in the center of the room a huge video screen had descended. An impressively detailed map of Killara filled the screen, dotted with tiny color-coded lights indicating the positions of all the ranch personnel. Brett knew that each employee wore a wristband containing a monitor/transponder that made it possible for them to be tracked and their physical conditions monitored constantly.

Cassie was wearing one herself. She had set up a secondary control panel on the desk beside the computer, this one specially designed to handle direct communication, through headsets the ranch hands wore, as well as to sort through the biological information provided by the individual transponders.

As Brett came in, she was saying, "Okay, I've got everybody on-line now, so I'll coordinate from base. Take your time, don't get into a hurry. Until we have a little daylight, the darkness is a bigger threat than the storm, so be careful. Ray, what about the yearlings in the southeast quadrant?"

The foreman's voice came through the communications panel, clear and calm. "Sharon says they've found the herd. Must have fell over 'em. Check for strays, will you, Miss Cassie? I've been out here an hour and *still* can't see a bloody thing."

She glanced up to see Brett approach, but didn't react except by a nod. Her fingers were busy on the computer keys, and immediately the huge video screen obeyed her commands by shifting perspective to a close-up view of the quadrant in question. There was a large group of red lights bunched together and loosely surrounded by numerous multicolored lights, with a smaller group of red lights several hundred yards to the north.

Cassie immediately flipped a switch on the communications panel. "Sharon, you've got at least a dozen strays in that little ravine north of your location."

"Roger, base, we'll get 'em," Sharon responded, laconically confident for someone maneuvering in almost total darkness.

Brett rested a hip on the corner of the desk and smiled at Cassie. "Motion detectors and heat sensors so sensitive they know the difference between cattle and coyotes, headsets and transponders providing instant communication between all the ranch hands and their base, and an electronic map of Killara so precise you could guide anybody to a particular rock or cactus without leaving your chair. Old Shamus wouldn't know what to think about all this."

Cassie leaned back in her chair, lifting her coffee cup. She kept her eyes on the screen until several multicolored dots converged on the red ones that denoted cattle. Then she shifted her attention to

Brett's face. "How about you?" she asked lightly. "I've heard some people say ranching the old way was more exciting."

Brett shrugged. "I can remember as a kid, when the technology wasn't so precise, but I don't know what it was like when the only electronic device you could find on a ranch was an adding machine, a calculator, or a simple personal computer—much less when there was no electricity, indoor plumbing, or running water. How can you miss what was never a part of your life? To me, all this is perfectly natural, and it would be both stupid and criminally negligent not to make use of everything available to help get the job done and safeguard lives."

"That's the way I see it," Cassie said. She leaned forward to adjust a switch on the comm panel as the ranch hands talked to one another, setting the volume a bit lower but keeping it loud enough so that she would hear if any question or problem was directed to her. Then she leaned back again and smiled wryly. "Besides, I have a feeling Hollywood glamorized the so-called excitement of ranching in the old days. I doubt any of Killara's hands would be pleased to find themselves back there, dependent pretty much on nothing but their own senses and experience to keep themselves and the stock alive—especially in the middle of a blizzard."

Brett glanced over at the video screen, watching the glowing dots moving busily, people accomplishing their work despite the fact that dawn had yet to arrive. "No. And some things never really change. Even with all the technical advances, ranch hands still ride horses and herd cattle basically the same way they did two hundred years ago. These days, it's just easier to find the strays and a lot harder to find yourself lost even in total darkness or lousy weather." He looked back at Cassie. "Speaking of which..."

"The forecast changed a bit overnight," she reported somewhat wryly. "The snow will likely start by noon, the wind begin to pick up shortly after, and by midafternoon we'll be in the middle of the worst storm to hit this area in twenty years. And ever since the experts found a way to patch up the ozone, the jet stream has dipped farther south than ever before; storms all across the southern part of the country have gotten more intense. This one looks like it might be a killer."

Brett whistled softly. "I'll say the forecast changed a bit. Okay, so how can I help, *boss*?"

Cassie didn't say anything for a moment as they looked at each other. His question had not been in the least sarcastic or condescending; right now she *was* the boss, the more experienced of the two of them, and it was simple common sense that she remain in charge throughout this crisis. The ranch was his, but a lifetime of stubborn resistance to learning more than necessary about the workings of the place and the past ten years completely away from it meant that he was virtually untrained. He was intelligent enough to know much of what had to be done, and he would remember quite a lot from his childhood and youth, but not enough to run the show.

Cassie drew a breath. "I wish you could stay here and coordinate," she said softly.

His smile was a little crooked, but his eyes remained shuttered. Today the guards were back up full force. "Because I'd be less trouble here than running around out there in a blizzard?"

Because you'd be safer, she thought, but didn't say. Instead, she said, "The comm panel is easy, and I could make a list of who should be where—"

Brett was shaking his head. "You know better than that. The person with the most knowledge of the people, the stock, and the layout of the place has to be here. That's you. You're the pivot holding everything else together." He hesitated, then added, "Look, I want to help without getting in anyone's way. So put me to work, all right?"

She couldn't refuse him. Not because the ranch was his, or because his ego would suffer if she openly tried to protect him, but because he could no more stand by idly and watch when Killara was threatened than a medic could ignore a man in cardiac crisis. That was, after all, why he had come back here after ten long years on the other side of the world. If she didn't put him to work, he'd put himself to work.

"Cassie?"

She opened the center drawer of the desk and pulled out a wristband. "Nobody goes out without one of these," she said, handing it to him. "Even Moira and I have one in case we go out. Put it on and keep it on; it's already set for you."

Brett put his coffee cup on the desk and fastened the band around his wrist, adjusting it until it fit snugly. It looked deceptively innocent, like nothing so much as a plain sweatband a tennis player might wear, but he knew it contained state-of-the-art sensors to monitor his vital signs and a small but powerful transponder that would constantly relay his position and bio readings to the tracking system.

Cassie typed a command into the computer, made a couple of adjustments, and then nodded. "Okay, you're online." She studied his bio readings, then looked up at him. "You have a strong heart."

"Have I?" Totally beyond his control, his voice deepened on the question.

Cassie seemed to hesitate, then opened her mouth to respond, but whatever she might have said then was lost, because Moira stuck her head in the door and told them that breakfast was ready. Cassie silently double-checked the video screen to make certain there was no trouble, then picked up a portable receiver to take with her so that she could continue to hear the ranch hands as they talked to each other.

Breakfast was the last quiet moment of the day.

It was just barely light outside when Brett left the house in a Jeep pulling a trailer that held four emergency shelters, various tools, and a generous load of hay. Three of the ranch hands had driven off in other directions carrying the same equipment. They were to drive to specific points and put up the shelters as quickly as they could. Each could call for help if they found it necessary, but was under instructions to complete the work alone if at all possible since every hand was needed elsewhere; it was quite possible for one person to manage under optimum conditions but was a bit tricky in very cold or windy weather.

It was cold.

During the next few hours Brett learned a deep respect for several things. One was the weather; he was bitterly cold despite protective clothing, which naturally made the work more difficult. Another was the shelters, which were marvels of engineering and construction, designed to withstand extreme weather, and yet relatively easy to assemble.

And his deepest respect was earned by Cassie. Throughout the long hours, he heard her voice in his headset, filled with a rocklike calm and utter confidence no matter what the emergency. She was never rattled, never uncertain, and never hesitated a moment when instructions were needed. Cassie always seemed to have anticipated the unexpected, because no one had to wait long for her to decide what to do.

Brett worked steadily throughout the morning, ignoring the weather as snow began to fall and trusting Cassie to tell him when he should head back to the house. She was monitoring what were now emergency weather broadcasts as well as all her people, and by noon had already called in everyone from the outlying edges of the valley.

Brett had spoken briefly to half a dozen people on horseback as they passed his position on their way to or from other places where work had to be done, but other than that he just listened to the reports and conversations on his headset. Each time he stopped to inspect and open the entrances to a shelter, he found himself virtually surrounded by a herd of cattle, all unnaturally quiet and eager to get into the shelter, where there was hay and protection from the rising wind. Several times he was forced to elbow an inquisitive nose out of his way, and at least once forgot himself to cuss at an overly affectionate heifer.

The responsive chuckles in his headset reminded him that his microphone was voice activated and that nearly every soul on Killara had heard him. It also reminded him again that he wasn't alone, that he was a part of something greater than himself. It was a nice feeling.

It was just after one o'clock when Cassie told him to return to base.

"I'm nearly done here," he reported.

"Five minutes," she said. "Then move, whether the shelter's okay or not. The weather's getting worse. I want everyone back here within fifteen minutes."

Brett heard a number of rogers, and added his as he worked faster. He took every one of his five allotted minutes on the job, and when he climbed into the Jeep for the drive back to the ranch house, he was granted an eerie sight.

He could *see* the storm moving in from the northwest, a wall of white eating up all the brown and rust of the Arizona countryside.

He barely made it back ahead of the snow.

Outside, the wind howled like a caged demon, and through the frosted windows of the house nothing could be seen except white. By the time an early darkness fell, even the snow seemed swallowed up by the stormy night, so that through the window was only blackness.

Inside, it was warm and quiet. The only indications of the raging storm were an occasional moan or whistle as the house withstood the fierce wind, or a sudden rattle as sleet was driven against the windows. In the rock fireplace of the den, the flames crackled and a cheery warmth spread outward into the room. It was a little before nine o'clock in the evening.

"Absolutely nobody goes out during the night," Cassie said from her position in the comfortable old wing-back. "If the storm's still rough tomorrow, the hands are under orders to do nothing outside except what is absolutely necessary."

Standing by the fireplace, Brett looked at her. "And you'll track them while they're out of the bunkhouse?"

She nodded. "The rule is, base is notified before anyone so much as opens an exterior door. The tracking system remains online constantly, of course, and an alarm sounds if the bio readings show dangerous stress or any other signs of trouble."

Her voice was just a little husky, and Brett knew the strain of today had been much greater than she was letting on. Though she'd remained in the house and out of the weather, Cassie's job had been the most draining of any on the ranch. She had remained in the study for hours, until every last person was safely back inside and Killara was as secure as possible.

There was more stress to come, Brett thought. If the storm lasted more than a couple of days, Jeeps would be sent out to check on the cattle in the valley, and Cassie would have to guide them through the blinding snow. And even if the storm blew itself out quickly, the snowfall would be treacherously deep, the drifts deceptive, and everyone would still have to be tracked electronically for the sake of safety.

"You should rest," Brett told her.

She lifted her gaze from the bright fire and smiled faintly as she looked up at him. "I am resting. I have been for the past few hours, in case you didn't notice."

"You know what I mean."

Cassie shrugged. "Even in the best of all possible scenarios, nobody will go outside tomorrow until nearly noon. I have plenty of time to sleep."

After a moment he nodded. "I suppose." They had been alone together for only a short time. When he had come in half frozen much earlier in the day, Cassie had been busy in the study with the final coordination to get all the buildings buttoned up to weather the storm and everyone inside. Brett had taken a hot shower and then later joined her, Moira, and Hank in the kitchen for a late lunch.

For the most part, the remainder of the day had been spent in the warm kitchen, the four of them listening to weather reports, drinking coffee, and talking quietly about nothing in particular as the storm outside intensified. There was nothing else to do. Killara was as ready for the fierce weather as it could be, and at least until morning they could only wait.

The waiting was rough on Brett; he'd never been good at it. He had spent a couple of hours before dinner working in the study, and had spoken yet again to Gideon, who had called, ostensibly and oddly, it seemed to Brett, to report on the weekend activities of one of their competitors in Australia. But the storm was such an audible thing, its sounds so curiously primitive that he was too restless to sit still for long. He supposed the need to be with others of his kind when nature raged so powerfully was stamped deeply into the human instinct. In any case, he couldn't concentrate on the information about Delaney Enterprises or the ranch, and he didn't like being alone.

He'd been surprised when Cassie joined him in the den after dinner. They had both changed back into casual clothes after the meal, but neither had lingered long upstairs. Why had she returned when, he sensed, she really didn't want to be alone with him? He could only guess that she was no more eager to spend time in her silent room than he was. This was one of those times when any kind of company, even the strained kind, was preferable to solitude.

But they were both too quiet, too wary, and he found their mutual constraint painful. He slid his hands into his pockets and leaned a shoulder against the high mantel, watching her steadily. He was very conscious of how alone they were tonight. Moira and Hank had gone to their rooms for the night, the house was very quiet, and outside the storm cut Killara off from the rest of the world.

Cassie seemed to read his mind. With her gaze once more fixed on the fire, she said, "We're still able to receive the emergency weather broadcasts, but the dish isn't picking up much else and communication outside the ranch is iffy. We're all right, though. Even totally cut off, Killara can keep its people safe and fed for weeks."

"You really love this place," Brett said quietly.

"That seems to surprise you very much. Why?" She looked at him, her eyes reflecting the firelight oddly. "It might not be mine, but it's home."

Brett was reasonably sure this was a mistake, that they were too tense with each other to get into this subject. And he didn't know if he was ready to face any of it, to decide what he did or didn't believe, but he knew there had to be some kind of resolution between him and Cassie—and soon. Just the prospect of days of being shut up in this house, virtually alone together, while they continued to be stiffly polite with each other, was enough of a spur to talk.

Besides, some part of Brett *was* ready, or at least was compelled, to confront all the painful questions. He needed to understand Cassie, and he had a strong feeling that if he were unable to do so, she would leave Killara after the first of the year. So he spoke carefully as he responded to her words. "I didn't mean it that way. Of course this is your home. I just meant . . . well, the Delaneys haven't exactly treated you with respect, have they? I certainly haven't, and from what you've said, neither did my father."

Cassie merely looked at him.

He tried again, and his voice roughened a bit. "I'm trying to thank you, Cassie. You've taken care of this place when I had no right to expect that of you. It would have served us right if you'd let the ranch fall to pieces."

"Us?"

He felt a little shock, and his short laugh sounded shaken to his own ears. "Me. I keep forgetting I'm the last of the line. I never thought about it much till I came back here. The last Delaney."

After a slight hesitation Cassie said, "According to what I know of the family history, there have been a number of times when there was only one son to carry on the name. And when it happened in the past, that Delaney son was . . . someone special. It ends with you only if you let it, Brett."

He shied away from that topic of the future. It wasn't something he was ready to contemplate. "Anyway, I want you to know I *am* grateful, Cassie."

"Don't mention it." Her face had gone expressionless, but her voice held a note of sarcasm.

Brett could feel himself tense. "All right, what have I said wrong now?"

She drew a deep breath and released it slowly, then rose to her feet. "Nothing. You know, you were right, I should rest. Good night, Brett."

He moved quickly, crossing the space between them and effectively barring her way. "Cassie, if you have something to say, then say it. We'll have enough trouble coping with cabin fever during the next few days without adding a lot of unnecessary tension between us." He felt an odd sense of relief, and realized that the stiff politeness between them was something he simply couldn't bear to have continue.

"Just let it go." Her voice was low, her gray eyes meeting his were shadowed.

"No. There never seems to be a good time to deal with us, so to hell with it. Now looks fine to me. What's wrong, Cassie? What have I said to make you angry this time?"

"Angry?" She shook her head. "I'm not angry. I guess I'm confused. It's very obvious what you're doing, but I don't understand." She paused. "Or maybe I do."

"What are you talking about?" Brett could feel his tension increasing, and a part of him wanted suddenly to back away again, to say never mind and turn away and avoid something he had a feeling was going to hurt him.

Cassie met his gaze squarely. "You don't know how you feel about me, do you, Brett? One moment I'm the girl you left behind, the woman you still want. The next moment I'm your father's widow. You want me, but you can't seem to decide what my place is in your life. So you keep falling back on the easy label, the impersonal pigeonhole, treating me as if I'm just another employee and thanking me for doing such a good job with the place—or offering to reward all my hard work with money."

"I apologized for that," he said.

"No, you didn't. You very carefully rephrased your question

when you realized I was furious, but you were still asking my price for staying here. And now you're thanking me."

"Am I not supposed to be grateful to you, Cassie?"

"*No.*" Her voice was emphatic; her eyes glittered. "I don't want your gratitude. I didn't do any of it for you, Brett. I didn't do it for Kane. I didn't even do it for all those Delaneys buried up on the hill. I did it for me. I did it to leave *my* mark on this place."

It was something he hadn't considered, and his question emerged slowly. "What do you mean?"

Cassie knew she was taking a big risk. By telling Brett how much Killara and being a part of the Delaney family meant to her, she was offering to a suspicious mind a very powerful motive both for marrying his father and for responding to Brett's desire so intensely. After all, her threat to leave might have been no more than a subtle bit of maneuvering, and the fact that she'd taken offense when he offered to pay her to stay could have been more of the same. To a suspicious mind, at least. If it was something he wanted to believe, he would have no trouble convincing himself that Cassie's ultimate goal was to remain mistress of Killara. Whatever it took.

Her hesitation was momentary, because there was only one way she could go. She had never lied to Brett, and didn't intend to start now.

"I mean just what I said. This has always been my home, Brett, I've lived on Killara all my life. I'm part of this place, and it's a big part of me. But as far as the family history goes, my name appears with Kane's in the family Bible to note a curious marriage that left me in charge of the ranch for a while. That's all. So history will record. My blood won't continue here, won't mingle with Delaney blood to make me a part of one very special family."

She drew a breath and looked up at his face with all the steadiness she could muster. "So I'm leaving my mark the only way I can. Killara will be better because of me. The ranch will be more successful, more profitable, and more famous—because of me. I may not be a Delaney, but I will be a part of the Delaney family history."

"Is that all you want?" he asked quietly. His hands rested on her shoulders, warm and heavy.

Cassie shrugged, very conscious of his touch. She couldn't read his expression; it was still and closed and gave away nothing. "Not that you'll believe me, but yes."

"And that's why you married my father? Only to protect Killara?"

She nodded. "I wouldn't have done it for any other reason. It was a business arrangement, Brett, from the very beginning. Kane wasn't sure if you'd ever come back, and he knew I loved this place. He knew I'd take care of it."

"He never tried to get you into his bed?"

She heard the disbelief in his voice, and managed a faint, wry smile. "I never said that. As a matter of fact, he did try—once. I reminded him of our bargain and told him that if he ever tried again, I'd be gone in an hour. Like you said, sex was something very casual for Kane. I was worth more to him as a manager for Killara than a bedmate, and he knew I meant what I said. So he never tried again. In the end he was more like a father to me. But he wasn't an easy man to love. I was every bit as ambivalent about him as you are."

That much, at least, Brett was certain of. Everything she had said about his father had implied or stated that Kane Delaney had been a difficult man whose faults had far outweighed his virtues, a man who, like a scorpion, stung others for the pleasure of wounding, because it was his nature. Obviously, she had understood him well. Yet she had married him, and she had taken care of his family home with total devotion both before and after his death.

"I guess I'm still ambivalent about him," Cassie went on in the same level voice. "I didn't like him very much, but I respected him in some ways. He was strong, no doubt about that. He was smart and he was tough, and he had the Midas touch in business. He was proud always, sometimes arrogant. He was very fierce in his loyalties, especially when it came to family, to his name. He loved you."

Perhaps oddly, Brett felt a little shock. "Did he?"

Without hesitation Cassie nodded. "Yes. But you were too much like him in many ways, and the two of you were not going to get along."

"I don't want to be like him."

"You're his son, Brett. Some of the things he gave you will be yours forever. But how much you choose to be like him . . . well, that's up to you. You're your mother's son too. There must be some part of Rebecca in you."

Brett was conscious of another shock. His mother's name hadn't been uttered in this house for a long time, at least not within his hearing. Kane Delaney had reacted with such violence to the car accident that had taken his wife that everyone around him, including his grieving son, had avoided any mention of her.

It was another wound Brett blamed on his father.

He cleared his throat. "She's been gone eighteen years, Cassie. I was barely fourteen when she died."

"Don't tell me you hardly remember her," Cassie said quietly. "I was younger than you, but I remember her very well. And she wasn't my mother."

"Of course I remember her! I remember everything about her."

"Then you must know you inherited as much from her as you did from Kane, at least physically. You move the way she did, Brett, with her grace. She gave you the shape of her eyes, if not the color, and something in your voice, a kind of inflection, is just the way hers was. Even the shape of your face is more hers than Kane's."

Brett had always thought, somewhat resentfully, that he was the image of his father, so Cassie's words were both welcome and a little surprising. If she was right, it was yet another indication that his own anger and bitterness had blinded him to something he should have been able to see for himself.

"You keep telling me things I didn't know—or didn't want to know. Why, Cassie? Why does it matter to you?" Brett realized that his thumbs were moving, probing through her sweater to find her delicate collarbones; his attention was being drawn to her and away from the conversation.

Cassie could see as well as sense what was happening. Those

devil-black eyes of his were becoming intent, heating, and his voice was almost absentminded, as if he weren't entirely conscious of his own words. She was torn between the pleasure and excitement of knowing he was so responsive to her and the frustration of knowing they had settled virtually nothing.

The conversation had wandered quite a bit, dancing all around the real cause of the current tension between them, and that, certainly, had only been touched on—not settled. She doubted that Brett believed her relationship with Kane had been platonic, and his disbelief made his motives, his desire, highly questionable.

Why did he want her? Because he felt like a betrayed lover who was determined to get that woman back? Because he really did believe she was the only weapon left that he could use against his father's memory? Because they had almost made love ten years before, and now it was simply a case of finishing what he'd started? Because he wanted her to continue managing the ranch, and he was ruthless enough to use any means to keep her here?

None of those possibilities made Cassie very happy, and she knew that if any of them proved to be true, it would certainly break her heart. But not even to save herself could she refuse Brett, of that she was utterly certain. He didn't know it, and would probably never believe it, but she had belonged to him since she was a child.

She cleared her throat, but her voice was husky when she spoke. "Even if I told you why it mattered to me, you wouldn't believe me," she said.

"Wouldn't I? Try me."

Cassie wanted to tell him, but the words wouldn't come. She was afraid, she realized. Afraid to tell him how she felt about him. There were still too many doubts and questions between them for him to believe her.

She had offered her love to him once and hadn't set eyes on him for ten long years. What if the same thing happened again? No, she couldn't say it. Not yet.

His dark, burning eyes searched her face, and his long fingers tightened on her shoulders. "I know what you want me to believe," he said. "You want me to believe you were telling the truth about never being in his bed. That's it, isn't it?"

"Yes," she replied simply, because she really did want that.

"Why? Why is my belief so important to you?"

There were many reasons she could have given him, but Cassie settled on just one. "Because if the situation were different, Kane wouldn't have believed me. And I hope you know me better than he did. Even after ten years away."

That was the first calculated thing Cassie had said. She wanted Brett to recognize that his suspicions and disbelief were reactions with which his father would have been very familiar. Kane had been incredibly slow to trust, quick to suspect, and even quicker to condemn. She didn't think Brett had inherited that from his father, but it would certainly do no harm to make him think about it a little.

He got the point, as she'd known he would. His face darkened and his mouth hardened, but the reaction was fleeting. With a slight shake of his head, he said, "Touché."

"Things are looking up," she said lightly. "At least this time you didn't go rigid or get angry."

"Maybe I'm getting punch drunk," he offered. "You've got a great right cross."

"When the fight means something," she said, keeping her voice light, "I don't pull my punches. I'm asking you to believe me, Brett. To believe *in* me."

6

WHY WOULD SHE LIE?

It was the question he kept coming back to, the one he'd brooded over all day. Why would she lie about her relationship with his father? He had thought of the worst possible motives, of course, but none of them seemed to fit Cassie. She couldn't have changed so much, he was sure.

No, what it really came down to, Brett thought, was that Cassie wanted *him* to believe—to know—there had been nothing sexual between her and his father. Why? Perhaps because of the memory of a summer night ten years ago, he thought. Or maybe Cassie still felt something for him, if only desire, and wanted it clearly understood, especially after his earlier accusation, that not just any Delaney would do.

He lifted one hand from her shoulder to touch her cheek, brushing back a strand of her pale, silky hair. He was dimly aware that every silence between them was filled with the muted sounds of the storm, encapsulating them.

"I don't know what I believe," he said finally, his voice harsh even to his own ears. "All I know is that I want you, Cassie. I can't think past that."

She had taken a gamble, but she wasn't entirely sure if she had won or lost. She had a feeling his reluctance to believe her now might, in the end, turn out to be a positive thing. Because once they made love—and they *would* make love—he'd have no doubt she was telling the truth, and that might just teach him a valuable lesson about his own quickness to disbelieve.

But whether or not that happened, she simply couldn't fight him now and she knew it too well. She had been in a kind of limbo ever since she had looked up and seen him standing in the study, waiting for this to happen.

She went into his arms without hesitation, her face lifting, and for an instant what she felt most of all was an overwhelming relief. Whatever happened during this stormy night, at least they were taking a step forward, a step toward each other, and nothing could ever be the same again.

Brett kissed her with a feverish intensity that seemed almost familiar to her now and yet was still stunning in its force. For the first time, she made no effort to restrain her own desire, responding to him with a matching hunger. She welcomed the possession of his tongue, her own eager, and stood on tiptoe instinctively to press herself even closer to the hardness of his body. A burst of heat exploded deep inside her, and she was only vaguely aware of the wild little sound that emerged from the back of her throat.

He held her hard against him, his mouth slanting over hers to deepen the kiss even more, and Cassie heard another whimper of intolerable need from her own burning, aching body. The last of her reservations vanished, lost beneath the onslaught of feelings too powerful to fight. She had wanted this, wanted him, for half her life, and even if he did leave her a second time, she knew she wouldn't regret this.

Brett swung her up into his arms, still kissing her. His impulse was to carry her only as far as the couch, because he wanted her so badly, he didn't much care where they were. But a stronger and deeper hunger made that impossible. He wanted to take her to bed, to see her golden hair spread out on his pillow, to lose himself in her, to hold her and sleep with her and wake up with her beside him in the morning. He wanted a night just for them, with a locked door and a storm isolating them from the rest of the world.

He had to stop kissing her to see where he was going, and felt his heart turn over with a lurch when she pressed her face against his neck and made a soft, shaky sound of need. Her slender body was light in his arms, warm and pliant, but he could feel tension growing in her. He thought it was the tension of passion, the same strain he felt himself, but managed to ask while he was still able to.

"I hope you're sure," he said huskily as he carried her up the stairs.

Cassie didn't lift her face from his neck, and her voice was so low he barely heard it, but her words were clear for all that. "I'm sure, Brett. I've never been more sure of anything in my life."

He paused on the landing, kissing her when she raised her head to look at him. Her response was instant, total, and again he fought an almost overpowering urge to simply lower her to the floor and make love to her right there. He had never in his life felt a desire so elemental, so urgent.

Her slight weight slowed him not at all as he strode rapidly down the hallway toward the master bedroom. He paused for just a heartbeat at the door to her rooms. Lamps glowed welcomingly inside, and a bright fire burned in the fireplace. Brett's hesitation was hardly more than a second or two, then he was continuing down the hall.

Cassie, her arms tight around his neck and her body held to him with his easy strength, knew why he had hesitated at her door. Not because it was closer and his patience was running out, but because it had occurred to him that his bedroom had also belonged to his father. He had hesitated to take her to Kane's bed.

She couldn't help feeling a pang, wishing that the competitiveness between father and son had been buried out there in Kane Delaney's grave, where it belonged.

She wished he could believe her.

But even that ache conjured no hesitation or regret in Cassie. She wouldn't have gone back even given the chance, not now. Her arms tightened around his neck, and she pressed her lips to the pulse beating underneath the tanned skin of his throat. She felt his powerful arms tense, drawing her impossibly closer, and she felt her own excitement increase at the evidence of his responsiveness to even a tiny caress.

Brett carried her into his bedroom, kicking the heavy door shut behind them. As in her room, the lamp by the bed welcomed and a fire crackled cheerily in the fireplace. The covers had been turned back, which was something Moira never forgot to do, and the room was comfortably warm.

Brett didn't want to let go of Cassie even for a moment, but set her gently on her feet beside the wide bed. He was conscious once again of the storm raging outside. Sleet rattled against the windowpanes and the moan of the wind was loud, but all he could see was Cassie. Her face lifted to his, the haunting eyes as mysterious as mountain fog, her beauty so great it stopped his heart. Her arms had remained around his neck, as reluctant to let go as he was, and his hands slipped down over her bottom to hold her even closer as he bent his head and kissed her hungrily.

Cassie trembled against him, kissing him back with a feverish craving that matched his. For a moment she remained like that, her body molded to his as if they could never be close enough, both of them straining a little to be closer. But there were barriers between them. Her arms slid from around his neck, her hands tugging at his flannel shirt to free it from his pants and then searching blindly for the buttons.

Brett groaned against her mouth, his desire flamed by her eagerness. He raised his head, finding the bottom of her sweater with impatient fingers and peeling it off over her head in a single motion.

She had to let go of him long enough to pull her arms free, but as soon as he tossed the sweater aside, she coped with the last few buttons of his shirt and pushed it off his broad shoulders as she impatiently kicked her shoes off.

Cassie didn't realize he had unfastened her bra until the satin straps slid down her shoulders, and she was only vaguely aware of brushing the skimpy material aside. She couldn't take her eyes off him. Knowing he wouldn't be going back out into the storm after his shower, he hadn't donned a thermal undershirt, and his powerful torso was bare.

The light flickered over his skin, painting shadows and highlights, making his bronze flesh gleam. He was a perfect sculpture created by the hands of a genius, the pure definition of what a man was supposed to be. Her mouth went dry, and her heart hammered against her ribs.

At that instant she remembered vividly another storm, a summer storm nearly fifteen years before. She had been thirteen and had run errands for her father, who had been the foreman of Killara then. He had asked her to ride out and check on Brett, who had been working with a young horse near the lake. It was the only kind of ranch work Brett had taken an interest in, and something he'd been good at. There was a storm on the way, and Cassie's father wanted her to warn Brett.

Cassie had ridden her own little mare out to the lake, and when she topped the hill she had seen him and the yearling colt near the water's edge. The colt had been fighting the halter and lead rope, and Brett had taken off his shirt while he worked with the young animal.

She remembered the sight so well. The strong Arizona sun had beat down, causing a glare to bounce off the water, and in that harsh light Brett and the horse had struggled. At seventeen, Brett had reached his full height, and though he had not been heavily muscled then, it had been obvious he was going to be an exceptionally powerful man.

Cassie sat on her horse, her gaze riveted on him as he fought the colt. The strong light played over his half-naked body, his tanned skin gleaming with sweat, the well-defined muscles of his arms and back rippling with every movement, and she had been mesmerized by the sight. It was like some primeval ritual, the fierce battle between man and beast, and it was beautiful in its raw intensity.

Then the expected storm began rolling over the valley, heavy clouds blocking the harsh light as the sun vanished behind them. Below Cassie, the primitive struggle lost its ancient aura and became something less fanciful, if no less beautiful. She could see Brett more clearly then, make out his features. His thin, intense face showed the stubbornness and pride of his nature, and for an instant Cassie was able to see clearly the diversity of his heritage.

Irish, Spanish, Apache, and Gypsy blood, the most noticeable legacies of his ancestry, blended smoothly in the strong body and handsome face of that very American young man. The mixture was a potent one indeed.

And Cassie, always a tomboy, her body still thin and angular with childhood, graceless and careless and innocent, gazed down upon him and felt her mouth go dry. Her heart hammered suddenly against her ribs, her hands trembled, and she couldn't seem to breathe properly. He gained control over the unruly colt just then and began to stroke it gently. A moment later he looked up and saw her on the hill.

That was when Cassie realized with a certainty beyond knowledge that she would love him forever.

The memory came back to her vividly as she lifted an unsteady hand to touch his bare chest. Not the same now, no. The promise of strength and power in his youth had been realized. His shoulders were broad, his chest was wide and hard, the muscles very distinct. Cassie slid her fingers into the thick, soft pelt of hair, watching the firelight dance over the gleaming black strands.

There was almost no give to his skin; the muscle and bone beneath was hard with innate strength. And Cassie's mouth was dry, her heart pounded, just as it had all those years before when she'd been on the threshold of womanhood and had first felt a woman's desire.

The memory came and went in a flash, leaving her with a more profound sense of what was happening between them. To her, it seemed destined, something that had always been meant to be. Inescapable. Fate. Because even then, even all those years ago when she was still more child than woman, she had known that someday she would be here with him, like this. That thirteen-year-old girl had never doubted it.

"Cassie," he said in a rough tone.

She looked up into his eyes, remembering that she was also naked to the waist because he was looking at her with eyes like black fire. His hands were light on her sides, and they drew her slowly forward until her breasts touched his chest. Staring into his eyes, she caught her breath at the sensual contact, seeing his response as the flames leapt higher and burned hotter. He made a low sound in the back of his throat that sounded like a growl.

Cassie was sure she had stopped breathing. And she couldn't look away from his burning eyes. He bent his head slowly and kissed her, very lightly this time, almost teasing, drawing a little sound of aching protest from her because she wanted so much more. Startling her, he turned suddenly and sank down on the edge of the bed, his hands at her waist guiding her so that she automatically turned toward him. She was abruptly looking down at him, standing between his knees, overwhelmingly conscious that she was half naked.

But before she could tense or become disturbed, Brett wrapped his arms around her and buried his face between her breasts. She felt his mouth moving on her, his big hands stroking up and down her back, and she forgot about everything except the erotic magic of his touch. Her own fingers lifted to slide into his thick, soft hair. She could hardly believe the sensations, and she was dimly shocked by the force of her emotional response to what he was doing to her. It was as if some part of her was completely caught up in the primitive act of mating.

Cassie bit her lip, trying to hold back a sound of unbearable pleasure when his mouth trailed up the slope of a swelling breast and closed over her nipple. She held his head, her fingers moving convulsively in his hair, and felt all the strength drain out of her legs in a rush. With a wordless whimper she sagged against him weakly. If his arms hadn't been wrapped around her, one beneath the curve of her bottom, she would surely have crumpled to the floor.

What he was doing to her was maddening. His mouth moved from one breast to the other, his tongue darting out to tease and swirl and torment until she didn't think she could bear any more. Her flesh responded to his touch like kindling to a match. How could her body contain such heat? One of her hands left his hair to wander over his shoulders and back, her fingers kneading the hard muscles restlessly, her nails digging into his skin when she felt his tongue flick over the burning, aching points of her nipples.

A moan escaped her. "Brett, please..." Her voice shook.

His arms tightened around her briefly, but then he put his hands on her hips and eased her back away from him. She was surprised her shaking legs would bear her weight, but they did, and she felt his hands at the snap of her jeans. He looked up at her face as he unfastened them, his hot eyes heavy-lidded and fierce, and she bent her head to kiss him urgently.

She felt the sudden release as her pants opened, then the heavy slide of denim down her legs, and managed to step out of the material and kick it aside. Then she felt his hands moving over her bottom, slow and shockingly intimate, the silky material of her panties providing a slippery friction. His fingers hooked into the waistband and pulled them down over her hips. She gave another little moan into his mouth and trembled when the scrap of material pooled around her ankles, barely able to master her quivering muscles enough to step out of the panties.

His mouth still holding hers, Brett rose slowly to his feet. His hands cupped her naked bottom and eased her against him, until she felt the roughness of his jeans and the shock of that final barrier between them. It was a strangely voluptuous sensation to feel her naked body pressed to his half-clothed one, to feel his hands on her flesh.

Cassie had never been so primitive, so at the mercy of her senses and the awakened needs of her body. She gloried in the freedom of it. Her mouth was wild under his, and her hands moved between their bodies to fumble at his belt until she got it unbuckled. She felt as well as heard him groan, felt his hard stomach tense even more when her fingers slipped under the waistband of his jeans. Somehow, she found the snap and then the zipper, unfastening both.

Still moving purely on instinct, she put her hands at his hips and slowly pushed the material of his pants and briefs down. She could feel him moving slightly, realized he was getting out of his shoes, and was dimly grateful that neither of them had worn boots. His clothing slid down, and she felt the hard muscles of his thighs beneath her fingers for only a brief moment. Brett groaned again, and then he was lifting her off her feet and onto the bed.

Cassie opened her eyes as she felt the softness of the bed under her, and looked at him dazedly as he joined her there. He had kicked his clothing away impatiently, disposing of the last barrier between them, and the lamplight and flickering firelight showed her a face that was hard and intent in desire.

"Cassie," he said, his voice shaking, too, now.

Her arms wreathed his neck and she whimpered as she kissed him back, her hunger for him so frantic that it would have shocked her if she'd stopped to think. But he didn't give her the chance. His mouth trailed down her throat, burning her with pleasure, and her body arched when his lips found the aching fullness of her breasts.

She couldn't be still; her body struggled to escape the rising tension, but she couldn't control herself. Her hands explored his back and shoulders and stroked his hair restlessly, and her legs shifted as the ache deep in her body intensified until she thought she would go mad with it. He was touching her breasts, his long fingers kneading gently while his mouth caressed, and her already swollen breasts grew tight and hard, throbbing with the heated blood of passion.

Then she felt one of his hands glide down her side, over her hip, and caress her thigh, and her tension surged dramatically. She wanted, and the craving was so acute, she thought she might cry out or sob or even die of it. He was kissing her again, exploring her mouth, the intimate touch of his tongue making her hunger stronger, even as it satisfied a part of the need.

Brett wasn't sure he could take much more. But his hunger for Cassie was so intense that the torture of prolonging the loving was almost essential. He needed to touch her and taste her and feel the rising heat of passion in her body, see it in her haunting eyes. Even though it was torment to hold back when every screaming nerve in his body demanded release, deeper instincts needed this every bit as much—and perhaps more. He had lived with a brief memory for so long that every touch of her now, every tremor of desire, every wildly exciting little sound she made, satisfied another wordless craving deep in his soul.

He felt her trembling legs part for him, and a shudder ran through him as his hand slowly stroked up the satiny softness of her inner thigh. God, she was perfect, utterly perfect, and he couldn't tell her so because he didn't have the words. He didn't have any words except her name, that was all he could say, and when he said it again, his voice was so low and raspy he hardly recognized it as anything human.

Cassie heard him, astonished that her name could sound like that, like something so vitally important it was much, much more than merely a name. It sounded like a prayer or a curse, like something ancient.

The thought fled. His hand was so close to the ache tormenting her, she suddenly could think of nothing else. The feverish heat he had ignited had centered deep in her belly, burning her until she wanted to sob with the awful pleasure of it, and between her legs the empty ache was unbearable. Then he touched her, his fingers gently probing her damp, swollen flesh, and the most exquisitely sensitive nerves in her body went wild at the caress.

The burst of sensation was so acute, Cassie didn't know if it was pleasure or pain. All she knew was that she couldn't take much more of it. Her head moved restlessly on the pillow and her nails dug into his shoulders as she gritted her teeth unconsciously to try to hold back the sounds she could feel clawing to be free. But the sounds, frantic, took wing in spite of her, and some part of her was startled at the primitive cry.

Brett shuddered, a low groan rumbling up from deep in his chest. He moved, rising above her and spreading her thighs wider as he slipped between them. Cassie felt the bold carnal touch of him as she cradled his body, his flesh hot and hard as it pressed into her softness, and the sensation was so incredibly erotic, it shocked her.

She had, naturally, thought about this, wondered how it would be, but nothing could have prepared her for the starkly intimate feelings. She stared up at him with dazed eyes, her hands gripping his shoulders, trembling, trying to catch her breath as her body began to accept him. All her awareness shifted, focusing on the slow, burning invasion. She felt an instant of pure panic that was mostly instinctive, the female's innate comprehension of vulnerability, of ancient risks and responsibilities that was the price she paid for this act, but even that faded in the face of her overwhelming need for Brett.

Cassie felt her body stretching, accepting him, but a sudden sharp pain made her flinch and jerked a soft cry from her throat. She had expected it but, again, nothing could have prepared her for the way it felt. There was a tremendous pressure as his body demanded entrance, and her sense of panic returned even stronger than before. Part of her wanted to fight him, to resist even as her body resisted, yet another part of her needed him so badly, she was willing to bear whatever she had to, pay whatever price he demanded of her as long as she could belong to him.

Tense, her body trembling, she stared up at him and saw the instant he realized what was happening, when he understood the truth. His black eyes flared, something she couldn't read leaping in the heated darkness, and on his taut face was a rapid play of emotions. Surprise. Understanding. Disbelief. And then a strange, curiously primitive expression she understood emotionally rather than mentally.

"Cassie..." This time his voice was a cry of emotion.

Her lingering panic vanished, and the tension caused by fear ebbed. Beyond her body's stubborn barrier was an emptiness she knew only he could fill, and nothing else mattered to her. Her arms slid around his neck, and she gave herself over completely to her desire, trusting him.

Brett made a rough sound when he saw that trust glowing in her eyes. The insistent demands of his body made thinking impossible, but some part of him understood what he was feeling even if he couldn't put a name to it. Then his desire rose even higher, sweeping everything else aside, and he concentrated fiercely on maintaining his restraint. She wasn't accepting him easily, her body resisting despite both desire and trust, and he didn't want to hurt her any more than he had to.

He bore down slowly, carefully, almost flinching himself when he saw her pain. He saw glimmering tears well up, and she bit her bottom lip with a smothered little sound that was like a knife to him. Her delicate body seemed so small beneath his, almost frighteningly defenseless, yet in a curious way she was the stronger at that moment. Her innocence had reined his strength when nothing else could have, and he was overwhelmingly conscious of it.

More than anything else, he wanted her memories of this night to be filled with pleasure.

He was as gentle as he knew how to be, one hand slipping between their tense bodies to touch her insistently, building her need higher as he pressed inward. Cassie moaned and whispered his name pleadingly. Then she cried out, her eyes widening in surprise and pain, but her arms were tight around his neck and the tension subsided quickly. The surprise was still there, and all her awareness seemed focused inward; the almost dreamy, absorbed look on her face was the most incredibly erotic thing Brett had ever seen.

And felt. Her body sheathed his with a silky tight heat as she adjusted to him, her legs cradled him with satiny strength, and her breasts were pressed to his chest as he slipped his arms underneath her to draw her upper body even closer. His heart was pounding so hard he thought it would burst, and all his muscles quivered with the strain of control. Staring down at her flushed, enthralled face, he felt primitive things he'd never felt before.

No matter how much his modern intellect might scoff at the uncivilized urge, the ancient male that existed somewhere deep in his being wanted to roar in wordless triumph in that stark moment of possession. There was something rawly primitive in the certain knowledge that she had given herself to him—and only him.

Cassie was completely caught up in sensation, the pain forgotten. She could feel him throbbing inside her, and his weight on her felt like the most natural thing in the world. Her body seemed designed to cradle his, yet she felt overwhelmed by the sheer intimacy of what was happening between them. She had never even imagined that this amazing closeness was possible between two people, and it was wonderful.

The fever was rising in her again, gripping her body in that other kind of almost-painful tension, and she lifted her hips just a bit, moving instinctively beneath him. She felt his arms tighten around her, saw his eyes close briefly in a spasm of pleasure, and a hoarse sound that might have been her name rose up gutturally from the depths of his chest.

When he kissed her, Cassie held nothing back. When he began moving inside her, she moaned and instinctively matched his quickening rhythm. She responded to him as always, with a hunger as deep and fierce as his own. She moved with him, and when he might have tried to be gentle, her intense sensuality burned away his restraint. She wanted him to lose control as completely as she did, and when it happened, a primitive sense of triumph swept over her.

Cassie couldn't believe what he was doing to her. The tension inside her was spiraling, winding tighter and tighter, the force of it almost frightening. She felt she was being carried on a rising wave, carried beyond herself, powerless to stop the headlong rush toward something her body desperately needed. And it was hot and frenzied and totally beyond her control. She could only struggle against it, against herself, against him, resisting the drive to give in until the last possible second.

Until, finally, she let go, and the tension shattered all her senses. Wave after wave of throbbing pleasure swept through her, convulsing her body in a release so devastating it felt like the last moment of life.

Cassie went limp, dazed, a melting weakness pulsing through her. She held Brett with what strength was left to her, drinking in the inexpressibly moving sight of his face, so profoundly primitive as he buried himself in her and shuddered with the overwhelming force of his own release.

Brett came back to himself gradually as his heartbeat slowed and his breathing steadied. He could hardly believe what had happened between them, the incredible power of it. And he could hardly believe what he now knew was the truth. She was his, all his. No other man had felt her fire.

No other man.

She had not lied about her relationship with his father. Their marriage had really been a business partnership formed purely for the benefit and protection of Killara and its future. And Brett could see now how it must have happened. Always a businessman first, Kane had obviously seen past her beauty to the potential in Cassie, her intelligence, leadership skills, and strong sense of responsibility. The future of Killara must have been on his mind after Brett left. He had needed someone he knew he could trust. With her every word and action, Cassie must have demonstrated very clearly her love for the place, and Kane had taken advantage of that.

It made perfect sense.

Brett didn't want to leave her yet, but eased himself up onto his elbows so that he could see her. She was, at that moment, more beautiful to him than ever, her face still softly flushed, her expression dreamy. He kissed her gently, wanting to say so much but somehow unable to. All he had was a question.

"Why didn't you tell me?"

She looked at him, and even though her lips still curved in a lingering smile of contentment, there was a touch of sadness in her mysterious eyes. Her voice, still husky, was low and curiously reluctant.

"I kept hoping...I wished I wouldn't have to say I could prove I'd never slept with Kane. I didn't want to have to do that. I didn't want this"—her fingers tightened on his shoulders and one thigh brushed his hip smoothly—"to be about proving something. That's no reason for two people to be together."

Brett stared down at her, and the sense of triumph he'd been conscious of vanished, replaced by a sudden rush of hot shame. All this time that he'd been asking himself why she would lie about it, asking himself what reason she could have for lying, he had been automatically suspicious of her claim, thinking of her as guilty until he could find some proof of her innocence.

And now he had it.

"Cassie..." He kissed her again, wishing he had the power to take back words, to ease the pain his disbelief had caused her. "I'm sorry, I'm so sorry. I should have believed you."

"I wish you had," she confessed softly, her smile turning a little wry. "But since you didn't, I'm glad I had proof. I...I don't think I could have borne it if you'd had doubts now."

Brett cursed himself for his own detestable suspicions. And the worst of it was that her last statement hit him hard. If she hadn't been a virgin, his hostility about her relationship with his father would certainly have remained, even intensified, and he hated to think of what that torment might have caused him to do to them both.

At that moment much of the hold the past had on him began to loosen.

"I'm sorry," he said again. His mouth found hers, gentle at first, but her response was a little fierce and it was like setting a match to dry wood. The feverish heat that had died down with completion flared again; he wanted to wrap his arms around her and lose himself in her once more.

Instead, he drew back slowly, then eased away from her. She tried to hold on to him with her arms even though she flinched slightly when his body left hers. The expression, fleeting though it was, didn't escape him.

His voice a bit raspy, he said, "I'm sorry I hurt you, honey." And he meant *all* the hurt, physical as well as emotional, the present as well as the past. She shook her head as if it didn't matter, but made a soft sound of protest when he left the bed. Brett bent to kiss her again briefly. "Shhhh, it's all right, I'll be right back," he told her in that same rough voice.

Cassie waited, closing her eyes as he moved away from the bed. She still felt boneless, and it seemed too much trouble even to get under the covers. But with the warmth of his body gone and the heat of passion banked, she was gradually conscious of being somewhat chilly. She could hear the wind wailing outside; maybe that had something to do with how she felt, because the room was comfortably warm. In any case, she didn't want to move, waiting for him to come back to her.

She heard water running in the bathroom, then a click as he turned off the light on the nightstand. She opened her eyes to a room lit only by the flickering fire, fascinated by the way the dancing light made his powerful, naked body look so primitive. He sat on the edge of the bed and bent down to kiss her, and as her arms lifted to encircle his neck, she felt him press a warm, damp cloth between her legs.

To Cassie, it seemed the most intimate thing yet between them, though she couldn't have said precisely why. He was kissing her so tenderly, caring for her so that the faint soreness she was conscious of eased, and she felt a sudden burst of love for him so overwhelming and vast, it seemed to fill her entire being.

A few moments later he tossed the cloth toward the bathroom

and joined her in the bed, drawing the covers up over them both. He pulled her into his arms, holding her close, one of his hands stroking her hair, her back.

Cassie was a little disturbed, realizing that there was too much tension in him. She thought Brett couldn't stop thinking about what his doubts could have done to them, and it wasn't something she wanted to continue. Her marriage to his father had become an issue even though it never should have; that was what Brett had to understand and believe. They would never put the past behind them until he realized that very simple truth.

Cuddled up to his side, her fingers toying with the black hair on his chest, she made her voice matter-of-fact. "Nobody told me it could be like that. You made me feel things I never even imagined."

His arms tightened around her, and his voice was more normal now, not so rough. "I can't take all the credit, Cassie. You were... pretty incredible yourself. You are sensuality itself."

Cassie almost agreed, still terrified he'd leave her when he knew the truth. Then she braced herself, and spoke steadily. "No, I don't think so. Remember you said that when you kissed me the first time, you knew it *was* my first time? You said it was as if I'd waited for you."

"And you said you had."

"Yes. I waited for you, Brett. I've always waited for you."

7

BRETT WAS VERY STILL FOR A LONG MOMENT, THEN HE SHIFTED HIS weight, rising on one elbow to look down at her. The firelight showed Cassie an expression she'd never seen before, and her heart began to thud against her ribs.

"What are you saying?" he asked huskily.

She drew a deep breath and struggled to keep her voice steady. "I've wondered since then what you really thought about that summer ten years ago. You've said something about it happening so suddenly. I suppose it all seemed sudden to you, because until you came home from college, all you saw when you looked at me was the foreman's bratty daughter. But it wasn't sudden for me, that wanting. It didn't just happen when you finally noticed me. I'd already been in love with you for years, Brett." She reached up and touched his cheek with trembling fingers. "Years."

"You were a child," he said slowly.

"Was I? Maybe so, in some ways. But I've known since I was thirteen there'd never be anyone else for me. It didn't make any difference that you had a dozen girls chasing you and catching you, that you never even looked at me. It didn't make any difference that you went away to college. It didn't even make a difference when you left without a word—and stayed away all these years. Loving you wasn't a choice, wasn't some decision I had to make. And once it happened, I couldn't change my mind about it or make it stop. It just was. Is."

"Cassie—"

She rushed on, her voice growing unsteady. "I don't want you to think I'm demanding anything, that isn't why I'm telling you how I feel. It's just . . . I think you're still bothered by the fact that I married Kane, and I want you to understand. That didn't make a difference either, Brett. I was never his, not in any way; that's why I didn't take his name. I could never have belonged to him or any other man. I already belonged to you."

Cassie didn't expect him to reveal his own feelings, whatever they were. As simple and absolute as her love for him was, she knew too well that right now Brett's emotions were tangled. He had come home with reluctance to his past, and until he sorted out his feelings about who he was, about his father, and about Killara, he couldn't begin to be certain about his feelings for her.

In the end he might love her. Or he might leave her again.

Because of that, because she didn't want him to feel pressured into responding to her declaration before he was ready to, she didn't give him a chance to try. She lifted her head from the pillow, kissing him, her arms winding around his neck. All she demanded of him was more of what he had already given her.

Against her mouth Brett said hoarsely, "I don't want to hurt you again."

Cassie didn't know if he meant he didn't want to hurt her physically or emotionally, but she didn't question him. And she didn't lie, didn't say of course he wouldn't hurt her, because she thought he probably would. Instead, she murmured, "It's all right." That was all she could say, and all that was necessary, because the passion between them flared up even higher and hotter than before.

This time there was no conversation afterward. They were left totally drained, both of them drifting from a sensual exhaustion into a peaceful sleep.

Brett didn't know what had awakened him. The room wasn't dark; the fire had died down, but a cold white light was coming through the windows. His mind registered that, and took note of the eerie silence. Then he realized he was alone in the big bed, and sat up abruptly.

He saw Cassie immediately. She was standing by one of the windows, bare-legged, wearing only his flannel shirt, her face intent as she gazed through the frosted glass. Brett looked at the clock on the nightstand, saw it was a little after two A.M., and tossed back the covers. He didn't bother to put on anything, he just went to her.

"Cassie?" He slipped his arms around her from behind, easing her back against him. She was pliant to his touch, her body warm and relaxed.

"Look," she said softly.

Outside, the Arizona countryside had been transformed into a winter wonderland. A huge full moon gleamed down on sparkling, pure white snow that covered everything. From this room Brett could see most of the outbuildings, and all of them looked beautiful and curiously peaceful. Nothing moved, not even the old weather vane atop the main barn.

The snow looked deep, so deep that Brett couldn't make out any of the dips and hollows he knew existed between the house and the barns. There was just a smooth blanket of white, rolling gently, seemingly forever.

"Is the storm over?" he asked, keeping his voice as low as hers had been.

Cassie shook her head slightly. "During the last few years, the storms in these parts have become like hurricanes. This is only the eye. The back side will be worse than what we felt yesterday."

"Will we lose much of the stock?"

She half turned to look up at him. In the curiously stark light, her lovely face was solemn. "Probably not. We have two big advantages here on Killara: the fact that we're in a valley with a lot of natural protection, and the fact that we're situated so far south. The temperature isn't much below freezing even now, and it should start climbing in another day or two. If the worst of the storm is over by tonight, and I think it will be, then we may not lose more than a dozen head. And many of those will be animals that broke a leg falling in a drift."

Brett knew that whatever the outcome, the count of lost stock would have been drastically higher if Cassie had not taken the precaution of bringing the herd in close and offering them as much protection as possible. But he didn't mention that. Cassie had made her point well when she had told him how much she resented his thanks. It was patronizing in the extreme for him to thank her for doing the job she had chosen to do. Instead, he asked, "What woke you?"

"The silence. I'm sorry, I didn't mean to wake you."

"You didn't." *Your absence did.* He didn't say it, of course. "But it's still hours till dawn. Come back to bed, honey. I'll build up the fire."

A slow smile curved her lips. "Which one?"

Something inside him responded instantly to that smile, to that soft invitation. To her. "You seem to have an exaggerated opinion of my stamina," Brett told her, but his voice deepened on the words and he was drawing her closer even as he said them.

"I doubt that," Cassie murmured.

As it turned out, she was right to doubt.

By six A.M. the storm was battering them once again, just as Cassie had predicted. The wind moaned and whistled as it swept around the house, and sleet pelted the windows. Since the moon had long disappeared behind heavy storm clouds, sleet, and blowing snow, and the sun didn't have a chance, the room was as dark as it had been at midnight.

There was no reason for her or Brett to get up so early, but it was virtually impossible for either of them to sleep late. Brett woke up a little before six to find her sliding from the bed, and even half-asleep he managed to hook an arm around her waist and drag her back under the covers with him.

"No," he said quite clearly.

Imprisoned by a painless but inescapable grip, Cassie could just barely reach the lamp on the nightstand to turn it on. Able to see him now, she twisted around to stare bemusedly down at Brett.

He was mostly on his side, one powerful arm wrapped securely around her middle, and he had both eyes closed. There was a satisfied, peculiarly male little smile on his lips, an utterly peaceful relaxation in his lean face, and he was clearly almost asleep again. If he had ever awakened, that is, which Cassie couldn't be sure of.

"Brett, I want to get up," she said softly.

His arm tightened around her, and he murmured, "It's still night."

"It's almost six. The storm's back, that's why it's so dark. Can't you hear it? I'm ready to get up. I've usually been up at least an hour by now."

"I knew there was a reason I hated ranching."

Cassie couldn't help but smile, because his tone had been the ornery one of a man who simply wasn't eager to leave his warm bed; he would have said exactly the same thing if ranching had been his passion, she knew. Still, there was probably more than a little truth in his irritable statement.

She should have felt a bit tired herself, Cassie thought. But, aside from a few muscular twinges from having engaged in an activity she was totally unaccustomed to, and an unfamiliar sensation that wasn't exactly soreness deep in her body, she felt remarkably fine. In fact, she felt energized.

"Brett, I didn't say you had to get up, so go back to sleep.

There's no work to do, I'm just—slept out. I want to go back to my room—"

Both his eyes snapped open. There was no doubt he was completely awake. "What?"

A bit startled, Cassie finished. "And take a shower, and get dressed. My clothes are there."

"Oh." A slight flush darkened the skin over his cheekbones. He turned onto his back, slid one hand to the nape of her neck, and pulled her down to kiss her.

Cassie was still puzzled by his reaction, but he quite effectively distracted her within a minute or two. In fact, she couldn't remember why she'd wanted to get up in the first place. It seemed like a very stupid idea.

Against her mouth Brett murmured, "The shower in here has room for two. And I have a robe somewhere you can wear to your room later, if you still want to get dressed."

She wondered if she would.

It turned out that she did, but it was well after seven o'clock when she stood near the bed rolling up the sleeves of Brett's robe.

"It swallows you whole," he said lazily, watching her from the tumbled bed. "But you look cute as hell in my clothes."

Cassie remembered putting on his flannel shirt when she'd gotten up to look out the window sometime during the dark watches of the night; apparently, he'd noticed. Tightening the belt at her waist, she eyed him and said, "Are you going to get up?"

"Are you going to crawl back in here with me?"

She found it both astonishing and a little frightening to feel her knees go weak when those black eyes of his rested on her with blatant invitation in their liquid depths, when his voice deepened with desire. Her willpower where he was concerned was practically nil. And she was rather amazed he could want her again, especially so soon after...

Clearing her throat, Cassie said, "I hate to mention such a prosaic subject, but I'm starving. If I don't have breakfast soon, I'm liable to collapse in a heap."

"I doubt that." Smiling, he sat up in the bed and ran his fingers absently through his still-damp hair. They hadn't dried off after their shower, too involved in each other to bother, so the sheets were damp.

Cassie ran fingers through her own damp hair, telling herself to leave for her room now but unable to stop looking at him. God, he was beautiful. "So you're getting up?" she asked, her tone somewhat preoccupied.

"I might as well, since you're being sensible." Then he laughed. "To be perfectly honest, I think I could eat a whole steer."

She glanced toward the nightstand, at the very compact intercom that an earlier Delaney had installed; there was one in almost every bedroom, and though the system was antique, nobody had bothered to have it updated or removed. Cassie went to the nightstand and pushed a button that would sound a buzzer downstairs in the kitchen. She used a particular sequence as a signal; it was something she usually did from her room to alert Moira that she was up and would be downstairs shortly.

This time her signal, familiar to them both, would register on the board in the kitchen—from Brett's room.

She looked up to see him watching her, and answered the silent question of his lifted brows. "So Moira will know we're up. She hates to cook breakfast and have to warm it over later. I always let her know I'll be down in a little while."

"Good idea."

Cassie hesitated, then said, "She'll know, of course. I mean... she'll know I didn't sleep in my bed. Do you mind?"

Brett got to his feet, gloriously naked and completely unconcerned about it. He put his hands on her shoulders and bent his head to kiss her, lightly but not briefly. "No, I don't mind. I don't care who knows. How about you?"

Cassie still felt that she was walking on eggshells, wary of every step she took. Though she felt so completely natural with him that it was easy to act casual, in truth she was terrified she would say or do something to make Brett feel pressured. So she didn't quite know how to answer, except with a shrug and a casual denial.

"No, of course I don't mind."

"Good. I'd hate to think either of us wanted to keep this a secret, as if we were doing something wrong." His voice was very steady.

She nodded, still matter-of-fact, and turned away to gather up her discarded clothing. "Then we agree. I'll go and put something on besides your robe, and dry my hair, and I'll be ready to go downstairs."

"I'll shave and dress, and meet you at your door."

Brett stood beside the bed for several minutes after she left, still not really conscious of his nudity. Her room. She had returned to her room. This one was his, that one hers. Despite the intimacy they shared now, their lives were separate.

He went into the bathroom to shave, unaware he was frowning until he saw his reflection in the mirror over the sink. He knew why it bothered him, of course. Despite her words of love, Cassie quite obviously had no intention of outwardly changing their relationship. He meant to make certain she spent her nights in his bed, and he knew she wouldn't object—but he also knew she wouldn't move a single item of her clothing or any other of her possessions into the master suite.

It bothered him. During the incredible night with her, he had discovered a depth of feeling in himself he had never known was possible, and even though his earlier fury about her marriage to his father was now gone, his emotions seemed more tangled than ever.

He wanted her love—he'd never wanted anything so much in his entire life—but it wasn't an easy matter of just accepting her love. Cassie was part of Killara, part of his past and part of who he was, and he was still uncertain if he could accept that.

It was all or nothing, he knew. With her own words and her fierce devotion, Cassie had made it plain how much she loved Killara. If in the end he turned away from this place, he would be turning away from her as well, turning his back on who she was and everything she had worked so hard to accomplish.

Whether Cassie knew it or not, he knew her love would never survive that.

Though she had not pressured him in the slightest—and wouldn't, he was sure, Brett still was conscious of a sense of urgency. There was the threat against Killara, the threat he had come back here to fight. It had never been out of his awareness. Time was running out.

The storm would leave snow on the ground, just as he had seen in the mirror, and that meant the danger was closer. If he wasn't able to identify his enemy in time, his chances of saving Killara were slight indeed.

The mirror . . .

Brett stepped back to look through the open bathroom door. The mirror was still in a corner of the bedroom, still crated. He gazed at it for a long time, automatically going through the motions of shaving.

Part of him wanted to have the crate hauled up to the attic unopened. Part of him didn't.

He listened to the part that didn't.

Cassie had decided to go downstairs alone when Brett finally reached her door. She started to ask him what had taken so long, but there was something in his eyes that made her swallow the question. Instead, she merely smiled and joined him in the hallway. He kissed her, which didn't surprise her, and kept an arm around her as they headed downstairs, which did.

"From the sound of it, the storm's getting worse," he said. "Nobody goes outside, right?"

"No, there wouldn't be much use. If the weather hasn't cleared by midafternoon, some of the hands will be sent to check the stock in the barns, but that's all."

"So the comm panel will remain active, but you won't need the computer?"

Cassie understood what he was getting at. "Right. And I can move the comm panel out of your way if you want to work at the desk, Brett."

He stopped on the landing and looked at her, his eyes restless. "I don't *want* to work, dammit, I want to spend the day in bed with you. But I'm feeling . . . pushed, Cassie. I need to check the rest of the house for fire hazards, but I doubt I'll find anything. The threat's coming from outside. And if I don't find out who wants to destroy the ranch, and soon, we'll have a hell of a lot more to worry about than a winter storm."

"I know. It's why you came home, after all."

Brett kept an arm around her as they continued down the stairs, and if Cassie hadn't known better, she could have sworn he muttered something under his breath, something that had sounded a lot like "Is it?"

Moira had breakfast ready for them, and not by a single word or look did she indicate she saw anything unusual or worthy of remark in the new and obvious closeness between Cassie and Brett. In fact, all she had to say was that Brett take his elbows off the table.

Sometime later, as he and Cassie left the kitchen, he said dryly, "I give up. As far as she's concerned, I'll always be an unmannered kid."

"Only until you have kids of your own." Cassie wanted to bite her tongue, and very carefully avoided looking at him.

They had gone into the informal den, where a cheerful fire blazed in the fireplace, and Brett didn't try to stop her when Cassie wandered over to stand gazing down at the flames. After a moment he joined her, and his voice was as matter-of-fact as she tried so hard to keep hers.

"We haven't talked about it, but we should. Cassie, when I left here, I had some wild idea of . . . just stopping it. The famous Delaney family. I wanted it to end with me. Or, at least, I thought I did."

"Even then you weren't sure," she murmured.

"No, I guess not. Because I could have taken care of the matter with a lot more finality than I did. I could have gotten myself sterilized. Instead, I just began taking the yearly injections."

She looked up at him silently, and he smiled a bit crookedly.

"Wonderful thing, technology. It's all so simple now. If you don't want to get whatever strain of flu they expect next, or catch some other stray germ floating around, or sire a child, you just take a shot." He shrugged. "After a few years it was more habit than anything else. The last shot I took was back in the summer, so that's something we don't have to worry about."

Cassie nodded. "I sort of thought you'd probably taken precautions, feeling the way you do."

"But you haven't, have you? There was no need."

She nodded again, not about to tell him that she would never have begun birth control measures simply because she had wanted to be able to conceive his child—just in case there was ever a possibility of it happening. "No, there was no need. Once I convinced my doctor that I really did intend to abstain, she said it was always her recommendation that patients never use any kind of hormone therapy, however safe, if it wasn't necessary. So I didn't."

Brett took a step to close the distance between them, and lifted his hands to surround her face. A bit huskily he said, "I don't know if I happened to mention it, but I'm glad it wasn't necessary. I'm glad you waited for me, Cassie."

She accepted his words simply for what they were, not a declaration of any kind. That attitude enabled her to kiss him back when he kissed her, and to smile at him when he raised his head again. As if that subject were closed, she began another one in a calm tone.

"Well, since we have a long day stretching ahead of us, and since you need to get back to the computer, I think I'll find something to occupy myself."

"Come help me," he invited her.

Cassie was tempted, but shook her head. "We've been over this before, and my reasoning stands. I know the ranch, not Delaney Enterprises—and the threat has to be coming from there. I wouldn't be any help, Brett."

Sighing, he released her with obvious reluctance. "Maybe not, but I think I'd enjoy the search a lot more with you beside me. Could you at least come and visit me occasionally?"

She kept her face solemn. "If you'll leave a trail of bread crumbs."

He looked a little sheepish. "Okay, so I'm not going to the ends of the earth, just to the other side of the house, and I plan to be there a few hours rather than days. Can I help it if I want you near me?"

"I hope not."

He turned away unwillingly, but paused at the door to look back at her. Almost absently he asked, "How do you plan to occupy yourself?"

She shrugged, her attention shifting a bit as a log slipped off the grate. Bending, she picked up the poker and opened the glass doors covering the fireplace to prod the burning wood back into place. "Well, I thought I might go ahead and decorate the Christmas tree."

Brett felt a chill as icy as the sleet rattling against the windowpanes. "The tree?" His voice sounded normal, he thought.

"Oh, I know it's early, but we might as well. Hank potted the tree I picked out more than a week ago; it's out by the breezeway, on this side of the garage. No problem to get at safely, even in the storm. It'll probably take me most of the morning to bring the decorations down from the attic and sort through them. I think it'll keep me busy."

Brett wanted to protest. In his mind's eye he could clearly see what the mirror had shown him. Snow on the ground. The Christmas tree in a front window. The rental car he'd driven parked out front. It was all happening, just as the mirror had shown him it would.

He wanted to stop it. But he couldn't try any more than he had tried to get a different rental car that first day. Because the threat against Killara had nothing to do with snow on the ground, or a certain rental car, or a decorated Christmas tree. Those were only signs to guide him, indications of a ticking clock, of time winding down to a particular moment. Some instinct told him that tampering with the signs would do nothing except deprive him of the warning they provided.

The huge tree he had seen would not be decorated quickly, Brett knew, but even without help Cassie would have the job completed by the next night. Decorations in place, lights on. And the storm would likely be over. Within a few days the roads would be clear. Killara would not be cut off any longer by the weather, would be accessible to any outsider.

At best, nothing would happen until the new year, weeks away; at worst, he could have only a few days left before someone tried to destroy Killara.

"Brett?" Cassie had straightened, her attention fully on him. She was frowning. "What's wrong?"

He almost told her. But again his instincts intervened to prevent him. It was plain to him that despite his telling her what he had seen in the mirror, Cassie felt that Killara was safe for now. Her immediate concern was the storm and its effects, which was logical and efficient. He had a strong feeling it was important that she remain as unaffected by his own worries as possible. She had unusual powers of perception, and it was something he thought he might need; the less she knew about the specific signs he had seen, the more likely she was to see something else, something he could miss.

"Brett?" she repeated, taking a step toward him.

He managed a smile. "It's nothing. I'm all right. Really."

"Coping with memories?" she asked a bit hesitantly.

Brett shrugged, hoping to God this was as close as he would ever come to lying to her. "Something like that. Look, I'm going to be on the computer until lunchtime, I imagine. By then I'll probably have to get away from it at least for a while. So you can help me check over the rest of the house and then I'll help you with the tree. All right?"

"Of course." She smiled suddenly. "Don't forget those bread crumbs."

In a light tone to match hers he said, "I'll lay a clear trail."

He didn't, of course. But she found her way to him without the bread crumbs.

* * *

It was nearly ten o'clock, and Brett was sipping the coffee Cassie had brought him a few minutes before, when he found what he'd been looking for. At first he nearly missed the significance of what he was scanning, but an inner alarm bell jangled and he set his mug down with a thud on the desk as he quickly scrolled back to take a second look at the relevant section.

He had been studying one of the many reports concerning the activities of Delaney Enterprises. This section dealt with something that had occured *after* his father's death, hardly more than six months earlier. It seemed that the board had voted to buy a small, struggling company against the wishes of the man who had started it.

This man, Duncan Lang, had not accepted the takeover with grace. He had stormed into a board meeting with alarmed security men at his heels, so enraged that several board members thought he might have a coronary. His tirade had been recorded for posterity— and recorded verbatim.

Brett read it slowly, and this time he paid very careful attention to every word. Lang had not made a specific threat against anyone in the room, but he *had* gone on at length about the "arrogance" of the Delaneys, about their "merciless" business tactics, and their "mongrel" bloodlines—that last in a sarcastic reference to the family's history of being publicly considered as America's own kind of royalty. If he knew there was only one heir to Kane and that Brett was on the other side of the world, uninvolved in the running of Delaney Enterprises, he didn't mention it.

Indeed, he seemed to see the Delaney "family" as the large and far-flung entity it had been in years past rather than as much smaller, as it was today. It was as if his grievance was so vast and painful that his bitterness and rage required a target far larger than one man ... or one executive board.

It was the last bit of Lang's tirade Brett couldn't take his eyes off.

I know two other men who've lost businesses to Kane Delaney's raids while he was alive—and now you vultures are continuing that fine tradition of greed. The Delaney family has spent two hundred years building up their power so nobody could touch them. They've forgotten what it feels like to lose something important to them. Maybe they need a reminder. Maybe if that fine house of theirs burned to the ground or this fine office building blew up, maybe you'd all know how I feel—

Brett swore softly, feeling his heartbeat quicken. A flat-out threat, for God's sake, and a damned public one. It had never occurred to him there would be a threat so direct, so bluntly obvious.

"Eliminate the obvious, dammit," he muttered to himself, angry because he should have done that at the very beginning—and would have if his emotions hadn't been overshadowing the problem.

He quickly gave the computer new instructions. What he wanted the machine to do was to list all reported instances of threats made against Delaney Enterprises, any executive or board member of the company, Killara, Kane Delaney, himself, or other members of the Delaney family. He narrowed the search to the previous ten years, knowing that few people would wait that long to carry out a threat.

While the computer was cross-referencing information with a speed the human brain could never hope to equal, a video call came through from Gideon Paige. Brett was nonplussed. Gideon had no news for him from Australia, no real reason to talk, but he was full of questions about Brett's progress and plans. He seemed . . . jealous? Brett shook off the question as absurd and went back to the problem of Duncan Lang. He noted the man's name and brooded over why he would have waited months to carry out his threats—assuming, of course, that he'd ever intended to.

Then Brett remembered. In going over the company's records, he'd begun with current information and backtracked; he recalled now that the year-end statements he'd gone over first had noted the fact that the acquisition of Lang's company was ongoing, not expected to be complete until the first of next year. Apparently Lang was fighting them with everything he had.

But he would lose, Brett knew. Lose a company he'd spent

twenty years building. That kind of thing had driven more than one man over the edge.

The first of next year . . .

Duncan Lang was such a remarkably apt possibility, Brett could hardly imagine why he would need to look further. Which just goes to show, he decided later, how idiotic it is to assume anything at all.

It took the computer nearly half an hour to finish its assigned task of sifting through ten years of records, and Brett felt more than a little bleak when he looked at the resulting list on the screen. Of the ten-year span, Kane Delaney had run the company eight years. And during those eight years, there had been *twenty-six* recorded threats, twelve made against him specifically and the rest more general.

That was the first eight years. During the last two, with Kane out of the picture and the board in control, three more threats—excluding Lang's—had been made against something or someone associated with Delaney family concerns.

"Thirty? You mean thirty people have made threats in just the last ten years?"

Cassie had stopped sorting Christmas ornaments when Brett had come into the front drawing room, and was watching him as he picked his way through the boxes and piles of shiny objects to reach the fireplace. A fire lent a cheery warmth to the huge room, but he was obviously disinclined to be cheered. In fact, the look he gave the old bogwood clock on the mantel was decidedly grim.

Nodding, he showed her the hard copy he'd requested from the computer, and placed the sheets on the mantel with a sigh. "Just for the hell of it, I asked for a second list, this one going back a lot further. Since my father took over Delaney Enterprises, there's an average of two *public* recorded threats per year against him personally. I knew he was ruthless—but, hell, didn't he know how to get what he wanted without destroying people in the process?"

"I don't think so," Cassie said simply.

Brett looked at her for a moment, then left the fireplace to sit on a footstool near her. She was sitting on the carpet, comfortably cross-legged, and he couldn't get closer without treading on the fragile ornaments spread around her on the floor. She looked fragile, he thought, in her oversize red sweater and snug black pants, her golden hair held off her face by a ribbon.

He couldn't help but think how amazing it was that there was enough steely strength and will in her delicate body to withstand Kane Delaney's ruthless nature, even to triumph over it for so many years.

With some difficulty he said, "My father was a real bastard, wasn't he?" He had said it before, and to her, but there was a difference. The first time he had said it, he had been blindly angry. This time he truly understood just how much of a bastard Kane Delaney had really been.

"Yes," she answered just as simply as before. Then she smiled at him slowly. "But that doesn't have anything to do with you."

"Doesn't it? You compared us a lot when I first came home, and I seem to remember being told more than once how like him I was."

"Past tense is right. Once you got rid of that chip on your shoulder and stopped trying to prove you weren't a Delaney, all the resemblance to him sort of faded away." Cassie's smile remained, but her expression was grave. "Brett, I honestly believe you got the best of the line that produced Kane—but very little from *him*. Just like that line on his headstone says, it was his nature to destroy. But it isn't yours. Believe that."

Brett was leaning toward her, his elbows on his knees. He looked down at his clasped hands, at the emerald ring glowing on his finger. Slowly he said, "It's obvious Dad trained the board too well. They've made some pretty ruthless decisions and choices since they've had control. The company might be richer for it, but I don't much like what I see."

Cassie didn't say a word.

He looked up at her and smiled crookedly. "You're not going to remind me, huh?"

"No. You don't need reminding."

Brett nodded. "True. I know I'm the only one in a position to change how Delaney Enterprises is run. If I step back into the picture, control reverts to me automatically. I can clean house at the company, replace every board member and executive, start from scratch if I want to. I can even reverse some of the decisions made in the last year or two."

Duncan Lang, he thought. If Brett stopped the takeover and offered instead to support Lang, to become an investor in his company or arrange a loan of some kind to help him through his troubles, the man would have no reason to follow through on his threats. That would, at least, turn one of thirty possible enemies into a friend, or at least a neutral partner.

Twenty-nine to go.

Ironic. In order to save Killara, Brett might well have to assume the place his father had always intended for him, because he could cope with the enemies of the Delaney family only from within the company that had bred those enemies.

8

Cassie didn't intend to help him brood over the decision he had to make. Reasonably, she said, "Well, since you can't contact anyone outside Killara until the storm breaks, there's nothing you can do about the situation now."

"Yeah." He gave her a wry smile. "It's almost funny. When I came back home, I thought I could fight for Killara the way some of my ancestors fought for the place, with sweat and blood. There was a part of me that was even looking forward to a good physical fight. Instead, it looks like my fight's going to be a little different—and not nearly so black and white. I'll have to wade into a company and find the conscience my father kicked out of it. Instead of struggling hand to hand with an enemy, I'll have to try to stitch up the wounds Dad inflicted."

He laughed shortly and sat up straighter, his hands flexing on his thighs. "Talk about the sins of the father."

Cassie rose gracefully from the floor and came to him, avoiding the fragile ornaments spread out everywhere. She knelt between his feet, her hands reaching to cover the restless ones on his thighs. "Does that matter?" she asked softly.

He frowned, trying to keep his mind on the conversation when her nearness and touch were having their usual effect on his senses. "Of course it does. Or should. Cassie, I've never admitted it before, at least not out loud, but I hated him. I hated my own father. The only reason I would have come home if I'd known he was dying was that I felt some battered sense of duty toward him. I hate him even more now when I can see what he's done, the lives he's destroyed."

She wondered if he realized how many times he had called this place home in the last few minutes. Probably not. But it was something that made her heart beat faster with hope. She threw caution to the wind, knowing there would never be a better time for him to see the truth.

Cassie's voice remained calm, soft. "Brett, your mother was wonderful. Your grandparents were terrific. If you look back, so many of your ancestors were exceptional people. There was the black sheep here and there, and there's been a strain of ruthlessness in Delaney blood ever since old Shamus, but by and large your family has an incredible record of producing good people. Strong people."

He nodded slightly. "Yeah, I know, but—"

"No, listen to me." Her voice became even more gentle. "You think that because Kane somehow wound up with all the twisted genes, the lousy traits and rotten flaws and the weaknesses, that it's somehow a reflection on *you*. That you *can't* be a Delaney, can't let yourself accept that burden because you don't believe you are good enough to live up to that magnificent ancestry."

She drew a deep breath, her haunting gray eyes holding his steadily. "Your feelings about Kane colored everything in your life, don't you see that? He dirtied the name of Delaney. You began to recognize that when your mother died and he no longer had Rebecca's influence tempering the worst of his traits. The best thing I know about him is that he grieved so terribly for her."

Brett cleared his throat. "It's the best thing I ever knew about him."

"Yes." Cassie kept her voice even. "After that he got worse with every year. You saw it. And that's when you began to—resist being a Delaney. Kane expected so much of you, but it wasn't only his expectations you struggled against. You could see what he was doing, see his ruthless disregard for others, his cruelty and hostility. He was making an awful reputation for himself, and you knew it. His name was Delaney. Wasn't that what you hated most? All those wonderful stories about the family, all those heroes. Then came Kane, your own father, to ruin the epic romance of it with his corruption."

It was painful, contemplating all this, but Brett forced himself to. He thought he'd avoided it long enough. "You said he loved me, but that we were too much alike to get along."

Cassie nodded instantly. "Yes, he loved you, and yes, you shared some traits with him. Stubbornness, temper, a streak of arrogance— and a passionate conviction that you were always right." She smiled to take the sting out of her words, and went on. "The difference, though, was that *you* were still very young, Brett. Those traits in you were the natural ones of a fierce young man; all you needed was time to mature. Leaving here was probably the best thing you could have done for yourself, you know. It gave you the time you needed without Kane's negative influence to grow into the man you were meant to be."

Brett lifted his hands to her shoulders, leaving her hands lightly gripping his thighs. "It wasn't a reasoned decision, and you know it. I went because of the mirror, because of what it showed me."

"That doesn't matter, not now. Brett, if you had never gone away, Kane's influence could have been devastating. Your anger and bitterness suited him and his plans because he thought he could turn you into a carbon copy of himself. And he just might have been able to do that."

Brett was silent for a moment, then spoke slowly. "Instead of coming back home with at least a chance of repairing some of the damage he caused, if I'd never left here, I would probably have followed his lead and learned to destroy people myself."

Cassie half nodded. "But that didn't happen. You *did* go away, and you do have the chance to make things right. Do you remember Patrick? That lone Delaney who saw his world torn apart by war while he was a young man? He could have let the awful waste of that war color his life, but he didn't. He didn't do anything especially heroic, not really. All he did was to decide that his family would flourish again. He rebuilt the Delaney family, giving it more than another century of life and prosperity and history. He didn't let the past burden him any more than those who followed let the past burden them. Don't let it burden you, Brett, not anymore. Just start it all again. Start it fresh and new, and put *your* mark on the future. After all, maybe you didn't come back here just to save Killara. Maybe you came back to save the Delaneys."

He couldn't look away from those incredible eyes. His fingers probed the delicate bones of her shoulders, and he thought again how remarkable it was that there was so much strength and will in her slender body. And so much wisdom.

"That's a tall order."

She was smiling at him. "No problem. You're a tall man. And your name's Brett Delaney. Have you realized that there isn't another Brett on the entire family tree? You're unique."

"Not as much as you are," he told her, pulling her against him. He barely had time to wrap his arms around her when a brisk voice in the doorway interrupted.

"Lunch is ready, you two."

Turning his head to glare at Moira, Brett released a sound midway between a laugh and a groan. "Suppose I told you we weren't quite ready for it?"

Moira lifted an eyebrow. "I would say it's soup and sandwiches. It'll keep." Then she calmly drew the double doors closed, leaving them in the room alone together.

"I'll be damned," Brett said.

Cassie slipped her arms around his neck, her body molding itself to his, and he forgot his astonishment because he had to kiss her. A few moments later he muttered, "All these damned ornaments. Most of them are older than I am, and quite a few date back to all those heroic people in my epic family. If we break any of them, everybody up on the hill is going to come down here and haunt us."

Her eyes were sleepy with desire as she gazed solemnly at him. "Oh, that would never do. But there aren't any ornaments on the couch, you know. I kept that clear. Just in case."

"Shameless hussy," Brett said.

They didn't break a single ornament, even though one of Brett's shoes narrowly missed a crystal angel. . . .

After their delayed lunch, Brett and Cassie checked for fire hazards in the remainder of the house. Since it was impractical to consider tearing out walls to check old wiring, they contented themselves with the most obvious dangers: frayed electrical cords, flammable liquids, objects or furnishings too close to heat registers. They were quick but thorough, and the search yielded nothing except a bit more peace of mind.

The storm eased up during the afternoon, and Cassie sent a few of the hands to the barns to take care of the stock there. Nobody stayed out more than a few minutes at a time since the weather was a long way from being clear, and she tracked them every second. The weather service was confident the storm would blow itself out sometime during the night, so she decided not to risk sending anyone farther out. The cattle could be better tended after the storm, and a few hours wouldn't matter much.

Watching her as she worked at the desk, Brett waited until the last hand was safely back in the bunkhouse, then said, "If the sensors know the difference between a cow and a coyote, would they be able to track something else? Say, a man?"

"You mean a trespasser?"

"Yeah. I know our people are wearing the wristbands now, so the system's set up to track them. What about someone else?"

"You don't really think even a madman would try to get through this storm to torch the house, do you?"

Brett shook his head. "No, I'm thinking about after the storm passes. I mean, this place doesn't have an external security system except for the locks and alarms on the buildings. We don't have the thousands of acres of Killara electronically fenced. Anybody could get on this land if they wanted. They could make their way to the house, and they wouldn't have to get inside to start a fire. Would this system alert us to that kind of movement?"

Cassie chewed on her bottom lip as she considered the question. "Well, this isn't a security system, so it isn't set up that way. I think I could reprogram it. The thing is, there'd be a lot of bugs at first, a lot of glitches, even if I could manage to do it. Our people, every one of them, would have to keep wearing the wristbands all the time, so the sensors would be able to identify them. That's no problem, but the difference between a cow and a coyote is several hundred pounds. How do I set the sensors to look for a man who is probably not on foot? If he's on horseback, the tracking system would just note the horse, and we have lots of horses on Killara. With all the vehicles we have going around here all the time—especially with snow piled up everywhere—there's no way the system could differentiate between a Jeep that belongs here and one that doesn't."

Brett held up a hand in surrender, his expression wry. "I had a feeling it wouldn't work, but I had to ask."

"If you're really worried, I can post some of the hands at strategic positions around the valley after the storm. They'd be able to spot a stranger for sure unless he was wearing Arctic gear or was otherwise invisible. But that'll leave us awfully shorthanded, Brett. It would take at least two dozen people to cover the valley with any kind of thoroughness, and I need every hand I can get to take care of the stock."

He brooded for a moment, then shook his head decisively. "No,

I think we'll count on the slippery terrain to keep him away for a few days at least. You can alert all the hands to keep an eye out for strangers, though."

Cassie nodded. "That's no problem. They'll all be close in for a few days anyway, because we have to clear away the snow."

Brett leaned down to kiss her. "Anybody ever tell you you're a hell of a rancher?" To his surprise, a quick flush spread delicate color over her cheeks.

"No," she murmured.

"Well, you are."

"Thanks. I had a good teacher."

"Not Dad," Brett said definitely. "As I remember, he pretty much left things to the foreman."

Cassie looked momentarily surprised herself, then shook her head a little. "You're right. My father. I guess I picked up more than I thought from him. Kane taught me a lot about the business end of ranching, though."

Brett pulled her up from the chair, smiling down at her. "You do try to be fair to him, don't you?"

"I suppose." She'd never thought about it. "For the most part he treated me with respect, Brett. Granted, it was probably because he wanted me to manage the ranch and I'd made it plain that if he pushed me too far I'd leave, but since the end was that he left me pretty much alone, I didn't care about the reasons. Oh, he taunted me from time to time, the way he did everyone, but I got used to that."

"Did he know—" Brett broke off abruptly and shook his head as if at himself.

Steadily, Cassie said, "Did he know I loved you? Yes, I told him before I accepted his marriage proposal. I don't think he believed me until—well, until I refused to share his bed." She hesitated, then said, "He taunted me about my feelings for you. That's the worst thing he did to me."

Brett held her close against him, meaning to comfort her because the pain in her eyes hurt him. But their bodies were becoming so attuned to each other that desire was never far away. He kissed her, slowly and deeply, then lifted his head reluctantly.

"At this rate, we'll never get that tree decorated," Cassie murmured.

"Bah, humbug," he said after a moment's consideration.

She laughed. "No Christmas spirit? Brett, I'm ashamed of you."

Because he didn't want to diminish her pleasure in the holiday, and because he had begun to feel confident that he could stop the threat against Killara just as soon as the weather cleared enough for communication with Tucson, Brett allowed his mind to be distracted from everything except her and his enjoyment in being with her.

Musingly, he said, "I've forgotten. Do we hang mistletoe here in the house?"

Cassie nodded, at the same time slipping from his loosened embrace and heading toward the door. "Uh-huh. In practically every doorway."

Brett followed her. "Good," he said, his heated gaze admiring her graceful walk.

They spent the remainder of the day together in the front parlor, stringing what seemed to be miles of old-fashioned lights around a potted tree of truly epic proportions. A Delaney-type tree, Brett observed, to which Cassie solemnly agreed. And there were also the aforementioned Christmas ornaments, enough for even an imposing tree to be proud of. From the very old wooden ornaments Shamus had carved for each of his sons and the golden baubles of a genuine treasure later claimed by one of those sons to the very latest thing in holographic decorations, the ornaments spanned all the generations of the Delaney family since they had put down roots in their new country.

Brett hadn't helped decorate a Christmas tree since he was a boy, and he enjoyed it very much. There was a strong feeling of tradition in performing the tasks involved, and an even stronger sense of his family ties than he'd ever felt before.

Or maybe, he realized, he was so conscious of his family, his heritage, because Cassie had helped him to sort through his emotions.

One thing he had realized, and come to accept, was that he was tied
to the past because everyone was. Past, present, future—it was a circle, a loop. Maybe he'd been so conscious of the past because at Killara it was all around him, but he lived in the present and looked
forward to the future.

In any case, he was feeling more and more like a Delaney with
every hour that passed—and for the first time in many years he was
enjoying it.

They stayed up till midnight working on the tree, and the storm
outside had quieted almost to silence when Brett finally climbed the
tall ladder and placed the magnificent holographic star at the top.
He came back down and moved the ladder away, then stood with
his arm around Cassie as she pressed a switch.

Sparkling with myriad lights in all colors, its every branch tipped
with a unique decoration, the tree was beautiful and dignified, grand
the way a shooting star is grand because it's such a fleeting thing.

"An epic tree," Brett murmured, honestly moved by the en-
chanting sight despite his gentle mockery.

Cassie looked up at him, trying to keep a straight face. "You're
never going to let me forget my choice of words to describe your
family's history, are you?"

"No. Epic is a wonderful word, a vast, complicated, glorious
word. Inspiring. Makes me feel like Ulysses off to conquer and pil-
lage."

"I don't think he pillaged," she offered.

"Of course he did. They all did. Even heroes pillaged in those
days. It was required of them."

She began to giggle, feeling lofty herself in the face of his enjoyment. "So I finally got you all fired up with enthusiasm, huh?"

"Something like that." Without a wasted motion he lifted her
and slung her gently over his shoulder. In the same calm and reasonable tone, he said, "I think we'll leave the lights on so the tree can get
used to them." Then he carried her from the room and up the stairs.

Cassie was too busy laughing to protest.

It was considerably later when she roused herself enough to notice they'd left the lamp on the nightstand on. Pressed to Brett's side, she thought about the matter idly and decided not to do anything about it. She just lay contentedly listening to his heart beat steadily beneath her ear.

Then her drowsy gaze probed one corner of the room, and she realized something was missing. "Brett?"

"Hmmm?"

"The mirror's gone."

"No. I uncrated it before I met you for breakfast. It's hanging in the dressing room."

Cassie was still for a moment, then got one elbow beneath her and raised herself enough to look at his face. He was awake, his black eyes meeting hers with tranquility but no sleepiness in their liquid depths. She thought he had the most beautiful eyes she'd ever seen.

"You hung it in the dressing room?" She waited for his nod, then asked hesitantly, "Did you—?"

"See anything? No, just my reflection."

Cassie hesitated again, but couldn't stop the question. "You wanted to, didn't you? See something, I mean."

Brett lifted a hand to brush a strand of shining gold hair from her face, his fingers lingering to stroke her satiny skin. What could he answer to that? The truth, of course.

"I had a dozen questions for it, demands really," he said quietly. "There was a lot I wanted to know about the future. But it's a contrary thing, that mirror. Stubborn." He shrugged. "I have a feeling it's shown me all it will. It sent me away from here and brought me back. I guess all the rest is up to me."

Again Cassie had to ask, "Do you believe the mirror *caused* events?"

He smiled. "No. Sorry. I know that's your theory, but I can't buy it. Although I suppose it's no more bizarre than believing the mirror can predict the future or show scenes of the past."

"But you believe it's possible to prevent what it showed you would happen?"

"Killara burning? Yes. I have to believe it, Cassie. Especially now."

She forgot about her worries over the mirror, his words raising a much greater anxiety. She thought he had decided to stay, that he was home for good, but she wasn't sure. So she waited mutely, her eyes locked with his.

He stroked her cheek tenderly. "I don't want to fight just for Killara now, I want to fight for it all. I want Delaney Enterprises to regain its reputation for honesty and fairness, even if it takes years and I have to restructure the company from the ground up." He smiled. "You've said a lot that makes sense, sweetheart, and I think you're right, at least about most of it."

"Then you're home for good?"

Brett nodded, and there was a glow in his black eyes she'd never seen before. His voice deepened suddenly. "If you'll let me come home, Cassie. Really come home."

She swallowed hard. "What do you mean?"

His thumb rubbed over her bottom lip in a slow, sensuous little caress, and his voice became even lower, husky with emotion. "I mean that I finally know how I feel, especially about you. All these years I was so blinded by my own anger at Dad, I couldn't see the truth about anything else. But now I can because you helped me to. I love you, Cassie. I've loved you for a long, long time. And I want this to be our home, together."

Cassie didn't realize just how much strain she'd been under until the relief of its ending nearly overwhelmed her. He was kissing her, murmuring words of love and desire, and she didn't remember how she'd wound up on her back, but it didn't matter. She kept her arms around his neck, and she thought she was crying, but that didn't matter either.

"You're going to marry me," he said fiercely.

She let out a little sigh, her eyes glowing up at him, and her smile was radiant. "I've been waiting to marry you since I was thirteen."

Brett kissed her, then lifted his head suddenly. His black eyes were very bright. "You weren't the only one waiting. Until today it was a memory, a whole bundle of feelings I couldn't let myself re-member. I was seventeen. You rode out to the lake, where I was working with a yearling, to warn me there was a storm coming."

Cassie felt her heart beat faster. "You saw? You knew that was the day it happened?"

"It happened to me too, sweetheart. I looked up, and you were sitting on that little paint mare of yours, bareback as usual. The wind had picked up, and your hair was blowing around your face like gold silk—and I felt like somebody had kicked me in the stomach. I thought I'd gone out of my mind."

Wonderingly but with a slight touch of indignation, she said, "You ignored me for the next five years."

He let out a low laugh. "Cassie, my darling, the law—not to mention your father—considered you a child. The way I felt about you scared the hell out of me, and I was pretty sure I couldn't control it. Of course I stayed as far away from you as I could. At least until I came home from college and found you reasonably grown-up."

Recalling the explosion of heat between them then, Cassie be-lieved him. Their passion *had* been like something that had been contained too long, just as the same overwhelming force had gripped them this time after ten years.

"I love you," she said gravely.

Brett kissed her, tenderness heating with desire. "I love you. God, I love you so much...."

A long time later, as Cassie sank blissfully into the most exqui-site sleep she could ever remember, she found the strength to mur-mur, "Epic."

And Brett must have understood, because she heard him chuckle drowsily as he pulled her even closer and finally turned off the lamp on the nightstand.

The next two days were frantically busy. The storm was gone, leav-ing behind it a foot of snow with drifts several feet in depth. The good news was that the temperature rose almost at once to begin a slow melt. The bad news was that in the meantime, everyone had to work despite it.

Brett had thought he might be able to regain control of the company while remaining at the ranch, using a conference hookup, but a moment's consideration convinced him that he didn't want to seem in any way distant, didn't want to set up the possibility in anyone's mind that his return and his hand on the company was anything but definite. So, after completing all the work he could at the ranch, he reluctantly left Cassie to deal with the aftermath of the storm, and flew into Tucson to begin asserting his authority.

He called a board meeting in the Tower Building, the headquarters of Delaney Enterprises, and he spent the hours while everyone scrambled to get there in reacquainting himself with the layout of the building and speaking to a large number of surprised employees. When the board was finally assembled, he listened quietly for nearly two hours, then promptly "cleaned house" so that only two members of the original board remained in place. He offered generous severance pay to those fired, but didn't listen to protests or excuses.

Ordinarily Brett wouldn't have moved so rapidly, but in this situation he had little choice. He knew that every decisive action sent shock waves throughout the company, but he couldn't afford to hesitate. He consolidated his power quickly, made it plain things were going to change—and then set about changing them.

He spent long hours at the Tower over the next few days, coat off and sleeves rolled up, making it obvious to everyone around him that he was taking charge with a vengeance.

Bewildered executives found themselves conferring with company attorneys to draft agreements, some of which concerned past business deals and decisions; computers hummed and phones buzzed; video displays showed puzzled faces as, one by one, the people Kane Delaney had injured were located and contacted. All were told that Brett Delaney now ran the company, that he would not stand for unfair treatment—even that which his father had been responsible for—and that he had an offer to make them in the form of compensation for the losses they had suffered.

All were skeptical, but Brett spoke to each directly as he or she was contacted. He was matter-of-fact and businesslike, explaining his reasons and his offer. He had worked hard to shape each offer for the individual, and that effort showed.

It was well after dark when Brett flew back to Killara each evening, and he had the satisfaction of knowing he was making definite progress. Of the half-dozen people they found in those first few days, all had accepted his offers, at least provisionally, and seemed willing to reestablish cordial relations with Delaney Enterprises. Even Duncan Lang, whom Brett had contacted directly with the offer of investment or a bailout loan, had been civil—especially since he'd just received the news from his own people that Delaney Enterprises had halted the takeover.

Brett had made certain to first contact the people he considered most likely to make an attempt against Killara, so he felt much safer now. None of the executives he'd fired had showed any disposition to make threats even against him personally and, besides that, he felt no danger from any of them.

When he'd mentioned it to Cassie on that first night, she was quick to understand his thinking.

"You mean none of the executives could possibly be responsible for Killara burning because when the mirror showed you that scene you had no plans to get near the office, much less do anything to cost them their jobs."

He nodded, but he was conscious of a peculiar feeling suddenly, as if something had lightly brushed his skin.

Cassie was obviously troubled. "Yes, unless your coming home and taking over the company was at least a part of the events leading up to what the mirror predicted."

Brett couldn't really disprove that theory. In fact, it left him uneasy. He couldn't help wondering if Cassie had had the right idea all along—or at least had come close. He still didn't believe the mirror had controlled events, but perhaps what it had shown him had been a prediction of what would happen *when* he came back to Arizona and assumed his rightful place as head of Delaney Enterprises.

His own actions in attempting to thwart fate could be the very ones that would cause it to work its worst.

Realistically, Brett knew he could second-guess himself until it drove him crazy. All he could do was what he had done—take steps to safeguard Killara. He had begun a course of action based on the assumption that the threat had existed before he had returned, and he had to continue along that path. He wouldn't be very effective if he rushed off in every direction, trying to fight real and imagined threats.

The ranch was recovering, the hands still working close in because that's where the stock was. Four head had been lost in just the way Cassie had predicted—from broken legs—but otherwise it seemed Killara had weathered the storm with little damage. The only threat was external.

His unease about the situation made Brett work even harder. He hated being away from Cassie for the necessary hours, but since they spent every possible moment together, it was at least bearable when he had to return to Tucson. He continued to put his plans into action, moving as quickly as possible to nullify every chance of a threat he had found.

At some point he called his partner in Australia and announced he was bowing out of their business there.

"What? Brett, for God's sake—"

"Look, Gideon, I know this is sudden, but I've made up my mind. I belong here. You can buy me out, or I'll become a silent partner—whatever. I can't run two companies on opposite sides of the world and be fair to either. You'll do fine alone."

Gideon Paige protested long and hard, but he didn't have a chance to change Brett's mind.

Truthfully, Brett was entirely caught up in Cassie, the ranch, and his work, and not much interested in anything else. The days slid past, busy and filled with his growing contentment as he felt more and more that he truly had come home. His relationship with Cassie was more exciting and satisfying than he had ever dreamed possible, Delaney Enterprises was shaping up as he wanted, and Killara, peaceful as the snow of the storm melted away, sprawled unharmed in the valley.

They had another light snowfall on the twenty-first, this one lovely without being dangerous, and since the temperature hovered just at freezing, it seemed they would have a traditional white Christmas.

9

ON THE TWENTY-SECOND, WHICH WAS A SUNDAY, CASSIE SPENT THE time after lunch wrapping a few last-minute presents to place under the tree. She was by herself in the front parlor, since Brett had ridden up to the cemetery. Although he had suggested she come along, she believed he needed the time alone there. She felt certain he was ready to make peace with his father, to accept the somewhat wry excuse engraved on Kane Delaney's headstone and put the pain behind him for good.

She was glad.

He hadn't been gone for more than an hour when Cassie started at the sound of the front door's chimes. She had thought she'd heard a Jeep sometime before, but there were Jeeps moving around quite a bit today, so she hadn't paid much attention.

She went to the front door and opened it, wondering if one of the hands needed her and had driven to the house to find her rather than call. But the man she faced in the doorway was a stranger to her.

He smiled quickly, a man of medium height, about Brett's age, with a thin, somewhat intense face and pale blue eyes. "Hello—you must be Cassie. I'm sorry to turn up here without calling, but I thought a surprise might be more effective." He offered a slim, well-shaped hand. "I'm Gideon Paige, Brett's partner for the last five years."

"He's mentioned you," Cassie said, shaking hands and stepping back to admit him to the house. "But I'm a little surprised he mentioned me to you."

Gideon smiled crookedly. "I'll have to say he didn't seem to be aware of it, but if I heard your name once in five years, I heard it a hundred times. And I heard about Killara too. This is ... quite some place."

"Yes, it is," Cassie agreed, a bit preoccupied by learning that she hadn't been far from Brett's mind even on the other side of the world and after years.

"Is Brett here? I understand he's been raising hell in the business world, but even God rested on the seventh day."

Jerked from her abstraction, Cassie felt a brief spurt of anger. Gideon was smiling at her though, so she dismissed it. He was just smarting a bit from losing a brilliant business partner, she decided, and that was why he'd spoken so sarcastically.

"He's—he's outside at the moment. He rode up to the old family cemetery."

"I could use a ride to get some fresh air after the trip. Is there a horse available? I'm no expert, but I've been riding for years."

"Of course."

Cassie called down to the barn to have a horse saddled, then led Gideon through the house and out the back. She pointed to the barn where he'd find his horse waiting, and then showed him where the cemetery was. From their angle Brett wasn't visible, but Cassie knew he was still up there.

She remained at the back of the house, absently hugging herself against the sharp cold since she hadn't put on a coat, and watched him make his way down to the barn. A few moments later she also watched him exit the barn mounted on a big sorrel paint gelding. He waved to her, a salute she returned, then headed for the cemetery.

She went slowly back into the house. Moira wasn't in the kitchen; she and Hank were spending time together in their rooms, which was their habit on Sunday afternoons. Cassie felt peculiarly alone, and increasingly restless. She found herself climbing the stairs with no clear idea of why. It wasn't until she was standing before the closed dressing room door in the master bedroom that she realized where she was going.

It was the strangest feeling, as if something were pulling her gently but insistently. Cassie wanted to resist, yet at the same time she felt a sense of urgency compelling her to look into the mirror for the second time in her life.

She opened the door that Brett hadn't bothered to lock, though he kept it closed. The light switch was easy to find. Cassie went steadily across the small room and stood in front of the mirror where it hung on the wall. She hadn't seen the mirror in a long time. When she'd had it sent to Brett, Hank had crated it, and Cassie hadn't felt tempted to look since it had been returned to its place in the dressing room.

She had forgotten how lovely it was, how mysterious. The dark bogwood frame so exquisitely carved, the glass so brilliant. It seemed to grow more brilliant as she watched—and then suddenly it wasn't her reflection she saw.

"Hello, Brett."

Startled, he jerked his gaze from Kane Delaney's grave to find he had a visitor. He'd been so intent on his own thoughts, he hadn't heard the horse, but now he saw it standing lazily beside his own gelding.

"Gideon, what on earth—"

"I hope I'm not intruding up here. Cassie said this was where you were, and I thought it'd be a peaceful place for us to talk."

Brett sighed, misting the cold air before his face. "Well, since you came halfway around the world, to say nothing of riding a horse up this hill, I guess I owe you that much. But if this is about the company, I'm not going to change my mind. I'm sorry, Gideon."

"Brett, I'm a behind-the-scenes man, you know that." Gideon's voice was steady. "I don't have your charisma or your brains. *You* won most of our clients, and it's you they're loyal to. If you walk out on me now, they'll go so fast, I won't be left with anything but a sinking wreck."

"You're exaggerating." Brett felt a little impatient but kept his voice calm. "And you're certainly selling yourself short. Just watch your temper and you'll be fine." He smiled at his ex-partner. "The only problem you ever had was a tendency to shoot yourself in the foot."

Gideon smiled suddenly, and his brief laugh hung in the air as gray mist. "Yeah. Okay, so you're staying here. Well, I tried." He flexed the fingers of his right hand, then blew on them absently. "Damn it's cold out here. I should have worn gloves." He fumbled to slide his hands into the pockets of his jacket.

This time Brett heard a horse approaching fast. He turned his head to look, feeling a shock as Cassie burst over the top of the slope on a wild-eyed roan. She didn't bother to stop the horse, and those next few seconds formed an oddly beautiful image Brett would remember for the rest of his life.

The reddish horse streaking toward him across the pristine snow, its breath puffing little clouds of white. Cassie on its bare back, just the way she'd ridden so often as a girl, her golden hair loose and flying. She wasn't dressed for the intense cold, wearing the snug jeans and oversize gray sweater she'd worn in the house, no coat or gloves. She was deathly pale, her eyes darkened to charcoal, her delicate lips pressed together.

And in her small hands was a rifle, held with expertise and incredible steadiness despite the galloping horse. She was aiming at Gideon, and before either man could move she fired.

The stun charge did precisely what it was designed to do—it knocked Gideon off his feet in an instant. He lay on his back in the snow, unmoving, not dead but unconscious.

Cassie halted her horse just a few feet from Kane's grave. She slid from the roan's back, still holding the rifle in one hand. In the eerie silence born from cold and shock, she walked to Gideon and knelt down at his side. She slid one hand carefully into his right jacket pocket, the one his fingers had never reached, and produced a small remote control.

"Gideon means 'destroyer,' did you know?" she asked quietly as she looked up at Brett. "He had plenty of time to plant explosives or incendiary devices, even in daylight. Nobody noticed him. Everybody was watching the distant hills for trouble, but he just followed the private road and drove right up to the house. The last way you expect an enemy to come."

Brett drew a shaken breath. "How did you know?"

Cassie put the remote down in the snow, careful not to touch the button on top, and laid the rifle beside it. She rose to her feet and walked toward him.

"The mirror," she said, and threw herself into his arms.

By Christmas Eve most of the furor had died down. The incendiary devices Gideon Paige had planted—a favorite of arsonists because they caused an incredibly hot and destructive fire and yet gave evidence of a simple electrical fire—had been carefully removed from two outside walls of the house. The danger was past. The police had charged Paige with attempted arson. A conviction would get him booted out of the country, and he waited in jail in Tucson. He didn't deny what he'd tried to do, only saying in a reasonable tone that with Killara and Cassie dead, Brett would have returned to Australia.

Any compassion Brett might have had for a man who was clearly deranged had been quite effectively destroyed when he'd heard that. He'd wanted to kill Gideon with his bare hands when he'd learned the man had hoped to kill Cassie as well as burn the house. Just thinking of what might have happened made his chest tight with fear, and made his arms tense around Cassie as they relaxed on the comfortable couch in the parlor.

The room was lit only by the sparkling Christmas tree and crackling fire, but that was enough.

"Stop thinking about it," Cassie urged quietly.

Brett made an effort to relax. "I know it's useless."

"Just one of the things beyond your control," she pointed out. "Beyond anybody's. Let it go."

He kissed her when she turned her face up, and it was easy to smile at her. "I'll do my best. All's well that ends well—even if I was no more successful at changing fate than any of my ancestors have been."

Cassie frowned slightly. "But you did."

"No, *you* did. I was blindsided, so busy looking for an enemy of my father's, it never occurred to me that it was *my* fault you and Killara were threatened. You were right, you know—the mirror did create events. It showed me something that would never have happened, except that what it showed me brought me back home with the threat right behind me."

Cassie turned a bit so that she could see his face more clearly. "Brett, I was wrong about that. What the mirror showed you was the destruction of Killara. True?"

"Yes. A destruction I failed to stop because I was so blind."

"But you did stop the destruction. You came home. If you had stayed in Australia, Gideon wouldn't have tried to burn this house down—but Duncan Lang might have. And even if he didn't, Killara would have been destroyed, just like Delaney Enterprises was being destroyed. Because you weren't here. That's what the mirror showed you. A prediction of destruction."

Brett hadn't thought about it that way, but curiously her analysis made sense to him. Perhaps, he thought, the whole point of the prediction hadn't had much to do with a burning building at all. Perhaps the point had simply been to bring the last Delaney home—and teach him a few things he needed to know.

"So you no longer believe the mirror creates events?"

Cassie smiled. "All I believe now is that the mirror is magic. Delaney magic. The epic kind."

Before Brett could respond, the hologram star atop the tree obeyed its programming and began to play a soft, tinkling tune.

"It's Christmas," he realized. He smiled at Cassie. "Merry Christmas, sweetheart. I have your present over there under the tree. Want to open it?"

"Well, that wouldn't be quite fair," she said solemnly.

"Why not?"

"Because you can't have yours yet. I mean, you won't be able to see it for a while."

Instead of repeating his question, Brett lifted an amused eyebrow in a silent query.

Keeping her voice grave, Cassie said, "Either that shot you took back in the summer was defective—or else the Delaneys really can overcome any obstacle." She took his hand and guided it to rest on her flat belly. "Because this Delaney wanted to get conceived."

Brett's gaze dropped, fixing on his hand, large against her slenderness. He had never felt such an incredible surge of emotion. Beneath his hand, inside her delicate body, their child was growing. Still so tiny . . .

"Are you sure?" he asked hoarsely.

Cassie had seen everything she needed to see in his face. Her answer was tender and content. "Yes, I'm sure. I went to a doctor yesterday while you were tied up with the police. Brett, it happened that first night."

He looked at her face, and he thought exactly what he'd thought ever since she was thirteen years old, that there was nothing on earth as beautiful as Cassie. "I love you," he said, simple and stark.

Cassie murmured a response, happiness nearly overwhelming her. She wanted to tell him that her phrase "this Delaney" was a bit inaccurate, but decided to give him time to get used to the idea of just one.

She'd asked the doctor not to tell her anything beyond the fact that their child was off to a healthy start, and the doctor hadn't. But Cassie had just happened to glance into the dressing room that morning, and into the mirror, and even though she wasn't due to take Brett's name until the quiet ceremony they'd planned for New Year's Day, it seemed the mirror had always considered her a Delaney, because it showed her the future for the third time.

The twin boys nestled inside her, safe and protected, would be only the first two of a strong and numerous new generation of Delaneys to walk the land their ancestors had named Killara. And that was a fate Cassie looked forward to.

"Merry Christmas, darling," she whispered to the love of her life.

"Cassie...God, I love you so much...."

She wondered a bit vaguely if the mirror would show him the wonderful images it had promised her. Maybe, but she thought not. She thought Brett had been right in believing he would never again see anything except his own reflection in the polished surface.

Because it wasn't necessary.

The mirror had sent him away to the other side of the world to become the man he was meant to be. And then it had brought him home when the time was right. When he was ready to see and understand what he needed to.

It had brought him home to her. It had brought him home to discover his love for his heritage. It had brought him home to begin again.

To rebuild the dynasty.

ABOUT THE AUTHORS

KAY HOOPER is the *New York Times* bestselling author of many novels, including *Sense of Evil* and *Hunting Fear*. She lives in North Carolina.

IRIS JOHANSEN has more than twenty-five million copies of her books in print and is the #1 *New York Times* bestselling author of *Firestorm, Dead Aim, No One to Trust, Body of Lies, Final Target,* and more. She lives near Atlanta, Georgia.

FAYRENE PRESTON is an award-winning, bestselling author who is approaching her silver anniversary as a published romance author. Her numerous novels include the much-loved *For the Love of Sami* and the soon-to-be reissued Swansea series. She lives in the north Texas area.